BROTHER TO SHADOWS

ANDRE NORTON

AVON BOOKS • NEW YORK

BROTHER TO SHADOWS is an original publication of Avon Books. This work is a novel. Any similarity to actual persons or events is purely coincidental.

AVON BOOKS
A division of
The Hearst Corporation
1350 Avenue of the Americas
New York, New York 10019

Copyright © 1993 by Andre Norton
Cover illustration by Daniel Horne
Published by arrangement with the author
Library of Congress Catalog Card Number: 93-13971
ISBN: 0-380-77096-2

First AvoNova Printing: October 1994
First Morrow/AvoNova Hardcover Printing: November 1993

AVON TRADEMARK REG. U.S. PAT. OFF. AND IN OTHER COUNTRIES, MARCA REGISTRADA, HECHO EN U.S.A.

Printed in the U.S.A.

RA 10 9 8 7 6 5 4 3 2 1

BROTHER TO SHADOWS

Jofre's chain weapon was a serpent ready to strike. There was a rising howl of sound and Jofre put his weapon into use. It twisted among the cords on the floor. He gave a jerk with full shoulder strength and the nearest of the broadcasting machines came crashing down.

Blaster beams were sweeping back and forth. There was struggling and the screaming of the women. Jofre tensed. He tightly gripped the weapon, expecting every breathless moment to be either cut down by a stass ray or fried by a blaster. He gave a leap which carried him over the wreckage of the wires and landed behind the Holder. In a moment his arm was over the other's shoulder, bringing pressure to bear on the Tssekian's throat.

"Be quiet," Jofre hissed in the other's ear, "and move—or you die!"

"SCIENCE FICTION WORTH SAVORING...
A FAST-MOVING, COLORFUL ADVENTURE"
Orlando Sentinel

"A HIT...FASCINATING ALIENS,
FAST-PACED ACTION AND INTRIGUE"
Booklist

"ANDRE NORTON CONTINUES TO LIVE UP TO
HER REPUTATION."
Hartford Courant

Other AvoNova Books by
Andre Norton

THE HANDS OF LYR

1

THE CHILL FINGERS OF THE DAWN WIND CLAWED. Behind the spires of the Listeners the sky was the color of a well-honed throwing knife. There was not any answer to time's passing in Ho-Le-Far Lair.

Brothers stood in the courtyard as they had since twilight, keeping the Face-the-great-storm position with a purpose that rose above any cramping of limb or protest of body. Only their eyes were apprehensive and what they watched was that oval set at the crown of the arch which marked the door of the Master's great hall. What should have showed a glow of light was lifeless, as dull as the stone in which it was set.

Now through that door, which gaped like a skull's lipless jaws at the top of a flight of stairs, came the long awaited figure muffled in robes the hue of dried blood—The Shagga Priest.

He spoke and his voice, though low-pitched, carried as it had been trained to do.

"The Master has fulfilled his issha vow."

No one in those lines below wavered, though this was an ending to all the life they had known.

Those two to the fore of the waiting company raised hands in Sky-draw-down gestures. Then they strode forward with matching steps while the priest descended further to meet them. He stopped, still above their level, so they must look up to meet his eyes. In the growing light their Shadow garments were a steel to match the lowering sky.

TarrHos, Right Hand to the Master, crossed his hands at breast level, drawing with action too quick for the eye to truly follow, slender daggers.

"It is permitted?" he asked of the priest, his voice as hard as the weapons he displayed.

"It is permitted—by the Issha of this Brotherhood it is so." The priest nodded his shaven head and his own hands advanced, like predators on the prowl, from the shadows of his wide sleeves to sketch certain age-old gestures.

TarrHos went to his knees. Three times he bowed, not to the priest but to that lifeless stone above. It was a blinded eye now; that force which it had contained had fled, no brother or priest could tell why or how. It had been, it was not, and with it went the life of this Lair.

TarrHos's weapons swept in the ritual gesture. There was no sound from the man who crumpled forward, only the moaning of the wind. Red spattered upward, not quite reaching the perch of the priest.

LasStir, Left Hand of the Master, took another step forward. He did not look at his dead fellow.

"It is permitted?" His voice, rendered harsh by an old throat wound, outrode the wind.

"It is permitted—the issha holds."

With the same dexterity of weapons LasStir joined his colieutenant in death.

The Shagga descended the last two steps, making no effort to draw back the hem of his robe from the spreading pools of blood coming to join as one.

Ten more made up that assembly left below, younger men, some near boys. Their short cloaks were black, the sign of those who had not made at least ten forays for the honor of the Lair. One in that line dared to speak to the Shagga.

"It is permitted?" His voice was a little too high, too shrill.

"It is not permitted!" The priest silenced him. "A Lair dies when its heart is no longer fed by the will of its Master. The unblooded and half-sworn do not take up the issha.

"Rather you shall serve in other Lairs still as is demanded of you. Ho-Le-Far has ceased to be." He made the Descent-of-Darkest-Night wave with his left hand—so setting an end to all which had existed here, erasing a long and valiant history. "Here no longer is there a Post of Shadows."

For the first time there was a slight movement in that assembly. This was a thing of disaster, almost of terror, and it was an evil fate to be caught in it.

The Shagga moved along the line slowly, stopping to eye each one, and to address that one alone:

"HasGan and CarFur," he singled out the first two on the left. "Draw supplies and weapons, go to the Lair of Tig-Nor-Tu. DisNov and YasWar, you will do likewise, but go over mountain to Ou-Quar-Nin."

So it went until the priest reached the last in that line. He had to look up to meet eye to eye with the waiting novice and now that it was fully light it was plain to see the sparks of malice in his sunken eyes, the vicious twist of his lips as he shaped words which he had long savored and held ready for this moment.

"Outlander—misborn—no-blood— Out with you to where you will—you are not of the Oath and by the Will of TransGar you never shall be. You are an abomination, a stain. No doubt the Master's force death has come through you. You will take no weapons—for those are of the Brotherhood, and henceforth you will go your own way!"

The hooded listener refused the Shagga the satisfaction of seeing how deep that thrust went. He had long known that the priest hated him, looked upon his being there as a blot on the honor of the Lair. Since the force stone had started to fail he had foreseen this and tried to plan beyond it. But so much of his life was tied here that it was hard to break the bonds of discipline, to think of himself as moving without orders on a wayward path which had no real goal.

Within the Lair only the Master had ever shown him any concern. He had been told why only three moon speds ago. The Brothers to Shadows, trained assassins, spies, bodyguards, had been in service on Asborgan for centuries. Rulers employed their services knowing well that, once oathed, they were absolutely loyal to their employer for the agreed-upon length of their bond. However, recently there had been a rumor that their particular talents were in demand off-world also and that was a new source of income for the Lairs. To employ one of off-world blood off-world would be setting that Lair to the fore of the new idea and the Master had been a forward-looking man—which was, Jofre thought, a hidden point of disagreement between him and the custom-bound Shagga.

Jofre was the Master's own find, a literal find, for the Master, on one of his scout training missions, had come upon the wreck of an escape craft, one of those which sometimes could make a perilous rescue from a spacer in dire trouble. Jofre had been the only living thing in that tiny vessel, a child so young he could remember only a few scraps of scenes of his life before he had been taken into the Lair to be given the grilling training of the Brothers.

Though in frame he was larger than the rest of the novices, he quickly absorbed all he was taught, proving more proficient in some of the necessary skills than others. At the same time the Master had seen that he was given lessons in the off-world trade tongue, passed to him information which seeped from the airport to the Lair, brought by traders and travelers. Though both Master and student knew well there were large and awkward gaps in what he absorbed with a will. His greater reach and strength as he approached manhood had awakened envy in his fellows, something he had long known that the Shagga Priest had fostered. However, he knew that he was competent enough for a mission and that the Master had had plans for him.

The Master and the force stone . . . Each Lair was endowed with such a stone and no one knew from where these came or what was the purpose—save that at long intervals their glow died. That was taken as a direct sign that the force of the Master had gone also and that he must pay for whatever secret failing had brought about the death of his power. With the stone died also the Lair as this one had here and now. But it had been a long time since any Lair had come to an end, and it was a bitter thing which brought a faint touch of fear to every other Lair when it happened.

Jofre continued to meet the priest eye to eye. The man would see him dead if he could. But he could not, for Jofre had passed the first oathing four seasons ago and Brother could not shed the blood of Brother. However, the Shagga was settling his fate in another way. This was the season of mountain cold. To be cast out of shelter without weapons or full supplies was a delayed sentence of death—or so the priest believed.

"I am assha if not issha." Jofre spoke the words slowly as he might ready his knives for a final thrust. "Weapons you may take from me, for they are of the Lair. I claim therefore traveler's rights under the law." On this point custom would bear him out and he would hold to it.

The priest scowled and then flung away after the others, who were already moving off to make up their packs ready for the journeying to their newly appointed stations.

Jofre faced the force stone again. Slowly he moved forward. The light which had centered it was certainly gone—it was now as dull as the age-worn stone which held it. At least ten Masters had lived and died in its light—the eleventh had the misfortune to see that light fail.

The young man skirted the bodies of the lieutenants and climbed the steps. He expected some outcry from the Shagga though what he would do was no profanation. However, that did not come and he passed into the darkness of the hall above, where the only faint light came from two lamps at the far end.

Between them lay that other body—the Master. For some reason Jofre needed to do this but he could not explain that reason even to himself. He came to stand beside the man who had saved his life, even though just perhaps because he saw in Jofre a tool to be well employed at a future date.

Jofre's hands moved Star-Of-Morning—Journey-into-Light. The fingers shaped that message in the air. Farewell-far-journey-triumph-to-the-warrior. As he did this there welled into him an inflow of strength, almost as if some of the will and purpose of the dead Master passed to him as a bequest.

Only a tenth night ago he had knelt at this very spot, had spread before him certain maps and papers, known the carefully hidden excitement of one being prepared for a mission.

"It is thus," the Master had spoken as one who shared thought, "these off-worlders change every world they enter. They cannot help but do so to us. We have lived by a certain pattern for ten centuries now. The valley lords have their feuds which have become as formally programmed as the IDD dances. They hire us as bodyguards, as Slip-shadows to dispose of those whose power threatens them or whom they wish to clear from their paths. It has become in a manner a game—a blood game.

"But to all patterns there comes a time of breaking, for weaving grows thinner with years. So it comes for us—though many of the Masters would say no to that. But we must change or perish." There had been force in those words as if the Master were oath giving.

"The Master of Ros-hing-qua has shown the way. He has oathed two Brother Shadows, one Sister Shadow off-world to men who seek easement to trouble on their own home globe. Word has come that they carried out their assignment in keeping with issha traditions. Now it is our turn to think of such a thing. There is news from the port that there has been talk of others coming from the far starways to seek the arts we have long cultivated. You are not of our blood, Jofre, by birth. But we claimed you and you have eaten of our bread, drunk brother-toasts, learned what was our own way. Off-world you can use all you know and yet not be betrayed by the fact you are born of us. Therefore, when the time comes, this mission shall be yours—either you will be sent to be the shoulder shield, body armor for some far lord, or you will be the hunter with steel."

Jofre had dared then to break the pause which followed:

"Master, you place in me great trust but there are those within these walls who would speak against that."

"The Shagga, yes. It is the manner of most priests to cling to tradition, to be jealous guardians of custom. He would not take departure from the old ways happily. But here I am Master—"

Yes, here he had been Master—until the issha and the door crystal had failed him. Jofre's lips tightened against his teeth under the half-mask scarf of his headdress. Could the Shagga have, in some way, brought this ruin here? There were tales upon tales of how they had strange powers but he had never seen such manifest and besides, were such a thing possible, all the Masters of Lairs would rise and even the Shagga would face death.

Jofre knelt now and touched his turbaned head three times to the floor, the proper answer to one given a mission.

"Master, hearing, I obey."

He was not being sent forth officially, no. For no Lair would offer him shelter with the Shagga against him, nor did he want to remain where he was not a true brother. Off-worlder they called him. But as the Master had pointed out he had certain skills which could well be useful on any planet where men envied other men, or feared for their lives, or sought power. The spaceport would be his goal and from there he would await what fortune his issha would offer.

Now he left the hall and its dead and went directly to the storehouse, in which there was a bustle. A line of burden quir were waiting with pack racks already on their ridged backs. Hurrying back and forth were the Brothers, already in their thick journey clothing, loading on those ugly-tempered beasts all which must be transported now to their future homes.

The Shagga priest stood by the door but as Jofre approached he turned with a whirl of his robes to face him.

"Off with you— But first— There—" he pointed to the ground at his feet already befouled by the droppings of the quir, "your weapons, nameless one."

Under his half-mask Jofre snarled. Yet, this too, was a part of the tradition. Since they declared him not of any Lair, he could not bear the arms of one.

His long knife, his two throwing sleeve knives, his chain-ball throw, his hollow blowtube. One by one he threw them at the priest's feet. At last he held but one knife.

"This," he said levelly, "I keep—by traveler's law."

The priest's mouth worked as if he would both spit and curse in one. But he did not deny that.

Nor did Jofre draw back now. Though the priest and the Brothers with their supplies tended to block the doorway.

"I claim traveler's right supplies," the young man stated firmly.

"You will get them!" The priest seized upon one of the boys just returning for another load. "Bring forth that prepared for this one. Then get you forth, cursed one."

The Brother ducked within and returned in a moment with a shoulder pack, a very small one, lacking much, Jofre thought, of what he would really need. Yet the Shagga had obeyed the letter of the law and if he protested, it would achieve nothing but to render him less in the eyes of these who had so recently been his oathed Brothers.

He took up the pack which had been tossed contemptuously in his direction and, without a word, turned and went toward the wide open gate in the wall. In that last meeting with the Master he had memorized from the map the route he must take. Of his destination he knew only what he had learned by study and by listening to the talk of the traders who now and then visited the Lair.

There was a road of sorts. However, that followed a winding way and he would lose time. By the heft of the pack he had little in the way of supplies. Though the Brothers were trained to live off the land, this was the beginning of the cold season and much which could be converted to food would be hard to find. The herbs were frost burnt and dead; the small animals had mainly retreated to burrows. It was at least ten days travel on foot before he would reach farming land and then he must be wary of attempting to obtain supplies. The Brothers were feared by commoners. A Brother alone might well be fair game. No, it would be better to strike straight over the Pass of the Kymer, if that was not snow choked by an early storm. In a way he would thus be seeking out his own roots, as it was on the slope of the Ta-Kymer that the escapeboat in which he had been found had made a crash landing.

Jofre did not turn and look back at the only home he could remember. Instead he centered all his concentration on what lay before him, marshalling all strengths to face the mountain path.

The Shagga priest stood in the middle of that narrow room which had been his own quarters at the Lair. There were blanks of lighter strips on the wall where the rolls of the WORDS OF SKAG had been hung only moments earlier. All his belongings were enwrapped in weather-resistant orff skin bags to wait by the door.

He plucked at his lower lip as was his habit in thought, though there was so little skin to be gathered there.

Outside the narrow slit of window the pale sun was being cloud hidden. A storm, early in the season, that might most easily answer his problem. But no man could count on the whims of nature. It was best to cover all possible points in planning an attack.

There was one other object there in the room. A cage in which a black blot huddled. The priest went to haul

out that occupant. He held something which was neither
bird nor mammal but a combination of both and faintly
repulsive. The thing expanded leathery wings, releasing
more of its disgusting, musty body odor.

Its head twisted and turned on a long neck as if it were
trying to escape, not the priest's hold upon its body, but
the glare of his eyes. Until at last the man's will overcame
that of the Kag, the turning head was still, and it was held
eye to eye with him as if being hypnotized, which it was
after a manner.

There was a long pause and then the priest stepped
quickly to the window and the Kag arose and was gone,
spiraling out over the countryside, but still as much under
his control as if he held it on a leash. It would follow, it
would spy. When death struck down that upstart its master
would speedily learn.

2

JOFRE NOTED THOSE SIGNS OF STORM, YET HE DID NOT quicken pace. For the first hour after leaving the Lair he had country comparatively easy to travel. For he could keep for awhile to the travelers' road. He swung along at the controlled gait for a long journey, with a divided mind which had come from his training.

One-half of his attention was for his surroundings and footing, the other probed into the future. He felt so oddly alone, though the Brothers, for the most part, operated singly, but always on a set task, and he was without that guidance. He set to gaining full control, first visualizing the map he was to follow, then examining in turn all the possible points of knowledge which could aid him in the future.

The history of the Brothers was thickly entangled with the intrigues and conspiracies of many small courts and kingdoms. All they knew of off-world came largely through hearsay. Many, such as the Shagga priest, wanted to keep it that way. Only because the Master had been far looking and ambitious in a new fashion did Jofre have those scraps he clung to.

A city had been already established on the plain where the first spacer exploring starship had set down on Asborgan. Now there were, in fact, two cities, the old and a new one which had grown up nearer the port landing and in which there were strange off-world buildings housing beings of different races, different species even.

On the outer fringe of this newer city along the port side there was a third collection of buildings, seedy inns, trading marts in which there were few questions asked as to the source of goods offered. Here the outcasts of both Asborgan's native stock and the scum which followed the star lanes as a blot gathered and held a strong hold of their own.

Jofre had heard of the Thieves Guild, which spread talons to seize across half the star lanes. There was said to be a branch of that which had gained a foothold here, incorporating into its very diverse assembly native talent. In addition there were those who had met with such misfortune that they had fallen to a point of no return. He had been told of drugs which drove men wild, giving them great power for a short time, but condemning them to miserable deaths. All the evil which an intelligent mind could conceive gathered there in that dismal sink.

Yet that must be his own first goal. As a Brother he could not shelter in the old city—for he wore no lord's badge. Also there would be a need for coins to pay his way. The better portion of the space city would see him as a curiosity and so suspect. No, he must dive into the dark quarter until he could find his way about.

In his decision Jofre had no fear of either the law or the lawless. The conception that a Brother could be taken anywhere, used at any time against his own will, or the will of his Master, was inconceivable. He had skills of body and will, honed mastery of mind to shield him there. But when he tried to think to whom he might offer those skills now he found himself at a loss.

Finally, deciding that sure attempts at foreseeing were only useless, he shut down that portion of his mind and concentrated on the journey itself.

It was twilight when he came to where he must take the cutoff for the pass. Long trained to scout work, he could slip through the bare-branched brush and work his way up into the heights easily enough. He sheltered that night in a half cave where two great rocks tilted together.

Once he had his fire, hardly wider than his two hands held thumb to thumb, and had chewed the tough trail mix of meat pounded with dried fruit into a strip, he turned to the fitting of himself for what might well be the trials of tomorrow.

First he sought out The Center of All Things, concentrating on the mental symbols which marked the existence of that. Then he visualized the inner workings of his own body, the muscles, the nerves, the blood and bones, the knitting of the flesh. From his toes he began to use The Flow of Inner Life, drawing it up through him, into his mid body, his arms and shoulders, until his hands, where they rested on his knees as he sat cross-legged, grew warm and each finger tingled.

Into his throat, his head, the flood continued. There was a feeling of elation but that he was swift to dampen. He was not summoning battle power. Only the strength needed for travel.

He breathed deeply three times, to lock in that warmth. Then he relaxed, aware that he had prepared himself as best he could. Now he set his sentinels of alarm that he might take a full night's rest. At least those were available to all travelers and so the Shagga priest could not refuse him them.

Jofre worked the three large pebbles out of their traveling bag and, with a knowing eye, in spite of the dark which had now closed in, he positioned them in the gravel about the rock. Such were quick to give alarm when approached by anything warm-blooded to which they had not been bound, as he had bound these with a drop of his own blood and the warmth of his bared hand.

Having taken his precautions, Jofre rolled in his double blanket and went to sleep, rest easily summoned by his long training.

There was no show of either moon tonight and clouds were heavy, though they had not yet loosed their burdens. Through their thickness sped the Kag. The creature lit on a spur of rock and hunched into a motionless blot of darkness, only to launch itself again and seize a warfin which had ventured out to hunt. Bearing the bird to its chosen perch, it ripped apart the body and fed ravenously, then settled to rest as had its quarry below.

Jofre awoke at dawn. He chewed another strip of journey rations, adding to that only a single finger scoop of yellowish paste from a small box. The Brothers did not depend often on stimulants but they had their own kinds of energy-inducing herbal concoctions. He gathered up his sentries, returned them to their pouch, and swung his pack up on his shoulder. However, when only a few feet from his last night's camp, he paused to eye something protruding slantwise from the rubble which must have descended in a small slide from the heights he must now face.

It was certainly not the remains of any bush, or sapling. No, he had seen—and used—its like before. This was a pass staff which, in the right hands, could even confront a steel swinging opponent. The flash of recognition sent his hand out to close firmly about it.

The slide held it well in grip and he had to work it loose. When he had it wholly free he could see that the hook at its end had been bent out of shape, but it was still a weapon of which he could make excellent use. His issha was assuredly strong—

But whence had it come? He took several steps backward so he could view the upslant of the way before him more clearly. Then he saw it—a clean angle which was not of nature. There had been—still was—a wall!

Jofre closed his eyes for a moment and drew to the fore of his mind the map. No, he was certain that there had been no hint of any such along the route he had chosen. How could he have gotten so far off trace? He turned his attention to the staff he now held. It was old but it had been painstakingly carven of armor wood—that precious growth which could be worked by a great deal of effort, but once shaped would perhaps well outlast its maker.

He pulled off his thick glove and took the shaft into his bare hand, allowing it to slide along between his fingers as he held it closer to centered sight. Then that grip tightened. His breath came with the faintest hiss.

Qaw-en-itter!

Dead Lair, long dead Lair! And by all the teaching of assha a site to be avoided lest the ill fortune of that place still weave some pattern to entrap. Even as his own home Lair would now be regarded by any chancing close to its deserted compound. However—Jofre slid the staff back and forth between both hands as he sifted logic from superstition.

The Master he had served had been one to discount much in the way of rumor and legend. His outlooking for off-world contracts had brought him a wealth of contradictory information which he had sifted patiently, and for the past half year Jofre had oftentimes served as a kind of sounding board—since the Shagga priest and the Master's Right and Left Hands were all of a conservative turn of mind. The Shagga doubtlessly believed, and would tell it near and far, that the now dead Master's loss of assha had come because of that very turning from orthodox ways. But something in Jofre had responded eagerly to whatever speculation the Master had wished to voice.

Now he could remember that small warning mark on the map. However, there was a far better way to the Pass if one tried the ancient route from Qaw-en-itter. He would save perhaps a day's journey time, maybe more. A glance at the lowering clouds, at that threat of storm to come, made him think it would be worth the try.

Slinging the staff to be fastened to the lashings of his pack took only a short time. He was moving upward determinedly, watching for the best footholds, almost at once.

Over the years there had been a number of slides here. He came to a place where his path was closed by blocks of masonry, perhaps a portion of the wall above, and he had to wriggle by. Then he came suddenly on a ledge which sloped upwards and showed the marks of very old tooling, undoubtedly one of the ways into the deserted Lair.

That was not what he wished. He must round what remained of the stronghold to locate the road on the other side. And the ledge was soon choked with debris. This was dangerous footing and Jofre walked with careful tread.

The half-destroyed wall arose on his right. There was the broken archway of a minor door but what he sought would lie beyond, and he shifted left, paralleling that offshoot of the wall. Something floated down, touched his sleeve—then another and another flake. The snow was beginning and, unless he would have himself walled from the pass, he must hurry.

Qaw-en-itter had been of moderate size, he concluded. Though so much of it was in ruin that he could not, without some waste of time, trace out its original ways. He tried to think of its history—there had been something—like a flicker, a scrap of memory came and went in his mind.

The master crystal here had failed, of course, or it would still be inhabited. But there was something else—the last Master—Jofre shook his head. For all his meticulous training he could not deepen that very faint feeling of having heard something.

The flakes of falling snow thickened, still were not enough to hide the way ahead. He had sight, if limited, and could keep from blundering off trail. Yet when he reached the point he had been seeking, where that other old path led upwards into the heights, Jofre hesitated. There was shelter here of a sort. Should the winds rise past the teasing point which they now held and he be caught in the open on the bareness of the upper slopes, he would be in a perilous state.

This was a first storm. Those of the Lair had been trained to be weatherwise; they had to be. Part of him urged pushing on, another suggested a prudent delay. He could not hope to breast the pass if the snow became a true curtain.

On a quick decision he turned towards the end of the wall where the ruins beyond promised shelter. Edging around a tumble of stones, he came into what had been the main court of the Lair. There was a tangle of autumn-dried brush where the land had set its first grasp back on the forsaken territory. Brittle and sparse though that was, it promised better than anything he believed was available at a greater height.

Jofre nearly tripped on the first step which had led to the Master's hall, so enbowed was it with dried grass and drift from storms. He hesitated. To go on into that dark cavern which opened like a toothless mouth before him would take him out of the storm. But enough of the Brothers' belief remained in him to warn him off.

Instead he chose a niche to one side, where there had once been a storehouse, enough remaining of walls and roofing portion to afford shelter better than he could have hoped for elsewhere. There he set up camp.

The brush he broke off, or tore from its frail rooting in the pavement chinks, to afford him fuel for his small fire. As he worked to gather that the snow thickened, becoming more and more of a concealing curtain, and he knew that his impulse to night here had been right.

At last he settled in the small space he had made as stormtight as he could, but he felt no desire for sleep. Instead he knew the alertness of a scout in an enemy territory, his hearing, his sight, every sense he had reaching out to pick up the small hint of something which was not of wind, or snow, or natural to this ancient place.

For he could feel it more and more; it was like an itch he could not scratch because he did not know its source. There was that here which was not— Not what? Jofre chewed upon that question and found no answer.

He set out his sentries at the entrance to his burrow. The portion of supplies he allowed himself was halved and he chewed carefully a long time before he swallowed each mouthful, as if that would stretch it to satisfy his hunger.

What clung here? Were there indeed bases to old super-stition and an abandoned Lair still held by the spirits of the last Master and his lieutenants? Without knowing that he did it, Jofre pulled the staff he had found across his knees as he sat cross-legged, was rubbing his right-hand along the shaft, his fingers tracing the runes set there to identify the armory from which it had come. Suddenly he was aware there was a warmth in the shaft which did not spread from but rather to his moving hand. And then there was a sudden sharp shift in the staff, which had certainly not come by his will or from any movement he had made.

"Ssaahh—" Jofre was so startled from his carefully main-tained calm that he hissed that aloud. What he was experiencing—yes, it was certainly that which he had heard tell of—had once seen demonstrated—and that by the Master on a scouting trip.

The half-broken weapon he had found on the rocks below was issha pointing! Issha? But the fact that this Lair was abandoned meant that there was no issha here—nor was he a Master to channel the power. Yet—this was happening!

In his now loosened grasp that shaft was pointing out-ward toward the snow. A long-set trap? He had also heard tales of such. Some of the Masters were rumored to have powers far beyond those of common men. He had dared to invade the accursed—was he now being drawn to the punishment for his impudence?

Because, Jofre also realized, he could not resist. He must carry through whatever action the weapon now urged. Loosing his knife for his other hand, he crawled out into the open, remaining there for an instant or two in the half crouch of Ward-the-attack-in-the-night.

Only the snow. Nothing moved through it or against the drifts it was building around the ruined walls. But the shaft was swinging in his grip with vigor, as if he were being pulled by a determined force on the other end. Now he was facing again the hall door.

"By the blood oath, Brothers.
By salt and bread, water and wine,
By steel and rope, hand and foot—mind,
By the ancients and the elders, Masters, and men,
Thus do I swear."

He repeated the oathing of the assha, even as he would have done had he been sent with the rest to another Lair.

And he followed, even as he would have had the long gone Master of Qaw-en-itter stood on the rubble-strewn steps gesturing him in.

But it was not to the dark that the staff led him. As he reached the top step, the staff swung in his hand, slipping fast to thud butt hard on the worn stone. He looked down.

That butt was near to touching a patch of darkness, a patch of black which seemed to have a— Jofre went down on one knee and held out his hand, his fingers cupped over the blotch. There was a spark, as if he had used his flint against steel for fire lighting. Almost against his will those fingers closed.

Warmth—even as had been in the shaft when it had driven him into this action. He raised his hand, bringing what he had picked up to eye level. It was an oval perhaps the size of his palm, smoothed like a gem for setting. Black, so black that it might have been cut from the darkest of shadows. But as he cupped it in his flesh it gave forth—

Assha glow! But no—it could not be! When a Master's stone died did it leave a ghost of itself? No legend he had heard had told of that. However, had anyone ever lingered in a cursed lair to make sure? He wanted to hurl it from him, his clutch was only the tighter. What he had found was a thing of power, that he knew. Only he was not one who might wield it—

"No!" His voice sounded through the night and the snow. "No!" But there was a bonding; he could feel it;

this was fast becoming a part of him. He strove to raise his own inner power to repudiate his find. There was no use—he could not hurl it away. Instead his hand, as if under the orders of a Master, went to his wide girdle and those busy fingers were working the stone into safe hiding there.

Jofre wavered as he stood. This—he could not summon any explanation for what had happened—but it would seem some power had fastened upon him.

He turned to make his way back to his camping place. Through the snow from above came a flying thing. He breathed a whiff of musty stench and ducked as it seemed to strike directly at his head. An ill omen indeed.

Jofre struck out in turn at the wheeling half shadow. It screeched, arose and was gone into the night. Nor did it appear again. He settled into his shelter. Twice he tried to reach for the stone that he might examine it better in the faintish light of his pocket-sized fire. But his arm, his hand, would not obey his will. However, he felt it against his body, within the windings of the wide girdle its presence even through the folds of his thick clothing.

He began determinedly to Draw-to-one, Self-warrior-heart, Mind-of-seeker, so slipped into the innerways of the one who hunted in a strange and forbidden territory—even though that lay within himself. But for all his searching he found no trail, and he came out of that half trance stiff with chill, the pressure of the find still against him, knowing that he had done the best he could to arm himself against the unknown—now he could only face what would come.

The Kag beat wings to which snow clung and was flung forth again. It circled twice the ruins below but it no longer screeched nor attempted to descend. At length it broke the last circle and headed out through the night, winging its way north, away from Qaw-en-itter. Morning broke while it still flew, yet it did not perch to rest. It was nightfall again when it circled another camp—though this a much larger one—and settled on the top of the empty cage.

A wrinkled hand and scrawny wrist was offered and the creature hopped onto that so that it was borne up to face eye level again the skull-sharp visage of the Shagga.

"Soooo—" the priest hissed at last. "He dares to meddle!" He considered the situation, weighing one thing against another. Tradition was strong; in spite of his hatred it bound him in some ways. None of the Brothers would move against one of issha training unless he had been denounced openly in a gathering of Lair Masters and the accused allowed speech in his or her own behalf. There was no knife or rope which could be dispatched openly against this four times damned off-worlder—not yet. But he must be watched—assuredly he must be watched.

As he thought he fed the Kag from a handful of wine-soaked herbs and put the now drowsy creature back in its cage. There was a second cage among the priest's baggage. As he approached that he looked up at the sky. Mountains would make no difference for his swift messenger and that one would reach the port city well ahead of that traveler he longed to break now with his bare hands.

He opened the cage and a farflyer pecked at his finger once and then came forth as the priest shrilled a summons. Again the priest and winged thing met in silent communication and then, with a practiced twist of the wrist, the man sent it up and out to complete its mission.

3

THE MAN CROSSED THE ROOM WITH A CURIOUSLY effortless ease, a gait akin, as an imaginative viewer might think, to the progress of a fish through water. His tunic and breeches were of a lusterless, sober brown, though discreet front latches showed the glint of red gold, and the buckle of his purse belt was set with small gems which would betray their perfection only to a knowledgeable eye.

He was known in several sections of both the old city and that quick growth which fringed the spaceport as one Ras Zarn, a merchant from the far north, of middle rank, a good bargainer, one who paid all obligations promptly and fully. In two other places he had another identity and one of those places was this narrow windowless closet of a room, the only light in which came from utilitarian wrought iron lanterns supported on brackets on either sidewall.

The furnishings were meager, a single seat cushion and the knee-high table before it, which was bare, but the surface of which was thickly marked with scratches and small pits as if someone had driven a knife point into it many times over.

His arm was held out from his body as he came and on the fore of it was perched a farflyer, huddled a little together as it clung so, as if it were indeed close to the end of its wing strength. As Zarn seated himself on the cushion he held out his arm and the creature gave a hop which placed it on the desktop, as it did so adding a new series of claw scratches to those of innumerable times before.

It seemed disposed to make no other move until the man's hands went out, clasped firmly about the feathered body, turning it about so that it faced him. Then the fingers of one hand swept up, jerking high the head, elevating that so that he could stare into its unblinking eyes. Time passed.

Once, twice, Zarn nodded as if he were assenting to some speech totally inaudible in that cramped chamber. Then he relaxed a fraction and out of his purse pouch he brought a pellet of dull green. He gave it a sharp squeeze between thumb and forefinger and then discarded it before the messenger, whose released head made a quick peck at the delicacy.

Once that was done and the reward received, Zarn sat very still, looking at the opposite wall as if he were searching there for some map or message which was of importance. At length he nodded for the third time and there was a small quirk of the lips, a flash which was gone hardly before it could be sighted. Once more he offered his wrist and the bird hopped to that perch. Then he went to the far wall, pressed the fingers of his left hand in a complicated pattern and a door slid back to allow him into the very prosaic counting house which he had leased for use during his exile here.

Warning had been given; he would set into motion the proper answer within the hour and he expected no ill results from his decided-upon plan. His weapon he had already selected and it would carry out his will as well as if it were his own hand wielding the silent steel or the choke of scarf-rope.

The storm which had imprisoned Jofre for two days in the ruins blew away during the second night and sun for the first time broke through those curtaining clouds. He was on the move at once. At this time of year such a respite must be made use of as quickly as possible. And some of the wind had moved drifts well enough for him to find the pass road.

He climbed steadily. It was not a road which would have suited a caravan of traders or any lowlander but to one from the Lairs it was as plain as that lower highway. Luck favored him in that there had been no slides here and the way was open, though he used the staff to sound the path ahead through any drift which did show.

The wind hit as he entered the pass and he clung to one wall of the cliff which formed it, moving crabwise at times lest some particularly forceful blast bowl him down. His inner strength was pushed near to the limit but the knowledge that once through this slit he would be on the downgrade again kept him moving.

Jofre was out of the cut and well down slope, to the first fringe of the evergreen trees which cloaked only the south side of the mountain range, before he paused long enough to eat. By sun height it was not too far from night and he must shelter out again in what protection he could find in the land. Also he was coming into occupied territory where he must make every effort to pass unseen. There were outlaws in the mountains, though most of them denned up in more accessible country, but there were also foresters and trappers in the greenlands he was entering.

Though he did not now wear the full uniform of his kind, his late kind, still he was recognizable to any really suspicious eye. The traveler's clothing he had taken on sufferance at the Lair was a mixture which few would wear. He had the girdle knife, and the haft of the broken pole-hook, and he had all the powers of weaponless training which had been drilled into him since childhood, but such were no answer to a lance beam such as the lowlanders had been introduced to since the off-worlders had arrived.

The Master had had studies of such weapons, gathered from accounts and snatches of information brought back by

Brothers who had served in the lowlands and returned once their service was done. But to obtain and master one of those weapons was something he had not yet achieved. The off-worlders were supposed to be forbidden to introduce such to a world where this craft mastery did not already exist. There grew up, therefore, a brisk smuggling trade. Only the lowland lords were as eager as the newcomers to keep such from the Brothers. Their long service as assassins and secret fighters had given them the label of being deadly with any weapon known to Asborgan. No one it would seem, save the Brothers themselves, wanted any new edge added to the murderous skill they already possessed. So though several of the Masters offered vast rewards for any strange weapon which could be delivered, so far none had come to them—instead only testimony concerning their deadliness and power.

Not only need he be on guard against foresters sweeping here for outlaw dens, but any lowlander would be his enemy on sight. Too many times had the Brothers on oathing been used by warring lords to put down rebellions or reduce some threat from the commoners. No, his safety lay in remaining invisible.

That night Jofre sheltered in a thicket of tree-tall brush at the lip of an ice-rimmed stream. He did not light a fire this side of the mountains and he allowed himself a very small fraction of his remaining supplies. Possessing no journey coins, eating and shelter in the lowlands would depend upon his wits and skill at thievery. Yet he was sure from what he had heard that there were those in the port city, could he reach there, who would be only too glad to add him to their following. The Brothers had no need to cry out their fame; history on Asborgan did it for them.

He had no coins, but he had something else. Not for the first time that day his hand touched his girdle and that lump within its folds. What he carried he did not know; but that it was valuable, he did not doubt at all. And he had heard Trader Dis, who had visited just before the end of the Lair, tell of the high prices one could get from off-worlders for any strange things from the old days. Jofre would not dare offer what he carried to any lord, it was too bound to the Brothers, but an off-worlder would not hold any such scruples. Yes, he would find a buyer; he would make sure of that. Having placed his sentinel stones, he set his mental controls to awake him at any change and at last slept. It was only a light sleep but enough to restore most of the energy he had spent this day.

It took Jofre a ten of days to reach his goal. He used every trick of a scout in enemy territory to feed himself. Clothing had been changed at a farmhouse where the family appeared to have withdrawn for a day to the nearest village and he was able to select for his needs. So he left there cloaked and tunicked over his field suit, taking his other clothing with him in a bundle which resembled the jumble of belongings any tramping the roads might carry. It was difficult to shed the turban and half mask of his calling. He felt strangely unprotected with his whole face bared. And catching sight of himself in a wayside pool it seemed he looked upon a stranger.

He had the height of his off-world race, whatever that might be, which had always set him aside from those of the native born. But his hair was as dark as theirs. Only his eyes, the color of a well-burnished blade, were again different from the uniformity of brown known to men of Asborgan. In this rough clothing he might well pass for an off-worlder—except that his knowledge of the star lanes was extremely sketchy and he could well make a betraying error every time he opened his mouth. Regretfully, on the last day before he reached the port, he broke into bits the remains of the pole. That was too patently a Lair weapon and no lowlander would have ever picked it up. He must venture now onto the open road but before he did so he found a thicket and burrowed his way in. Once more he sought the Inner Life and drew upon it. His hands shaped the gestures—rising thought, keen eye, listening ear, ready hand, fleet foot. He drew deeper and deeper breaths as if he were pulling visible strength into his lungs now with each gasp of the chill air.

His eyes no longer saw the world about him as it was but rather as symbols etched in the air, each having its meaning and worth. That which grew was rooted, as strength must be rooted within him, the wind which blew, the declining sun, draw in their spirit, their force—

Now Jofre bared his dagger. This would be no oathing ceremony, for oathing had been closed to him—except the oathing to himself, his inner need. He had shed his glove and with the point of the weapon he touched the tip of each finger in turn with strength enough to raise a bead of blood.

A stiff shake of his wrist sent those flying. Then he put his hand to his mouth and licked each tiny wound, willing them closed. He had shed ritual blood and was now prepared for what would lie ahead, even though he had no mission except the search for such.

Ras Zarn excused himself with polished manners to the off-worlder. He knew exactly who this stranger was, that a linkage ran back and tangled through this man to others spaceflights away. Though he knew also that this Rober Granger had no idea that he knew.

"Your pardon, Gentlehomo." Zarn bowed again. "At this strike of the hour I have a meeting I cannot set aside, much as I would wish it, for indeed what you have to say is of the utmost interest. However, that which summons me will not be of long duration and I ask of your kindness that you wait for me—if you find that possible. I truly believe, Gentlehomo, that we can well strike a bargain."

He sensed the other's irritated anger at such an interruption. However, he was also aware of how much this one needed what he, Zarn, controlled and he had no doubts he would find the man still there when he returned.

The house in which they had met had once been the town hall of a minor noble. Now it was cut into a warren of smaller rooms and narrow passages which might have bewildered any visitor who had not been furnished with a guide. Zarn turned right, left, and came to a room which had a second door on the outer world. The occupant there was already looking for him as he entered.

"Welcome, Lady." The merchant sketched a bow towards the cloaked figure. She could have been of any rank since that covering, though of good glas-wool, was of drab color and without ornamentation.

In answer to his greeting she inclined her hooded head but did not speak.

"You have had the message; you know what is to be done," he continued. "Remember, this one was high-rated. That renegade Master made of him a true Shadow. He must be taken so that which he now carries may be brought to us."

For the second time she nodded. Then spoke in turn.

"Honorable One, there is already laid on me a mission."

"Yes, but this can be accomplished before that is advanced. This is the oath-order."

"It shall be." Her voice was low but steady. Without any farewell she went out the other door into the open street beyond. Zarn rubbed one hand against another as if between them he was grinding something into dust. She would succeed of course; was she not the best he had ever seen in action? Another mission and perhaps they would have other plans for her—plans for the good of all.

He returned to his fuming visitor his mind fully at ease. With such weapons at one's command one was already the victor in any game. Now to business with this off-worlder and those behind him, and those behind them— Zarn speculated for a moment as to how far that line did actually reach.

There was no wall nor gates to hedge in the sprawl of the new city at the port. Though the merchants and administrators, the tourists (a few of them were coming now, mainly for the larox hunting in the west) and other law-abiding inhabitants were housed in five- and six-story buildings, some even with gardens, but all contained in barriers manned by private guards very much in evidence.

There was no place here for a penniless man, Jofre understood well; he pushed on at the steady gait of someone who knew exactly his goal toward the fringe where were the hurriedly built buildings put up after First Contact near a hundred years ago now. These had been "quickies" in the workman's tongue of that day, shoddily built, and never maintained past the bare necessity of keeping a roof on and not allowing too many holes in the doors.

Many of these housed traders too, those who sold a wealth of intoxicants from both continents of Asborgan, plus stray near-poisonous mixtures brought from off-world. To add to the wealth of drinkables there were the dealers in flesh, who made their wares visible in half-curtained windows during the busy hours of the night, and innumerable forbidden drugs. The police of Asborgan, the old city, had long ago washed their hands of any responsibility for what went on there. Those inhabitants who were permanent might look after themselves, which most of them were viciously able to do, or disappeared for good, and those off-worlders of the better sort kept out of the "Stinkhole" and maintained their private protections. A few spacers now and then would wander in, but they came in pairs or trios and with stun guns in open holsters well displayed. Those natives from the lowlands beyond the city were seldom fool enough to even think of penetrating into that foul morass and anyway, having come to town, they automatically hunted shelter and amusement of the kind they had always known in the old city.

Jofre's hands moved twice. He had set "No see" pattern in his mind before he had started down the street which ran to the Stinkhole. Though he was well exercised in that maneuver, he had never employed it before except as an ordered drill. But all he had heard suggested that it should work. It was not that an invader could actually render himself invisible, rather that he projected some type of thought which shuttered him from casual sight of those he would move among.

The fetid odor gripped at one's throat. Coming from the austere cleanliness of the mountains, the order of the Lairs, this was like a foul fog. Almost one could see the vapors of decay and excrement rising from the broken pavement. The hour was one strike past sundown and the quarter was coming to life.

Several paces ahead Jofre saw his first spacers. They were clad in close fitting one-piece suits, a brownish-grey which almost matched the discolored walls about them, but was relieved on standing collars and shoulders with colored patches, not all of the same design, symbols he supposed of either rank or duties. This trio were young and they walked with caution, glancing from side to side. He did not understand the remarks which floated back to him but somehow he sensed that they considered this visit to be something of a challenge.

Because he had nothing else in the way of a guide, Jofre kept in their wake. When they halted before a wide open door which was hung with a billowing curtain of grease-stained faxweed stuff colored a sun-brilliant orange, he paused, too, a step or so before him the opening to an alleyway.

There was a clangor of Whine drums from that doorway loud enough to drown out what the spacers were saying—they seemed to be in argument on some point. In fact those wailing notes were loud enough to drown most of the noises of this portion of the street.

Sound might be so blocked but not instinct. Jofre's head jerked to the left. Trouble—back in that black pocket of an alley. Not any cry of help to be heard with the ear, rather the reaction of someone fighting against odds. And in spite of the nature of the Stinkhole and the fact that its dangers should not be lightly taken Jofre moved—into the alley.

4

JOFRE COULD SEE THOSE STRUGGLING SHADOWS ONCE he was within the mouth of that noxious way. There was slime underfoot and he adjusted to that danger. Backed against one of those oozing walls was a tall figure and moving in a concentrated attack three smaller ones. Jofre shifted the thong of his pack and went into action.

No steel here, unarmed tactics, he decided in a flash of thought—there was too good a chance of the victim being brought down in a mixed conflict. The side of his hand chopped between neck and shoulder of the nearest of the rat pack and even above the drums he could hear a cry of pain as the fellow reeled away. Something metal dropped from the attacker's hand to ring on the fouled pavement as he clutched at an arm now swinging uselessly.

"Yaaaaaah sannng—" The cry came from Jofre unbidden as he whirled to strike out again, this time with a lifted knee which sent the second assailant backwards. But their victim took a hand now. There stabbed out of the dark a spear of light no thicker than Jofre's thumb. It struck the reeling man, then snapped to the left and showed for an instant a face rendered grotesque by a wide, near toothless mouth.

Both of those the ray had touched slumped. The man Jofre had first tackled was already careening down the alleyway, slipping twice and howling as he went.

"My thanks, Night wanderer." The words were oddly accented and Jofre stiffened. With all his need for caution he had betrayed himself with that battle cry. This other was addressing him by the name given by lowlanders to his kind.

Now the shadow which was the stranger stood away a little from the wall, stumbled, and would have gone down had not Jofre, without thinking, caught at a shoulder to steady him.

"You are hurt?" he demanded.

"I am—bruised—in my self-confidence as well as my flesh, Night wanderer. That there would come a day when such as that could move in on one of the Zoxan clan—alas, one is indeed led to face shame."

"If you need shelter—" Jofre began. He was not oathed to this stranger but neither could he walk away and leave him to be food for another pack of rats.

"Night wanderer, unless you have some mission of your own, I would welcome company—at least into the outer ways of this festering pit," the other replied frankly.

His forward move was a lurch and Jofre was again quick to steady him. There was something wrong about the arm the other had half raised to regain his balance; it was short, too short—was this stranger maimed?

Not only was he seeming short of part of an arm but he was plainly limping as they made their way out into the crooked street. The spacers were gone and for the moment there seemed to be no one else nearby.

Jofre turned his head to survey the stranger he was aiding. Only long training kept him from betraying full astonishment. He had heard that other species not akin to his own were star rovers. However, this creature was so far from anything he had ever seen or heard tell of—except there was a faint relationship perhaps to one of the "demons" of old tales—that he was shaken.

The other more than matched Jofre in height, perhaps being a handsbreadth the taller. His uncovered head was domed and hairless, but about his neck, rising like a great frilled collar, was a fringe of skin which pulsated with color—now a dusky scarlet, though that was fading even as Jofre set eyes on it. The skin of the face and head were scaled, minutely prismatic. In the somewhat fore-pointed face, which was chinless, a well-marked and toothed lower jaw showed no fullness, the eyes were very large and by this garish light appeared to reflect small points of flame.

The stranger was wearing a spacer's suit monotone in color and with no badges to be seen. He was busy now settling one of those fabled off-world weapons into a holster at his belt. His other arm, that which Jofre still held onto in support, was but half the size of the right one and completely covered with the sleeve of the uniform which was turned back and fastened over it.

Having holstered his weapon, the stranger turned his attention to Jofre.

"Well met, Night wanderer—or do you agree?" Those large eyes seemed to narrow a fraction. The voice had a hissing note which tended to distort the words a fraction.

"Who are you?" Jofre was startled enough to demand, bluntly.

The frill had lost its color, subsiding now to lie about the stranger's narrow shoulders like a small cape collar.

"You mean—what am I? There are no others of my kind on planet now, none that I have heard of. We, too, are wanderers of a sort but circumstances have led me to exceed the reach of my fellow clansmen for a while. I am a Zacathan—my call name Zurzal."

Zacathan! The Master had spoken once of that race. Old, far older than Jofre's own kind, their history stretched back into time mists so dim that no one now could penetrate them. Not a warrior-producing race, on the contrary they were scholars and students, the keepers of archives, not only of their own kind but of all those others they had contact with throughout their explorations into the pasts of many worlds. There were Zacathans to be found among the First-In scouts, for their particular senses and minds made them excellent observers and explorers. And there were fabled repositories of knowledge for which they were responsible, their long lives (when compared to other races) making them excellent record keepers.

Zacathans occupied a strange niche in the galactic world—serving at times as diplomats, peacemakers. Their neutral status was acknowledged and they were made free of any world they wished to visit.

But to find one in the Stinkhole? That Zurzal wore one of the stun weapons was only prudent for anyone venturing here; but why would he have come in the first place?

"I seek a man—"

Jofre tensed. Was mind reading also one of the arts this lizard man knew? If so, he wanted none of that art to be exercised upon him. He loosed his grip on Zurzal's shoulder.

"No, I did not read your mind, Night wanderer, I merely called upon logic. You, of course, wonder why I am here." He uttered a low sound which might have been laughter. "It is no place for a man of peace, that I agree. But sometimes one must overcome a number of obstacles to assure one success."

There was a silence between them. If the Zacathan waited for some reply, Jofre did not know what he should give him. Was the other hinting that he needed help in his search? If so, he had appealed to the wrong one.

"Master of Learning," Jofre gave him the honorific he would have given to one of the few scribes who jealously guarded the history of the Shadows. "I am new come to this place; I know no one herein. You must seek another guide."

"Are you oathed?" That demand came swiftly and with such force of authority that Jofre found himself replying at once with the truth:

"I am not oathed—the Brothers are no longer mine."

He was aware of the sharpness of those eyes which stared at him as if the Zacathan could indeed pry open his skull and sift out some answer.

"There is no outlawing of the Brothern that is recorded," the Zacathan said. "But also none will deny an oath. But— you are not of Asborgan and never have I heard of the Brothers taking into their midst a man of another race."

"I do not know my race, Master of Learning. I was found in the wreckage of a space lifeboat and I was so young that I had no memory of what chanced before the Master of the Lair brought me forth and back to be one of his followers. His issha failed, and the Shagga priest, who long wished none of me, denied me thereafter. But it remains I am issha-trained." And with that he ended confidently. It was no boast but a statement of fact.

"Do you wish an oath binding?"

Was that not what had drawn him here? Though in truth he had not dared to hope for any lord to offer him a House tie.

"Would not any in my position wish such? But I am not backed by any Lair now and the weight of the Brothers will not vouch for me."

The Zacathan nodded. "However, there may be an answer to two problems in this. Will you come and listen?"

It was a strange stroke of fate—there was almost something to be suspicious of in such a quick offer but at least he could hear the off-worlder out. Perhaps after his late experience Zurzal saw the need for a bodyguard. Well, Jofre was trained to that as well as the other uses of the Shadow ones.

"I will come."

He matched step with the Zacathan, walking on the side with the maimed arm. Already he had gone into bodyguard action, assessing each and every spot from which an attack might come. But though they met others, they were left alone and Jofre found himself beyond the Stinkhole and into that section of the port settlement where there were the hotels to shelter travelers.

They approached the largest of the buildings set aside for visitors from off-world, a tower which reached some ten stories above the ground to dwarf the highest of the old town's defense. Here was a clear circle of light about the wide door, showing in warning detail the guards, mainly, Jofre thought, of off-world stock and alert as their training demanded. However, at the sight of the Zacathan the one to the right raised his hand in salute. Whether he triggered some unseen mechanism or not, the door slid back without any needful touch to admit them into a place which, for all his training to be ready for the unexpected, almost brought Jofre to a halt.

Before them was a large hall chamber, one which might have swallowed up half the Lair. And it was divided by a series of tall walls into transparently sheltered circles, squares, alcoves. Some of these were vacant, others having company within.

The floor was not matted but in some places carpeted, in other sections grounded with what seemed stretches of sparking sand, in one place with what had all the appearance of thick mud, and in several what could have been well-cultivated grass starred with colored blossoms. However, the major roomlets were more conventional with a floor of thick carpet into which the boots sank. Here were no seating cushions and knee tables. Rather what looked to offer the same welcoming support of cushions were supported by frames raising them some distance from the floor. And in two of these so furnished there were parties of spacers, plainly of officer rank by the prominence and color of their badges.

Zurzal was threading a way which wound between window-walled units and Jofre followed, though for all his efforts he could not keep his eyes from straying now and then to the occupants of other roomlets they passed.

In one which was floored with the grass (if it were grass) there were planted two of what looked to be misshapen trees, wide trunks extending horizontally. Perched on these were two beings of surely a very alien stock. One was fragile of body, the proudly held head was covered with what seemed to be curled silver white feathers. The eyes in an oval face were very large and set rather to the side, while the mouth and nose were united in what could almost be termed a beak. From a wide gemmed collar about the slender throat floated a series of panels of gauzy stuff, the color shading from pearl-white to rose, constantly rippling with every movement of the slender body they were apparently to adorn rather than cover. Jofre thought this must be a female, for her companion, plainly of the same strange species, had a feathered head with an upstanding crest, and feathers extended across his shoulders and down the outer side of his arms. The hands he used in quick gestures were more taloned than fingered. His clothing was more practical perhaps, what there was of it, as it consisted of breeches of a shiny material and boots quite like those of any spacer.

The birdlike couple were neighbored by a stretch of sand wherein several large rocks had been assembled. On these squatted things—Jofre could not at that moment accept them as sentient beings—not emotionally—they were too much like, or rather suggested, carvings the Shagga priests used to express the forces of evil. Yet their shelled, near-insectal bodies were at ease and two of them held with foreclaws what were plainly large mugs into which from time to time they would dip a long tube tongue from between fanged jaws. Their attitude was so much like a trio of elders discoursing on a formal piece of business that Jofre was shaken.

He grasped the significance of this hall; its builders had made a conscious effort to suit not only humanoids but those of alien cultures. And for the first time it struck firmly home to him how very diverse life-forms along the star lanes must be—how utterly different, perhaps even repellent to his kind, some of those other worlds might seem, and how narrow his own life had been.

Zurzal reached the end of the corridor which ran between the "home world" sections of the lobby. Overhead this space reached to the top of the tower and was there roofed over with a yellow, partly transparent oval covering the whole of the circle through which any light outside would

filter down changed into the likeness of sunshine. The
Zacathan beckoned to Jofre and stepped upon a platform,
which, when it held both their weights, arose, passing by
two levels of balcony until it locked against the side of
the third, and the railing there swung back. They were
faced by the outlines of a door in the wall and Zurzal
stepped forward to plant his hand flat against that. The
panel moved and slid away and once more the Zacathan
waved his companion forward into what was undoubtedly
his own private quarters.

The glow of the lamp was very dim, but not enough to
disguise the anger on the face of the man who stood facing
a visitor. That he had not expected company was plain, for
he wore a loose chamber robe belted with a twist of cord
about him. Behind him was the pile of sleeping cushions
from which a private alarm had drawn him and in the air
was the faint scent of the brewing herbs intended to settle
nerves and drive away the day's cares—so much had the
man called Ras Zarn taken to lowland customs.

A loose hanging curtain was pulled to one side and his
unexpected and undesired visitor entered.

"There is no need—" Zarn near spat the words; at his
side his hands twitched as if he wished nothing more than
to make plain his resentment with a physical blow.

"There is every need," returned the other, low-voiced.
Her cloak was all concealing, but with every movement
its folds loosed a second scent into the air. "I have con-
veyed to my Master your instructions. He returns this:
None that he oaths undertakes another commission until
the first oath is blood erased. He is angry that you have
questioned this and tried to lay a new duty on me. Though
it does not greatly matter, as the path I follow now leads
off-world and I will not be here to serve as your hound.
I will be star borne at sunrise." She spoke without emotion though the other's growing rage was almost a tangi-
ble thing.

"By the Death of Shagga—"

She had been on the point of turning to leave, now her hooded head was on her shoulder.

"Master's oath—not Shagga—is my bond, and so it has always been. Apply to the Master for the weapon you wish, priest."

And she was gone. He twisted his hands together as if he had them about her neck. Fools, worse than fools! Traitors if what he and others suspected was true! Now—there was nothing he could do this night, save think. And think he must.

5

JOFRE SAT UNEASILY AND TOO COMFORTABLY ON ONE OF
those platform-raised cushion chairs. He was facing the
outer wall of the room, which was a curve as transparent as
were the divisions in the lobby below. There was a faint
sprinkling of watch lights from the old town, reflections
of the more brilliant illumination here. At his side, on a
waist-high table, stood a drinking vessel, seeming so fragile
a too quick grasp might shatter it, the green of verjuice
showing through its sides.

Zurzal, having equipped himself with a drink also—
which as mysteriously appeared as had the verjuice in a
wall space after the Zacathan had pressed some buttons—
seated himself opposite his only partly willing guest.

"You say you are not oathed."

"I cannot be—there is no Master who will coswear with
me."

Jofre had dropped his pack by the door. It would be ready
to hand when he left.

"You are issha—is there any way that you can retreat
from that?"

Jofre stiffened. What games did the alien want to play?
Surely fortune had not been that good to him that he could
find employment so easily, even for a short time.

"I am issha."

"I know something of the Shadow Brothers," the Zacathan continued. "It is part of the nature of my race to learn all we can about the ways and customs of others. It is true that your services are always contracted for through a Lair Master. How much power has this Shagga priest of yours?"

Jofre considered. "In oathing the Masters alone control us. The Shagga sometimes serve as special eyes and ears, they are advisors to the Masters—"

"The Masters can overrule them then?"

"Twice in our history it has been so. But to those who disputed with the Shagga misfortune came later—they were assha lost."

"As was your Master," Zurzal pointed out. "Could it be that he was a target then for Shagga ill will?"

Jofre swallowed. "He did not listen to advice he thought was too conservative, too lacking in a desire to learn new."

"So he therefore became one of the Elder Shadows."

"How do you know what—" Jofre flared.

"I told you, I would learn all that I can. There is talk in the old city of the Brothers, perhaps some of it rumor only; but even in rumor there is a core of truth. Think, Night wanderer, your Master was not a second voice for Shagga and he is now gone. Just as you have been hunted forth from the fellowship. You are freed by the very one who would condemn you, the Shagga. You have no Master save yourself. Therefore as a self-master you may be oathed."

Jofre swallowed. Dimly perhaps he had known a little of this but some back-looking part of him had not allowed him to put it so frankly.

"You want an oathed issha?" he asked now, trying to read the alien's face, which provided no features he could interpret after any pattern which he knew.

Zurzal took a long drink from his glass. "After tonight do you not think that I need a bodyguard? For a while I am not even a whole man." He set down the drink and his hand went to the sealing of his suit. With a quick jerk he had it open to the waist and back from his left shoulder and arm. For there was an arm there—or the beginning of one—a length of bone and flesh and a child-size hand.

"One of the attributes of my people," he informed Jofre. "We can regrow a lost limb but the process takes time and it is time I do not have right now. Therefore, I need aid."

"There are surely off-worlders who are guards—like those below—"

"They are not oathed men. You see, I know your customs, issha-trained. With an oathed man out of the Shadows I need have no fear of any treachery or carelessness. I lost this," he moved the small arm, "because I could not be ever on guard. I need you, Night wanderer. I offer you oathed status."

There was a pause and then the Zacathan continued. "What I wish to do here on Asborgan is only a beginning. Oath with me and it will mean the stars. You or any other in your place must have such a warning."

The stars—then what the Master had thought was true. On other worlds there were doubtless the same feuds, the same intrigues, the same covert wars for power that the lords here played. And this Zacathan had already suffered maiming—which meant—

"You have a blood feud?" Jofre asked—such he could understand and be prepared to undertake.

"Not as those of Asborgan see it. But that is not discounting any danger, and such lies ahead. You are out set from your Brothern; in a manner of speaking I am also. But that I shall discuss only under oath. What is your word—?"

Jofre's right hand closed about his dagger and he drew that one long weapon left him. Holding it now between both of his palms, he went to one knee before the Zacathan.

The scaled fingers came to meet his instantly and the dagger was drawn from the sheath of flesh in which he held it.

"By the Great Oath"—so this off-worlder *DID* know enough of the Brothern to follow the form—"I call you out of the Shadows and into my service until my purpose is achieved or life is ended." Zurzal reversed the dagger awkwardly with his single hand and managed to press his forefinger down on its point. Dark blood welled in a thick bead and he smeared it on the dagger and held it out for Jofre to once more clasp double-handed so that that smear of blood was imprinted on his own flesh.

"I am bound—" he said shortly, making no move to wipe that mark from his hands as he returned his weapon to his girdle.

"So done. The hour grows late. Have you eaten, sworn man? Drink up, for I have much to talk of now and time itself is snapping at my heels."

"I have not eaten." Jofre's hold left a faint bloodstain on the drinking vessel. "But if time is limited, that is of no importance."

The Zacathan's long jaws opened in what must have been a smile. "I assure you I am not so blind to the needs of any employee. As it happens, I myself have not eaten." He crossed back to the opening in the wall from which he had taken the drinks. A button brought up light in a square and Jofre saw marks in a series cross that.

Then the Zacathan busied himself with the lower line of buttons before that light square was gone. "They do vespar well here," he said, "it is considered, of course, in this setting a novelty. And there are some other things I think you will find to your taste. We are not too unlike in our eating habits, we two peoples."

As quickly as he had gone to one wall so now he turned to another and set fingers in a ridge to open another door.

"This is the fresher," he said, "and here," he had found another doorhold and opened that also, light streaming up even as the portal went back, "are sleeping quarters. Settle in while we wait to be served."

Jofre merely glanced into the sleeping room. There were two bed places which looked to be as luxuriously soft as a district lord might aspire to. But the fresher drew him most.

Austere and barren to city eyes as the Lair might be, it was always meticulous clean and cleanliness was part of issha training. This tiled chamber did not resemble the bathing place he had always known but it promised a relief.

The Zacathan had opened another door within that place of ease to display a cubicle and now he indicated various small levers jutting from its inner wall.

"Hot steam or water as you wish, cold, soap power spray, and air-drying hose. Make yourself free—"

Then he was gone. Jofre rummaged in his bundle and brought out much creased but clean underdrawers, and shirt. But before he tried the amenities of that strange room he made a careful inspection. There was no entrance save that through which he had come and there was certainly no place where there could be a place of concealment. Not that he had any fears of this being a trap—he was oathed and, therefore, as tied to Zurzal now as if he were one of the Zacathan's scaled kin.

It took him a little time to master what the fresher had to offer and inwardly he marveled. No Lair Master could hope for such luxury as this and he savored the feeling of cleanliness afterwards; almost he wished he did not have to rewear his travel-stained outer clothing. But he made very sure that the stone he had found at Qaw-en-itter was again well secured in the wrapping of his sash girdle.

Zurzal was waiting in the outer room beside a larger table to which were drawn up two of the tall seats, these not so encushioned as the others. On the table itself were set out covered bowls and platters and two plates. By the side of each of those there was an array of knives and spoons and some odd-looking cutlery which ended in a set of points and which Jofre could not identify.

"It was good, lord," he glanced over his shoulder at the now closed door of the fresher, "my thanks for your offering—"

The Zacathan had already seated himself and whipped the cover from the largest of the bowls so that steam and a smell, which made Jofre suddenly very aware how long it had been since he had last eaten, filled the air.

"I am no lord." Zurzal was now busy ladling some of the contents of the bowl onto the plate before Jofre as the younger man slipped rather awkwardly onto that elevated seat. "I am Zurzal, I do have a title—which means nothing on most worlds other than my own. I am called a Histechnic which only means that I have completed a series of studies to the satisfaction of my elders and betters. I am Zurzal. And you?"

"The Master named me Jofre."

"Jofre—" repeated the Zacathan, "sky given. Because of your finding, I suppose."

Jofre was again a little shaken at Zurzal's quick grasp of his name meaning, for that was a word of the high country and not the lowlands where a visitor might have traveled enough to learn something of the native tongues.

"Yes—" He eyed his plate now, drawing his knife to cut at the generous portion of smoking vespar which had been served him.

"Your Master made no attempt to report your finding to the port authorities?"

Jofre shook his head. "The Lairs have their own ways. He could have sent me to one of the valley lords but he did not. He was a man who kept his thoughts much to himself."

"I have heard that the Brothers are indeed secret in their ways; it is part of the faces they turn to the world. At any rate he gave you a trade, this Master of yours."

"He judged me issha," Jofre said and remembered his inner pride, which he had taken precautions to hide on the day he had received the Three Weapons and the Cloak. Not that any of those had come with him on his being exiled.

He was having a hard time curbing his hunger now, making himself chew and swallow slowly. The food was diverse. As he had spoken, Zurzal had heaped on the plate before Jofre large portions from at least five of the dishes.

"You need my services—" Jofre was perhaps too abrupt in turning from his past to the immediate present but he had no wish to dwell now on what lay behind him.

"I do."

"What lord has declared blood price against you?"

"It is no feud, as I have said, like those of your nobles. There are those who are opposing me openly, and recently I have learned that there is an even greater problem in the nature of some who want what I am working upon for their own purposes. Those you took me from tonight might well not have been seeking my life, but rather my person and what I know."

Though earlier he had admitted hunger, Zurzal seemed more intent now on talking. He sipped from his drinking vessel, but, though he stabbed at a portion of vespar on his plate with one of the pointed pieces of cutlery, he did not yet raise it to his mouth.

"You must understand those of my stock," he said. "To us knowledge is everything. And one of the sources of knowledge which we hope to find are records—records of the Forerunners—"

"Forerunners?" That was one term Jofre had not heard before.

"We did not come first into space. There are worlds upon worlds, some very old. It is a pattern with sentient people that they rise to a high point of civilization and then some inner lack or flaw within them saps the energy which sent them climbing and they decline, sometimes to actually disappear and be forgotten. So we are not the first rovers of the lanes; there were others before us and they left their traces here and there. There is a great reward posted for any major find which is made of such peoples— for they certainly were not all of the same stock or even the same time. Their civilizations may well have been as varied as our present ones. You saw in the lobby below life-forms which did not share a common beginning with yours. Yet all those are now citizens and equal under the galactic laws.

"Thus we have tantalizing hints on this world and that of other peoples, some we are sure were not native to the planets where they left these remains, but space rovers such as ourselves. One of my colleagues was able to find an entire planet city, stretching completely round the world which supported it, of a highly technical civilization. There are experts there now studying it under supervision.

"So many finds come by chance alone—but if there were some way that such could be traced—" There seemed to be tiny cores of light in the Zacathan's eyes; his neck frill was rising to frame his head and shading into a green-blue.

"And there is a reward for such discoveries?" Jofre thought he understood.

"Yes—but greater than any reward is the knowledge itself!" Now Zurzal's frill was a vivid fan.

"You are hunting such? But I have never heard of any old things on Asborgan and the Shagga priests have very ancient records. If there was knowledge, they would have sought it out."

"No, I am not hunting Forerunners here—rather a man. I was in trace of him this evening. He may be the key to a great discovery— We have records and also we have access to special knowledge. I have a discovery I must try. At present I am not well accepted by my people; they believe that my research for the past few years has been for a very childish and no-purpose reason. I am young, as my people count years, and oftentimes the young are dismissed for thinking something can be done in a different way.

"There was a discovery made and ill-used on a world named Korwar. The results were so terrifying at the time that the man who backed that expedition saw that—or thought he saw that—the instrument used was destroyed and all the plans from which it had been manufactured were completely wiped from the records.

"But the idea of what had been done could not be denied and there was an undercover rumor of what had happened which spread. That there could be an artifact which would summon up an accurate picture of the past had now to be accepted. But the machine was gone and even mention of it was thoroughly suppressed.

"Not so well suppressed that it was totally forgotten, however. Two planet years ago those plans were rediscovered in a mass of material turned over to my home section of the archives by the Patrol after they had raided a Jack outfit. There was a mixture of reports, some log books of old ships taken by Jacks—and it needed sifting for anything of value. I was given the task of that sorting—mainly because I was the youngest member of our group and considered the least responsible.

"But what I found was a complete plan for a probe, such a probe as would make any Histechnic give perhaps all his fangs for. I took this to my superior. He was not interested, pointing out this had been tried once with dire results and that my people would not tamper with anything of the sort. He confiscated what I had found and told me to keep quiet.

"I did. But I had those plans here." Zurzal laid aside his eating tool and tapped his forehead. "And keeping quiet I went to work until I had that scanner rebuilt. I ran one trial in a place I knew of and the result was astonishing, but it came and went in a flash and I knew that the remains on which I tried it were so well-known that I could be accused of falsifying evidence—which among my people, Jofre, is akin to oath breaking, if you can imagine that. Therefore, I must find someplace unknown where I could hope to tap into history totally newfound, and I also worked steadily on a true scanner, hoping to produce a way for it also to make a permanent record of what it draws from the past."

That the Zacathan believed in what he was saying was very apparent. That it could be done—well, Jofre would want to see for himself. Meanwhile it was more important to know who might be the enemy.

"It is your leader who would hunt you down now?" he asked.

Zurzal shrugged. "If he knew, he would oppose me legally, then I would have the Patrol on my heels. No, so far I do not believe they suspect what I would do. But the information on which I based my work was from a Jack hold, and that means it could have been kept to be sold to the Guild—surely you can guess what possibilities their Veeps could see in such."

"Treasure hunting." Jofre could see. However, if the Thieves Guild was to supply his potential enemies, he had accepted a very direful oath indeed.

"Treasure hunting," Zurzal conceded but the Zacathan did not seem upset at the thought of taking on the most dangerous starwide organization—next to the Patrol—which existed.

6

"**H**OWEVER," ZURZAL HAD TAKEN TIME TO CONsume a good portion of what was on his plate, as if he must also do a little arranging of his thoughts, "it is not what the Guild might consider treasure, adaptable in their consciences as they are. No, what I want is knowledge—to find a place where there was a storehouse of records—"

"Does such exist?" Jofre had cleaned his own plate and was watching the Zacathan's neck frill a little bedazzled. It continued to glow as ripples of rich color spread along the creases.

"I spoke of the world found by one of my colleagues where a vast city covered the major continents. There were archives there and—maps—"

Zurzal swallowed another bite. "Star maps. Though the language of the archives is yet to be broken down for translation, there were certain symbols which we recognized. That was indeed a Forerunner world, a planet where a technical civilization had reached a peak before the end and yet they were in turn latecomers to the star lanes, for they had museums, they had visual records, of much older civilizations which had preceded them. There were hints of finds to be made, which some freak of their own time prevented their making. My people impounded all such records with the blessing of Central Control. And it was my good fortune to be allowed some access to them.

"No, I do not hunt what the Guild would consider useful—the only market for my hoped-for finds would be my own people and, therefore, no market at all. I search for archives and perhaps the only way I can find them is by reaching into the past with the scanner for long enough to pinpoint the position of what I seek. Having made such a find, I will have redeemed myself in the eyes of my colleagues as well as added to the sum of our knowledge. None of my race could wish for a greater treasure hunt than that."

"Here on Asborgan—?"

Zurzal gave an impatient shake of the head. "No, as I said, here I seek a man, if he still lives. He did two band moons ago but he is in the last stages of graz addiction and I can only hope he still exists. He was the member of a First-In expedition to a world which, on Patrol charts, is named Lochan for the man who first made landfall there. What its inhabitants—they are listed as extremely primitive and at least nine points away from human—name it we do not know.

"As a primitive D class world it is off-limits to all but the smallest of Free Traders, those who nose around the lanes for the crumbs and are regulated by the Patrol as to what they may carry. There IS trade, however. A kind of clay which, when ground into sand texture, is highly desired by the potters on Reese, and there is some exchange for unusual furs and other oddments.

"But there is also a ruin which was reported by the First-In scout and then partially explored by the first expedition. They made certain records of the finds, one of which—" The Zacathan left his seat and went to a set of shelves on the other side of the room. He came back holding a box hardly bigger than his hand, which he put down before Jofre with the instruction, "Look!"

There was a round of glassy substance not unlike a mirror in one end of the box and into that Jofre obediently looked. The surface of that disc was changing color and now he could see what might have been a picture of a portion of a strange landscape. The ground was dull, black-sprinkled grey and would seem to be bare earth with no form of vegetation. From that sea of coarse, dull colored sand projected a straggle of rocks, so eroded that one could not tell whether they were a showing of the planet bones or the work of men.

The picture was moving, drawing closer as if he were approaching closely one of those rock humps. Here there had been a clearing, the sand had been dug or pushed away, and then it was as if Jofre stood at the edge of that pit looking down. The uncovered base of the rock reached deep, until it joined another at right angles. And on that second there was a flashing marking.

"The F ray brought that out." The Zacathan was beside him. "It must have been set with great care to have lasted so long a time."

"What is it?" Jofre was completely mystified.

"It is a symbol which has been found twice before and each time it indicated a storehouse," Zurzal informed him. "Only there was to be no follow-up; the expedition was attacked by desert dwellers. Two men escaped, one dying before they reached the landing port, the other very badly injured. He managed only to bring this recording with him but he was unconscious and could not explain its value nor even where they had been excavating to discover it. His brush with the natives appeared to plunge him into a deep trauma—for a year or more he was plagued by nightmares and had to be kept sedated. He resigned his position, dropped out of sight, and turned to graz. It was as if he had faced something so terrible that he dared not live conscious of the past at all—"

"The natives?" Jofre looked away from the small mirrored picture.

"Perhaps—very few of them come to the port and those that do any trading with off-worlders keep much to themselves. They seem to travel in fear themselves. There must be some menace which they do not discuss with outsiders.

"However, this," Zurzal took up the box again, "and the memories of that man are all the clues we have to what may be the greatest discovery of this generation. That same symbol elsewhere led Zammerly to the cache of star maps on Homeward, and the same sign brought Zage to the lost library of the Woland Priest Kings. It is as if some of the Forerunners deliberately marked such sites either for preservation or for a future exploration which never came to be. Thus Lochan is the goal, and the site of this," he tapped the box with one finger, "depends on the memory of one Garsteon z'Vole, who is now living out what is left of his life in the Stinkhole."

"They say graz rots out a man's mind. His memory may be already gone," Jofre pointed out. To him this seemed a business in which there were too many loopholes through which failure could thread. But he was oathed and it was now his business as well as he could carry it out.

"That can only be determined by meeting the man. Which perhaps we can tomorrow."

To that Jofre was ready to agree. He refused the comfort of the second bed in the Zacathan's inner chamber, taking his proper place, as a bodyguard should, in front of the doorway. The carpeting in the room was far softer than any sleeping pallet he was used to and he knew that no one could enter without his knowing.

That the Guild, having heard of Zurzal's boasted scanner, would be interested he could well believe. Even in the mountain Lairs they had heard tales of how the vast criminal network took into its clutches inventions and discoveries which it kept for all time. Jofre could understand that if what Zurzal claimed for his find was true, it could well be put to other than archaeological searches. As for himself he would believe you could see into the past when such a scene was directly before his eyes.

In a Lair tower to the north at that same hour, which was near midnight, a Shagga priest bent his shaven head over a brazier which gave forth a trickle of reddish smoke, drawing that deeply into his lungs. His eyes were shut and he rocked his body back and forth in a rhythm which matched the words he mouthed in a hissing whisper. He was going deeper perhaps than was prudent. Hate had set him on this road in the beginning; now there was a touch of fear. The contempt he had earlier felt had diminished; this adversary was stronger than he had ever conceived he would be.

He collapsed at last, huddled in upon himself as if he would hide from what was about him. The arts of the priesthood were very old; those which they transmitted to assha and issha were only the surface of what powers they could summon. He had been a teacher all of his ordained life but at times he had also been a seeker, probing into some ways which, if not completely forbidden, were warned against. It was only his fear which drove him to try this.

Jofre awoke from his doze immediately alert and ready as his training had prepared him to be. For a moment he did not stir; he looked through only slits, keeping his eyelids near closed to deceive any watcher; at the same time he readied himself. That he was not alone, of that he was so sure that his hand moved serpent still and quick under the edge of his sleep cover until his fingers could close about the handle of his dagger.

Still he waited. His ears quested for the sound of breathing. There was a faint light from the upper part of the walls where they joined with the ceiling, enough to give him full sight. He heard nothing, saw nothing.

Then there was a stab of heat, great enough to bring him up to his knees, his hand at the stretch of his girdle on the right side of his body. There was a lump there, the stone he had brought out of Qwa-en-itter! And through the cloth which hid it he could feel warmth, for the worst of that touching flame had eased.

At the same time that sense of another presence was gone, as if he had snuffed out a Lair lamp. And the warmth went with it. Shagga—Shagga tricks! He was as sure of that as if some priest still stood there leering at him.

The priest who had expelled him from the Lair company had certainly held no kind thoughts towards him, but why would he want to carry on any feud now that Jofre was no longer contaminating the Brotherhood? That pain— he worked the stone out of the girdle folds. There was no light in its depths now—it was opaquely dead. But there was still warmth in it as he handled it, turning it around in his hand. Whatever it was it answered to Shagga power. Perhaps it would be far better for him were he to discard it now. Yet he could not. It was as if the artifact had a will of its own and had oathed itself to him.

Jofre shoved it once more into hiding. He took the position of far-seeing—the door was made fast and he must dare thus for caution's sake. Nonetheless he planted his shoulders against the portal it was his duty to guard, firmly enough so that he trusted any movement there would alert him, before he began the Descent-to-the-heart—forcing his breath into the slow, regular pattern, using his will to wall away all thought.

He had always excelled in this since he was issha made— in fact to the point that the Master had used him several times without advertising the fact, in his own affairs. Perhaps some quirk of his off-world–born brain adjusted easily to this skill.

Now having reached the Center, where was the path? He might be standing in a circle of light from which led radiating rays to form roads. He sent out thought and was again in live memory, in Qwa-en-itter, his hand reaching for that ovoid he still carried. There was a flicker of light, a spark, as he touched it. Yes, a thing of power—very old power. And the Shagga— Jofre tried to find the path which would lead back to that one who had come spying. But nothing remained on which he could fix to draw himself.

A lash of will took him out of the Center. His hands began to move in the ritual patterns which summoned strength—to both mind and body. He could feel the rise of that strength, the way it filled him. The rest of the issha preparation he could not continue. He had only his dagger—the small knives, the sword, the flask of blinding powder, the hooked rope which could be either a ladder or a weapon, those he had been forced to leave behind. He felt their loss now; not being able to complete the Readiness worried him. If the Zacathan truly wanted him as a bodyguard, then with the day's coming he must see about acquiring the familiar weapons he had been deprived of before he would be fully at ease, a formidable trained issha. Where in this lowland country such weapons could be found, Jofre had no idea, but he must make plain to Zurzal their lack might cripple him in the future.

However, with the morning he had no time to speak of his need to the Zacathan; the other had anticipated him.

"You must have supplies," Zurzal said briskly, having summoned another of those very satisfying meals out of the wall. "I have heard that you or the Brotherhood can accomplish much with bare hands—but there is no reason to try and prove that. We shall see about more conventional ways of defense."

Seeing about that brought them to a warehouse-shop where Jofre, trailing Zurzal into a smaller room, nearly gaped as wide as any field laborer as he viewed racks of weapons, cases of them, an armory so superior to that of the Lair that the latter would seem a play place for children. However, a second and more measuring survey showed him that there were few of the conventional issha arms here. Those small throwing knives easy to be hidden—he could see none in the case which held mainly daggers and some blades long enough to be short swords. There were no whirl chains, no hook ropes.

"Over here." Zurzal was beckoning to him. The seller of these wares was a lowlander, though he wore the formfitting clothing of the spacers. A Tarken, Jofre placed him, one of the hereditary clan of merchant guardsmen. He had opened another case and was taking out those storied off-world weapons, such as Zurzal himself wore, the sidearms which could either stun for capture or burn to a crisp an enemy.

"Take your pick," the Zacathan bade him as Jofre joined the other two by the case.

Jofre looked uneasily to the salesman. He had his own needs, but to reveal them now would instantly label him for what he was in front of this lowlander. On the other hand were he to be summarily equipped with weapons with which he was unfamiliar, he could well be defeated in an attack before he started.

He stared down at the stunners. Then put out a hand hesitantly and picked up the nearest. It did not have the familiar balance of a dagger or sword, did not fit easily into a trained hand. Though as he examined it more closely it appeared to be a simple enough mechanism—one closed the fist thus, then within easy reach of the forefinger were two buttons. Jofre raised it and squinted along the short barrel at the wall—yes, just so must one aim it. He laid it back with its fellows and picked up the next. A man must feel at home with his weapons, not just take the first offered, thus he hefted them all before nodding and making his choice.

"This—" It was the one lying in third place, and somehow in his hand it felt the best. "However—there must be other things—" Again he looked across Zurzal's shoulder to the salesman. How much dared he reveal by his choices?

It was as if the Zacathan read his thoughts, for Zurzal turned to the Tarken and at the same time reached out and laid his hand on Jofre's shoulder.

"Ras Quan, this issha is blood oathed to me," he spoke deliberately. "As his New-master-one I must equip him properly. Let him then choose what he believes will serve him best."

Tensely Jofre waited for the Tarken's reaction. But there was not so much as a flutter of the eyelid to suggest that such a request was in any way out of the ordinary.

"Seek, Night wanderer." At least he was giving Jofre the name lowlanders bestowed upon his kind. "We have very little call for the Shadow weapons here; you may find that most are lacking."

Jofre nodded curtly and swung on his heel, going back to the display of knives and swords, eyeing as he went the various arms hanging on the walls. There were two small knives which might do for sleeve weapons, though whether they could be easily concealed in any clothing save the wide-sleeved coats his kind favored he was not sure. However, they looked enough like those he had practiced with for many hours to be familiar and he indicated them. A sword—if they were bound off-world into places where the weapons would be those lasers—swords would be useless. He eyed them wistfully for a moment and then shrugged.

A climbing rope he could devise himself but he found with some excitement a large bowllike container full of polished hooks, well barbed, and of those he selected a dozen, running his fingers across the metal in search of any flaws. Such he could conceal in a turban wrapping if he must.

There was no use, he was sure, to search here for a sleeve box of poison dust, nor other subtle weapons of the Lairs. And he had to be content with what he picked out, the hooks being fastened for transporting within his sleeves, the knives and the stunner joining his dagger in his girdle.

But it seemed they were not yet done with shopping for the Tarken led the way into another room and within a short time Jofre found himself with a totally new wardrobe, the suit of a spacer, a cloak which the Zacathan said was meant to shed water, underclothing, new boots which felt curiously heavy as they were soled with the plating for ship-bound travelers. In addition there was a bedroll and some of the aids to make easier camp life. Though Jofre privately could see no reason for such pampering of one who was out of the austere life of the Lairs.

He wondered now how Zurzal was to pay for this. As a sworn liegeman Jofre was entitled truly to weapons, the livery clothing of his employer's house, just as he would be entitled for, as long as the oath held, transportation, food and lodging. In the natural course of things a wage sum would have been transferred to the coffers of the Lair from which he came—but that would not be necessary in this transaction.

But no bar pieces passed between Zurzal and the Tarken— rather the Zacathan merely showed the other a band on his wrist on which glowed a number of markings. Then in turn Zurzal pressed this to a pad the Tarken produced.

As they went out of the place Zurzal explained and turned his wrist well out into the daylight to show Jofre.

"Each world has its own form of exchange for goods and services. But there are ways of transferring such credit without having to pass it into the form of another planet. Thus—" He flexed his hand and the wristlet was a gleam in the thin sunlight. "I have funds on several worlds to draw on, and pay from those funds may be demanded by merchants on other planets. It is a simple system—"

Jofre thought he could see the flaw in it. "If that is stolen and used—"

Zurzal shook his head. "It is blood joined to me alone; it will not work for any other. Now, let us go ahunting for this spacer."

He turned quickly into a side street, threading a way he seemed to know well, heading again for the Stinkhole. Jofre slipped a hand across the new weight of those recently added knives. Last night his unarmed skill had been put to the test; he wondered if this time his ability with steel would be called upon.

7

THERE WERE NO BURSTS OF EYE-TORMENTING LIGHT from any of the smoldering doorways, no whine of drums. Today they might be walking through a sink of long-deserted squalor. One or two muffled figures kept close to the verges of the pavement, since the center of that was a riverlet of corruption. Only the thick stench was the same, puffing out at them from the opening of every alley as if the Stinkhole itself had life and nauseous breath.

Zurzal seemed to know where he was going. Jofre was a step behind, every issha instinct alert. He did not like what he could not see but was sure was lurking in the stained walled buildings, in every one of those alley mouths; he did not like what he heard—which was nothing at all. Certainly there should be some sound.

As Zurzal took a sharp turn to the right, a moment's glance around placed Jofre. This was the same place where he had come to the rescue of the Zacathan the night before. To venture into such a trap was more than foolhardy.

At least a small measure of light had come with the day and Jofre could see the path ahead, choked as it was with rubbish. The alley was dead-ended by a portion of the building on their right which extended at a sharp angle. There was a door at floor level and up the narrow slit of this wing a series of windows, all covered with boarding.

They passed the site of last night's skirmish. The noisome debris underfoot had been churned and there were signs of some heavy object having been drawn along through the muck—doubtless one of their opponents taken away. A sound brought Jofre into action. He was before his patron, a punch of his shoulder sending the Zacathan back against the moisture-running wall while he half crouched in defense. Out of the disturbed muck and nameless mounds ahead poked the nasty white snout of a ku-rat—the largest Jofre had ever sighted.

His hand went from the hilt of his dagger to the far less familiar grip of the sidearm. He brought the weapon up, sighted and fired. There was a screech, then the twisting body arose from the rubbish in which it had sheltered to curl into both silence and a motionless ball. Jofre stared at the creature. A lucky shot certainly, he had had very little time to practice—save in dumb show—before they made this expedition and he must not believe that his accuracy with the off-world weapon was more now than rank fortune.

"The power of the first part," Zurzal observed from behind him as Jofre still sheltered the Zacathan with his own body, "is enough if we meet more than rats—to stun is allowable. I think that a burn-off even in this place might bring some retribution down on us."

Jofre made the adjustment before he returned the weapon to his unfamiliar overbelt. He had changed into the new clothing before they had started and he regretted deeply the loss of his wide-sleeved overshirt, though he retained the girdle which had always supported hand weapons. To be reduced to a dagger and this stunner-blaster meant double caution on his part.

In two more strides the Zacathan reached the door in that wall which blocked their path. It looked as set-in as the boarded-up windows above, as if it were sealed firmly. Yet the off-worlder did not appear to be baffled by this. He drew the taloned fingers of his useable right hand down the splintery surface, scratching into wood spongy with rot.

At waist level those fingers stopped to circle about as if outlining some lock which did not appear. Then Zurzal drew his own weapon, examined the setting critically before he made a small adjustment, and put the barrel to the door. There was a flash and a crackle of sparks ran from that point of contact. A moment later the Zacathan resheathed the weapon, put palm flat against the door to push. Reluctantly the barrier gave, showing a thick gloom within.

"This is a back way," Zurzal's voice dropped near to a hissing whisper. "What we seek lies there." He jerked his head toward the wall of the building from which this portion angled.

Jofre's hand was quick. His fingers closed about the Zacathan's sinewy arm.

"I first," he made that an order. "Which way?"

"Right. There should be a stair near. The man we seek has lodging, such as it is, near the top floor. He is, I think, very near the end. The report made to me is that he has not been seen for three days now."

Within the house there was a thick effluvium of old filth, the result of beings of more than one species being crowded in long-uncleansed quarters. The two invaders found the stairs easily enough, for there was an orb light, near exhausted by the feebleness of its glow, suspended over the well of the steps.

Now there were sounds, grunts, the rumble of speech, and once the throb of a hand drum, a smashing of what might be glass, and again a scream which held both rage and pain. Zurzal continued to climb; Jofre, eyes darting from wall to wall of the stairway, ears and nose alert, edged after him. They reached the third level of the stair and Zurzal stopped, fronting another door.

This time there was a waiting latch and he caught at it, throwing the door open. The room on the other side had once been of fair size, but a partition which did not reach clear to the ceiling had turned it into a pair of alcoves. The stench was now overpowering. In the nearer of those alcoves was a sleep mat and on that lay a body wrapped in a discolored length of bed covering.

Zurzal felt in the pouch which was clipped to his belt. He brought out a package which, without opening it, he squeezed vigorously in his one hand. Now another scent joined the rest, a cloying one which seemed thick enough to be visible in the room.

The bundle on the mat stirred, shifted, sat up. A bloated-faced head wobbled on a neck seemingly too thin to hold it, then a bony hand came out of hiding and made a wide circle through the air. The eyes in that puffed face, which at first had looked unfocused, now centered on the Zacathan. A slobbering tongue crept out from between swollen lips and then a voice which was thick and hardly to be understood spoke a single word:

"Give!"

Zurzal ripped open one end of the drug bag and that wavering hand strove to flatten and hold steady as the Zacathan shook onto the palm a wad of seeds and leaves. Dropping some of the stuff in his haste, the man on the pallet crammed it into his mouth and those jaws so hidden by fatty tissue now moved as he chewed.

The effect came within a few moments. The sagging body on the sleep mat sat straighter. There was a certain dim intelligence back in the eyes to be sighted in the constrained light through a half-masked window.

"You—" The word was mumbled around that cud which the spacer still chewed.

"As I promised," Zurzal returned calmly. "Enough of this to take you to the end—" He gave the bag a little shake and once more the smell of the drug was wafted about.

The bulbous head nodded. "Fair—fair bargain." Then the mouth moved as the speaker spat the pulp of his chewing onto the rotting floor. "I have—" Now two hands emerged from his wrappings and he was tugging at that covering, pulling away from his body.

He was bare of any clothing Jofre could see. In spite of the bloated face and head, his body was a rack of bones covered with greyish, grimed skin. But he wore around his neck a chain which sparked in the light—iridium! How could such a derelict possess that? Supported from that chain was a round medallion of the same precious metal. Long broken nails scrabbled at that until it opened and a tiny dark roll fell out. The ex-spacer weighed it in one hand, and for a moment, in spite of the ruin of that face, Jofre thought he saw a flash of another man who had once been.

"Fair—fair bargain," the spacer stuttered a little. "But—you may find it not so good. Not so good." He shook his big head from side to side. "Give!" he demanded.

Zurzal dropped the packet of graz in the seated man's lap and took the roll, slipping it into his belt pocket.

The spacer's one hand clamped on that opened bag as if he feared it might be taken from him. But with the fingers of the other he swung the pendant from which he had freed the roll back and forth.

"Beyond—call—duty—" He looked up at the Zacathan and then he laughed horribly, his huge face a mask such as one of the Shagga imagined demons might wear. "Get out! You have what you want, lizard man." The more he spoke, the firmer his voice, the clearer his words became. "You have everything but luck, remember that." Greedily he pawed at the bag, brought forth another wad of the drug and crammed it into his mouth, dropping his head back on the bed place. It was plain that he had nothing more to say.

"What do you have?" Jofre asked as they edged out of that horrible box of a room.

"The coordinates of the place on Lochan which I must visit. He was a hero once—did you see that medal? Through everything he held onto that."

Zurzal's voice was somber as they retraced their way down the staircase. "He is very near the end," the Zacathan continued. "The supply I took him will surely see him out and he will die in what poor comfort that has left him. He was a hero—once—" The repetition of that phrase rang in

Jofre's head as they stepped once more into the alley and headed back into what was a cleaner and brighter kind of life.

Ras Zarn stood again in that small private chamber of his, and again he held a farflyer. There was a weariness about him these days. Sometimes fortune turns against a man—then to fight his way through obstacles becomes twice the battle. He was no longer as young as his appearance made him seem to these townsmen lowlanders. And he had been long away from the north and close touch with that which demanded his inborn allegiance. Just as those who gave secret orders were far removed and uncaring about his problems.

They were set in the old ways as tightly as a sunken worm in its shell and perhaps all which would ever get them out was how one dealt with that worm—smash the shell itself.

Zarn shivered with a quick glance from one of the walls to another. The bird in his hands raised its head and quickly he put his other hand over that, cupping it gently, blinding the creature. No one knew, would ever know, just how farseeing the Elders were, nor what strange powers they could call upon. It needed only one small misstep, one planting of a seed of suspicion, and he himself could be a target no matter how well he had served in the past.

Sighing inwardly, he seated himself at the floor table and set the farflyer on its well-scratched surface. Lifting the shielding hand, he looked into the eyes of the north-bred creature.

He gained no comfort from that voiceless communication. His lips drew into a bitter grimace. They made their own rules, disregarding the fact that this was a spaceport, that a section of it was not under planet law, but rather that of the outlanders who policed travelers as long as they stayed within the confines outlined for their supposed safety.

An emissary could be sent in but he would be as visible, in spite of all the preparations of the Elders, as if he marched behind a challenge drum. Oh, the watchers were out; Zarn had learned much these past few days. However, the fighter was now oathed—to an off-worlder. And only this very morning had the news come that that off-worlder was ready to leave planet, taking the subject with him. If they meant him to be followed off-world—but why? Such an expenditure was beyond anything Zarn had ever been authorized to put out.

To arrange now for an assassination was to ask for not only failure of that mission but perhaps the uncovering of at least part of the net he had been cautious years in weaving. He could only report facts—those apart seemed to expect miracles.

Zarn stared at the wall. The feathered messenger uttered a plaintive sound and the man's head jerked. His hand went quickly to his belt pouch and he brought it out again with the globule the creature gobbled before settling down on the tabletop, scaled eyelids closing over those large eyes.

The merchant arose stiffly. They gave him very little choice and part of his present burden was the fact that they refused to make plain to him why and wherefore. What had this renegade Shadow done which made him the focal point of such a stir? What was it he carried? That spark of cupidity which had made Ras Zarn an excellent merchant flared briefly. If he could learn that and turn it to his advantage! But how—how?

Zurzal checked once more the carry bags. The labels were firmly attached.

"We shall transship at Wayright," he said. "Luckily that is a refit planet and sooner or later a trader bound for Lochan will planet there. Then we shall have cramped quarters for the rest of the trip." He looked at Jofre. "You are not space wise—some cannot adapt to such confinement. On the passenger transport it is another matter. But a trader is built first for cargo and only takes passengers on reluctant sufferance."

Jofre shrugged. "What has to be, is," he commented. However, inwardly he had begun to wonder. He had never, before these past few days, even been near one who traveled the star ways. Yesterday they had gone to the port station and he had seen the waiting ships standing nose skyward— there had been such a difference in them—from a swift courier of the Patrol, to a wide-bellied Company freighter. The passenger ships ranked somewhere in between and, looking at them, Jofre had felt an odd small chill, to venture into the unknown in one of these— But men had been doing it now for hundreds of seasons. There were disappearances and wrecks, dark stories of ships devastated with strange plagues, which wandered with a crew of the dead until they were blasted by a Patrol cruiser or were caught by a sun. Space was not kind nor cruel; it was the fortune of travelers which made it one or the other.

As for him, there was no choice. He was oathed and if that took him into space, so be it. He would move into this new world as he would move into an unknown strip of territory, with every sense alert, even though what he might have to face would not yield to any weapon he knew.

He again wondered at the Zacathan's seemingly inexhaustible funds. Jofre's passage had been promptly paid. In fact Zurzal had opened for him an interplanetary account and showed him how one could draw upon it. Into that his wages would be fed automatically every quarter. For himself, however, he was dubious about such a pay method. And surely the Zacathan must be wealthy beyond the means of even a valley lord to so arrange matters.

He had booked passage for them on a passenger ship due to depart before sunset tonight and they were on their way now to board. There were small scooter carts belonging to the hotel which loaded both passengers and their luggage. Having heard so much of Zurzal's scanner, Jofre was silently surprised that no box or container which could contain such was loaded aboard the scooter they chose. But it was not his place to ask questions.

However, there was a feeling of uneasiness which settled on him as they approached the landing stage, where groups of passengers before them were filing onto the lift, to be hoisted aloft into the ship. Did that come from the shrinking of the planet-born who had never been in space, or was it a cautionary impulse triggered by something else?

Whichever it might be Jofre was on guard. There were a number of attendants around but none of them showed the characteristic features of the Asborgan-born. These were mainly off-worlders and some were truly alien. However, it was one planet-born who centered Jofre's regard. In this very mixed group he might not have attracted the general eye, for he was wearing the livery of a high lowland house and accompanying a young Highblood.

His livery was not in any way suggestive of what might really be his duties but to Jofre there was no mistaking a Shadow—even though he had never seen the man before.

The position he was careful to keep, about two steps behind that of the young Highblood, was that of a guard, even though only the hilt of a ceremonial sword showed at his girdle. So another of the Brothers was bound off-world on an oathed mission. Jofre might have given a surreptitious gesture of recognition, but his own status was too equivocal. The chances were that they would never meet.

These two were well ahead of him now, almost as if the young lord was very eager to get aboard. And the Asborgans were already swinging upward on one of the lifts by the time he and Zurzal reached the takeoff mat.

They stepped onto their own transport, one of the attendants sweeping their baggage up beside them, and began to swing upward. Jofre fought his sudden, and to him shameful, reaction to that rise. Instead he made himself stare determinedly down at the port, and beyond it the old city, and beyond that—the only world he could remember.

8

WAYRIGHT WAS A CROSSROADS FOR THE STAR LANES. The many differences between races, species, sentient beings, which Jofre had been introduced to at the spaceport hotel on Asborgan, were here set forth even more plainly. He had to keep tight rein on himself not to turn and gape after the passing of what might be a vast lump of dough riding on a small antigravity plate and putting forth now and then eyestalks to survey something which caught the fancy of that particular traveler. Even an imagination honed and trained by issha teaching could not supply an idea of the world from which *THAT* had come.

Though the humanoid form was the more prevalent, there were also insectoids, some scuttling along on six legs, others, taller even than the Zacathan, progressing on powerful hind legs alone, using their upper and middle limbs in quick gestures to augment their click-clack talk. He caught a glimpse of one of the crested males of the bird people and, next to him, a warty-skinned, broad-bellied creature which resembled one of the pond dwelling amphibians of Asborgan. What passed here began to be like a nightmare in which eye refused to accept what was to be seen. Jofre fell back on an issha's refusal to be tricked even by his own senses.

The street was divided down the middle by a board rail of what gleamed like metal. Down that glided seated platforms which picked up or dropped passengers along the way. But Zurzal had chosen to walk. The Zacathan was apparently absorbed in his own thoughts. He had not spoken since they left their quarters.

This thoroughfare was lined on either side by many-storied buildings of an architecture new to Jofre. The first floors were square, as were those above; however, each was smaller as the structure rose floor by floor. And that larger section so left as a balcony surrounding each floor was occupied by potted and tubbed vegetation interspersed by seats and tables of different sizes and shapes to accommodate very dissimilar bodies.

This was a way planet, a meeting place for several of the major star lanes. Its principal industry and the livelihood of its natives was based almost entirely on serving the needs and desires of travelers en route to hundreds of different worlds. Beyond the inner city there were parks, carefully landscaped to catch the eye and tastes of a very mixed lot of visitors and there were amusements in plenty to fill any idle waiting hours.

The building towards which Zurzal headed was one of the more imposing ones. There was a deeply set insignia over the wide door and the automan that stepped aside when the Zacathan showed his identity disc was, Jofre was certain, armed.

The door opened automatically and they were in a wide hallway with many doors along each side. Zurzal did not halt his confident advance until he had reached the third of those on the left side. Again a door slid at their approach to admit them into a room thickly carpeted, containing several easirests and a wide table behind which, half-crouched, half-resting its thorax on a high cushion, was one of the insectoids.

As Zurzal approached, the alien, with one of its middle limbs, pushed into place between them a square box crowned by an upstanding, fan shaped attachment. The insectoid's claw tip touched a button at the same time it chittered its unintelligible speech.

"Welcome, Histechneer Zurzal. Our resources are at your command." The words clicked mechanically from the direction of that fan, and Jofre realized it was a translator.

"Rest and refresh yourselves, far travelers," the insectoid continued.

Jofre, however, did not follow Zurzal's example as the Zacathan seated himself in one of the easirests, rather he stationed himself in a proper guard position by the door, a point from which he could keep the whole room and its occupants in constant sight.

"Greetings to you, Fifthborn," Zurzal spoke directly to the fan and was echoed by a series of sharp clicks. "It is well with hive and hatchlings?"

"Well. And with you, Learned One?"

"Well." Zurzal's return was as terse as the other's. "I would take now that which is mine."

The insectoid's middle limb clawed at another of a range of buttons running down one side of the desk. "There has been an asking—" The fan squawked.

Zurzal shifted in the seat which instantly accommodated itself to his body. "Sssssssooooo?" The hissing which underlay all his speech suddenly was more apparent. "What kind of an asking, Fifthborn?"

"From one of power, Learned One. This one also has dealings with the Hivehold and to no small profit. He is one to be listened to."

"Sssss—" again that hiss. "And the name of this powerful one, Fifthborn?"

"He is—" the insectoid appeared to hesitate, "well-known enough—the Holder of Tssek."

The metallically sharp words brought silence. Jofre moved a half step forward. His issha sense caught that silent tensity in Zurzal's body, a sudden rigidity of spine. The Zacathan was not pleased by that answer, rather he found it disturbing.

"The Holder of Tssek," he answered now, slowly, spacing his words as if he would keep all emotion which might underlie them carefully hidden, "is known. I am not. What does he want with one who has been discredited even by his off-world peers? There is no reason to be interested in me."

"The hive repeats only messages given for the relay, Learned One. There is one named Sopt s'Qu, who is a highly placed follower of the Holder. This one is now at the Inn of the Three Fountains and wishes speech with you. He left the message some five daybreaks ago. There was no other message save that that one would see you as soon as possible."

"Well enough." Zurzal had relaxed a fraction but still it was apparent to Jofre that he was disturbed. "My thanks to the hive for the courtesy of message passing."

The insectoid made a gesture of assent and then pushed another button. "That which you left to hive care we return to you, Histechneer Zurzal." The words bore some of the formality of a ritual.

"I have been out of touch with many things for a space," Zurzal remarked. "There have been changes which a prudent being should know?"

The insectoid placed the sharp elbows of its higher pair of arms on the desk and latched that set of claws together. The feathery antennae on its head inclined towards the Zacathan.

"Changes? Not many and minor ones only, such as occur with the passing of time and can never be countered against nor truly foreseen. There are rumors of Jacks operating in the Alaban system, and there is the usual unrest on Vors—but there they are never happy unless they are unhappy—a most strange people. Of course Tssek is about to celebrate its Holder's Fiftieth."

"An auspicious occasion." There was a dry note in Zurzal's answer to that, as if he personally disagreed.

Before the insectoid could answer, if he were inclined to do so, a section of the wall at the left opened. Jofre was at half crouch at once, hand to belt butt, and then straightened, but did not release his hold on that weapon hilt as the small antigrav plate raised to the height of the tabletop and made for a landing on that. The insectoid lifted off its cargo, a black case with a handhold set in the top but no sign of any hinge or fastening on its smooth sides.

"Your hive desposit, Histechneer."

Zurzal was on his feet and approached the table, his hand out to close about that handle.

"I accept. My thanks, Fifthborn, for the courtesy and the aid of the hive."

"May you prosper in your going, Histechneer Zurzal."

"May the hive prosper with many hatchings, Fifthborn," Zurzal returned. He half bowed and the insectoid echoed him a little awkwardly, its body not made for such action.

As they issued forth from the building Jofre would have taken the handled box from the Zacathan but the other shook his head. "This I take—then if any harm comes to its contents I am alone responsible. But I do not like what I have heard."

"About the Holder of Tssek?" deduced Jofre.

"Just sssssooo—" again that hiss. "The Holder is bad news in any instance. Why he should be interested in me I have not the least idea but I am going to keep glancing over my shoulder from now on—"

Jofre shook his head. "The looking is mine, I am your oathed. But a man should know what he can of his enemies—who is this Holder and why is he considered a man of power?"

"It's a story, all right," Zurzal returned. "Let me get this back to our inn and into their safe room there. Then I'll tell you what I know. Which is common knowledge to most of stellar space in this quarter. My people have had no dealings with Tssek." He seemed to be speaking his thoughts aloud now. "What was there, suitable for inclusion in the archives, was routed out long ago. It is an old world and mainly inlooking, being occupied with a number of bloody events in the past."

Jofre was alert as they returned to their lodging but there was no sign that he could detect that any of that mixed multitude thronging the streets had the least interest in them. After Zurzal had turned his burden over to the security captain the Zacathan led the way onto one of those terraces ringing the building and took a seat at a table which was screened on three sides by the potted growths and well away from its nearest neighbor.

Having dialed drinks from the button menu on the table, he settled back in his seat, looking thoughtfully at Jofre.

"The hive tenders do not mention things they consider of little interest. Therefore, this business of the Holder is important enough to lead them to pass it on. They are the conservers and transferrers of credit; their vaults are entirely safe and have never been raided; they are keepers of a great many secrets. Doubtless even a number of the Holder's!

"Now—we come to the matter of Tssek. Over the centuries since First-In contact that world has not been too healthy a place, not only for off-worlders but for its own people. There appears to be some quirk in character there which leads to constant intrigue and war. For a long time there was no stable government, merely a string of very quarrelsome and warring small nations.

"A little more than a century ago there was born one of those individuals who appear in all our histories from time to time—a person of charisma and with inborn qualities of leadership to make him supreme. On Tssek this was Fer s'Rang. He set about vigorously and within twenty years he had united one continent under a government which for the first time appeared stable and likely to last. From there he went on to bring the eastern continent also under his control.

"Not only was he a born leader but he had the happy gift of being able to pick just the right followers for each job. And Tssek settled down into peace for the first time in the memory of that world. Things went very well indeed. Fer s'Rang, after he was proclaimed Holder, opened the spaceports for trade; he sponsored manufacturing and raised the standard of living and was generally what is seldom found, a genuinely benevolent dictator, and Tssek prospered.

"There was some dissatisfaction, of course; there could not help being, given the past history. But it was growing less and less. Then there came the Great Ingathering.

"All the clans which had been warring were invited to this. War was already a thing of the past and it was to be a peaceful celebration. In the midst of the festivities Fer s'Rang died. It was also a peaceful death, expected since he had been ailing for some time, though it was accepted that the exertion he had been put to in the last weeks of his life had told on him. He fell dead while receiving the homage of the last of the families who had caused him trouble.

"His second-in-command at once took over and it seemed for a space that there would be no change in what Fer s'Rang had started. However, the government began to tighten here and there, to dominate quietly, to take over. Now Tssek is a tight dictatorship and from all rumors a very unhappy world.

"The present Holder keeps aloof, as far as I have heard, from any off-world contact. And, as you know, only when a world is one of the Great Council can there be any examination of its internal problems. Tssek has never applied for such an inclusion. The rumor is that Fer s'Rang was on the verge of it when he died.

"There is a good amount of trade with Tssek. They provide a number of very much needed minerals as well as manufactured goods. But off-worlder contact is limited to the spaceport, as it is on any non-Council world, even as it was on Asborgan. There is good reason to believe that the Holder is anything but beloved by his present subjects. However, that is not for off-worlders to meddle with."

"But this Holder wants contact with you—" said Jofre slowly.

"Just sssoooo—and why? Not for anything I think I would have an interest in," Zurzal returned.

Jofre's movement was so sudden that it might have been intended to deceive the eye. The nose of his sidearm appeared on the surface of the table, pointing past the

Zacathan at the screens provided by two of the potted plants which were large and thick enough to be considered bushes and far too good a cover. The Shadow was on his feet in one supple movement. Though the eyes of his companion glittered and his frill stirred Zurzal made no move himself. Instead he raised his voice a fraction.

"Company expecting welcome moves in the open," he stated, then swung around in turn, though he produced no weapon of his own.

Their answer came from another direction: a man advanced into the open with the casualness of one moving about his proper business. He was fully humanoid—perhaps even Terran stock—but small. And he lacked the heavy browning of skin developed by a spacer. Against the high collar of his tunic his chin was jowly, and his eyes were small, set in darkened pouches of unhealthy grayish-appearing skin.

They were half-shadowed by the bill of a uniform cap generously embroidered with glittering thread, a matching device worked also on that high collar, and modifications of it up the sleeves of his tunic. The color of that tunic was a dead black, as were his tight breeches and the boots beneath. He also sported a wide belt from which hung, close to hand, a blaster sheath.

Jofre's second move had taken him crabwise, so that he was now in a position to defend the Zacathan from both this newcomer and that bush screen behind which his alert senses told him there was at least one more lurker.

Slowly the uniformed man smiled. "You are to be commended, Learned One, on the alertness of your guard. Harse"—the bush in the pots shook a fraction—"come out, man. We have no quarrel with the Learned One. On the contrary we come with open hands." And he held up both of his, palm out, demonstrably empty indeed.

From behind the screen of vegetation moved now a second man, much taller than his officer but wearing the same black clothing, though this was plain except for a shoulder patch in the jagged form of a red lightning bolt. He walked a little stiffly, holding his hands carefully away from a belt on which there were a number of loops all well occupied by rods of various sizes and lengths.

The officer clicked his fingers and Harse, if that was the subordinate's name, wheeled so that his back was to the three of them, forming a barrier between the table and the trio now by it and the outer world.

The Tssekians might be playing the part of being harmless in the most straightforward forms their culture recognized; however, Jofre did not relax. His trained senses could not pick up hints of anyone else in concealment. However, he had little idea of what weapons that festoon of belt equipment might represent and he was not to be caught off guard. Nor did he retreat from his position of guardianship for his employer as the alien officer moved closer to the table.

"I am addressing Sopt s'Qu?" Zurzal had leaned back in his seat with the appearance of one fully at ease. Yet Jofre sensed that the Zacathan in his own way was as wary as he was.

"News travels fast—" Was there or was there not a note of irritation in the other's comment? "Yes, I am Horde Commander Sopt s'Qu at your service, Learned One." And he sketched, so neglectedly that it bordered on an insult, a salute. "You are doubtless one who does not wish to waste time in formalities, thus I will say plainly that I have business to discuss, Learned One, a proposition to benefit us both."

Zurzal, with a flick of his good hand, indicated the chair from which Jofre had arisen. His oathed took two steps back, still in a position to view both the Tssekian officer and the firmly planted back of his subordinate, now playing screen for this meeting.

Sopt s'Qu's thin lips still sketched a half smile but he plainly was not pleased with Zurzal's greeting. He was undoubtedly used to a more receptive audience when he spoke of business. But he seated himself and was at a slight disadvantage with the greater bulk of the Zacathan looming at the other side of the small table.

"Since we have set aside formality," he continued, "I shall come directly to the matter. My Great Leader," his hand flapped up again as if he were saluting, "was informed that you were to be found here. He also knows that you have suffered from the refusal of your peers to believe in your splendid achievement of past retrieval. You seek now for an occasion—and a site—to demonstrate the value of your discovery. You are offered such with every facility which you may desire—you need only ask—"

"Most interesting." Zurzal's faint hiss was still to be detected. "And what moves the Great One to such a generous offer?"

"Belief in you, Learned One," came the prompt reply, "and in your discovery. You wish to prove that you can show the past; this is the fiftieth year of Our Leader's rule, of the sad death of Fer s'Rang. We can offer you an opportunity which will bring you fame, not only planetwide, but which will reach the stars, convince all doubters you can do what you claim to do. The Holder invites you to Tssek, to install your time scanner at Marlik and bring back the death day of Fer s'Rang. At the moment of your retrieval of this great event there shall be ready a planetwide broadcast to carry the scene to all of our people. Can you ask for more in the way of making known the value of what you have discovered?"

"Your Illustrious Holder must have heard also," Zurzal said, "that this discovery of mine is far from being perfected. That the former trials had no more than a very fleeting success. I can promise no better results and because of that I cannot, of course, accept this offer. Were the Holder to arrange such an impressive audience and occasion and then there was a failure—it would be more than a disappointment—"

"You are too modest, Learned One. Our Leader has made a close study of your achievements in the past. He believes that you are far nearer to complete success than your words now warrant. And he will see that you are well rewarded—"

"No." Zurzal was unusually curt. "I do not promise what I may not be able to produce. My thanks to the Illustrious Holder, but until I am sure of the worth of what I have to offer, I will not risk the disappointment of any who would seek to back my experiment. He will understand the logic of that certainly."

Sopt s'Qu's features had taken on a rigidity. "My Illustrious Leader is not a man to be easily disappointed."

Zurzal stood up. "No man accepts disappointment easily. But neither does any life flow with continued smoothness. I am sorry, Horde Commander, but my answer remains no— I am Zacathan and we are sworn to the gathering and preservation of knowledge. Yes, I wish to use my discovery in that cause. But until I am sure of success I must keep my actions to myself. If I can find the proper rhythm for the scanner by experiments, then I shall be only too glad to allow it to be used on any world to recreate such scenes of planetary history as the inhabitants wish to experience for themselves. That will be a proud day, but it is still far off. Thank you, Horde Commander, but make this point clear to your Illustrious Holder: I do not offer that which is not well perfected."

The Tssekian arose also. "I am sorry, Learned One. You have just thrown away that which would have brought you great glory."

"If so the loss is mine." But the Zacathan did not sound in any way disappointed. He nodded his head in a small salute as the Tssekian with no other word left them, his man falling in behind him as he passed the sentinel post.

"Now," Zurzal said slowly, "I wonder what lies behind that. I think perhaps I should speak a word or two in some places. There may be an interest in Tssek I have not heard of formally. Oh, well, we shall not be upshipping off to the Holder's hold, that is certain."

Only, of course, it was not.

9

T HE STRIKE CAME IN THEIR OWN QUARTERS AND JUST at the first sign of dawn. Jofre had been uneasy ever since their meeting with the Tssekians, as he was sure that Sopt s'Qu was not one to consider the argument finished. He thought once of the possible theft of the scanner but at his questioning, Zurzal had informed him that no one but himself understood its use. The various modifications he had been adding to the discovery originally made were not ones which existed now anywhere except in his own scaled head.

Though the Zacathan went to sleep early, Jofre continued to prowl their suite, slipping from wall to door to wall as if he expected each time he entered one of the three rooms to find a foe waiting and ready. He had asked the Zacathan about the various weapons Harse had apparently carried in plain sight (and if he had those in sight *WHAT* might he have in concealment?) and Zurzal had admitted that it was certainly true that the very warlike breed on Tssek might have perfected something new—or rediscovered something old, not yet generally known in the space lanes.

The outer door was locked on their palm signatures. As long as they occupied these rooms and made sure to set palm to the plate if they wished to be undisturbed, there could be no forcing that—short of equipment which would alert the whole inn. The windows were also sealed and locked where they opened onto the terrace outside. Jofre himself had taken the precaution of moving tubbed foliage out of their carefully symmetrical pattern in order to clear the space to the banistered edge of the balcony offset. He had in addition dropped two of his warn buttons at strategic places on that terrace.

Yet with every precaution taken he could not relax. The issha sense was awake; that which he had been so long trained to do was taking over. It was well within reason that the Tssekians might attempt to capture Zurzal. With the Zacathan and his machine both in their hands they could believe they would have no trouble in forcing the action they wanted. But why were they so determined? Zurzal had questioned that himself several times during the evening. He seemed sure that if they had full knowledge of what he wished to do, they also knew how chancy would be the success. To link the experiment to planetwide broadcast and then fail would discredit the Holder as much as the Zacathan himself.

"They play some game," Zurzal had said at last. "But it is not ours. I wish we had better luck in our passage. Lochan is a fourth place world, the only visitors are Free Traders. I do not have unlimited funds—for I cannot draw upon the resources of my House since they have disowned what I would do. Thus we have to wait for a Trader already bound for Lochan to take passage—I cannot just charter the ship on my own. However, this is the port from which such take off, and sooner or later one will appear."

To the wary Jofre such waiting, especially now, was like a silent war. This city was a maze of strange buildings of which he knew very little, though he made every attempt to study maps and mark out the principal reference points. The throngs of visitors (many kinds of whom he found it very difficult to name as "people" at all) added to the general dissatisfaction the whole port raised in him. The

sooner they could be free of this place the better—it was
far too removed from all he knew and he had almost begun
to wonder if all those skills which had been assha honed
would hold in such diverse surroundings.

For the third time he made the round of the rooms,
moving noiselessly, his night sight enough to take him
in the circuit. He would pause every few steps to listen,
sniff, call on his warn sense to pick up anything out of the
ordinary. This was the second night he had spent so and
he could not stand guard thus forever.

It was the faint flicker of one of his warn stones which
brought him along the wall, flattened against that, to peer
out on the terrace. His stunner was in hand, but in the
other he had one of the throwing knives on which he
would first depend, since it was an old and familiar arm
and he knew his skill with that.

There was something moving in a slow sweep in towards
the edge of the terrace. A grav-raft such as he had seen
in use for transport through the city. Jofre raised the
stunner—

It fell from fingers suddenly rendered limp, a grasp which
would not obey his will, anymore than his knees would
continue to hold his body upright. He crumpled forward,
facedown, and found that he could hardly breathe, as if
the muscles of his chest, the power of his lungs was being
crushed out of him.

If assault had been meant to cause his death, the attackers did not know the quality of their victim. Jofre's inner
defenses rallied instantly. He went into withdrawal, his
only answer to the unknown until he could learn the
nature of the weapon being used.

Though sight, hearing, other senses were dulled to near
unconsciousness, he was still aware enough to know that
there was movement now in the room, confident, assured,
as if those invaders had nothing to fear. Would they take
the commonsense action and kill him as he lay? So far they
had moved around him, heading towards the inner room
where Zurzal slept.

The pressure holding him immobile remained steady. Only issha defense kept him breathing shallowly! Then— he had been seeking the Inner Heart, the core of strength to hold to. There was a sudden flash, a shock as if he had heedlessly thrust a hand into a fire. He was aware of that hand now instantly. It was crumpled under him at an awkward angle, the fingers still curled as if about the stock of his missing sidearm. But he could move those fingers— a fraction. And the strength for that came from— The find he had made in the mountains—that he had brought out of Qaw-en-itter—the stone!

His thoughts seemed to slide in and out of a cloaking darkness as if he were bog-trapped. He fought to hold to them. Then there was a sudden explosion of pain in his side as he was struck a sharp blow there. And very faintly followed an explosion of sound, hardly more than a whispering, which seemed to be an argument of sorts. The answer came when he was roughly hoisted and dragged out of the room, over the terrace, to be dumped on a surface which vibrated under him—the lift platform.

A moment later a weight rolled against him and he smelled the musky scent of the Zacathan, who was plainly also helpless in the hands of these captors.

The platform gave a quick bound upward and it seemed to Jofre that it was whirling around. His precarious hold on consciousness grew even less, though he had somehow been able to move his hand so that the palm lay across the very slight bulge which concealed the mountain talisman.

There was clearly no move he might make now; he must wait until he could work around or break whatever the compulsion was which held him so pinned. But he could hold to the Inner core and so far had been able to survive. While a man lived there was always chance— which favored one who was ready to seize upon it.

How long they were airborne Jofre could not tell. It was much lighter and though he could not turn his head and dared not even lift those eyelids more than a slit high, he surveyed what he could of his surroundings.

The craft on which he was unwilling cargo was just that, a transport for cargo. And it had at least three passengers besides him and the limp and silent Zurzal. Two of them crossed his very restricted line of vision. One was Harse, and the other could be his twin. The third member of the party remained at an angle behind where Jofre lay and he could not see who it might be. But Harse's presence made plain that this dawn raid was a ploy of the Tssekians.

The lift gave a sudden drop, bringing Harse, who was in line of sight at that particular moment, to mutter a guttural sound or two and clutch at the rail, waist high, behind him. Another downward fall and they landed on some surface, with force enough to raise Jofre's body a fraction from the lift flooring and let him slam back again.

That slight change in the angle of his carefully masked sight showed him a tall reach of space-scoured metal. They had made landing close to a ship. Having done so, they were now in a hurry to get this particular cargo on board. Harse and his fellow ducked under the rail and then showed again with boxes which they dumped on the lift. One on the top tottered and fell forward, its weight bringing a red wave of pain through Jofre's leg. Once more the lift arose and was maneuvered closer to the side of the sky-towering ship. And into the cargo hatch of that he was slung along with the Zacathan, though the latter was immediately carried out of Jofre's very limited sight.

Harse appeared again, turned Jofre's body over with a kick and proceeded to search him for weapons. His belt knife and sleeve knives were jerked out, and hands felt over him but the Tssekian seemed to be quickly satisfied that his prey was now totally unarmed—too satisfied.

Though much of what Jofre could depend upon for offense and defense was gone, no issha was unarmed as long as he had control of his body. To regain that was the immediate task in hand. Jofre had not dared to experiment with even the smallest move while he had been under the eyes of his captors. But his hearing was slowly sharpening once more and he could detect now the sound of metal-shod space boots going away. Nor had they apparently left any guard.

He had been able to straighten the fingers of that hand which lay against the hidden talisman. Which was a suggestion he could not overlook. In his mind Jofre built a picture of that oval stone as he had studied it many times over. The dead, opaque darkness of it did not repel, rather it drew attention, as if there was a need within it—

The stone—dare he cut concentration from his surroundings to focus fully on that? Yet he felt that such a reckless move was the only one left for him to make.

Thus it was—his inner sight shut out the world, concentrated on the mental picture of the stone—he sought thus with all the intensity of assha strength of mind.

His hand raised a fraction from where it had fallen across his body when they dumped him here. The fingers moved in one of the Six Signs, those which led to the Great Call. Still he held the stone in mind grasp—thus it looked, thus it was!

The second hand tingled as life returned. He was dimly aware of that and raised it to join the other, so that the fingers could interlock in the pattern of "Seeking Strength of Mountain Winds."

He drew each breath a little deeper, moving sore ribs where that kick had struck. Slowly, with infinite care, he shifted one leg and then the other. There was a dim light in this cubby, enough for him to see boxes and containers which might be cargo or supplies. There was air enough to breathe, there was—

Jofre's body tensed and then he forced it to relax. That sound through the walls. This ship was taking off and, unprotected by any cushioned seat in a passengered cabin, he must face the brutal pressure of lift-off.

It came as a blow delivered by a giant fist and brought with it darkness. All he had so painfully won was negated in an instant.

* * *

In one of the upper cabins a woman lay breathing shallowly, her face drawn into a grimace. Then they were planet free, but she did not immediately loose herself from those restraining straps which had assured her safety. Her strained grimace was now a frown and she had the appearance of one listening.

At length she shook her head, as if denying some disturbing thought, and did arise from her resting place. Only to reseat herself cross-legged, her hands lying one on each knee. The movements of her body were now infinitesimal yet they were following a pattern as formal as might have part of a ritual dance. Her face had smoothed into a mask, ivory pale, in which blacklashed eyes were closed. The brilliant scarlet lines of her lips moved, shaping words which carried no sound. She began to sway back and forth at a more noticeable rate now. Her hands lifted—were held out before her. However, she did not open her closed eyes to watch the intricate patterns she threaded finger-wise through the air.

This was good—good! She could feel the power rising in her, arming her as these off-world louts could never dream one might be—

There came a shock, sudden, hard. Her eyes opened wide, her mouth shaped a cry which was not uttered. NO! This was impossible—beyond all knowledge—this could not exist—here!

Zarn—almost as swiftly as her thoughts had been interrupted and her weave strength shattered, her mind tugged at memory. Was—this what Zarn hinted at when he tried to seduce her from her mission and send her on a quest he merely hinted at?

She was frowning again, calling on every scrap of that memory. Truly Zarn had been excited to a point she had never seen. And the Shagga priests—they prided themselves highly on their imperturbability. But here—on this ship? The last time she had touched that kind of power had been back in Rama-di-frong when she had fronted the Lair Master and been given this assignment, proud that she would be a pioneer in off-world dealing. This was something which was so incredible that it must not be allowed to go unnoted, direct as her mission was.

Reaching for a box of prismatically glittering metal clamped for safety on a shelf behind her, she loosened its thumb lock and brought out a round hand mirror, raising it to the level of her face, inspecting her reflection critically. She had no vanity; that was never a part of issha training and was quickly dealt with whenever it arose. What she did now was view one of her weapons carefully. She had value and she could raise that value; she had been trained since childhood in the various ways she might use that particular weapon.

Now, she allowed the mirror to fall to her knee and gazed sightlessly at the near wall of the cabin. This new mystery—it was intriguing and demanding, yet it must not get in the way of her assignment—nothing must defeat that! However, these Tssekians were not particularly clever. Devious, yes; truly clever, no. There were ways people gave away their secrets though they did not speak them aloud nor inscribe them in reports. Supposing—just supposing this Sopt s'Qu had learned something of issha lore, had managed to obtain for his master that which she had sensed was now on board. That would be a danger. In the right hands it would mean a full control—of her. Her hand tightened into a fist.

They had taken off very suddenly. She had kept to her cabin as the role she would play demanded. But those others had been working on some plan—she was only a side issue, she had been sure of that—had meant to make it certain that her worth advanced highly before they reached this Holder. Thus it might not be to control her—though she must leave no suspicion unexplored—but for some other purpose.

She must now make very sure of her territory even as a hover spy soared over the land of some mountain lord. Rising, she began to make certain preparations which required access to several pieces of baggage, the contents of which had been most carefully selected.

There was the taste of blood in his mouth, a runnel of it from lip corner. The practice must have been a fierce one today. Jofre opened his eyes, but not on mountain sky. He was looking up at a ceiling not too far above him. His body ached with an ever-growing reach of pain and it was very hard to draw a breath.

This was certainly not the Lair arms court. Nor were these smooth walls around, as he painfully turned his head to discover, the rough stone of a Lair chamber. Where—where was he?

He allowed his aching head to drop back the few inches he had been able to raise it, stared at the roofing overhead and tried to remember the immediate past. Then he was aware of the vibration which thrummed through his body, spreading upward from the floor on which he lay. A—a ship—! Slowly it came, though it was adding to his pain to probe and hunt for that memory.

10

JOFRE WAS NOT GIVEN LONG TO MINE FOR MEMORIES. There was a thrust of brighter light into his prison and he made himself go limp. Better to discover the nature and number of any opposition before he put his own drained powers to the test. His almost closed eyes once more limited his field of vision but he knew that at least two had come to stand beside him and there was a guttural exchange over his body.

Hands pawed for a hold in his armpits and his feet were gathered up by another. The two of them edged out of the store cabin with his body and made their way down a much better lighted corridor. He was able to peer surreptitiously at the one transporting his legs—a man nearly as bulky as Harse and wearing the same uniform. They came to the foot of a ladder and he was dropped unceremoniously to the floor. A rope fell over his head, the loop of it crammed under his arms, tightened about him. He heard the click of boot plates on the flooring, saw that one of the men was ascending the ladder while the other dragged and pulled at him, getting his body into place at the foot of that climb.

He was to be hoisted up like some inanimate object but better still to let them believe that he was still unconscious. Were he indeed aboard a ship, as he was almost certain now was the case, there would be little chance of escape anyway. Best to let them believe that they had a really helpless prey within their hold.

The sharp jerking of the rope taking his weight from above aggravated the aches which had now grown beyond his power to count. That captor coming behind steadied his body now and then but certainly not for Jofre's comfort, rather for the aid of the one hauling him up.

They passed two levels, coming to a halt on the third. Once more he was dropped flat and this time they worked the rope off him. Then he was carried again, down a short corridor, until they entered a cabin of some size opening off that. Jofre plunked to the floor, only under him now there was a padding of some type of carpet and the air was not so stale, rather carried an almost fresh scent.

"As you see, Learned One, your fears are quite unnecessary—we did not leave a dead bodyguard behind us." The voice was familiar; Jofre fought to match it to a face.

"It would hardly have served your purpose to do so—" the hissing note in that voice he did recognize was exaggerated. "You will release him at once!"

"Learned One, we are ordered to give you all possible assistance—as long as you, in return, agree to consider yourself our guest— As a guest you certainly will not need a bodyguard—the Holder's hand would fall sharply on anyone daring to do you harm."

"You will release him," the Zacathan repeated. "You have given me no proof that your Holder has any peaceful thoughts toward me either. You have stripped my oathed of his weapons, he is harmless. Look at these bullies of yours, each overtops him by a head—could make two of him. Do you fear a man who has been held in stass until you have leached the strength out of him?"

"You are a man of peace, Learned One. It is well-known that your kind do not offer any threat to sentient beings. Why do you care what happens to this?" The toe of a well-polished boot swung into Jofre's very limited view, prodded him.

"He is the opposite of all you believe in, one who lives to kill, is that not so?"

There was a moment of silence. Then Zurzal answered, "This man is sworn to me, after the way of his own people; his trust lies in me, mine in him. You would have something of me. Very well: bargain, Horde Commander—or have you never heard of that?"

"Hmmm—" It was not a word, merely murmur of sound. Then there came a cackle of laughter, harsh, having nothing of humor in it. "So, at last we have touched you, Learned One. Good. You can have this one—as long as you conduct yourself as our . . . guest."

Jofre's body jerked. No one had touched him but that near rib-crushing weight which he had battled all these hours until it seemed as much a part of him as his body suddenly lifted.

"We leave you to yourselves then, Learned One—" There was the clang of boots, then the sound of a metal door slamming into place.

Jofre rolled on his side. He was dragging deep breaths. Getting one arm under him, he managed to raise himself to a half-sitting position. Zurzal stood by the bulkhead where the door showed its outline. By the Zacathan's position he was listening intently. Jofre rolled a little on his knee until his shoulder struck against a well-padded seat secured firmly to the floor. Gritting his teeth and calling on his reserves, he somehow got to his feet and stood, supported by that.

Now, when his own struggle was somewhat eased, the full force of what had happened struck home at him, almost hard enough to set him reeling again. He had failed in his task of preventing the very thing which had happened to them, betrayed the issha. There was only one answer to that, but one which he dared not make, not yet while the Zacathan lived and he was oathed.

Zurzal turned back from the door. His neck frill was extended and he raised a hand to smooth it down. In two strides he reached Jofre, swung the younger man around and pushed him down into the chair which had been his support.

"No warrior is the less if he comes up against the surprise of superior weapons." The Zacathan struck directly to the heart of the shamed confusion in which his cabinmate writhed. "They used a paralyzing stass ray; by the look you took it full force. Nothing save titanium armor can withstand that and neither of us were so equipped."

"I am your oathed—" Jofre muttered, unable to accept any such excuse. "I should have kept closer watch—"

"You are my oathed," Zurzal struck back sharply, "and as such you are on duty. And so shall it be until I release you. It is a marvel that you are still alive." He eyed Jofre up and down as if expecting to sight something unusual. "They could not leave your dead body—they brought you along—to space the evidence. But on my demand they had to produce you."

The Zacathan had come to stand directly before Jofre and now the long taloned fingers of the lizard man moved slightly. Jofre tensed and then, with all his will, relaxed. He did not know where Zurzal had learned the finger speech of the Brothers and indeed his messages had been somewhat clumsily delivered, but they were forceful enough. The two of them were under surveillance, perhaps, Jofre thought, by both eye and ear.

"We have something of a voyage before us," Zurzal continued speaking, though his fingers twitched in a different pattern. "They are transporting us directly to Tssek. It is the Holder's desire to use the scanner to produce a viewing on the fiftieth anniversary of that event, the passing of the leadership long held by the Illustrious Fer s'Rang to himself. I am to employ my time en route to making sure that the results will be just as he wishes."

Watch, wait, listen, look, those fingers spelled out, the orders given to any spy about to be planted in an enemy lord's holding.

"I am at command, Learned One," Jofre found his voice which sounded unusually harsh in his own ears. "What aid I can offer is yours."

"Well enough. Now," Zurzal went to the wall and pushed some buttons, "we shall see you fed. The stass leaves a man weak. Then—well, I have notes to be studied and perhaps a few experiments to run. Some will not require training and your aid will be of assistance."

A tray had come in answer to the Zacathan's order and he carried it, burdened with sealed containers, over to place on Jofre's lap.

"Eat—ship's rations, of course, but they are palatable and nourishing."

There was a drift of mist-thin weaving lying across the backed seat in the woman's cabin. She plucked up a fold of it between thumb and forefinger to eye critically. This was of fabulous worth, twice-woven spider silk—the cost more than even a Lair Master could raise. The color was strange—or perhaps one might say unfixed, for, though the basic shade might be a very pale green, as the folds rippled there were rainbow flashes along each edge, patches which glowed and faded with every move of the length.

Her own personal taste was for richer, deeper colors, but training, severe and critical, had taught her to suit her robing to the demands of her mission. Such stuff as this was truly the gift of a world ruler and when the time came she must show it off to the very best advantage, both of the gift and of she who had the wearing of it.

No jewels—except the moryen fire stones for a simple girdle to refrain the fluttering stuff so that it might outline her body, bracelets of the same to make certain the eye was led to the delicacy of her wrists, the slender beauty of her hands. She would not use the cheek lacquer overlay; rather a moryen fastened between the near-meeting arch of her brows—she considered her choices and made up her mind. Then, deftly, she refolded the robe, which seemed to cling to her hands as if it did not want to be laid aside, before seating herself and lifting her eyes to the expanse of the wall.

The metal casing of the ship's cabin was not starkly plain

here, rather there was a heavy scroll of pattern which was gem-brilliant in places. Her lip curled a little. Much as she inwardly rejoiced in color she found this display too ornate, lacking in taste. But it was not the patterning which she was viewing, rather she searched for a point which days earlier she had discovered, a water stone, into the blue-green depths of which she could channel her thoughts to outreach—

There was no true reading of the minds about her. To her knowledge barriers had never been pierced to that extent. Body language she was well versed in and she could pick up emotions, especially when they reached a certain intensity. However, that ability had served her well and she applied herself to it whenever she could be sure of privacy and quiet.

They were very satisfied with themselves, these Tssekians. So long had they held power that they had forgotten the useful curb of a little self-doubt. Certainly they were very apt to underestimate what they did not fully understand—a fault which might be safely used if the necessity arose. This one who named himself Horde Commander—her dealings had been with him and he was as clear to her as a cup of springwater from the Neeserdene heights.

There was the ghost of a smile about her lips as she considered the matter of Sopt s'Qu. Any issha-trained woman could have controlled him in three meetings, maybe less. She knew him for what he was, but she was after much bigger game.

There—that was this Sopt s'Qu; she caught a touch of his vast conceit, which was like a whiff of smoke in the air. Yes, he was very pleased with himself, swollen with success—too swollen. She considered that quickly. He was pleased with more than just her presence—the thought that he had in her a new toy for his master—he had achieved something else.

Her fingers moved. What else had he on board, or knew, or would receive in the future, to move him to such a fatuous belief in his own rise in the world?

She could not leave this cabin. It had been made plain to her that her presence on board this ship was not to be generally known. And she had accepted that, knowing that privacy would give her time to build her inner strengths for what would come. But now she wanted some touch with the ship world, to learn what was happening outside the walls of her own luxuriously furnished cabin. To perform, any issha must have all the information possible.

The only contact through which she might learn was Sopt s'Qu. So be it. She concentrated her gaze on that spot of sea-bright green on the wall and unwound her will to spin it as an intangible noose to summon the Horde Commander.

And the faint chime of the cabin bell came soon enough. She spoke only one word to loosen the inner locking:

"Enter."

Then as the Horde Commander strutted within, his bright eyes sweeping her up and down, she made a graceful obeisance, her own eyes lowered submissively, her attitude one of gentle waiting on his will.

"You have all you wish, Gentlefem?" Almost he spoke a little uncertainly as if he were not sure why he had come.

"You have given me of the best, Horde Commander." She made a small gesture to encompass the cabin and all that was in it. "I have specially to thank you for the tapes." One slender finger pointed to a small pile of discs. "It was most thoughtful to provide me with such information concerning your world—and your Illustrious Leader."

"What do you think of Tssek then, Gentlefem?"

"That it has very much to offer in every way," she returned promptly. "I think fortune smiled on the day we met, Horde Commander. You have shown me a very bright future."

Without being asked he settled himself in the second chair near that part of the wall which held the stone she held in focus. In her there was a prick of anger. He was making very plain what he thought of her. And she must make no move to destroy his summation of her character—the varl toad!

"So you like what you have seen on these." He indicated the discs. "Ah, Gentlefem, how much more will you like it in reality! And the Holder will indeed make you free of a very pleasant world. He can be very generous—when he is pleased."

She allowed herself a slight lift of eyebrows. "And you think that he will be pleased?"

"By you? He would have to be man without a man's body not to admire you, Gentlefem. Also we bring him not only your peerless self, but also the lock he can place on his future."

"You speak in riddles." She must be very wary, but also she must learn what she could.

"Riddles of time, Gentlefem. We have on board one who has mastered time—in his own way. And he shall master it for the Holder. You have doubtless heard of the Zacathan race?"

She triggered memory. Her briefing on Asborgan had not been too wide; there had not been time for as much as she would have wished.

"They are a race who study the past." Out of some corner she brought that.

"The past dealing with the Forerunners and on many worlds," the Horde Commander amplified. "Now and then through their delving comes some great discovery, for they are ingenious at following clues to ancient mysteries. We have one of their trained Histechneer's on board, who is to do just that for the Holder."

Sopt s'Qu looked very pleased with himself. "He will be greatly beholden to our Leader, who is giving him something his own people have refused to allow him: a chance to penetrate the mystery of time itself. This will be a discovery which shall make Tssek famous."

"And how does this Zacathan master time?" She was genuinely interested. All space goers knew of the Forerunners. And now and then rumors of finds from that ancient past filtered along the star lanes.

The Horde Commander grinned thinly, his lips seeming to find it difficult to shape such a move. "He claims he has a way. Our Leader is inclined to believe him—and the chance to put it all to the test lies now on Tssek. Our Holder approaches the fiftieth year of his taking power. He wishes to show to all the planet the event which transferred the rule from Fer s'Rang to him."

She allowed her eyes to widen in a calculated expression of wonder. "What a happening! How pleased this Zacathan must be to be a part of such action."

Sopt s'Qu lost his smile. "He is very modest, this Learned One. He objects that his preparations have not been successfully tried. But of course those who have knowledge which leads to power have no desire to share their secret. Once he has talked with the Holder and understands the advantages of the chance offered him, he will be quite ready."

But, she fastened on the thought, the Zacathan was not a contented party to this experiment, whatever it might be. She knew so little of his people. How effective could opposition from him be and what might such opposition do to impinge on her own mission? She wished she had at her command learn tapes—not like those which the Horde Commander had showered upon her, showing all the best of his Tssek, but those same which would give her an insight into what might prove to be a complication.

Then, there was that other—that touch she had made earlier. Surely somewhere on board was an issha-trained mind. And, since she alone had been assigned to this mission, she feared interference from that mysterious other. Who was the prey of the stranger? Why sent and by whom, that other lurker in Shadows? She dare not ask; though, as she eyed Sopt s'Qu, she longed to be able to enter his round skull and tunnel it, seek that information which meant so much to her.

The Zacathan was a player she had not been prepared

for. Was the lurker she had sensed connected with him, sent to spy on this strange time reader? Or a stranger from another Lair hired to perhaps a similar mission as her own? She felt anger again. She was issha, fully able to account for victory by herself alone.

But who and where was that other?

11

JOFRE HAD KEPT SILENT AFTER HE HAD CLEANED UP TO the last crumb all the food in the container Zurzal had shown him how to unseal. The Zacathan had produced a small black box which he tapped on one side and then stared intently at some curling lines of different colors which writhed, tangled and wove across the slick upper surface of that artifact.

In spite of what the Zacathan had said Jofre bitterly chewed upon his own failure. It was plain that much of what he had learned in the Lair would not apply to weapons which could be used from some distance with devastating force. Therefore, he must set himself to assess what he had that he could use. Would these off-worlders also be impervious to such dealings as the Shadow use of practiced invisibility? Might they be made, as any lowlander, to look at him and not see—see in the sense which would alert their thoughts? Would they even have a readable body language? He could not be sure until he tried. At the same time any experimentation on his part must be very carefully done.

Zurzal clicked off his small screen of patterns and Jofre, out of his desperate need to learn the worst, broke the silence.

"Learned One, you have traveled the star lanes very far, have you not?"

"Not as much as many of my kind. By our standards I am quite the beginner—a novice with the blade as your arms instructor would put it."

"I know only the ways of one world—truly. It might be well that I know more if I am to be of service to you, Learned One."

Zurzal nodded and smoothed his neck frill, which continued to show a fluttering at the edges, betraying his uneasiness though he appeared to be lounging relaxed in his seat.

"You deal in weapons," the Zacathan began abruptly. "Very well, we shall begin with those." He launched in the even tone of an instructor who expected full attention from his audience and he had it. As he continued Jofre could almost have been startled into a denial that such things were possible. For Zurzal went from hand-to-hand combat to the fiery destruction of worlds, and back again, outlining the innumerable ways of dealing death among the stars.

Jofre's first shame became a misery eating at him. He had been so believing that there was nothing the issha could not in the end defeat and now he heard of weapons so outré that they sounded like the demon myths of the Shagga priests. Most killed at a distance—killed, or—as the ray which had brought him down—rendered the victim entirely impotent. The stunner he had been so wary and yet proud of owning now measured by these brutal tales, for the Zacathan spoke plainly of the different deaths which could be met, had no more value than a rock some land grubber of the plains might pick up in the futile desire to defend himself against an osscark on the prowl.

Issha training—even the hints of his Assha-trained Master—was enough to assure him that this must all be true. Therefore, oathed though he was, he was worth nothing to Zurzal off-world. Why then had the Zacathan taken him on?

"There are the like of the Brothers along the lanes, are there not?" Jofre was trying to frame that question so that if they were overheard it would not reveal too much.

"You have seen the guardians of Tssek—felt their power. Each world has their elite guards and fighters."

"Learned One, what use is such as I on these worlds you have spoken of?" Jofre forced the point; he had to.

Zurzal did not answer in words. The forefinger of his useable hand twirled, tip pointing down—Spear-seeking—grave-ground—then it flicked in a sudden sidewise movement to suggest the covering of that hole.

Jofre caught his lower lip between his teeth. Where had the Zacathan learned that? It was a death order such as was given among the Shadows to a designated killer. From the hand which had stopped moving he raised his eyes to meet Zurzal's.

By all the rules of the issha trained, he had not only been confirmed in his oathholding but informed that he would remain so in full trust even under death threat. And Zurzal met him full eyed, so that he realized that the Zacathan meant just what he signed.

"A man who is weapon trained," Zurzal spoke again in his lecture voice, "can be taught those weapons which are new to him if he is open to the learning and not so tightly confirmed in his beginnings that he cannot see the value of change when the conditions are right. There is something else—most of these ably armed and trained men of other worlds do not possess issha. Nor any equivalent to that—therefore, they are in a way maimed when they meet one who possesses it. Consider that well, my young Shadow."

He leaned farther back in his chair and closed his eyes as if he had indeed finished with instruction, leaving Jofre to take to pieces and consider, near to word, all he had been told.

There were the outside weapons and even among his own kind those were diverse and many. But there was the inner strength—issha and assha cherished. Jofre set himself on that inward journey to assess what he did have—to build upon any shred he could find, not spend time regretting what he did not. The Quietness of the Center—that enfolded him and he opened himself fully to it. He "saw"—saw the muscles which lay under skin and knew what each could be called upon to do—saw the steady beat of heart blood through his veins and knew what must be done in time of injury to seal off the vital parts. His body was a weapon and that belief had been pressed upon him with brutal force from the beginning of his training—the body first—and then other arms—even makeshift objects which could be called upon to expand the reach, toughen an assault, raise a tight defense.

Deliberately his memory turned to the arms field of the Lair, refought rough battles there, where broken bones and sometimes even life itself was the payment for a moment's inattention or folly. These off-worlders cherished weapons afar—which meant that one must somehow nullify their range, reduce a struggle to the body to body—since he lacked throwing knives, poleax, sword.

What he had was himself and, of his bones, blood and flesh, he must make the best possible use. If any of these strange weapons came within his reach and he could gain mastery of them, so much the better, but desire was not a fact and it was facts he must cling to.

There would be, he thought as he came step by step, breath by breath, from the Center and fastened again on the outer world, little chance to try any ploy while they were aboard ship. Even if by some totally unheard of smile of the Assha Gods he might be able to somehow seize control of the ship, he would still be helpless within a metal shell, surrounded by enemies, and unable to command the forces which would take them planetward.

Therefore—wait—the patience of the issha was well-known, another of their unseen weapons. Wait and learn. He must know more now of this Tssek, of what they might face upon disembarking there.

He shifted his weight a little and Zurzal looked at him. "What is the nature of Tssek, Learned One?"

The Zacathan nodded as if he were answered a question he had not asked.

"It is what is termed a heavy metal world. There are many great cities wherein factories turn out machinery for mining—not only the mines of the north mountains which appear to be bottomless in their promise of rich ore—but also for shipping off-world. Machines work and the people labor with them. It is very different from Asborgan."

Well, he had half suspected that he would not be favored by fortune even in that much. Jofre nodded. He was being shunted into an entirely different life. But he had one rock to cling to—issha training. That was not of machines, but of men. If men came to depend upon machines so greatly, would they strive to keep also in balance with the Quiet of Center?

"It is a contentious world," the Zacathan was continuing, "or once was. Parts of the land are rich in minerals, or in soil able to produce bounteous crops. The people are—or perhaps we should say were—inclined to greed. Generations ago there were a number of nations which warred, each striving to take over some advantages they believed their neighbor controlled—a good port, a fertile valley, mines newly discovered in the upper ranges.

"It was then that they forged ahead in the making of weapons. Rumor suggests that some of the dissatisfied dealt with the Guild, buying up off-world weapons which they might copy in their own way. Which may not be too far from the truth, for the Guild is noted for fishing in disturbed waters.

"Then, as has been many times over in the history of numberless worlds, there arose to power their leader of genius. In a single generation Fer s'Rang, as I have said, united the Tribes, united them as a whole world. He proved, however, to be unusual in the fact that after he made himself Holder of Tssek that act indeed meant the saving of his world. Peace brought trade and the factories turned out products which could be sold off-world. The people prospered—except for a handful of the old noble families who resented their loss of power and made of themselves an irritation to the Authorities.

"Fifty years ago—these of Tssek are long-lived and their medical science was much advanced by their wars—there was a final meeting arranged between Fer s'Rang and the two most important rebels. Fer s'Rang died—"

"Assassinated!" Jofre could follow this kind of politics very well.

But Zurzal was shaking his head. "No. He seemed to have died quite naturally, though he was still, by the standards of Tssek, only in middle age. They believed some inner hidden weakness hit. At his death he had made plain that he was to be succeeded by the man who is the present Holder and was then his trusted second-in-command. It is that ceremony which the Holder wishes to reenact by the time scanner for all of Tssek."

Jofre used finger speech. "Then there is something he must prove." To follow this idea was easy.

"He wishes," to Jofre's surprise the Zacathan answered him aloud—did he not care that there might be those same ears he warned of earlier? "He wishes to recover the past for the glory of Tssek, for the edification of those born since that historic hour."

Words which held a very clear meaning. It was necessary somehow that this Holder make plain the fact that the rulership had indeed passed peacefully to him and by the will of his own lord. Therefore, there must be those who did not believe this; there were questions being asked somewhere—and with force enough so that the Holder must make his answer very plain. Even though Zurzal had warned this messenger that perhaps the time recaller would not work—the Zacathan had never claimed that it could, he only hoped that it might. Which meant—Jofre's lips turned up in the thinnest of smiles—the Holder had some plan he thought would make the experiment foolproof. That was something to consider. The Brothers had taken part in subterfuges of one kind or another—played major roles in some. *This* was not a strange and alien form of warfare.

"Learned One," he said in the quiet tone of one stating a fact, "if anyone can show the Holder what he wishes from the past, then that one must certainly be you."

They were not visited again by the Horde Commander. Twice Harse appeared with messages from his officer, asking if all was to the Zacathan's liking and if there were anything he wished. The pretense of honored guest was now being played to the limit.

On the appearance of the Tssekian guard Jofre made himself as inconspicuous as possible while he studied every movement of the man's body. At first Harse had kept his back to the door, outside which Jofre could hear some movement—which suggested he had come with backups. But on the second visit he was forced to cross the cabin to give Zurzal a tape case and explain that this was a mock-up of the ceremony of which the Zacathan was to be an important part, sent to him to study.

Jofre could have taken the Tssekian during that short meeting, he was sure of it, but it would avail him nothing. Not on board ship. In the meantime he might seem for periods to be dozing himself, but instead he was actively exercising issha fashion.

When the tape was run and Jofre invited to look at the small screen of the reader there appeared a building of formal and austere architecture with a wide audience hall. Centered in this was a two-step dais on which were several chairs alined. Though the tape was in color the apartment was bare, grey-white wall and showed no attempt at decoration. There was nothing to view except the static dais and the chairs.

Then flashed on a second scene in bright color but so static that those in it might have been caught in the same paralyzing stass which had held Jofre prisoner. They wore brightly colored clothes with the look of uniforms and there were a sprinkle of jeweled insignia everywhere. A voice, using trade tongue, came out of nowhere in explanation:

"The historic meeting between the Holder Fer s'Rang and the Lords of Nin and Vart as shown in the painting of Re s'Dion."

Five men were seated in those chairs on the dais; the sixth stood among them, one hand upheld as if to underline some point of speech. Two of his listeners were leaning forward as if very intent on what he was saying. The other three did not appear so moved. Now Jofre sighted a seventh man on the lower step of the dais towards the back where the shadow overhung and nearly erased him from sight: the present Holder in attendance.

Jofre could see very little of the man, his head was turned away so that his face was only a slice of cheek. Yet there was something—Jofre wished there was some way of sharpening the screen or bringing the scene closer that he might catch more details of that near-hidden man. He could only guess, but it seemed to him that the position of one hand was odd. It seemed to be raised breast high and flattened horizontally as if it supported a weight and yet there was plainly nothing resting there.

From the time the Zacathan had told him the history of this scene Jofre had fastened on the relationship between Fer s'Rang and the man who had succeeded him. If this shadow figure *was* the Holder-to-be, why was he not in a more important position at this meeting? Certainly he was not on the dais, where one expected the second-in-command to stand.

"Learned One," Jofre asked, "after the death of Fer s'Rang was there any trouble? Any claim that he was the victim of some attack?"

"Far from it. His personal physician revealed that he had been suffering from a fatal illness for several months, that he had really made a supreme effort to rise from his deathbed to cement the alliance pictured here. It *was* cemented over his body by those shocked into fellowship by such a loss."

Still—Jofre was too well versed in the devious tricks played by the valley lords to completely accept that story. It was far too convenient for the present Holder—an alliance at the death of his predecessor, sworn to by men who had doubtless been completely stunned by that death—too much a whim of fortune. He had heard tell of other deaths, carefully executed to order by issha trained to complete anonymously action requiring months of tortuous intrigue. Not that it mattered now what had happened fifty years ago—unless Zurzal's time scanner could produce a copy of just what they were viewing now.

"Can it be done—that scene brought into being again?" He wriggled one finger at the screened picture.

"You can answer that perhaps as well as I can." Zurzal's good hand arose to rub across the growing stump of his maimed one, as if the renewing flesh and bone itched as might a wound in the progress of healing. "I have had some fleeting successes, it is true."

He did not continue but Jofre thought he could pick up what the other was leaving unsaid, that Zurzal was honestly wary of any success in this venture. Which meant that they could have only a fleeting value to their captors.

Frustration bit at Jofre but he could do nothing, save prepare as best he could for the first chance he would have which would promise even the remotest chance of escape.

In the days which followed he had to fight against the constant urge for action. He refused to let himself walk the floor as sometimes his body demanded, wanting to be free. All he could do was draw upon the Center—

There was one small thing to which his mind continually turned—the fact that when he had been, he was sure, very near death from the stass weapon, contact with the stone from Qaw-en-itter had somehow given him the strength to hold on. He took to studying the stone and made small discoveries, though he was cautious about it—it came from a cursed place and some of the darkness which gathered there could well cling.

He found that if he held it cupped between his palms when he did his Center seeking, he was brought much more quickly to the state of body awareness he wished. Once, when trying a memory exercise he pressed it to his forehead and then nearly dropped it when he was answered with a painful burst of jangled images which even left him partially blinded for some very frightening moments.

Something kept him from showing his find to the Zacathan. He only brought it out when Zurzal was resting or deeply occupied with the studies which had to do with the scanner. By now Jofre was convinced that what he held could only have broken off of the Lair stone whose death had signified also the abandonment of Qaw-en-itter. No one—except the Masters and the senior priests—knew the relationship between men and the Lair stones. Those were assha—of the innermost of the Shadows. Nor had Jofre ever heard of anyone possessing an artifact such as he had found.

Perhaps a prudent man would have left it where he had discovered it—any Brother would—but—it remained that he was not by birth or blood a Brother—he was an off-worlder. And when he thought of that he knew a trickle of cold within. From what world had he sprung in the beginning? How did that other breeding limit—or aid—the issha now ingrained in him?

There would be more than one trial ahead to test both his limits and his successes, and all he was must be pushed to making certain he faced all squarely and alert.

12

THEY DID NOT TOUCH FOOT TO TSSEKIAN SOIL ONCE they had earthed. Rather Jofre found himself squeezed in between Harse and one of his look-alikes on the second seat of a flitter which had made a precise connection with a landing platform. While Zurzal was wedged in with the Horde Commander and the pilot on the fore seat. Just as his first glimpse of Tssekian architecture via the vision screen had impressed him with stark utility and no concessions to any softening of line, so did the loom of the buildings between which their present vehicle streaked its way offer a vague threat, as if each was a sentinel on duty and those of the population about were prisoners.

They did not linger in that somber pile of a city but rather sped on into open land beyond. Jofre could not move enough in his seat to see what lay below them. But the walls were gone and, except for sight of a distant skeleton-like erection or two, they were now in the clear.

Their craft apparently had reached maximum speed and was being held so. However, they were not alone in the sky. During their flight through the city they had passed a number of similar craft and, once they had reached the outer ways beyond that stand of buildings, a second flitter hung close, a little behind, but apparently bound for the same goal.

Jofre had made no resistance to the somewhat rough handling which had steered him to his present seat. Neither of the guards broke silence, and their craggy features were set in stolid, almost stupid, patterns. However, Jofre was well aware that in no way must he underestimate these followers of the Holder. He was lucky in that he had not been placed in bonds and would continue to be most biddable while he noted all he could pick up from his surroundings. Both of these guards were trained, though not, he believed, in the more outré systems of the issha. Armed or not, and given the smallest of chances, he could take them both. But that must wait upon a time when such a move could be made profitable. At least they had not stassed him again and he was given that small freedom.

The flitter fell into a circling pattern and began to descend near a building some four stories high. It was not the stolid block of the city structure but rather was a different design altogether. There had been some ornamentation about the windows and one could catch flashes of color through those as if they were curtained. Then their craft set down on a perch extending from the side of the building just under the rise of the top story. Facing them one of those windows had been expanded into a doorway by which a man in a brilliant yellow tunic stood waiting.

At the sight of the Zacathan he bowed—apparently the subterfuge that Zurzal was a welcome guest was to be carried on. Jofre was given a sharp dig in the ribs to send him after his employer as the flitter took off, just in time to clear a landing spot for that second craft which had followed them from the city.

The yellow-tunicked man was waving Zurzal in before him and a meaty hand on Jofre's shoulder hurried him in the same direction. He gathered, by the placing of that goad and a certain tenseness of his two guards, that they did not want any passenger which the second craft might have brought to be seen.

She did not have to be seen. The strict training of years kept Jofre from any halt in his step. He did not turn his head as every atom of him wished. Here—! Who was she? *What* she was he knew from that faint whiff of scent which had reached him. Only in the Lairs was that distilled, to be one of the minor weapons of the Others—the Sisters, of whom he had seen exactly two in his full lifetime, and then only from a distance. Daughters were few in the Lair and those were born there, not recruited from the land at large as the Brothers mainly were in childhood. Their fabled prowess in their own field was the bed from which legend and rumor both grew mighty tales.

One of the issha—and a woman! He allowed his arm to swing loosely by his side, twice brushing the thigh of the guard who had herded him to the doorway. His forefinger and thumb moved. She might never sight that signal, nor sighting it, have any desire to reveal herself. Certainly she was here on a mission and he could not believe that that had anything to do with him or Zurzal. But the fact that she would be under the same roof—or so it would seem— was a new factor to be considered.

She certainly was not following them. He caught no trace of sound and that faint touch of scent on the air was gone as he passed into the room beyond that door. Nor did they linger there, for the Zacathan's guide had already reached a matching portal on the other wall of the small chamber and was bowing Zurzal through. While Harse and his companion, paying no heed to any such formality, propelled Jofre along in their wake.

A twist down two corridors and they entered a room where the walls were an eye-searing riot of color, great sweeps of brushwork in vivid shades seeming applied with no reason in sometimes crisscrossing directions. The floor was thickly carpeted in a material possessing the texture of some kind of fur—and there was furniture gilded, carved, and inlaid, within tawdry splendor which fought valiantly with the walls. It was a room in which to keep the eyes shut if possible.

"Ask whatever you wish, Illustrious Learned One." The man in the yellow tunic was speaking trade language in an oily voice which matched his moon-round face and thick-lipped mouth. "All is at your command."

Jofre's guards had not crossed the threshold; that hand on his shoulder had merely propelled him within. He stood where he was and Yellow Tunic had to take a side step to pass him in order to reach the door. As soon as that closed Jofre went into action. A single stride brought his ear flat against the panels and then he nodded. They had been locked in.

Zurzal's snout grin was plain to read. He put the box he had refused to let anyone touch on a table which stood in the middle of the room.

"We are indeed honored guests," the hiss underlay that observation.

Jofre had been forcing himself to eye those riotous walls. The Zacathan had been sure on board ship that they were under observation—how much more certain that must be here in the enemies' own home territory. He had to blink and blink again; staring too intently at any of the swathes of color hurt his eyes. Perhaps that was exactly what was intended—to keep any inmate from a prolonged examination of the walls.

"For how long?" He thought he dared ask that aloud.

"For as long as is necessary to satisfy the Holder's need of us."

That was an answer which could be translated two ways and one of them deadly.

Jofre set himself to inspect their quarters. They had been favored with a suite, all lavishly furnished—including a room with a pool of water which bubbled a little at one end from which there arose a cloying scent. Zurzal stooped and dabbled a finger in that.

"Sooooo— Yes, we are indeed honored guests—and well prepared for. This might well be my Zoxan home quarters—even the vantan pool for relaxing."

Jofre had gone on to another discovery. Although the walls of this building had been pierced by those windows he had sighted during the descending circle of the flitter, here there were no openings on the outer world at all. Nor was there any sign of another door such as the one through which they had entered the apartment. They were sealed in as much as if they had been escorted into some valley lord's deepest dungeon.

There was a sound—Jofre's head twisted so he looked to the wall from which that had come—a thin wailing, shrilling which made him wish to raise hands to cover ears. It slid up and down a scale worse than any Whine drum.

"Yesssss—all the comforts of home," Zurzal continued. "Now that is the second movement of Zamcal's Storm Symphony. It is a pity I am not a lover of Zamcal's work—something a little lighter would be more to my taste."

As abruptly as it had begun that wailing ended. Jofre shot a side glance at the Zacathan and saw a taloned finger move in assent. They were under observation. But he also commented aloud.

"It would seem, Learned One, that your voice is enough to summon or dismiss."

"Yessss—how very enterprising of those who designed these quarters. We shall doubtless find much here for our benefit. Now, I see that our luggage, such as it is, has preceded us. Shall we deal with that?"

Jofre was surprised to discover that his own shoulder pack had indeed appeared along with Zurzal's personal baggage. It had been ruthlessly ransacked and anything which could be classed by the inspector as a weapon had been taken. However, as he crouched on the floor, Jofre slipped his hand along the edge of the overflap and felt that reassuring resistance to his fingers. So—the Makwire remained to him and, even though it might be nothing against a stass gun, he felt a surge of satisfaction. Every inch of that hidden chain was known to him by weight, by feel, and he knew just what it could do in close quarters.

Zurzal was prosaically stacking his clothing and other belongings away in a chest but Jofre merely dragged his pack to one side, allowing his shoulders to sag as he did so. If he were in luck, any watcher would believe that he learned of his weaponless state and was cast down by it.

It had been midafternoon when they had earthed on Tssek—it must now be close to evening. Where was that other he was now sure was under this same roof—and what did she prepare—and for whom?

She was making herself felt indeed. One glance at walls, nearly as violently disfigured as those in the Zacathan's suite, had brought an instant and vigorous protest. Screens had been hurriedly found and set here and there and even lengths of cloth hung to cover those eye-torturing lines. Her own baggage was extensive and she refused to allow the maidservant they had produced to touch most of the contents, inspecting the girl's hands disdainfully and dismissing them as being too rough to be entrusted with her fine belongings.

All the time she was bending these Tssekians to her will in this enjoyable fashion, another part of her mind had fastened on one thing. Those other two, plainly prisoners who had preceded her from the ship to this place. One was a Zacathan, so of course, the one Sopt s'Qu had been so vocal about. The other one— Without thinking her right forefinger touched the thumb beside it. Issha—! She had been right. And—surely it would be too much of a coincidence to believe that this was other than that outlaw Zarn had been so intent on eliminating. He was certainly taller than any of the Brothers she had seen—but she must be wary. To make any move before one knew one's path was the way of a fool.

Besides her own mission must and would come first. She would take the first step to insure that this very night.

* * *

The messenger they had expected arrived at last. As the man who had ushered them into these quarters, he wore a yellow tunic, this also garnished by gold lace as if he strove in part to outglitter the walls about.

"Illustrious Learned Ones," he introduced himself, "I am Dat s'Lern at your service. Is all to your liking?" He addressed the Zacathan only, but his eyes had lingered for a second on Jofre who sat cross-legged against the wall, his shoulders a little hunched, his demeanor very much of one helpless and sulking because of it.

"Your hospitality, Dat s'Lern, leaves nothing to be desired," returned Zurzal blandly, "except of course the small matter of our freedom."

"Freedom? But, Illustrious Learned One, that is, of course, entirely yours—"

"In return for?" Zurzal was lounging in one of the casirests, showing no form of polite return to any effusiveness the other might offer.

"In return for your word, Learned One, your word that you will be willing to await a peaceful meeting with our Leader." The man's right arm swung up in a stiff salute. "He wishes nothing but your comfort, truly, Learned One. This is his country place for rest and relaxation; it has many amenities; please make yourself free of any you wish to sample. Your—guard, however—" That stare was turned once more in Jofre's direction.

"Yesssss—" Zurzal hissed as the man paused, "What of my guard? You have left him empty-handed, disarmed. Do the noted warriors of Tssek fear attack by his bare hands?"

"Learned One, it is only by special favor that he shares your quarters. The regulations state that personal guards are permitted only by the favor of the Holder and he does not give that often. Perhaps—since your service is about to mean so much to him, he may make an exception. However, even if your guard is made free of this place, he will bear no arms; that is forbidden!

"Now, Learned One," he had stepped back towards the door, "I am to summon you to a meeting with the Holder; he has most graciously invited you to share his evening meal. The Holder lives simply here—he does not dine formally, rather wishes to be able to converse easily with those he has a particular desire to meet."

Zurzal arose from the easirest. "Since I have also a particular desire to meet him at the present moment, this is very fortunate. Lead on, House Master."

As the Zacathan passed Jofre his hand shaped the message:

"Watch out!"

As if he needed such, Jofre thought, with a small bitterness—though his *NOT* watching out, being prepared for all eventualities, had landed them right here. The door closed behind the Zacathan and the Tssekian, and he was left to brood.

Except brooding was a waste of time. Either his eyes had become somewhat accustomed to those flashing walls or else some of the strident color had been dimmed. Perhaps the whole effect was meant to distract newcomers into these apartments, throw them somewhat off guard. Now he made no move to rise from his position near floor level but he began a squinting survey of the nearest spread of flashed, crooked lines, and splashes of raw color.

Within a short time he believed he had located at least two spy holes in that length. Jofre gave his eyes a rest by centering outward sight on his two motionless hands and concentrating the inner strength. He was alert enough not to be startled when the door slid open—foresense had given the proper alarm.

Harse entered with a tray which he dumped unceremoniously down on the top of the table. He stood, hands on his hips, fingers brushing in passing significantly against his festoon of belt weapons, his thickish lips snarling as he stared at Jofre. Then he grunted something in the guttural local tongue and went out.

The issha-trained needed no ear to door to assure himself that he was locked in—perhaps even with a guard at ready. But—his tongue swept across his lips as if he savored the seldom known taste of lar honey—he could have taken Harse. He knew that as certainly as if the action had been carried out in full.

One studied each tiny movement of the enemy, each flicker of eye, which foreran action. These Tssekians made so plain their contempt for their opponents, their overwhelming confidence in their abilities, that they held and handled themselves as awkwardly and transparently as the youngster new come to the Lair arms court. Yes, he could take Harse—and when the time came he would. But he must know more of what lay beyond that door.

With the quiet pad tread of a hunting ossack Jofre went to the table and uncovered the dishes. Drugs? Poisons? He did not think the latter—but the former might just be in the Holder's program for keeping his unwilling guests under control.

There was a rich and mouth-watering savor rising from the larger plate. Jofre touched fingertip into the thick gravy about the chunks of unidentified meat there, and transferred that taste with a lick of his tongue. Though each world might have its narcotic drugs—with all those of Asborgan he was familiar, he could sense nothing of that like here. But—

Jofre thrust fingers into his girdle and freed the talisman from Qaw-en-itter. It was the only touchstone he had and assha matters were quick to warn of danger. Hiding what he did by cupping the stone within his palm, he passed it closely over the dish and then squinted between his fingers at the stone's surface. There was no hint of life within that ovoid though it felt warm to his hand as it always did. So—well, life was full of chances—he had long ago been rendered immune to the poisons of Asborgan—he could hope that held here. They had supplied him with no eating knife and his own was gone. He was forced to use his fingers as might any land grubber who shared a common pot, but he ate, slowly and chewing each bit to the limit, alert to any change of taste in any mouthful, though that did not come.

They had supplied him with a square of cloth on which he could wipe his greasy hands, and as he did so with slow strokes he went back to his study of the walls, through narrowed eyes as if that lethargy which comes from a full stomach was already creeping over him.

13

"**I**LLUSTRIOUS LADY," THAT GIRL ACTUALLY STUTtered and she had a harsh voice into the bargain. If she who now named herself Taynad Jewelbright was to be properly served, she would have something to say about the selecting of her servants. These off-world lar beetles were going to step smartly to her gripharp sooner or later.

Taynad was surprised, however, though of course she would not show it, at the summons that pompous fool of a house master had just delivered. She had expected a first interview in private, not to be told to report to a food table and eat in public—even a valley lord had better manners than to approach the highest rank of Jewelbright so. But what could be expected from those who had no proper issha shaping?

The robe she had long ago selected for this first meeting must be the one, though it was not entirely proper for such an occasion. However, one would not expect this Holder to be aware of the nice graduations of formal robing as practiced in a Jewel House.

She stood to allow this inept maid to settle it over her shoulders, but for the rest she pushed the girl away and clasped her own girdle, plucked the hold collar into just the proper angle, and then leaned forward towards the wide

mirror—at least they had not stinted her there—to place
the moryen gem on her forehead. Moving back a little she
examined her whole reflection with a very critical eye.

Her specially bleached skin was faintly rose under its
firm ivory surface. The hair so carefully cared for and
induced to grow over the years to a proper length for a
true Jewelbright beauty was very dark in contrast to the
ever-changing colors of her near transparent garment, but
it was not black, rather when she moved there were glints
in it of deep rich red. Her features were well shaped and
had been schooled into the masklike expression to be worn
in open company.

Well enough, she had prepared her weapons—now it was
to the arms court to see how well those could be used. She
saw the maid's face reflected over her shoulder in the mirror
as she arose fluidly. The stupid child was in the proper state
of awe—let her hope that a like effect would fall on the
company waiting to be met.

The maid hurried to open the door and Taynad swept
through, the veiling which was her gown swirling in ever-
changing color about her. At least she was being given a
proper entourage. There were four of the hefty guards statue
still at attention, their eyes not daring to follow her, as they
came to life and fell in about her. While the house master
trotted like a ushound back to his master at the fore of
their small procession.

They passed down the hall, passing several open or half-
open doorways and Taynad was well aware that she was on
view. She also fed upon the emotions which the sight of her
awoke. Easy—easy these Tssekians—it certainly must be
that they were totally unacquainted with the Jewelbright.
Were all their women as clumsy and heavy bodied as the
servant they had inflicted on her? She probably had no
rival, though she must not be overconfident. Sometimes
the tastes of off-worlders ran in strange patterns.

The house master ushered her into a high-ceilinged room
with the same color-scrawled walls which made her sup-
press a shudder. In the exact center of what seemed an

overlong room for the purpose was a dais crowned by a table and several chairs, each one upholstered in a vivid color which inclined to war with the hue of its neighbors.

One of the occupants of that dais had arisen and now stepped down, his arm swinging across the breast of his overly ornate jacket in what was doubtless meant to be a gesture of greeting. The Horde Commander—

Taynad inclined her head at just the proper gracious angle, indicating that she acknowledged his right to so meet her. However, it was the man who had not stood, who instead sat, slightly hunched, in the mid chair at that table, who was the important one. She placed two fingers on the back of the hand Sopt s'Qu extended and matched step with him as he turned back to the dais.

Below the first step she dropped the touch and curled gracefully forward in the First-Time-House-Greeting obeisance, bringing her two hands together, fingers pointed upward, under her chin and lowering her head, but not so far that she did not have full view of the two at the table.

One of them had arisen in proper courtesy and she knew him instantly for the Zacathan. The other continued to sit, staring at her, though she had not missed that sudden widening of his eyes. He might put on the seeming of one encased in boredom, one who must be coaxed and teased into whatever these Tssekians deemed was the proper height of pleasure, but certainly he had not seen HER like before.

"This Jewel one," she used the trade tongue, though she might have spoken in his own guttural sounds—only it was far better that these believed her lacking in knowledge of their speech—at least for awhile, "arrives, Illustrious Lord of Many Lands and High Towers."

He made no move except for one hand and he snapped the fingers of that. From somewhere below the level of her sight, hidden by the folds of the golden cloth which enveloped the table, arose a furred creature.

It was about the size of a two-year-old child and humanoid enough that, as it jumped to the arm of its master's chair, it squatted on its haunches and held its upper limbs and paws as one would use arms and hands. Its body was covered sleekly with a tightly curled fur growth of dull grey-blue. The head was round with the snout seemingly pushed back towards the skull, so that the flesh there was wrinkled. Eyes which were apparently pupilless, like opaque copper gems, were overlarge and were now regarding Taynad oddly. She gave it a quick glance, unable to judge what it might be.

Ears long, shaped like pointed leaves, the tips of them bearing tufts of fur, flanked the skull on either side, set well back on the head. Those tufted tips now tilted in her direction.

Issha knowledge gave a certain rapport with all living things. Those of the Lair had contact with and made use, on occasion, of flyers, creepers, runners which were native to the mountain heights. But Taynad sensed here something which was not quite animal. Was it a potential danger? The Shagga priests, she knew, had such control over some creatures as to even make of them weapons. Had this Holder such a protection in this thing?

She could not continue to hold her position of formal greeting without losing face—that command of the situation which she must retain at all costs. Was this thrice-cursed world ruler never going to make her any welcome?

He was leaning a fraction forward again and this time she felt a little more at ease; there was no mistaking that she had begun to awaken his interest. Shoving aside the creature he had summoned a moment earlier, he got to his feet.

As Sopt s'Qu he was a short man, seeming almost of a different race than the tall guards—which, of course, might be true. His skin was very fair and bore no trace of beard, nor did he show any great signs of age—the life span on Tssek must be a greatly advanced one. His hair came to a sharp peak over brows which slanted a little upward and was nearly as dark as her own. On one cheek there was a distinct pattern of red lines as if he had been tattooed.

"Our house is honored." The timbre of his voice was oddly rich, almost he spoke as would a legender of a lord's hall, trained to make the most of every possible inflection. It held warmth which drew but which was in contrast to the man himself. "Will the most Gracious Jeweled One guest with us?"

Shoving back his chair a fraction, he moved around the table and took two steps down from the dais. Beside her Taynad heard the indrawn breath of the Horde Commander—apparently she was indeed in the process of being given some extraordinary honor.

Then the Holder held out his own hand as his subordinate had earlier, and with confidence and the air of one only claiming what was rightfully her own, Taynad advanced to touch fingers. Only it was not polite and formal finger touch which greeted her, rather he actually grasped her hand in his and she recognized the gesture of one taking possession. The first encounter—he must believe that it would be wholly all his desire. She meekly allowed him to steer her up to the dais and install her in the chair next to his.

The furred creature had made no sound but had continued to eye her, and Taynad felt a tinge of uneasiness.

"This is our good friend," the Holder had gestured toward the Zacathan, who bowed where he stood. "The Histechneer Zurzal, who will lend the fruit of his great learning to our project. And"—he let his hand fall so that his fingers slid from the nape of the furred creature's neck down its back—"this is Yan." He gave no other explanation of what purpose the creature served. Instead he reached out and selected a round blue fruit from a dish before him and dropped it into eagerly reaching paw hands.

Servants appeared with food and it would seem that the Holder did not encourage speech while eating, for his eyes were mainly on his plate, several times sending a portion of some proffered dish to either the Zacathan or Taynad by a finger flicking gesture alone.

She ate daintily and lightly, sipping very carefully the full-bodied drink poured into the crystal goblet by her right hand. It was an epicure's meal rightly enough and she would have had a hard time putting names to the contents of the dishes.

The Zacathan was as much a teasing point of interest as the Tssekian ruler. It would seem that he was now an honored guest. Did that mean that he had agreed to whatever project the Holder had in mind? Listen—not only to words, her thoughts urged, but to the inflection of voices if and when these about her began to converse. Very much could be learned from that.

With the passing of time the violent patterns on the wall had dimmed. Jofre moved from room to room of the suite, each time apparently on some small errand which he dutifully carried out, searching for other spy vents, to learn that they would certainly be under observation, for all the chambers that made up their quarters were so supplied.

During their last days on the ship he had managed to make plain to Zurzal that he must learn something of the Tssekian language. The Zacathan had the ability of his species to pick up an alien tongue quickly but Jofre did not trust himself to do likewise. Asborgan speech and dialects he knew in plenty, even as he knew finger speech. And the trade tongue had been required study for several years in the Lair, but other-world tongues were difficult.

He was well aware that space travelers often encountered peoples whose physical makeup alone kept them from sharing a common speech with strangers—then the translators such as he had seen in use at the hive bank were in common use. But he must be able to learn enough on Tssek to operate. Jofre refused to believe that he would not get the chance to strike for their freedom sooner or later.

Now he deliberately made use of one of the appointments of the suite that Zurzal had pointed out earlier in passing. There were buttons to be pushed on the rim of a box set into the wall. Then on the screen above that flashed into life scenes of people, bursts of talking, even of music which was sometimes harsh and sometimes stirring. He seated himself before this now and brought the screen to life. Not only his ears but his eyes were trained on what he watched with issha concentration. There were movements of the mouths which sputtered and spoke, very faint changes of position, all which could be studied. Zurzal had given him a short briefing in the local dialect—limited even more to trade tongue which everyone knew could not contain the real nuances of constant speech.

He began to catch words whose meaning he did recognize and repeated them under his breath. What he was watching he took to be a sharing of general news. Then that faded and what followed appeared to be reenactments of some kind, for the Tssekians employed in the action wore clothing unlike any he had seen so far and they moved with a certain formality which almost aped ritual ceremony.

To make any sense of this was difficult but Jofre persevered. It was an exercise, just like any other of training, and only constant usage made any exercise profitable. He was frowning intently at a scene wherein a bound Tssekian had just been deprived of his head, apparently to the dismay of a number of females who had been forcibly lined up to watch this disaster, when the screen went black for a second, only to come to life again showing a face so enlarged that it nearly covered the whole area.

"—enemies—die—in honor—unite against—the Great Destroyer—"

A click and the face was gone, but the scenes it had superseded did not return, and, though Jofre fingered the control buttons in every possible pattern, he could not gain any change in the dark screen. But he was very certain that that face had had nothing to do with the program he had been watching and the few words he had understood were intended to be an arousal for those who heard them.

There had been anger and fear—the anger for the moment overriding fear—in that shouting voice and issha instinct picked it up easily.

Jofre was still trying to gain back some life from the machine when the click of the door behind him brought him to his feet. Had his use of this installation triggered some trouble with the Tssekians on guard? His hand went to his girdle where earlier he had carefully wound in the Makwire.

However, it was Zurzal who entered, though the door was shut so quickly behind him that it was close to a slam, as if his escort was glad to have him safely back under lock and key again.

"You have had a profitable evening, Learned One?" Jofre asked.

It was plain to see by the yellowish tinge of the Zacathan's neck frill that he was not completely at ease. What a mercy that the issha kind did not have such betraying body part. To learn control of something such as that might tax even a Lair Master.

"After a fashion. We are not the only guests the Illustrious Holder has seen fit to gather to him. She must have shared our ship—even though we knew nothing of it. It seems that Sopt s'Qu has truly thought to please his master; he has imported a Jewelbright!"

So—Jofre had his answer. Not all jewels of any establishment were issha—Sisters of Shadows—but it was a very useful cover for any assignment those were given.

"A Jewelbright," he echoed the Zacathan but, at the same time, holding his right hand where only Zurzal might see it in spite of all those spy holes. Jofre sketched the thumb to forefinger, the recognition signal of his own kind.

The reptilian eyes of the other narrowed only a fraction. Jofre knew that Zurzal had picked up that identification and that now they must both wonder what this new player, whose part in the game they could not guess, was about to do.

"It costs more than four lords' ransom," he said as one commenting on a wonder, "to select a Jewelbright for personal service. This Horde Commander must indeed wish to curry favor—"

Gain favor, Jofre wondered, or had Sopt s'Qu imported a weapon, the danger of which he himself was sure no Tssekian could gauge?

14

JOFRE KNELT ON THE TILES WHICH ENCIRCLED THE large bathing place of their quarters. Zurzal's body was stretched out in apparent ease, a turgid greenish liquid hiding much of his length. But he had one shoulder hunched over the edge of that miniature pool, the one which ended in the very slowly growing arm replacement, and the small fingers of that undersized hand were moving along the tiles, trailing through a violet soap smear.

Though the oathsman was apparently just waiting with a roll of towel across his shoulder, he did not miss the least movement of those small fingers. Zurzal was mapping out for him the ways outside these rooms as far as the Zacathan himself had followed them.

But what the Zurzal spoke of audibly was something entirely different.

"The Illustrious Holder," he commented, "is well served. He also possesses a Jat."

"Learned One, a Jat is—?"

"Something one would not expect to find this far from Varingholm. There is a ban on their export therefrom—"

"A Jat is?" Jofre persisted. That the Holder had another possession which was or seemed to be as rare as a Jewelbright of Asborgan meant resources—or power.

"No man really knows," Zurzal continued. He had brought the palm of the baby hand down on the soapy tile, splashing away any marking. "They are not animals; though they are apparently unable to communicate except through the vague mental images, they do not live in communities or apparently share any of their lives with another of their kind. Nor are they, by most of our standards, yet judged to be sentient beings. There was a nasty traffic in them some years ago—their home planet raided by slaving Jacks. And those who could be located and liberated were returned to Varingholm."

"Of what value are they—their hides?" Jofre persisted.

"By the Teeth of Naman, no!" Zurzal appeared to be honestly shocked as he clambered out of the bath and reached for the towel Jofre held ready. "Even a Jack would be fire-blasted by his own kind if he suggested such a thing. They are—it is difficult to put it into words—the brains of Central Control are not sure how they do what they do— but they are calmers, possessing an odd ability to project to those they company soothing thoughts, and, in some indefinable way, actually appear to heighten the mental processes of their owners as well as warn against perils to come."

"How could they be enslaved if they possessed such capabilities?"

"Easily enough—through stass. They were carefully kept incommunicado until they were purchased and then and then only were they released. They bond at once with the person who provides them with food and water when they are again alert. But they are a very valuable warning signal against anything which or who threatens their bond master and they never willingly leave that owner."

Another shield for the Holder then—this Jat. But it was not the Holder against whom he must now act. And he was going to make his first move this very night. Brother to Shadows they called the issha—very well, he would now appeal to Shadows for cover.

He had signed to Zurzal what he would do, and, though the Zacathan, it was plain, did not altogether approve, he did not forbid. Perhaps he thought Jofre did not have a chance to go exploring.

Jofre had selected his first shield with care—a large cushion. So big it was more a body rest than a promised patch of comfort. Zurzal was going to bed, leaving the liquid to gurgle out of the pool. Jofre followed him as far as the doorway of that chamber and then flopped down across the portal on his chosen bed, as any bodyguard must do, were he weaponed or not.

He made a fussy business of settling himself, seemingly finding his choice of bedding difficult to arrange to his satisfaction. While doing so he slipped the Makwire from his girdle. Then he dropped near the edge of the cushion, his left shoulder against the door itself. The lighted walls had dimmed yet again—perhaps the Tssekians' own cleverness in trying to provide guest comfort was going to work for him.

Slowly, Jofre edged the floppy cushion rollaway from him, subsiding behind it. He had made much of arranging his pack for a pillow and that remained in place. Then, an inch at a time, he began to move along the wall. It all depended upon the angle of those spy holes. They had been set, as far as he had been able to determine, so that those who used them could survey the most of the room—but that meant they were aimed mainly at those walking or sitting. He shifted over to his stomach and was digging his fingers into the carpeting, keeping to a worm-flat advance along the wall.

He thrust the thought of time from him, rather drew upon that shadow-sight-hide trick for a spy. The corner of the wall faced him. With infinite slowness he came into position to head down the next with which it had right angled. Another corner and he had reached that wall which held the outer door. For a very long pause he lay facedown, sending out every possible extension of his senses to reconnoiter for him.

They could well have fastened on him by now, even watched him, waiting for him to make his big attempt and then fasten upon him, to deliver a double blow. That idea he forced away. His study of Harse and the other guards had suggested that they were not subtle thinkers, perhaps not skilled in any unusual form of fighting either, depending only on their chosen weapons and brute strength.

Once at the door he came to real danger as he must get to his knees to deal with the lock. They did not use the sophisticated body heat locks he had seen in the hotel on Wayright, rather he had been aware every time they had been visited of a faint click.

Now his fingers crawled up the surface of the door, the end of the Makwire caught between two. The forefinger located the small depression and he felt a surge of satisfaction which he instantly suppressed. With the most delicate touch he turned the fine end of the wire, to pass back and forth across that depression until it caught!

Using it as he might the finest of tools, Jofre pressed. To his joy it sank a fraction and then hit a barrier. Now—the hair-thin wire he had worked out of the length of Makwire twisted under his bidding. There followed a click, the hair slid cleanly in, and, as quickly, he jerked it out and resealed it into the thicker part of the coil.

He was on his feet in one movement so swift it might even deceive any watching eye, his palm flat against the door, the wire a-swing and ready in his other hand.

The door gave no betraying sound under his urging. There was a whiff of odor which he recognized as that which clung to the clothing of several of the guards due to their smoking of crumpled native leaves.

That scent alone was a guide. Outside the door the hall was lighter than the room within, giving Jofre a good sight of the man who was leaning against the wall, his shoulder only inches from that doorslit. Suddenly the Tssekian yawned widely and straightened a little. Jofre froze but the man did not turn toward the door he was guarding.

Did not turn, no, but with that small movement rather
delivered himself squarely into Jofre's hands. The issha sent
the door open and his right hand through in a blur of
movement. His fingers thudded home on the neck of the
Tssekian before the befuddled guard knew what happened
and the man folded forward. That nerve pressure had not
been enough to kill, Jofre wanted no bodies to betray him,
but it would keep the fellow unconscious for a space of
time, perhaps even leave him unable to account for what
had happened—it sometimes worked that way.

Jofre squeezed through into the hallway, pulled the bulk
of the guard to a cramped seating position with his back
to the door which he had drawn closed. He stood assaying
the situation. There did not come the sound of any alarm.
Which, of course, did not assure him that such might not
have been given.

But he had gained freedom, at least for a space, and he
must use that to the best advantage he could. Also, and
that healed a fraction the wound to his self-esteem which
their kidnapping had dealt, he was in the act of proving
that issha training had some answers to even off-world
technology.

He did not rise to his full height, rather scooted along at
a crouch, but he was swift and he reached the end of the
corridor where it linked to the next in seconds. This was
the way to the dining room which Zurzal had outlined in
the soapy rings.

It was deserted, there were no signs of guards along it,
and all the doors were closed. There could be someone in
wait behind any of those but Jofre had to take that chance.

This was not to be an escape but rather a reconnaissance,
thus he must take no chances. He slid into the dining hall.
The light here was very dim, and only night sight alone
was able to assure him there were no watchers. There were
two other doors, wide ones which could be thrown open
to accommodate a whole squad of visitors at a time. He
opened each in turn cautiously. One showed another hall
of closed doors, the light very dull. But not enough to hide

that other guard. Jofre pulled back instantly and waited, Makwire ready. He dare hardly believe he had not been sighted.

However, there was no alarm and he slipped around the wall to that other doorway. This gave abruptly onto a terrace and the open night. He could smell the scent of growing things and hear the splash of water as if from a fountain. Several steps below the terrace lay a garden and into this, with the ease of one coming home to the familiar, Jofre quickly faded.

Many of the scents were strange, growing things particular to Tssek, issuing from various forms of vegetation. He flitted from one welcoming shadow to the next, surveying as well as he could his surroundings. This garden did not give on the open countryside, but rather was set in a well with the four walls of the building standing to form its limits. There were doors at intervals in those walls, but for the moment Jofre did not test those.

He had early sighted the lighted windows a full story above the garden level. The light was dim, cut by drawn curtains, and the three windows from which it issued on a line. Someone was awake there, of that he was sure.

Moving in immediately below that beacon he surveyed the wall. With the proper equipment—now denied him— he would have found it an easy climb. At the same time any such action would spotlight him against the pale wall at once to any other intruder in the garden. Regretfully he decided against that.

It was while he was still fingering the wall's roughish surface, reluctant to leave such a chance to spy, that he was interrupted by a sound. Instantly he went to cover and from his brush-screened position he saw a figure flit from the door in the wall below those intriguing windows.

The invader did not come boldly, rather showed something of the same stealth Jofre was employing. And, his curiosity fully aroused—for why should any rightful inhabitant of this pile act like a rooftop thief?—Jofre moved closer and then took a limited step or two along the path the other followed. The newcomer emerged from the thickest shadows when reaching the pavement surrounding the central fountain.

A woman! The enveloping cape the other wore, even the hood to veil the head, could not disguise the swing of body and telltale signs of sex for an issha. For an instant he thought of the Jewelbright—if this were indeed she, he might have his chance to learn more of this unknown Sister.

But the small breeze stirring branch and leaves about brought no whiff of the betraying perfume. Then she whom he spied upon pushed back her hood a fraction so that he could see features which certainly could never be assigned to any peerless beauty.

She crouched down beside one of the two benches set to face the fountain and, though the long cloak masked her movements, Jofre thought she was in some way hiding or withdrawing from hiding some object.

He could catch, even through the continued tinkling of the fountain a faint scraping sound, even a click. Then she was on her feet again, hurrying back the way she had come. He watched her disappear before, like any trail hound, he went to sniff at the place she had been busy.

His fingers touched moist earth, crumbs of it. She had not taken time to sweep entirely away the traces of her work here. His nails caught under the edge of a flat stone like those which paved the section of earth between bench and fountain and the rock yielded to his pull. Carefully he used his fingertips since it was too dark in this corner to depend upon his eyes to explore the find. What he examined by touch was a roll covered with some slick material, the whole perhaps as big as his hand. Jofre was greatly tempted to take it. To his exploratory pinch the contents within that narrow bag yielded a little—nothing stiff or hard. He could, in spite of all his prodding, discover nothing solid. This might not be a conventional weapon nor even the fruits of some theft—unless what had been taken was some type of record.

At length he decided to leave it where it was. If he had time to stand spy here, to discover if what he had uncovered was merely a way place for message exchange and not a secure depository, he could doubtless learn—but that time was not his—not this night.

He had already been away from their apartment too long. To be sighted by the reviving sentry was the last thing which must happen. Regretfully he replaced the stone and this time he made sure there were no crumbs of soil about to betray that it had been moved at all.

Back he prowled through the dining hall, down the corridor. To his relief the guard was still wall supported and yet as unconscious as he left him and he was able to squeeze within the narrowly open door and begin the same worm's journey back to his sleeping cushion.

Once stretched out there he allowed himself to relax, loosed the strains he had put upon every sense during that night's journeying. And that relaxation allowed him to slip into the slumber which he had banished so ruthlessly earlier. He did not try to relive his exploit, to wonder about what he had seen—there would be plenty of time for that later.

Though there was no sun beaming through a window to waken him, the daytime glow of the walls appeared to arouse one with the same efficiency. He stretched and became aware that the Zacathan was standing near, watching him.

"Only one with a quiet mind can sleep so well," Zurzal observed. "No dreams, Shadow, to plague you? That is well. We need clear minds and ready spirits—"

Jofre sat up. "We need these minds and spirits to a greater degree than ordinarily, Learned One? I await orders."

"The Illustrious Holder has thought that he would like a demonstration—"

"I thought—" Jofre was startled enough to begin when Zurzal interrupted.

"It seems that there are those the Holder would like to have see a small exhibit of what can be expected. The crew who are to arrange for the broadcast of the Fiftieth time scene believe they can work better if they are shown what to expect."

"The time scanner in the hall—"

"Ah, no. The Holder wishes something a little less impressive. There are some ruins from the old days within a short distance. It has been arranged that we visit those with the scanner—and a selected number of guests—this morning."

And if it does not work Jofre wanted to ask but thought better of it. He believed that Zurzal had been given little or no choice, that the Zacathan was caught earlier than he had expected in a tight web of what must be deception. Oddly enough, however, Jofre detected no sign of disturbance in either the Zurzal's voice or actions, his frill had not risen.

It was midmorning before they were escorted out of their quarters by Harse and his usual squad of guards, Jofre being ordered at Zurzal's demand to carry a bag which the Zacathan insisted held auxiliary equipment. Once more they entered a flitter waiting on a terrace approach above ground level and took off, heading out towards a range of hills which appeared to lead upward, like the beginning of a giant flight of stairs, into fog-dimmed shapes of mountains.

Jofre saw that other flitter already landed as they set down and standing by it the Holder and— This woman was as well robe-wrapped as the one he had spied upon the night before, and yet he was sure of her identity. The Jewelbright had also been brought to watch this phenomenon of time past.

He was able to pick out the weathered ruins which were their goal, so time eroded that there was little to be seen above the drifted earth. This was a country of rocks and what vegetation existed was a meeting of small drab plants clinging to crevices and the rough parts of the stones.

Jofre had favored the Jewelbright with a single glance. Though there certainly was not much of her to be seen, even her hands were concealed within the wide, enveloping folds of the cloak, and the hood was drawn well forward to shade her face. That cover-up might have been in protection against the furies of grit which breezes, funneling down the cut in which they stood, whirled about them.

Sopt s'Qu was very much to the fore but he was not a happy man, rather one who displayed every sign of nervousness. Perhaps even more than Zurzal he feared failure. But he spoke up loudly as they joined the other party.

"This is a place of which there is no mention, even in the First Archives. The Holder wishes to see what the time scanner will make of this. Perhaps there can be little hope of such far reach—"

Was the Horde Commander trying to provide them with an excuse? If so, Zurzal did not fasten on it. In fact there seemed to be very little uncertainty about the Zacathan— he was all business, beckoning to Jofre who went down on one knee and unrolled the bundle he had carried, setting together the rods within as Zurzal had earlier demonstrated, to make a holder for the scanner. In order to steady that on this rough ground it was necessary for Jofre to hold it in place while the Zacathan worked.

At last Zurzal looked over his shoulder. "I have set it to the farthest extent possible, Illustrious One, since this site is said to be so old. We can only hope that it comes within range. Now!"

Jofre nearly jumped, for that last word had the force of an order as Zurzal reached out with his good hand and pressed firmly down on a lever.

15

THERE WAS A SUDDEN UPRISING OF THE GRIT-FILLED wind between them and the well-eroded stones. Or was it that? Jofre blinked and blinked again. That mist appeared to be thickening in places, thinning patches showing between spots. Color—a warmth of that. But it was like trying to see through a bog mist which swirled and eddied, enveloped and revealed.

Figures—yes! At least dim shadows which were not fixed, but appeared to move backward or forward. He saw with sudden clarity a single face which held so for no longer than it took him to expel the breath from his lungs, but he would take full oath to the fact he saw it.

It did not hold long, that mingling of denser shadows in a mist. Then it was gone as Zurzal clapped the edge of his hand down across the lever.

"No—!" That protest had come from the Holder; he alone of their company had found a voice.

"Yessssss—" Zurzal hissed. "Would you put such a strain on this," his hand caressed the scanner, "that it cannot be used without lengthy recharging? You have a time limit set for that which you wish to see the most."

"Yes," the Holder nodded, "yes, that is so. But—why do you say this scanner will not work, Learned One? Have we not just seen it in action?"

"Have you seen clearly, anything more than unidentifiable shadows?" the Zacathan countered. "It is a clear
picture, a full one which I seek. Now I must rework the
setting on this, make very sure that it will serve as well as
it can the next time it is called upon."

What brought Jofre's glance upward to the heights which
backed those anonymous ruins he never knew. But a glimpse
of that flash there sent him instantly sidewise, to sweep
the Zacathan from his feet, rocking the scanner perilously
askew.

There was no sound, but a smell of scorching fabric.
He felt the smart of a burn graze along his shoulder as he
continued to grind Zurzal down against the rock, shielding
the other with his own body.

The others were shouting; he heard a crackling and, even
though he did not see them clearly, he knew that blaster
beams were cutting back and forth overhead, aiming at a
point well above, perhaps that from which the first beam
had come.

Zurzal was struggling in his hold and for a moment Jofre
resisted the Zacathan's fight to free himself. Then he
realized that the other was attempting to move away from
that exposure into the lee of one of the crumbling stands
of weathered block. Jofre aided that with a stout push. Now
they were crouched tightly together in the small measure of
protection that hollow offered them.

The Holder's flitter took off, seemingly by a straight
upward leap, whirled and turned back towards the outer
plain. Their own craft was also quickly aloft, heading not
after the first ship, but along the range of the heights with
now and then the crackle and flash of a blaster beam aimed
from it to spatter and slice rocks. There was no sign of any
return fire.

Not that that would mean they themselves were in the
clear. Jofre, surveying as much as he could see of those
rock walls without offering himself as a good target, fully
expected an attack from above. And he was not the only

one to so judge trouble. Though the flitter which had
transported them was hunting aloft, the guards who had
been so ready to keep him under control were both still at
ground level. Against the light grey of these rocks the dark
shade of their uniforms made them visible, though they had
taken cover as quickly as he and Zurzal.

He watched Harse twist a little in a crevice between two
piles of the ancient masonry and wriggle a tube loose from
that fringe of arms he wore at his belt. Sliding back a little
so that he could gain all the protection possible from his
cover, the Tssekian fitted that rod to the weapon he had
already openly in hand, making the barrel near twice as
long. Again he plundered his belt arsenal and produced
something he cradled in the palm of his hand until he
could fit it into the mouth end of that barrel.

Having so prepared, Harse inched forward once more to
the very end of his cover and the weapon in his hand
moved slowly, pointed well up towards the heights. At
length he apparently had it centered to his satisfaction.
There was a click sharp enough to be heard even over
the crackle of those blasters being fired indiscriminately
above.

What he released arose almost lazily, angled inward
toward the cliff face. Then it struck and Jofre flung up
his arm a little too late to save his eyes entirely from a
torturing burst of vivid white light. A second later sound
beat at his ears. When he could again see through his
watering eyes there was a glowing scar down the rock face;
a good portion of wall had simply vanished. Harse sat back,
his hand slipping along his weapon almost as if rewarding
its action by fondling it as he might a living thing.

The flitter had ceased firing and was now coasting along,
quite close to that scarred wall as if those aboard were
inspecting the results of the attack. Then it spiralled down
towards the level space from which it had earlier arisen.

Could they believe it was all over, Jofre wondered. He
absently brushed down his side and then snatched away
his fingers. That beam had come close! The fabric of his

tunic was blackened, he ripped it a little to look at that line of smarting flesh his earlier touch had awakened into protest. However, save for the burn graze he could see no great harm.

Then his hand was jerked away and Zurzal bent over him, pulling the brittle cloth apart.

"It is nothing," Jofre said quickly. "No more than one would get being careless at a campfire."

"Yessssss—" Not only was the hiss very loud in the Zacathan's speech but his frill was extended to its furthest extent, throbbing an ever-deepening shade of crimson. "You have served, oath bound." There was a certain formality in those words and Jofre forced himself not to allow himself any credit. What he had done was only such actions as he had been pledged to. He drew together his slitted tunic.

"Someone wants you dead," he said slowly. Zurzal had been directly in the line of that first fire.

"Me dead—or that out of commission—" The Zacathan had sense enough not to stand up as a target to any who might still linger above, but he was wriggling toward the scanner.

That was tilted on its tripod; Jofre himself might have pushed it out of place when he had made that jump for Zurzal. On the ground there was a blackened line inches away from the machine. No, Jofre was sure, it was the Zacathan and not his scanner which had been the prime target.

Harse and the other guard were on their feet and walking freely toward them from the flitter. Of the Horde Commander there was no sign and it might well be that he had joined with the Holder's group in that swift flight.

"Move it—" Harse approached the two by the scanner. "We go—now!" He jerked a thumb at the scanner and then at Zurzal and Jofre. The latter glanced upward. There was only that new blackened scar on the cliff side and it would seem that these believed the battle—if battle it had been—was now over.

The man with Harse advanced purposefully on the scanner and Zurzal swung out his good arm to ward him off.

"No hands on that—" His now blood-red frill was still up. "We shall do it." He beckoned to Jofre.

Together they dismounted the scanner, nor would Zurzal pay any attention to the attempts to make him hurry as he examined it carefully and supervised Jofre's two-handed disassembling of the stand. Only when that was packed away to his satisfaction would he pick up the carrying case of the scanner and start for the flitter by which most of the squad were obviously impatiently waiting.

Jofre was occupied with speculations.. The attack, he was sure, was truly meant to take out Zurzal and perhaps the scanner—but first the Zacathan. He was sure that the Tssekians were well aware that only Zurzal could properly set up the machine—or was he wrong there? Did they believe that, after this rehearsal, one of them could do as well? Still he was very sure that that attack from the heights had *NOT* been part of any plan made by the Holder. Leaders of nations did not use themselves as bait.

Therefore—who—?

He was chewing on that as they packed into the flitter once more. But this time he had shoved past Harse and taken his place beside the Zacathan. When the Tssekian tried to shoulder him back the Zacathan faced around.

"That is my bodyguard. I am alive right now because of him. No thanks to you and your men here. He rides with me, he stays with me—from now on or I shall not be coming out of my quarters. This I shall make very sure of with your Holder himself!"

Harse scowled but did not seem sure enough to protest and Jofre found himself in the fore of the flitter with Zurzal as they winged back across the plain.

From this more open seat he could better see the countryside. Up to the foothills it was level, apparently much of it covered with a thick vegetation which on Asborgan would have made it pastureland. But he could sight no beasts at graze there and he wondered if this world had any species that lived so. They were about halfway back when they were passed by a flight of six larger flitters flying in formation and boring steadily towards the place of the ruins. If the Tssekians had decided that they were not yet sure of the fate of the one who had launched the attack, they were going to make very certain now.

As they came down to the landing stage on the Holder's headquarters Jofre gained some idea of the size of that building. It was certainly larger than any on Asborgan and any inn on Wayright. Surrounding the outer wall were a series of small domes, slits in them open toward the sky. Through those slits pointed what could only be the barrel tips of weapons too large for any one man to wield. It was plain that this was an armed camp, which meant enemies— who—how many—where?

The teachings of the Assha Masters swept to the fore of his memory. Weaken your enemy from within, lead him to believe that his own trusted underlings will turn against him, the strongest fortress can fall to inner rot. But he needed to know more—much more.

Was this a hint of a power struggle between two leaders—the Holder and would-be ruler—Sopt s'Qu for example? The importation of a Jewelbright as a gift—how much did the Horde Commander know of the true nature of the woman he had brought? Trained issha she was— even the hair on her head could become a weapon at her will. The skills of the Sisters were legendary. They never came for any purpose but that of secret war—she would not have been oathed except for that and she would not be here were she not oathed, no matter what amount of treasure an off-worlder offered for her.

Was the Zacathan in some manner an unknowing weapon in a hidden struggle? It would seem that he was feared or his death would not have been intended. But one small point of good had come out of that—he had, as Zurzal had certainly been quick to recognize, now the right to demand the constant attendance of Jofre—might even gain back for the bodyguard some of the weapons of which he had been shorn at their capture.

They were speedily escorted back to the suite of rooms which had been their prison. Zurzal had spoken only once, as the door had been opened and they were motioned within:

"My life has been threatened. If I am the guest the Holder proclaims, then I must be told by whom and why I should be fried by blaster!"

Having delivered that, he turned his back on the guards and stalked within, the case of the scanner still held carefully in his arms as if that were something he would do all he might to protect.

Once the door was closed Jofre instantly laid ear against it. Yes, they had stationed a guard outside. At least the one who had been on duty there last night had never reported any difficulty. When the Tssekian aroused he probably had been afraid for his own skin; he might well have believed that he nodded off on duty.

Zurzal placed the scanner carefully on the table as Jofre dropped the bundle which contained its supports on the floor. Some of the red had faded from the Zacathan's neck frill and now he swept up his hand in the impatient gesture Jofre had seen him use before, striving to settle the fluttering skin to his shoulders.

"The scanner," Jofre broke the silence, "it worked. I saw a face—"

"The timing," Zurzal shook his head, "it was too inexact. How could it be tuned when one did not know the general setting one would need? Yes, it worked. But it has worked even better before when there was a more definite dating to be calculated. What is important now is who doesn't want it to work at all?"

"Could they believe that with you dead they would have control over it?" Jofre advanced what he believed could be a very logical argument.

"There is always a good measure of stupidity in this or any other world," hissed the Zacathan. "However, they have not pressed me to discuss this," he rested hand on the scanner, "with any of their men of learning who might be considered able to grasp the principles of its controls. No, I do not think that that is the answer. The Holder wants me—he wants me to use this—he does not want a dead man and a useless piece of hardware to spoil his plans."

He turned away, to face Jofre squarely. "Meanwhile, let us see to you, oathed. Off with that tunic—"

Jofre protested, but to ears not prepared to listen. He found himself speedily divested of tunic and shirt, seated on the edge of an easirest while the Zacathan squeezed a jelly from a tube he produced from among his luggage.

"You were very lucky, oathed." Zurzal's hand had the lightest of touches as he spread the ointment over the reddened skin and slapped a flesh seal over it. "That was on full or you would not have taken so wide a scorch as you did. There will be no scarring and there is no reason why it will not heal well. However, we shall not let them forget that you seem to be the only one who was marked in that action, and because, weaponless, you fulfilled your oathing. On Asborgan I believe I could demand a wound price from them."

Jofre flushed. "It is no real wounding," he muttered. "I failed you once—when they took us—did you expect me to fault every time?"

"I cannot see there was any failure. You fronted a weapon you knew nothing about, were caught by something which could well have caused your death. You are a very tough fighting man, oathed, to have survived stass holding as well as you did. The issha are certainly highly regarded, I know, but I was not aware they had ribs like tillenium to keep them breathing—"

Jofre had pulled on shirt and tunic and was being careful with his girdle, holding as it did both the Makwire and the talisman. But not careful enough, for the ovoid slipped out of hiding, struck on the floor and landed near the Zacathan's feet.

16

JOFRE SWOOPED FORWARD BUT HE WAS A FRACTION late; Zurzal had already half stooped to eye the artifact more closely. Against the light shade of the carpet it presented the appearance of a giant drop of some unknown liquid frozen in shape.

The Zacathan put out his hand. However, when it hovered over the ovoid, he jerked it aside just as Jofre made a determined grab for it. From his stooped position Zurzal was staring up at his bodyguard with a keen measurement.

It was almost as if he were questioning the younger man's possession of such an object and Jofre responded to that sensed demand.

"Mine!" His hand closed about the stone and he felt the familiar flare of warmth in the cup of his palm.

Zurzal straightened. "Yours," his word came in agreement. Too quick an agreement? Was the Zacathan trying to placate him?

Slowly Jofre opened his hand; he had no true explanation for what he held. But if an oathed could not trust his lord, then he was indeed a man without hope or being.

"I do not know what it is—" he said slowly.

"A thing of power." There was no doubt in Zurzal's quick return. "And without a doubt very old." He was shaking his head as if to deny one of his own thoughts. "But there is no record of any Forerunner remains on Asborgan—perhaps that is from off-world—"

It was Jofre's turn to gesture denial. "It is of the assha." At the moment he was sure that all his speculation concerning his find was correct. "I found it in Qaw-en-itter—a Lair which died four generations ago. I—I am sure it was part of the great stone—the Master's assha heart—though I have never heard before of any such retaining any life after the fail of assha—"

"This retains life?" Zurzal's voice came quietly, hardly above a murmur.

At that moment Jofre remembered where they were—that those eyes in the walls might well be turned upon them. Rather than answer in revealing words, he hunched a little, bringing the stone up between their bodies and loosed the tight grip of his fingers. He could see that point of light at its heart—could the Zacathan? Or was it all some ancient spell set by one of the Shagga?

"Interesting—" was Zurzal's comment. "It is a luck talisman then?"

Jofre's lips tightened. Let this off-worlder dismiss his find as one of those luck pieces such as the lowlanders gave credit to—sometimes wearing them on chains about their necks. Very well, let this be thought a talisman—a superstition. He did not raise his eyes but—he sensed—this was what the Zacathan wanted—that he be lessened in the sight of any spy, a ruse. He dared to give the ovoid a toss, catch it lightly.

"Well, Learned One, I have a good measure of luck since I found it"—or, his thought added, it found me—"so I shall not deny that." He tucked it away again in the folds of his girdle. "One of my calling needs any help fortune may send."

"And we need luck that this has not been injured by our recent skirmish." The Zacathan turned back to the table where he had parked the scanner. Taking the machine from its case, he set it on the tabletop and then crouched down so that he could view it at eye level from a number of angles.

Jofre watched with interest, though he understood little of what was going on as the Zacathan's one good hand touched here and there, his large eyes squinting along the surface as if he were bringing to bear on some target one of the large weapons of the Tssekians. At length he settled back on his heels.

"As far as I can say without actual testing, it has not suffered. As for testing—" Now he stood up and laid the scanner on its side, hooked a clawed finger at the side of a small plate there and jerked it up. Within that cavity were two coils of fine wire of a particularly vivid blue-green wound in even patterns around what would appear to be a core of another substance—that a sullen grey-black.

"Sssooooooo—" the hiss as well as the lifting and coloring neck frill of the Zacathan suggested agitation of some sort. "Power—perhaps one more viewing and then it must be recharged. We have no chance to experiment."

"When is this viewing these Tssekians want? Can they provide the power you need?" Jofre wanted to know.

"The viewing is within two days. As to the other—I shall find out." He shut that pocket in the side of the scanner. "That was folly, errant folly," he hissed again, "to waste what I had on that peep show this morning!"

"I do not think you could have said 'no,' " Jofre observed. "This Holder is not one to have his wishes denied. And— it worked! You proved that, did you not?"

"Worked? Raised some shadows and near got itself—and us—fried. I can do without such examples of its proficiency," snapped the Zacathan. "What is done is past— there is what lies ahead. At least they can give us a proper dating this time and not too far in the past."

Jofre noted that "us" the Zacathan used so easily. It was as if he had suddenly advanced from a mere oathed to an accepted kin sworn. And that brought a quick touch of warmth within even as the assha stone had given him in the past.

*   *   *

Taynad turned the thread-slender stem of her wineglass between two fingers. Her lips smiled provocatively as her thoughts raced. The Holder's performance this morning—the man was afraid for his precious skin! This—this weld-worm was what she must court with all her skill, soothe into contentment, encase in feeling that all was right with his world and there was no need for fear. She could have spat the wine she had just taken into her mouth into his face! No, control, control that contempt, make of it a weapon.

At least she had had a chance to learn much these past hours. Now as soon as she could get this booby occupied with all the various acts to make sure of his continued safety she must start piecing together her scraps of true knowledge.

The first was, of course, that the Holder of Tssek believed himself anything but secure in his exalted position. In the past sweeps of the timekeeper since they had returned to this fortress of his she had heard orders given, raids planned, lists of suspects made—names marked for death, for imprisonment, for questionings.

There had been returning reports also. Of suspected nests of rebels which had been found deserted when the raiders moved in, of the disappearance of a number of those whose names appeared on those lists. It was as if the failure of the attack upon the Zacathan and his machine had been a signal, somehow broadcast farther than any mirror flicker or flyer message, to take cover.

And with each reported failure that man by the table had tensed the more, spoken fewer words, become more—dangerous! Yes, perhaps she had indeed misread him—even a vomink caught in the trap could flay the hand of the hunter who did not brain it in time. The orders for death were now outweighing those for imprisonment. And such summary deaths began to be listed a few at a time.

Would this put an end to whatever game the Holder wished to parlay with that machine of the Zacathan? She did not yet believe so. He had spoken twice of the ceremony and of those who must be brought one way or another to attend it.

It was true that the Zacathan did possess something which could not be explained save as what it was, a recreator of the past. She had gone to view the action at the ruins very much a skeptic, and had been practically convinced that he could do what they said he could. However, were his scanner to turn up nothing more than ghost-mist forms such as they had seen that morning, she did not understand the Holder's dogged demand that the ceremony of the great Ingathering be so reenacted.

She was suddenly aware that there was a lull in the constant flurry of officers reporting and being dispatched again. The Holder had arisen from his seat and was approaching her. Taynad set the wineglass down and went immediately into the welcoming obeisance.

"Your pardon, Jewelbright," he put out his hand and she straightway set hers in it, allowing him to so draw her to her feet, "these matters are harsh; I am sorry that you have been witness to them. But all is now arranged, so that we have time for more pleasant things. I have not yet shown you the inner garden. The langian are in bloom and you who are such a connoisseur of perfumes will find these to your taste—"

As he spoke he was drawing her on. There was a scuttling at his other side. The Jat that had not been present at the morning's fiasco was there now accompanying the Holder closely. If all they said of that creature was true, and she had heard much from the maid last night, then it was certainly a good weapon against any close attempt at assassination. She allowed herself to speculate on whether the creature could be won away from its allegiance, though as yet she would not make any move in that direction. Instead she used the speech of the Jewel House, meant to soothe, to compliment, to enhance the ego of the patrons—not with bold and open flattery but rather with the most delicate innuendo.

The garden proved to be in the heart of the fortress-palace, the four walls rising to encompass it. She could hear the play of a fountain, and even the sounds made by insects. A flying thing with huge wings outspanning a body no larger than her little finger hovered before her. Without thought her hand went out and it settled, so lightly she could hardly feel its touch, fanning wings of brilliant green which appeared spangled with inset gems of blue and gold. Its beauty was enough to startle her out of her thoughts for the moment.

"A lashlu." The Holder was regarding her with something close to benevolence. "Have you any such on your world, Jewelbright?"

"Not such as this." She held her finger very still, hardly daring to breathe. In those few seconds it chose to remain with her it was as if she had stepped out of time, away from all she was and what had brought her here, all that she must never forget.

It was the Jat which broke that moment of otherness. For the first time since she had first seen it the creature uttered a cry, scuttling ahead and out onto the pavement of flat stones which ringed the place of the fountain. There it went down on all fours, its wrinkled-in nose close to those stones, clearly on the trail of something.

The Holder had halted and his hand brought Taynad to a stop also. He was watching the actions of the off-world creature as it fastened its attention on one of those grey squares. Its forepaws, which were so like hands, suddenly sprouted claws as if it could extend normal nails to far greater distance on demand. These it curled about the edge of the stone and heaved, the rock turning easily in its grasp as if very lightly set in place.

A fast scoop of paw into the hollow beneath the stone tossed out a lump of grey-brown which might be a bag. With the very tip of its claws the Jat urged that find towards the edge of the pavement well away from the two standing watching.

"So—" The Holder dropped his touch on Taynad and took a step or so closer to view that small round of what might be plumped-up hide. All expression had been wiped from his never too expressive face. He reached for his weapon belt, not as heavily laden as that of his followers but showing the jewel-inlaid butt of what could only be a blaster.

Then that was in his hand with one quick movement.

"Away—" he made that sound almost a whistle and the Jat obeyed instantly, leaping backward to them.

The spat of fire caught the bundle cleanly and from that core of flame burst smoke and a strange scent—Taynad found herself coughing, her head shaking from side to side as if she could banish that odor or escape it so.

Smoke and flame were gone, there was nothing left but a charred black mark on the stone where the Jat had rolled it. The Holder, blaster still in hand, stood over that now, looking down at the charring.

"Sooo—" he said again. "Here—?" He made a question of that last word but Taynad had a feeling that it was not addressed to her. Then he came back to her.

"Fair One, it seems that this servant of mine," he snapped his fingers and the Jat moved closer so that he could draw his hand caressingly across its rounded skull between those two stiffly up-pointed ears, "has nosed out some contrivance which was ill meant. This place," he lifted his head and stared beyond her at the rich wealth of growing, blossoming life, "was meant as a sanctuary—but even here there is no safety. I must crave your pardon, for this is a thing which must be carefully examined and I must ask you now to excuse me."

He escorted her with punctilious ceremony back within the building and then left her with the guards and that maid she could not yet rid herself from, dismissing her so in a way she found irritating. He was not going to explain just what menace he had blasted out of their path, that she had to accept. But it did not please her—there was too much in his attitude now of one who considered her only something to be thought of in an idle hour, not a real part of his life. That lack of true interest in *her* she must deal with, and by every way she knew. She must become more important to the Holder than the Jat or the blaster—far more.

Though they had not left their quarters (they probably would not have been permitted to do so, Jofre had thought from the first) the two prisoners were aware that much must be going on in the fortress-palace. Jofre strove to free senses for outer-questing—always an uncertain thing but needed now. He must assess what he could pick up—at least a little of what was in progress. Issha touch caught—as if a fog invisible to the eye but very apparent to one's inner consciousness seeped through the walls. Something which brought with it the same feeling of ever-abiding dangers and evil as hung over the dark alley of the Stinkhole. Save that there he had been free to defend, and here he could not even be sure of what weapon the enemy might produce—or whether there was but one major enemy or more to be reckoned with.

He firmly dismissed all conjectures and concentrated on his inner exercises. The Makwire was always there in his girdle for seeking fingers, and those very fingers themselves were ready to be weapons. The Zacathan for the first time showed signs of worry, prowling back and forth across the room, going now and then to inspect every inch of the scanner as if he expected it to be somehow invisibly attacked unless he kept a careful watch.

They were fed from trays brought by guards, though Harse was not in charge, rather the fetching and carrying was done under the supervision of an officer who did not address them and whom the Zacathan made no attempt to question. The food was good and Jofre was almost sure that it could not have been tampered with. This close to the time when Zurzal's skill with the scanner would be demanded, the Tssekians certainly would not in any way attempt to drug them.

Three times Zurzal called again for the tape Sopt s'Qu had supplied of the scene of the Great Ingathering and sat for a long space of time before it in study, as if by his will alone he could somehow transfer that picture to the scanner and have it appear when desired. Yet it was always the same and the Zacathan would shut it off with a hiss of exasperation.

His neck frill was in constant agitation and the colors, while not bright, ran through a variety of hues. Zurzal was not taking this waiting with the same philosophical adaption to circumstances as he had earlier shown. Jofre debated concerning a second assay at exploration by night and decided against it. The Zacathan was plainly not ready to settle in and he had no desire to leave the other alone.

In spite of his attempts to forget her, his own thoughts played with the puzzle of the Jewelbright. That she was assuredly issha he had not the least doubt, yet she had not responded to his Slip-shadow recognition signal— if she had seen it and somehow he believed that she had. That she was on an oathed mission must be the truth—otherwise she would not be here—no issha would willingly leave Asborgan on some whim. No, she had been introduced into the Holder's household for a very definite purpose, even as others of her Sisters had from time to time found themselves in the halls of lords they were oathed either to protect or bring down. And somehow Jofre did not believe that this one was here to protect—no.

He felt a certain frustration that he could not share his speculations and doubts. Not only did there remain the fact that they might be constantly under observation through the loopholes those violently patterned walls contained but he had no right to interfere or betray another oathed.

They spent a restless night and in the morning Zurzal attempted to view the world through that screening device Jofre had earlier watched.

"That is their monument to the past." The Zacathan identified a building which flashed onto the screen while a voice blared out in the native tongue a stream of words so fast Jofre could identify perhaps only one in ten.

The screen viewed the structure from slightly above, as if they were seated in a flitter swinging in there for a landing. Jofre caught sight of something to the far right.

"Spaceport!" He was sure that he had seen, through an opening between that forest of grim buildings, the rise of a ship on pad.

"Yesssss—" the hiss of the Zacathan was low. "To the south, I think."

They would surely be transported again by flitter Jofre believed. If they made their move, once aboard that, could they hope to reach the port? But what good would that do—

Zurzal might have picked that question out of his mind. "There is a Prime Control base there—otherwise off-world ships could not land. Reaching that—"

"The Patrol would protect us?" Jofre allowed his doubt of that to be plainly read in his tone. "The port at Wayright must have been patrolled—yet here we are."

Zurzal nodded. "Yesssss—that is sssssooo—but we were but helpless baggage then and they treated us as such."

"And as we come in with blasters ablaze and demand aid here—" Jofre could not believe that the other could be so naive as to believe that.

"I am Zacathan," Zurzal said. "My race has immunity on most worlds. Also, when we raise our voices, planet lords listen. I think we would have a very good chance to claim sanctuary."

"But first we have to get out of there—" Jofre jerked his thumb to the scene on the screen. That had changed somewhat. They were now looking at the loom of the building from ground level facing an impressive flight of stairs. And those were occupied, with rows of statue-straight, well-armed guards, and behind them a massing of people moving restlessly back and forth as might waves kept out by the barriers of a portside landing.

"Just sssssoooo—" replied Zurzal, but he was looking now, not towards the screen, but at Jofre. If the latter had also been befrilled that appendage might have gone into a rising flap. He was being challenged in a way and he found that there was that within him which was rising with a fierce eagerness to meet that challenge.

17

THE TSSEKIANS, IT WOULD APPEAR, HAD ALSO FORE-
seen that the task of ferrying Zurzal, Jofre, and the scanner to the place where they wanted them was going to
be a problem. Perhaps they could not reduce the two
to the point of becoming baggage to be towed around
with impunity, but they mustered such a guard that each
of the off-worlders was wedged in between two towering
Tssekians and under constant eyes of those matching step
with them.

There was no way in this compact and ever vigilant
company, Jofre had to admit to himself, that he could
make a move towards freedom. When the flitter landed
them in a cleared space which guards held open with
cracks of riot staffs before the steps of the Ingathering
hall, he needed only to see that seething sea of a crowd
to realize that massed bodies alone could wall them from
escape.

Through the subdued roar of the voices about them even
the commands of their guards did not carry and they were
shoved in the direction of the steps leading upward.

So they came into the long hall which had been shown
them on the viewer. There was the dais, the chairs which
had been midpoint of that older scene, but there was no

one on that perch now. Gathered below and to one side was a clot of brightly uniformed men with here and there a woman in rich robes and bejeweled. To the fore of that small assembly was the Holder with the Jewelbright a step or two behind him, the Jat reaching up one paw to grasp the edge of his brilliant golden tunic.

Between the newcomers and the chair was a spiderweb of wires, interlocking a number of installations all set at different angles and heights but meant to focus on the dais. These were under the control of men also in uniform but intolerant of the guards, giving harsh orders now and then.

"They prepare the broadcast." Zurzal had somehow managed to come near to Jofre.

They certainly must be very sure of the results they wished, the Slip-shadow thought. But how could they be? There was some trick in this—there must be. Only he could not ferret out what it was nor how it would work.

The guards pushed the two of them on, Zurzal insisting on carrying the scanner as usual. They had to be careful of those crossing lines on the pavement as they advanced. Zurzal opened the case; Jofre, as before, unrolled and made ready the supports. The Zacathan lingered on sighting the scanner so that it was aimed at just the angle he wished. Behind them rang out orders from one of the broadcast experts.

Jofre shot a glance to the left. The Holder looked at perfect ease, exuding such an air of confidence that Jofre's own wariness became like a taut string within him. He continued to steady the scanner with his right hand but his left rested on his knee not too far from the end of the Makwire in his girdle.

Having made a last finicky adjustment, the Zacathan turned his head toward the Holder and nodded.

Jofre had turned his attention in another direction— in time to see one of those attendants at the nearest of the broadcaster machines hurriedly slip a cone over the forepoint of his machine. Had there been a mistake in the setup that must be remedied at once? The off-worlder had no idea how those machines worked but there was something in that hasty action which, to his watchful eyes, presented a suggestion of trouble.

Their guards were impatiently motioned away by those running the other machines, though there were protests until one of the officers from that brilliant group marched over and snapped an order which made them move. Zurzal and Jofre were alone well beyond arm's length of any of the Tssekians for the first time since they had left their quarters.

The Holder raised his hand at the same time Jofre's fingers closed about the end of the Makwire. With a supple twist of the wrist the issha freed it, to lie three quarters of its length among the mass of wiring. The possibilities he had before him now had doubled. And he was sure that, aided by the last few days of practice, his wrist had lost none of its cunning.

Zurzal reached over and pushed the control of the scanner. Three breaths later there was a shimmer on the dais, which had more life and gathered more quickly into definable shapes than that mist had evoked at the ruins.

From the massed group of notables to the side arose a hum of astonishment. It was plain to Jofre at least that they had really not expected this response. What had they then expected? Something to issue from the unknown machines about them?

The shimmer was gone; they might have been looking at an enlargement of the same scene Jofre and Zurzal had studied on the record given them. But this was no frozen picture. These people on the dais moved, shifted in their seats. The representation of Fer s'Rang moved, raised his hands, spoke—words which rang out and even seemed to echo hollowly down from the ceiling above.

And the picture held, grew bolder!

Jofre shifted weight. Those about him seemed bemused by what they were watching. His chain weapon was a serpent ready to strike.

*   *   *

Taynad stared at the dais and then quickly looked to
the Holder. He had taken a half step backward as if he
had been confronted by some sheer surprise which he had
not thought to face. Beside him the Jat jerked at his tunic,
waved its other paw in the air, plainly distraught by the
emotions broadcast now from the man it was bonded to.

The Jewelbright sent one swift glance at the other man,
the Horde Commander. There had been a smirk on his
face, but now there was forming another expression altogether, one rooted in fear. Her fingers moved as she flexed
them. Emotion was so thick that it lay about them like
a mountain fog exiling each from the other, and it was
true fear!

However, almost all eyes were fixed on the dais, on those
actors out of time. Jofre looked now for the one who had
puzzled him in the painting they had been shown, the man
who had lingered on the lower step. His hands—

On impulse Jofre gave a small shove to the scanner and
it seemed, in answer to that, that figure became not only
brighter to the sight but somehow more dominant in the
scene. Its hands went to mouth level in a swift movement
as the representation of Fer s'Rang turned to address one
of the other seated lords.

The Great Leader made a sudden movement, raised a
hand to the side of his throat. He took a step forward, his
other hand sawing at the air and then he crashed down.
While the man on the step below was already in motion
upward to raise him, his hand sweeping across the dying
man's neck as he did so.

There was a rising howl of sound and Jofre saw that
those at the machines about were frenziedly busy. He put
his weapon into use. It twisted among the cords on the
floor. He gave a jerk with full shoulder strength, aware
that Zurzal's scaled hand had joined his in that hold.

The nearest of the broadcasting machines crashed down.
There were screams and cries and that scene on the dais
abruptly disappeared. Zurzal was again back at the scanner.

A blaster bolt of fire skimmed from the mass of officers. There was struggling there and the screaming of the woman. Guards moved in—two of them towards Jofre and the Zacathan. But Jofre was ready. He took a leap, not away, but at the men and the wire flicked to imprison a wrist holding a blaster. The Shadow jerked the one who had held it forward into the line of his own comrades' fire. Again Jofre struck and the other guard dropped his gun, caught at his face, hands over his eyes, as he screamed thinly.

Other blaster beams were sweeping back and forth. Jofre grabbed up the weapon one of his victims had dropped and tossed it to Zurzal. Pacifist the Zacathans might be, but they were ready to protect their own lives and Zurzal fired twice. Jofre was jerking at that mass of wiring across the floor, sweeping it back and forth until its tangles brought down two more of the guards.

Then he had their weapons, the precise blows he gave both of the entangled men putting them speedily out of the fight.

He looked back over his shoulder to the Zacathan and gestured with one of those hands in which he tightly gripped the weapon, expecting every breathless moment to be either cut down by a stass ray or fried by a blaster.

Hostages? Jofre looked to that milling mass of spectators. There were uniformed guards plowing into that for there were apparently a number of small fights in progress. He saw bodies in bright uniforms lying underfoot. And some of the guards had apparently turned against their own officers.

The Holder? The man was gone from his position.

Jofre tensed. It was as if a voice had shouted in his ear, someone at his side had screamed aloud in fear. Yet it was not sound but raw emotion and he swung towards that. He had reached the edge of the dais, that man whose fear was being so broadcast. Dragging at him as if to urge faster flight was the Jat and behind those two by several steps the Jewelbright.

Jofre gave a leap which carried him over the wreckage of the wires and landed behind the Holder. In a moment his arm was over the other's shoulder, bringing pressure to bear on the Tssekian's throat.

"Be quiet," Jofre hissed in the other's ear, "and move— or you die!"

The Jat was kicking at him, but not with enough strength to shake that hold. Now another moved beside him.

"These witless waglogs have turned on each other to the death. It is as if the Old Ones have sent them mad!"

He knew her scent. At least she was not oathed as bodyguard or he would have now been dead.

"Move!" He shoved the Holder around the end of the dais to where the Zacathan, blaster in hand, stood over the scanner. Jofre could see over his prisoner's shoulder now. There was such wildness in the struggle in the audience hall that the Jewelbright might indeed have been right. These Tssekians could have all been struck mad, for they were fighting each other. Now there dropped on ropes from above other armed fighters, both men and women, wearing no uniforms except a band of green about the upper arm, and these moved in upon the fighters.

To reach the outside they would have to win through that mess on the floor and Jofre was not sure they could. He was trying to evaluate all possible advantages, if there were any, for this action or that, when a party of those who had come down from above began to draw in upon the four of them in a grim-faced half circle.

"Pass us—or this one dies!" Jofre shouted in the trade tongue, hoping that he would be understood.

The leader of those confronting him, a man as tall and wide-shouldered as Harse, and certainly with all that guard's grim presence, made no move to lower his own weapon. Jofre staggered; a sudden and more vicious attack from the Jat had nearly rocked him from his feet. But a moment later the Jewelbright took a hand in the matter and captured the creature in a grasp strong enough to pull it back.

Zurzal had shouldered the scanner, paying no heed to its tripod stand, using a side strap above the maimed arm to support it, as he covered the distance between them in two strides.

"Pass or this one dies!" Jofre tightened his hold on the Holder's throat. The man was already gasping for breath, his hands flailing out to no purpose as he had no weapon now and Jofre was positioned out of reach behind him.

"There is a problem here." The leader of the opposition had again edged closer so that his voice carried even through the clamor. His weapon hand was steady but Jofre, reading the subtle change in the other's eyes, did not think that he was about to be crisped at once by blaster fire. At least the fellow was speaking trade tongue. "You have what we are very anxious to get—yield your prisoner—"

In Jofre's grip the Holder struggled wildly. It was plain to the issha that this was not a friendly party seeking to rescue their leader.

"Why?" It was not he who asked that question but Zurzal. The Jewelbright said nothing, merely held to her place beside Jofre, both hands gripping the upper front limbs of the Jat in spite of the creature's frenzied fight for freedom. That she possessed issha-trained strength was very plain to see.

"He is more our meat than yours, Learned One," the green-banded leader returned promptly. "We have certain plans for him."

One of his squad moved closer and growled a sentence. The melee in the chamber seemed to be dying down. Here and there a knot of uniforms still fought, but it was apparent that those who had swung down from aloft were fast gaining control of the conflict.

"Plans for us also—" Jofre stated. "What are those?"

"Not perhaps what you might fear," returned the other. "Learned One," now he spoke directly to Zurzal, "you have served our cause even inadvertently." With his free hand he pointed to the scanner which now dangled down the Zacathan's back. "We are a little in your debt—even more when you turn that one over to us. I think you will find us grateful."

Two of the squad, one of these a woman, Jofre noted, split off now and came inward, one from either side as if to box in him and his captive.

"These are rebels." For the first time the Jewelbright spoke and flatly.

"Partisans of freedom, lady." The leader was smiling now, almost gallant in his attitude, but there was no lessening of alert menace in those still edging towards Jofre.

"And our coming—was it part of a plan which you also shared?" asked Zurzal. "Well," he did not wait for any answer, "perhaps we can deal after all. Though I think that your party had another end for me in view two days ago."

The leader shrugged. "We have hotheads, such are the bane of any party, Learned One. Those who made that decision have been disciplined for it. Now—give us that man—"

Jofre interrupted. "One does not throw away a weapon untried, Commander," he gave the man the only rank he could guess. "You admit that your followers tried to burn us down at the ruins. How can it be that we are now to forget that? You did not take this prisoner; we hold him—"

"So you can decide what is to be done with him?" queried the other. "How long can you stand there, guard, and hold him? You need both hands to the purpose, are you then able to sprout another pair to beat us off?"

"He will kill—" It was the woman approaching from the left who spoke then. "We need that one for—" She stopped abruptly, near in mid word as if she realized that she might be giving away something of importance and the commander favored her with a quick frown before his eyes clicked back to center on Jofre.

"What do you want?" he demanded sharply then, plainly impatient to settle the matter—if he could—as quickly as possible.

"What you spoke of earlier, Commander," Zurzal had adopted the same title, "freedom. We are here against our will—we were kidnapped to order. We want nothing more than to ship out from Tssek and go our own way."

The commander studied the Zacathan, then his attention turned to Jofre, and last of all to the Jewelbright.

"This off-world female was not brought here by force but to play another game of her own. She cannot claim otherwise."

"Any game she was to play," Jofre said, "is now ended. She is off-world—she has not meddled with your ways—can any speak against her?"

"She is what she is," the scorn in the woman's voice was near as hot as blaster breath. "We want none of her—let her return to her own kind and swim in their dregs."

"Let us reach the port," Zurzal said swiftly. "I do not know what ship may be there ready to lift. If there is none then let us enter Patrol custody—do you not agree that that will keep us away from any meddling here?"

"We need give you nothing," the man who had earlier spoken in Tssek to the commander, burst in. "Stass rays—"

Jofre stiffened. It was true, they could be taken again as easily as he and Zurzal had been back on Wayright. As long as he must keep his hold on his prisoner he could do nothing to prevent such an attack.

"You forget, At s'San, we do have something to thank them for. Did they not show us the true death of Fer s'Rang—though that service was quite unintended." The commander smiled thinly. "No, we shall give them what they wish—the female also since we have no use for her kind—and even that squalling thing," he pointed to the Jat who was crying out in a thin wailing. "Such are not for our world; let them go. Escort them to the port and turn them over to the off-worlders who keep the peace for their own kind. But first—give us—him!"

Could these orders stand? Could he accept the word of this rebel commander? But Zurzal was nodding in agreement and Jofre must accept the bargain as became an oathed.

He loosened his grip on the Holder and at the same time gave the prisoner a push forward. Those two who had closed in from the sides were on him in an instant, and one pointed with a rod straight at the Holder's head. He stiffened with a jerk which nearly raised him from his feet and then toppled forward, caught in stass and so completely helpless.

Three of the squad bore him away but six more fell in around the off-worlders, forming a hollow square, moving forward at a trot which they were forced to equal. The Jewelbright had swept her shimmering robes up with one hand. She had tweaked out of her cloak of hair one of those hidden cords the same color and texture of the tresses in which it had been fastened and thrown that in a noose around the neck of the Jat, so pulling the creature along as one might a hunt-hound.

There was still fighting in progress and twice they had to battle their way past opposition from one of the stubborn pockets of beleaguered guardsmen. There was no flitter waiting for them, rather a ground transport into which they were crowded while their guard took position around them, weapons ready.

They turned abruptly from the main streets where struggles were still in progress, winding a road through lesser ways, some nearly alleys. There were bodies to be seen here and there. Once there came a blaze of blaster fire crisping the side of their vehicle inches away from where the Jewelbright crouched. She winced but made no sound and Jofre was so tightly jammed against her other side that he could not see whether she had been burned by that fire's touch.

The transport skidded around a corner and they could now clearly see the space port. The great gates had been firmly closed and within their perimeter were to be seen the black and silver uniforms of the Patrol as well as the grey worn by the space employees. Also there were weapons very much to the fore.

But there was no warning to stop as they approached. Though neither did anyone move to open the gate. The nose of their vehicle was nearly touching that when they came to a halt.

The Tssekian guards stepped aside and allowed the three off-worlders and the Jat to face the barrier. A man wearing Patrol dress and one in space grey, who had the insignia of Port officer on his right shoulder, moved a little forward.

Zurzal hunched the strap of the scanner higher on his shoulder and raised his good hand in the peace salute.

"We claim refuge under the Code of Harktapha." His frill was high and a deep crimson and his hissing near serpent-strong.

The Patrol officer took a stride which brought him to that section of the larger gate which might be opened separately as a small door.

"Who are the hunters?" the officer asked.

Zurzal's frill fluttered and the hue darkened. "We are not hunted, First Officer. These have brought us out with orders that we reach here. We are from off-world and there is war on Tssek which does not concern us."

"You will drop all weapons and enter singly," came the command. "You will abide by the code, surrendering to judgment concerning that which brought you here."

Zurzal nodded. "Agreed, First Officer." He tossed to one side the blaster he had belted when he had given the peace sign. Jofre wound the Makwire about his hand into a coil and sent it earthward. The Jewelbright produced from somewhere about her person, so swiftly he could not sight where it had been hidden, a slender but, as he knew, most deadly knife and added that to the collection on the ground.

Moving one by one, Zurzal in the lead, then the Jewelbright with the Jat on leash, and finally Jofre, edged through the gate door which was opened only far enough to give them tight passage. Jofre's empty hands stirred in a sign he did not know he was shaping:

"Out of dark, into light."

18

THOUGH IT WAS WELL PAST THE MID-HOUR OF THE night, there was still a lamp alight in an upper room of the old town house. A shadow swept across the wall in an even pattern as Ras Zarn paced the room. This night he was ridden by the need for physical effort, to somehow expend the tension which crippled him during the day, which made it more and more difficult to make decisions swiftly and correctly.

Might the Night Gnawers of Garn feast upon their lives! He fought to keep control, to not throw back his head and voice the howl of frustration which seemed near to suffocate him. Could any one of them in his position have done better? All well for them to issue orders, but the ability to obey was not in their power to enforce—unless they would decide to make an example of him and set up some other fool who, given the same situation, could certainly do no better.

THEY could hunt across the hills as they had in the past to bring down prey. There was no way any one man could hunt the star lanes. It would require centuries to even sift through a small portion of the star ports. Such a search was madness even to think of!

He had given them one solution but they would not

accept it. Secrets—they were not prepared to share their secrets! But there was no other way. If the Guild accepted that they were to hunt for a man, if the matter could be presented to them solely as an act of vengeance—a chance. Though for the most part a Veep of the Guild would not concern himself with such a minor matter, under certain circumstances he or she could be led to give such orders. That was a kernel of understanding on which he, Zarn, could build—though there would be a price.

However, there was the problem of the prey—had he yet learned the value of what he had stolen from the cursed Lair? Supposing during a hunt the Guild would discover what their quarry had in his possession?

Zarn's fist was at his lips and he gnawed on his knuckles. This night he had sent his strongest message. It must be acted upon at once, for the Guild contact was not going to wait on the favor of a priesthood they did not recognize nor consider of any import in their own deliberations.

Time was fast running out. They must either depend upon these others who had the wide-flung organization which could locate a man off-world, or they must admit defeat. And to do that was to perhaps open a future which would—

Zarn shook his head. He went back to the low table, dropped down to the mat seat behind it, his fingers scrabbling among a number of small sticks littered there. Each was notched in a different pattern, one which could be read by touch, even in the dark. But he had no need to try to sort out again those orders, threats, demands.

There was a muted sound, hardly louder than his own labored breathing. Zarn's head came up, he was on his feet at once, to pass through a concealed doorway into that narrow room where there was a panel high in the wall open to the night sky. Through this his awaited messenger had come to perch on the desk table. It uttered two plaintive sqawks as the merchant reached it.

His hands went out to stroke and gentle the flyer. Then met those avian eyes with his own compelling gaze. This was one of the best trained of the shrine flyers. At least they had accepted that the task demanded the very best weapons they could bring to the field.

Zarn plucked the message from brain to brain. His tongue tip swept dry lips. His life—well, he had known in the end it would come to this—his life in the balance against victory. But they *were* giving in, if reluctantly; they were agreeing that his suggestion could now be the only way.

So—in hope he had already made certain moves; now it was time to follow those up. He gave the flyer its reward and left it squatting on the desk top, the opening in the roof unclosed. There would be no message he could send now—that he wanted to send. What he would do needed no interference from those at a distance who had never encountered the players he must draw into the game.

Dawn was smoky pale in the sky as he began to set into action the plan he had labored on. He sent another messenger, this one two-legged and from his household, with a very ambiguous report that he had lately obtained certain wares from the north which might interest that particular buyer.

Down in the larger chamber devoted to business he oversaw the unpacking of two bags, the setting out of his bait—star stones worked by Hemcreft himself. The High Shagga had parted with those as easily as if they had been implanted toothwise in his jaws—but they were unique enough to hold this Xantan.

He had time to compose himself fully, to practice the Six Exercises of Quiet and Preparation. So it was with his usual composure that he faced the woman who answered his summons.

She was clearly an off-worlder, a thin-bodied figure with elongated arms and overlarge hands. Her dark skin had a metalic sheen and looked very smooth, almost as if she were indeed encased in some hard coating. A great deal of it was exposed by her scanty clothing which consisted mainly of strips of shaggy material which might be the fur of some strange beast and was of a violently vivid flame color,

showing even brighter against the grey-black of the body it
wreathed around. Her head was swathed in a large turban
that flashed a border of jewels, the seeing of which gave
Zarn a hidden satisfaction. It was plain that this envoy of
the Guild had a liking for gems, so that what he had to
offer should prove tempting.

"Gentlefem"—he bowed and escorted her to a pile of seat
mats well raised above the floor to accommodate her longer
limbs—"you honor this house of trade."

She raised her first set of eyelids and opened the inner
ones halfway. Her narrow, almost snoutlike, mouth was not
meant to shape a humanoid smile but it twisted somewhat
in what might just be the equivalent of such.

"The wares of Ras Zarn," her trade tongue had a rasp as
suggestive of metal as her body, "are well known to produce
treasures. It was spoken to me of a special shipment—"

She had not glanced once at the display on the table.
However, Zarn believed that she had not only surveyed it
but at the same instant had been able to value it.

"As you see, Gentlefem." He waved a hand toward the
gems set out skillfully on a darkened strip of leather which
enhanced their incandescent silver and gold natural
coloring.

Now she did turn a little on the mat seat, that exercise twisting her long neck (looking far too slender to
support a large head made even more bulky by the turban). Both her outer and inner eyelids were fully open.
She made no move to lean forward a little farther to
touch the gems, merely regarded them. Zarn did not doubt
in the least that she knew to a quarter star credit their
value.

"A showing, Merchant Zarn, a showing. But—"

"A buying—no?" he said quietly. "Ah, well, it was the
Gentlefem I considered first when these came to me, knowing how great is her ability to pick the best and make the
finest use of such. But if they do not suit your taste, then
I am most sorry to have troubled you."

Her mouth worked again and those second inner eyelids

half closed, surveying him now, rather than the display of
stones.

"We buy and sell, both of us, merchant. If I buy, what
then is the price?"

Inwardly Zarn relaxed a fraction. She was willing—at
least enough to discuss matters. But any deal with the
Guild was tricky, very tricky.

"There is a story to be told, Gentlefem."

She made a sound which might either have been a sigh
of boredom or one of impatience. "There always is when
one of you wishes to deal with us." She was frank enough
anyway.

"We seek a man, a traitor, one who has betrayed us blood
and bond."

The woman raised a hand as if to straighten the mound
of her turban.

"Your world is wide, but I do not doubt that you have
the means for tracking him—Shagga!" She mouthed that
last word almost as if it were an accusation, but Zarn was
not taken unawares. No one could deny that the Guild had
their own seekers of knowledge, that they kept account
and learned all they could of any they might have future
dealings with.

"Unfortunately he is off-world. Before we could put
hand on him he blasphemously used the code which had
been stripped from him and oathed with an off-worlder—
a Zacathan."

"Ah, yes." Now the woman did reach out, and, with one
of her long equal-length six fingers, tapped the table below
the first jewel in line.

"That lizard skin is one I have heard that your own
people have an interest in." Zarn ventured the first push.
He must assume more authority or else be defeated before
he began.

"We have an interest—slight. Not one that moves us
particularly at present," she said.

"We are ready to award interest with payment—" His
very slight gesture indicated the array of jewels.

"That could be taken under consideration." She arose from the pile of mat cushions. "Word will be sent before nightfall."

He was forced to be content with that, but he was hopeful. The rumor which had reached his own well-enlisted spies was that the Zacathan was of particular interest to the Guild. They could already be laying a web for that one. However, any company their prey might have at the time might then be summarily disposed of unless a neat profit would change that part of their program.

Had he been able to use his own eyes and ears as well as he wanted to, his relief would have been the greater. The woman made her way directly to the spaceport and there in the lounge where those who waited for a ship to take off she had taken a seat and sat as if only idly interested in what was about her. She did not wait long before a man in spacer suiting but obviously of her own species came to stand before her. She greeted him with the slightest of nods and he sat down at the empty seat facing her.

"That mud-based toadling," the language she spoke was not trade and it was a murmur of words run together until they seemed to be a single sound, "offers a respectable amount—the Shagga must have combed out their private treasure boxes."

"For what?"

"The Zacathan oathed a renegade of their tamed killing order. They want him back—they are highly primitive in their thought processes. This traitor of theirs went off-world with the Zacathan."

"They want him dead?"

"No, I believe that the death dealing is something they desire to be strictly their business—they want him."

"As an oathed guard he will defend the Zacathan."

"Yes. However, there are ways and means— The main point remains that the Zacathan be allowed to proceed as he himself wishes until the proper time. I understand that there has already been some difficulty on that point—"

"The Tssekians were not in the picture as we knew it then. We have to sort that out."

Her mouth moved in that twist of a smile. "Doubtless there has already been set in motion a plan to deal with that. But—do we accept this other offer—the renegade to be taken and returned here? The price they offer is tempting."

"And this Shagga can be depended upon to come through when the deal is properly completed?"

"He is no fool. Guild bargains are kept, as he and all the stars well know. This can be done I am sure—and the extra bit of sweetening he is ready to offer will please the Council. They just must be sure our merchandise is not harmed in any future action."

"Very well, make what arrangements may be demanded." He stood up. "We lift at the fourth moon hour. Shall I see you aboard?"

"Of a certainty, yes, and with some interesting baggage. These star stones, Talor, are worth even perhaps a fourth grade organizer's ransom—should some sum as that ever be asked."

Zarn had made his first move; he did not linger before following through on the second. Once more he sorted out the rune-inscribed sticks, setting them first in one pattern and then another as if striving to find one which suited him best. There was no possible other choice. Yes, one of the Shadows had gone off-world as bodyguard to that young lordling. He was not of top grade, nor experienced, and the reports on the renegade had been clear.

Outlaw that he was, he was well trained, though he had never been sent on a mission. But that mind-twisted Master of his had given him special instructions—some the Shagga on station in that Lair did not even know; he could only suspect. *He* was certainly a fool also—the renegade should have been assigned another Lair and quietly disposed of there. But instead he had been loosed—

Luckily that brain-empty skull of a priest had had him

monitored when he crossed the mountains or they would never have known what happened in the dead Lair. But that Shagga was now busily repenting his first stupidity and would be for some time to come; no one need worry about HIM.

However, they must accept that their prey had training well past novice grade, perhaps approaching that of a Hand, young as he was. And with what he carried— No, they could not, even if the oath law permitted it, detach the young lord's guard.

Nor must they depend solely upon the Guild, even if the latter were willing to seal a bargain. The Guild wanted the Zacathan—or rather what they hoped to wring out of him. While the renegade was oathed and would defend his charge to the death. Not even the Shagga who loathed him would deny that he was truly issha-trained and firmly set in their pattern.

Also— Zarn tapped his fingers on the tabletop inches away from the sticks. What if the renegade began to understand what he had taken out of Qaw-en-itter? What if he would become—a Master? Assha strength might defeat even the Guild entrapment.

Who—? It must not be left to the Guild. What if they (and he had the greatest respect for their Veeps and experts) also did a little delving and discovered that taken from the dead? They might even strike a bargain with the renegade— his life for his find—taking as an excuse for such dealing that the Brothers had deceived them in not mentioning the prime reason for their hiring.

Zarn shivered. Were that to happen— He would envy for the days of life still left to him the fate of the Shagga who had first loosed this blot upon the Shadows. To dispatch another issha—one of greater training and experience— off-world? He had no time to wrangle with the Shagga Over Heads for that. The longer the renegade remained loose off-world—and only the Foul Three of Trusk knew what he was doing besides guarding the Zacathan's back— the more chance of his becoming greater than they could hope to handle. He might even be able to give the Guild a surprise or two.

Which left only one choice and he had already been denied that. However, under the circumstances this time she would have to agree. Her oath could be dissolved with the permission of the Sister of the Inner Silences. Such action had been taken several times in the past—need must overreach custom when there was demand.

But how then was he to reach her—off-world? There would be only one organization—outside of, of course, the ever-present Patrol—which could bear such a command along the star lanes after having first located her to whom it was to be given. The Guild again—

Zarn sighed. He poked at a roll of leather. Wealth beyond the raising of any one Lair—at least four of the richest had been stripped to gather that. And the Guild were no unpaid benefactors—they would demand more for such a task. Still—deep in him he was certain of only one thing: he could not trust the Guild to the point of blood oath— the Sister who had already gone starward would carry out any true order to the death.

Get her free from her present bond—and he had only until the Guild Veep returned to do so. He swept the sticks together and rolled them into a bag he thrust into a concealed holder under the low table. This he must do himself.

The roll containing the jewels he took to the wall behind the seat mats and touched several places there to open a small cavity. But before he stowed his packet inside he surveyed the present contents of that hiding place. With a sigh he flicked another box into place beside the packet, and then closed the cavity.

For him to approach the House of Jewels openly in daylight and be sighted, would cause talk—and not the kind of talk his position in the old city welcomed. But there was no help for it. He could only depend on a hooded cloak, such as one of the mountain priests wore, or a disguise— a very flimsy one.

The Mistress of Jewels received him in her own chamber and listened to his terse outline of what had to be done and why. She frowned.

"This you ask casts a stain on honor. We are also issha, and we live by the Five Oaths! Once a mission has been honorably taken and the Shadow oathed, only a successful completion—or death—releases the Sister. You ask much—too much!"

"This is a threat to us all." Zarn dared not tell her the truth; only a handful knew it and if he spoke without permission he would be word-broke—disgraced until he could not even redeem himself with his own life taking.

"In what way, Shagga?" She was not going to give in easily. He could feel the sweat beads gather at his hairline in spite of all his inner effort to appear above emotion.

"I cannot be word·broke," he decided that he could be this frank with her, "but it is such a danger that we have not known since the Refusal of Gortor." The mention of that portentous action which had nearly wiped out all the Shadow breed was never uttered idly. Surely that would impress her!

Her eyes had widened slightly and now her fingers sketched Ward-off-Perils-of-the-Far-Night.

"You swear this?" she asked.

Zarn's knife was in plain sight. Deliberately he extended his heart-finger and pressed the tip of that sharp narrow blade into the flesh, until a bead of red showed. Withdrawing the knife he held out his hand where the drop of blood welled larger. The woman looked straight into his eyes and then down at that finger. With her own heart-finger she touched his and Zarn knew inwardly a great relief. She had accepted, she would do it!

"The oathed one has gone off-world, there is no way a Shadow message can reach her—" the woman continued.

Zarn shook his head. "There is a way, that I also oath swear."

For a moment she looked dubious. But the promise he

had just given her was so binding she had to accept that
he believed he could carry it out.

"Very well. The word is Flow Cloud."

The word which would trigger oath release—Zarn almost
shivered. That was something sacred, by custom used only
by a Lair Master to release one from a mission accomplished. To pass such to another was a perilous thing, but
in this he had no choice.

Once again in his own chamber, the packet and box from
the cavity prominently ranged before him on the table, he
busied himself with another small twiglet of stick, this of
a dull black in color and no longer than his heart-finger.
With a very small tool, such as one who set gems would use,
he made his scratches on the stick. First the release word
and then the second oathing—one which would bind the
Sister to her second and most important mission. He was
barely finished in time, for one of his household came to
announce the return of the Veep. If she agreed—but she
must! He called on that inner way which, it was said, one
truly in difficulty could use as an inducement—holding to
it like body armor as the off-world woman came in.

19

"**Y**OU UNDERSTAND THAT UNDER THE CODE 1732X you must be held." Patrol Captain Ilan Sandor eyed his listeners coldly. "If the Tssekian government demands that you be turned over to answer charges of fomenting riot, of plotting, you cannot claim sanctuary here."

"We are escaped prisoners." Zurzal's return was as evenly voiced. "We were brought to Tssek against our will and in defiance of interstellar law. I have not yet heard that kidnapping is a legal form of obtaining immigrants."

"You have one story—"

"Backed by a truth reader," Zurzal interrupted. His neck frill was stirring. "We had no voice in our coming here; we were kept prisoner by the then recognized government—forced to accede to certain demands made upon us."

"And you precipitated a revolution!" the captain snapped.

For the first time the port officer spoke. "As you have seen, Captain"—he motioned to a number of reader discs lying on the desk between the two parties—"there was preparation for such a rising long in the making before the arrival of this Learned One."

"With"—the captain showed no softening—"this infernal machine of his! That at least we can take care of—"

Zurzal's frill flamed a violent yellow-red. "It is under the seal of the Zacathan explorative service, Captain. I do not think that even your all-powerful organization is going to dispute ownership."

"You, Learned One," retorted the captain, "are no longer a member in good standing of your service—and because you meddled with this very scanner of yours! Any protest will have to be entered through your Clan Elder and, since we are half the galaxy away from your home, that will take quite a time to resolve."

"I am on detached service, Captain. Consult the authorities if you wish. You will discover my credentials in order. My search. Before my journey was so brazenly interrupted, I was on my way to Lochan. I have already shown my authorization for such a study. That this has occurred on Tssek, is, I assert, no fault of mine."

"It remains that there is a civil war in progress on the other side of that fence," the captain waved at the nearest window opening onto the port, "and that you have had a hand in stirring it up, willing or not willing. You have transgressed against the creed of your own people as well as the central law of noninterference."

"Captain," again the port commander spoke, "is it not better to wait and see? There is abundant proof which you yourself have viewed," again he waved toward the discs, "that a strong underground movement was underway even before this Learned One and his bodyguard were brought here. That the attack came at the time it did was also certain. They had knowledge—my listening service is not a questionable one—that the Holder planned to broadcast his carefully edited version of the Great Ingathering. The overturn of his plan was caused because two of the technicians selected to set up the already prepared broadcast of his own editing were members of the underground party. They were prepared to sabotage his efforts. When the Zacathan was brought in it added a new factor they had not planned on. But in fact, Learned One," now he addressed Zurzal, "you did show what might have been the truth fifty years in the past. This was a support they had not counted on, but one they speedily turned to their advantage. For what your scanner showed was broadcast over more than half of the machines, picked up by underground installations and passed on. The broadcast had already been arranged as the signal for the uprising, and they moved in."

"Their control is not yet complete," the captain stated. "It is difficult to believe that they will prevail over such fortresses as Smagan or Wer."

"Thanks to our friends here," the port officer nodded to the three on the other side of the table, "they have the Holder. As do all who rise to power he has for years systematically weeded out all below him who could question his authority, depending on those linked to him so tightly that his fall would mean theirs also. They may hold out in pockets because it means their lives, and even ras-rats will turn and fight if they are cornered, but there is no longer any leader to rally them and there has long been jealousy and infighting among them."

"You have been watching the building of this situation for long, Commander?" Zurzal's frill was lightening in shade.

"As the one responsible for this port I have had to make observations," the other agreed. "Every form of government sooner or later reaches a plateau from which there is no longer an upward advance. Since the lives of sentient beings do not remain static, there follow changes. As your people know so well, Learned One. So it happened here. But when the rebels win they will have something to thank your guard for—that they have the Holder."

"As I have said!" the captain scowled, "interference with the native government—"

"You would rather, Captain, that we be dead?"

Startled, it was not only the Patrol officer but all the rest of them who turned now to look at the fifth member of the party. Gone were the floating, seductive garments of the assured Jewelbright. Taynad had asked for and changed speedily into a spacer's drab garb. The long waves of her hair had been tightly braided, and were now bound around her head, though the wealth of that hair made it seem she must be wearing a turban.

"Yes," the captain had almost instantly adjusted to her entrance into this meeting, to the implied criticism of her question. "There also remains you, Gentlefem. I believe that you arrived here by the invitation of the Holder, is that not so?"

"Having done so," Taynad returned calmly, "there is no reason for my remaining once he is no longer my host. My very presence in his company would probably have damned me with these rebels. I owe my continued existence to the Learned One and his guard. And I am duly grateful. I hardly think, Captain, that you are going to hand me over to Tssekians—"

Jofre was sensitive to what she was doing, using trained will-power. Even though she had not turned it on him, he could feel the gathering force of it. And he did not believe that this Patrol officer, disciplined as he might be, could stand against the issha assurance of the Jewelbright.

"Why did you come?" It was not the officer but the port commander who asked that bluntly, and she answered as fully:

"The Holder had (I saw *him* cut down in the hall and so he is no longer my employer) a Horde Commander who was ambitious. He had gone off-world hunting the Learned One here as an offering to his master, and on Asborgan he chanced to learn of the Jewels. As was custom he bargained for my services. I was to be another gift. He had plans—" She shrugged. "I was a weapon; he did not have time to use me."

"Now that we have discussed a number of explanations and scraps of news," Zurzal cut in, "may we return to the main point of this meeting? I have suffered a crude and unnecessary interruption to plans I have been making for years. It is my intention that I carry those out and I do not think that anyone, Captain, is going to produce a good reason why I cannot."

"You will wait until there is a settlement here!" returned the Patrol officer flatly.

Zurzal spoke then, not to him, but to the port commander. "Commander, you have shown that you have ample reason to believe that my coming here had in reality nothing to do with the present embroilment. You also know that my appearance on Tssek was entirely against my will. By Stellar Law can we be held in this fashion?"

The commander looked neither to the Patrol captain nor to the Zacathan, instead he was studying with great interest the nails on his right hand.

"He's right, you know," he observed. "We have proof of the kidnapping, of the fact that he was being used against his will. He has claimed refuge under the Code of Harktapha—that has held since the first spacers met with his kind. We have no quarrel with Zacathans—their knowledge is ever at our service—their persons are diplomatically sacred—"

"This one presumes too much!" the Patrol officer interrupted.

"In your opinion—" The three words brought a sour silence from the captain. His hands clenched on the edge of the desk as if he would upend that innocent piece of furniture and send it in the general direction of those three across from him.

"So, Learned One," as if he need expect no more interruption the commander turned again to Zurzal, "what is your will?"

"I would return to Wayright and carry out those plans of mine," returned the Zacathan. "My guard goes with me and this gentlefem also, if it is her will."

"It is," Taynad agreed. She added nothing to that and Jofre wondered what thoughts clustered now in her head. Since he who had oathed her was dead by what the issha-sworn would consider chance, she was free from employment. Would she, once more on Wayright, seek to return to Asborgan?

"Also," she was speaking again, "there is the matter of the Jat."

"That can be easily attended to." The Patrol officer must have been glad he had a clear and definite answer to that. "It will be returned to its home planet."

"In the condition in which it now exists?" she queried.

The officer looked to the port commander for an answer.

"Unfortunately, the creature has gone catatonic and cannot be roused," he reported. "The bond between it and the Holder was so harshly broken as to send it into a coma. The medic reports that nothing he has been able to do will restore it."

"It might be well to let me try." To Jofre's surprise the Jewelbright spoke. "A broken bond might indeed break a mind, but a transferred bond—"

"Can this be done?" the commander questioned.

She hesitated for only a second. "My kind have certain powers, Gentlehomos. I have developed a liking for the creature and I saw more of it when it was with its bond master than any of you. Let me try to transfer the bond."

"But it still must be returned—"

"Let that be decided after we see how this will work," said the commander. "Yes, Gentlefem, I shall give orders that you are to try this—and may you be successful."

To Jofre's complete astonishment she turned her head and surveyed him. "This is one of my world," she indicated him. "The training he has been given grants him a certain rapport with other species. I will need him to give me aid."

Jofre had no chance to talk to her alone. She had admitted obliquely that she knew him for what he was. But that that would constitute any tie between them was chancy. The commander escorted them over to the medic quarters and there they looked down upon the small body which had balled itself almost into a knot on one of the bunks.

"It still lives," the medic reported, "but it has had no food nor drink, and the heartbeat is very slow. It is close to death."

"Yan searches for he who is gone, that one who became his other half." Taynad seated herself on the edge of the bunk and leaned over, to gather the Jat into her arms as if it were a hurt child.

"Medic, on our world we have certain training which can unite us with other living creatures beside those of our own species. It may be that we can reach Yan and bring him back. We can only try."

The medic shook his head. "Gentlefem, I fear it is hopeless. But if there is anything you can do—"

He went to seat himself on a stool at the other side of the room, watching them intently.

Taynad, the Jat still held against her, moved carefully around on the bunk, so that as much of her back was now presented to Jofre as possible. He could guess the next step. Though he had never been a part of such linkage, yet he was well aware there were cases in which it would and had worked.

Now he seated himself behind Taynad's back and dropped his hands on her shoulders. The inner commands he knew and gave one by one, each taking him further to the Center. As yet he was aware of nothing but his own search for full control.

With one hand Taynad stroked the small body which she cradled so close to her. She began a soft crooning in which there were no words to be distinguished, only soothing sounds.

Jofre within himself found and fastened upon that strength he sought. Now he drew—launched—as he might a dart—what he shaped. He could feel the feed of it from his center, along his arms, into her body— Then—!

Touch, immediate linkage, being borne along by another's demanding will. A wall against which that will struck, and then began to beat in a heavy pattern, seeking a weakness, a way of entrance—

Swifter grew those blows, steady and unrelenting the draw upon Jofre. He summoned up more and more to feed, to strengthen—

The resistance lessened reluctantly, as if a bit crumbled, and then another. Before him now was a whirling chaos of terror, alien and therefore threatening. Jofre braced himself and held. What they shaped together now was not the battering ram which had found them a way into this place of rolling terror and loss, but rather a thread to be caught up by the churning of what abode there, twisted, tangled. And they were content to have it so for now—though the payment was heavy as there was feedback of that terror, those waves of negative force. They must not only hold their small contact, but protect themselves into the bargain.

Now! She had not spoken, but the order reached Jofre as if it had been shouted like a battle cry. He sent forth a surge of power, the thread tightened as she spun. It was well enmeshed now in the chaos, it held. Yet it formed a path for them. Dark, cold, nothingness slipped along towards those two who dared to touch.

The room was gone, Jofre was aware only of a battle which he could not see, only sense. This—this— Frantically he hunted a shield, a weapon, something to stop that dark counterflow.

As if it lay heavy in his hand he knew now what he must have. The stone out of Qaw-en-itter. Asshi—if it were assha—force—if it could bring him that force. Though he continued to hold to the thread the Jewelbright had spun, yet he groped within him until he in turn touched! Yet this was no chaos—rather ordered energy. His inner self buckled as he strove to harness it. Too much—he was like one filled with fire which ate outward until all which he was might be consumed.

Ruthlessly Jofre fought to turn that wave, that fire, to harness it to the thread. And so it did—whether by his efforts, or perhaps because it was attracted in turn to what they were spinning out from issha strength.

The thread had wound and now was in a whirl which had begun to thicken, to encompass the darkness as if that had substance. And the darkness drew in farther and farther upon its own core until it was like a single nugget of pain and fear. This the thread netted and drew towards its own source.

Jofre was aware again of the woman beside him, of her body trembling in a hold he had tightened to keep her erect and steady. Then the last remaining fragments of the break-bond spread into him and his clap on her shoulders would have fallen away save that there rang from her to him the issha touch—enough to steady him.

He accepted the break-bond as he would swallow some bitter potion if such an act was necessary. Then made one more call, issha—assha—he could not tell which answered but, as the blowing out of a lamp, the flash of a blaster, the darkness was gone.

Into its place there flowed something else—a warmth which was not of his own, not issha at all—alien—yet with no harm—rather lightness of spirit, peace of mind and heart. Jofre realized that their linkage still held but what it had done was more than they had thought—the Jat was free of that despair which would have killed it—but it was—rebonded—with them!

He could see over Taynad's shoulder that the creature was no longer a hard ball in her arms. One of its small forepaws was raised, drawing the blunt finger growths down the Jewelbright's cheek. It chirped inquiringly and she gave a small cry and hugged it closer, rocking a little back and forth as might one who had feared for a child and now found that fear had gone.

"Friend—" Jofre's head jerked. The Jat had moved in Taynad's hold and was now looking over her shoulder to him. Again its forepaw advanced, to stroke caressingly his hand which still caught at the Jewelbright. From that touch came the warmth and peace which he had earlier felt, but increased, as if fueled with the same power as one of the starships.

"You have done it!" The medic was standing over both of them, staring down at the Jat, which kept its hold on Jofre as well as remaining within the circle of Taynad's arm.

For the first time Jofre heard the tinkle of the Jewelbright's laugh.

"Perhaps not as the Patrol captain might wish," she

returned. "I am afraid that he will be unable to follow orders even now—Yan has rebonded with—" She glanced at Jofre. Her face had a slight softness which had gentled the masklike beauty she had always turned upon them. "Yan has bonded with—us!"

"And," Jofre swiftly spoke for himself, "I do not think that you can try a second time." He was surprised at the warmth of his own feelings. Issha were not bond-worthy except by oath, and certainly no oathing had passed here. Or had one which was deeper and wiser than that of Lair knowledge?

The woman also, he was sure that some of his feeling at least had been shared by her, known to her now. Which was a muddle—they had indeed wrought thoughtlessly, for it would seem that the two of them were now linked in a way unknown to their breed before—by one small, warm, and peace-spreading creature. He wondered what complications they had both drawn to them by what they had done.

He loosed his hold on Taynad, feeling a little awkward, but he reached forward to draw his hand in a half caress across the bobbling head of the Jat, between those up-pointed ears.

"You are sure?" The medic was demanding. "This is going to present a problem—"

"We are sure," the Jewelbright answered calmly. "Though we could have done no other to save the little one's life. Bond-breaking," she shivered and her arm tightened a fraction about the small furry body, "is deadly."

The medic looked at them both indecisively. "I shall have to report—" And with that he was gone.

Taynad waited until the door closed behind the spacer. Then she squared her body around on the bunk so she was facing Jofre as well as she could.

"Brother." She had freed her one hand from the Jat and gave him finger greeting.

But dare he answer her as Shadow to Shadow? That was deceitful and not issha way.

"I am no longer of the Brothers," he said, watching her face carefully, waiting for that small softening of the expression to vanish. "The story is a long one, Jewelbright. But thus it stands—" And quickly he sketched all which had happened to him since the morning when the Master had paid the Dead-Stone-price and he himself had been denied. Though he did not mention his night in Qaw-en-itter nor his find there, for that was something he felt he could not share—there was too great a secret about it and he must have the unlocking of that first himself.

"You are issha—for all the blathering of the Shagga," she returned unexpectedly. "Have you not followed the proper pattern and oathed yourself—and to a lord who is well worth the serving? Do you think we could have linked to free this one," she glanced down at the Jat and then to him again, "if you were not a true Shadow? The Shagga sometimes take too much on themselves."

He was startled by her questioning of authority. Perhaps in some fashion she, too, had had something to be angry over after some priestly encounter. But that she accepted him—with a lift of heart he solemnly made the gesture of welcome and dared to change it so that it was not just to a Shadow met in passing but to one who shared a common goal.

20

ONCE MORE THEY WERE GATHERED IN THE OFFICE OF the Patrol captain but this time two more had been added to their number. These were Tssekians but not in the uniforms the unwilling visitors had seen everywhere during their travels in the city and at the keep of the Holder. It seemed to Jofre that they were trying to make a special effort to break with the restraints of their former clothing. For one wore a one-piece suit of green girded by a brilliant scarlet belt and the other a loose shirt of crimson over dull purplish breeches. But both were armed, carrying a fringe of various weapons about their waists and slung across their shoulders, and the speaker for the duo was a woman.

"We have no quarrel with the Learned One," she spoke the trade tongue with an accent as if it was one she was not used to using. "He and his guard were brought here against their wills and what he would have used for the purpose of increasing knowledge was not misused—it showed us the first great treachery of that one—" Her lips moved now as if she would spit, though she did not. "That which is his and that which belongs to his man, we have brought with us."

Zurzal inclined his head in a small formal nod. "My thanks for your courtesy. I bear no ill will to those of you who now rule here."

"This other," the woman had only nodded curtly in answer to the Zacathan, as if she had already dismissed him from her mind and all dealings with him were completed. Now she was looking at Taynad. "This other was also brought here for a purpose—but one differing from your case, Learned One. Therefore, she is not to be judged as you—"

Jofre stirred. He had had little time to do more than acquaint Zurzal with the news that the Jewelbright was issha and that her mission was aborted with the fall of the Holder. Now he saw her head come up and she met the Tssekian woman eye to eye, almost in direct challenge.

"Why did you come—plaything?" There was scathing contempt in that last word. But Taynad showed no sign that any sting of that reached her.

"It seemed that the Horde Commander Sopt s'Qu had some thought of pleasing his overlord," she returned calmly. "Thus I was included in this plan."

The Tssekian scowled. "Sopt s'Qu is dead," she said flatly. "The one he served will be held to face the wrath of the people. What should be done with you?"

Jofre tensed but Taynad spoke before he could make any protest.

"The man with whom I made my bargain is dead; the man for whom that bargain was made will be otherwise occupied. My reason for visiting Tssek has ceased to exist."

The Tssekian woman continued to measure the Jewelbright and there was nothing soft in that harsh stare.

"Your kind are without value," she almost spat the words. "We want no taint of you in our lives. Since you had no time to work any true mischief here, we shall send you off-world with these others."

"That is your right," conceded Taynad, "nor have I any wish to remain here."

"You brought with you gauds—"

"To which you are now entitled," Taynad interrupted. "Since such were of the Horde Commander's gift and so belong to Tssek. I do not ask for any accounting of them."

"Well for you!" The woman was determined not to be bettered in their subtle struggle. "So, off-worlder," she now looked to the Patrol captain, "these are now your responsibility. Let them return to their own places, we need nothing of them. The Council meets tomorrow; we shall be speaking with you again concerning regulations for off-worlders—some of those will be changed."

She stood up, adjusted a fraction the swing of her weapon slung across her shoulder, and moved towards the door without another word or look.

"Well, it seems it is all decided," the port commander said briskly as the two Tssekians disappeared. "There is no reason, Captain, why these three must be retained to answer questions now—or at least I cannot imagine any. According to the wishes of this planet's people the sooner they are gone the better. There is the courier attached to the port service which is due to lift for Wayright. Quarters may be a little cramped," he spoke now to Zurzal, "but the courier service is fast and there is no other ship due for some time. In fact the local disturbances here may be a warn-off for freighters in company service. They will want to be sure the new regime is well rooted before they start negotiations again."

The Patrol captain was frowning.

"Learned One, I intend to send a full report of this whole matter to headquarters. This is very close to interference with planetary affairs, and, if proven, that can keep you safely out of space wandering. You, Gentlefem," he said more slowly, "were also undoubtedly intended to interfere with matters as they stood. That you did not have a chance to do so was merely fortune. I shall recommend that you be returned to your Asborgan and not permitted off that world again."

She did not answer him but the Zacathan did. "Send your report, Captain. You will be following the proper procedure. But know this, I shall also offer an explanation of what was done against my will; also I intend to speak for this gentlefem who was legally hired by the laws of her own world, brought to Tssek and then, not only dismissed from service but deprived of the payment promised her. She dealt in good faith and therefore cannot be held responsible for what another deems she might have done—a very unsure assumption.

"For the present I consider her as one of my party and ask that she accompany us to Wayright without prejudice. You cannot condemn anyone for a crime which was not committed and perhaps never would have been except as you speculate."

The port commander was nodding in time to the last words. "He has the right of it. Submit your report, Captain, and I shall also submit mine. The Tssekians find no fault with these people; instead they freely admit that the Learned One was kidnapped. That his machine worked in part, even aided what they had planned to do, for it betrayed the fact that the Holder had been a traitor to his predecessor. I can believe that such glimpses into the pasts of all of us might turn up some unpleasant and dangerous decisions and events. However, it is the Learned One's desire to use his scanner only in the field of archeology—to present a past so far removed that its summoning will have no effect on the modern day."

"It is wrong—" the captain exploded.

"As you see it. But let us leave such judgments to the higher authorities. What happened on Tssek was a forced use of what might be a very important thing. Now," he spoke once more to the Zacathan, "you will leave with the courier and I promise you as quick a trip as possible. I cannot assure you there will be no questions raised when you reach Wayright—but that will be your concern."

"We shall be most pleased—" Zurzal said. His neck frill, which had shown some traces of color and a tendency to flutter at the edges, now lay peacefully at rest.

When they had time to themselves the Zacathan spoke to Taynad. "Since they have deprived you of your wardrobe and other necessities of travel, allow me to make up that loss at least in part."

"You are very generous, Learned One." Her answer came in a colorless voice. The Jat had hunted her out and now cuddled against her. "I cannot promise any repayment. In the eyes of those I return to I may be considered one who has failed."

"Death cancels an oath!" Jofre broke in. "Sopt s'Qu is dead. And the Holder will soon be, judging by the attitude of these Tssekians we have just seen. Also—were you oathed directly to him or to his subordinate?"

"To the Horde Commander."

"Who is, I repeat, dead. You cannot serve a dead man."

She could, of course. That, too, was part of issha training, but there was no reason for her to use her knife on herself in this situation—the oath was not a full service one he was sure.

"At any rate," she returned, "we have to wait on the fate shadowing us. Much is changed by time."

Their voyage back to Wayright was both swift and smooth. For Jofre it was a far more comfortable one, even though their quarters were crowded. He had hoped to establish some closer communication with the Jewelbright. But she spoke only of service things, mainly of the Jat. And it was that creature which drew the two of them together.

Jofre was startled to learn that he could exchange vague thought-speech with Taynad if the Jat was with them both. This was something new in his experience and in the Sister's also he believed, though she did not admit to it. Zurzal was greatly interested and set up some tests, but when he himself strove to try the same form of transference of ideas it was a failure. Apparently only the shared bonding allowed this.

At ship's night measure before they planeted the Zacathan made a serious suggestion to Taynad.

"Gentlefem, I know of your way of life, and also that you are issha-trained. Perhaps what I have to offer is too far removed from that which you know and desire. But I would like to ask you to join with us—not oathed but as a partner in what is to be done on Lochan. That is a planet about which we know little—and where we would venture is wilderness. It is, I have been informed, a harsh world and not one to tempt a visit. There is danger to be found there. However, danger is not new to the issha-trained and your success with this small one who is alien to all of us, might be a factor for success or failure of what I would accomplish.

"For if you can bond with a Jat, then binding with other alien wildlife can certainly be hoped for. And where I would go the wildlife is said to be one of the greatest perils."

She was smoothing her long fingers down the Jat's furry back, sending the creature squirming and uttering small mews of pleasure. Away from her fantastic robes, dressed in the severeness of the spacer garb she had obtained at the port, she looked like another person.

Taynad studied the Zacathan. What she had seen of the man suggested trust. She was not sure that Jofre had been right, that death had broken her oath-binding. After all, by his own admission, the guard was no longer a true Shadow Brother. If she returned to Asborgan—if she would be able to return there—she had no funds and those possessions which she might have been able to pawn to secure such had been taken by the Tssekians—she might find herself in a difficult position. Doubtless on other worlds there existed the equivalent of Jewelbrights with their own manner of life—but to her that was a mask, a disguise only, and to think of it as ALL of one's life was distasteful. The Zurzal's suggestion promised hardship, but she had come from perilous and sometimes near-vicious schooling; she had no fears that she could not do as well as Jofre if it became a matter of survival. There was much in this offer which did interest her.

The binding with the Jat was something which still made her feel warm and good inside. Suppose she could indeed develop such a talent with other forms of life? It was truly something to consider seriously.

"Learned One, I cannot make answer until I know what awaits me in Asborgan. It may be that I shall be tied by another's will. But—let it be as you wish for now!"

"Fair enough," Zurzal returned. "We may have a period of waiting at Wayright port, for ships to Lochan are few."

Taynad continued to gentle the Jat. Good, time she could use, not only to settle her own possible future but to discover what there was about this disowned Brother— she shot a glance at him as he stood checking some list the Zacathan had handed him—which gave her always the sense of hidden power.

His off-worlder blood showed in his greater height, even though beside Zurzal he was made to look small, slim, boyish—He had ice-grey eyes also, instead of the brown ones she was used to seeing, able to warm with fire, when the issha displayed skills in the arms court. Yet he moved with the unmistakable ease of any Shadow she had seen.

What had Zarn said concerning him when the disguised Shagga had attempted to get her to forego her mission and go after him? That he was a renegade, one who was the first in generations to break the Code of Vart, that he had stolen something of power— Still Zarn had been very wary in that part of his explanation of why Sister should turn against Brother.

She knew well that what Jofre had told her about his outlawing from Ho-Le-Far was the truth. Deep-trained could not so deceive deep-trained. He believed that it was Shagga hatred which had denied him his proper life and certainly it was Shagga hatred which had set Zarn scheming to bring him down.

They had linked to free the Jat and linkage would have speedily revealed to her any darkness in him. But—there was something—that power—a strength which she was well aware he possessed. Oddly enough she was also sure that he did not realize what he had—it was as if a man carried a bit of stone, perhaps as a luck piece, not realizing that what he grasped in truth was a gem of great price.

What made one Asshi? Oh, there were ceremonies and trials, all manner of testing. She had never been at such a raising herself but she had heard talk of such. Could it be that this off-worlder who was not of the true blood possessed that necessary extra core of power? Then—yes, it would explain the Shagga hatred—all the rest. They would never allow among them a Master who was not born of their own breed.

Nor would they—her thoughts carried logically forward—would they wish one with issha training and perhaps such dormant power, to really escape them. Better the death the Shagga had planned in the mountains, they would think. And perhaps most of the Brothers and Sisters would agree. Assha were jealous of their standing; it was the base of their inner powers, something which must not be questioned.

Taynad summoned now her own inner reactions to this outlaw. There was no hatred—why should there be? Hatred could be seeded, grown, used judiciously when it was needed to enhance inner power, but one did not nourish it without cause. He had been ready to stand for her before the port authorities; she had sensed that as completely as if he had spoken aloud.

He had linked, securely and well. And he had bonded—with the Jat—and perhaps also—at this new thought her head jerked a fraction—bonded with her? But that was impossible! There had been no oathing. Nor had this Zurzal offered that either when he had spoken of Lochan. He would take her free of any loyalty tie and this Brother would accept her so—she was sure of that.

The Jat had fallen asleep and she laid the small body on one of the cushions of the bunk. She gave a sudden shake to her head and loosed the curtain of her hair as it must be before she sought the Center. The other two in the cabin were very intent upon the tapes the Zacathan had borrowed from the captain of this ship, data of distant worlds. If they noticed her, Jofre would realize what she did and would not disturb her.

Deep, slow breaths, control of mind, closing out of all which was about her. In—in to the Center. Her hands moved in the long familiar patterns although she was no longer aware of them. In and in and in— She knew the calm, the waiting force, and encushioned herself in it. As she would do before any trial of strength, Taynad fitted herself with that armor, those weapons, no living being had ever seen.

It was like being free to swim in some pool of pure and fragrant water, turn lazily and circle, feeling the flow of that force about her. Yet there was the prick of warning which came now. Not too long—one dared not linger here too long. Reluctantly she roused once more her will, out, away—it was sluggish that response, then it grew stronger, swept her out into the world once again. She was once more Taynad, save that for a while she would be a little more than she had been. No Shagga, no Master, no Mother-sister, had ever learned how to hold to that force for long, how could a lesser issha hope to do so?

It remained that she must wait for a period—learn if those who controlled her would reach for her again. When she entered into this bargain there had been no time limit set on her off-world stay. She had not been dispatched to deal death but rather to subtly bend a man to another's will, and that she and those who had selected her were sure she could do. But there had been no promise that this would have been a short mission or that when it was finished she would not return to her Lair.

They planeted on Wayright in the late afternoon, using that part of the giant port which was reserved for couriers and Patrol ships. There was none of the heavy traffic here which engulfed one at the passenger port some distance away.

Jofre had expected that they would be met by a guard, marched off to another debriefing by the Patrol. He had his suspicions that the officer on Tssek had no intention to forget them and the danger he believed them to be. However, they were picked up by an antigrav ground transport and, with their scanty luggage, transferred to the city, back to the pyramided inn from which they had been snatched— was it weeks—or even months ago? Space-time and planet time differed in a way Jofre found amazing.

As the outer door closed behind them they were received with the suave diffidence shown them before under this same roof, speedily escorted to a suite of rooms on the second rise of the building. Jofre made for the windows at once and examined the latching, even though he hardly believed that the same trick would be played on them twice. Surely there was not a second dictator ready to have his past scanned.

21

"**W**ELCOME, VEEP TETEMPRA, WELCOME INDEED!"

She noted the exact depth of his bow as well as the carefully cultivated joy he was so quick to express at her appearance in the conference chamber where he had had his temporary rule. This Salanten was harboring some thoughts he believed unguessed. She would have to take steps sooner or later. Just now there were more important decisions to be made.

"Glad hour to you also, Salanten. There arose no difficulties during my absence then?"

She fitted her gleaming body, bending her stick-thin limbs easily, into the waiting seat at the head of the conference board. Her turban flashed two new jewels, her personal selection from that hoard the Shagga Voice had reluctantly bestowed.

"Nothing of great import, Veep. Routine merely." He was of the old Terran stock, and the pride of such sometimes got out of hand. Though he had come up through the ranks and knew exactly how he stood and how firm that standing might be considered at present. Now he began to rattle off his report and Tetempra listened, twice condescending to tap out a note on her own recorder.

There was a new market for Kamp opening up in the

northwest sector. And the illegal trade in Varg furs was showing a generous profit. So good a one it might even be well to see that the Jack outfit in charge of that poaching be replaced by one of the Guild's own fleet. Have Fengal evaluate that. The rest was petty, planet-bound stuff. He was deliberately smothering her in such details, hoping to bore her so that she would be adverse to more than very random checkings on such activities as he had managed to corner under his own control. There were a number of those—yes, this servant must be bound to the orders of those over him and not free to meddle on his own.

But she allowed him to come to the end of his dull reporting and did not interrupt. Although twice she made mental note of matters her own special eyes and ears were going to check on.

"And you bring us new business, Veep—?"

She narrowed the slight slit of her inner eyelids. He certainly must be watched. Business for "us" indeed! Did he rank himself as one who could speak at any time for the Guild?

"There will be a conference at the hour of the second moon rise," she made no direct answer to such effrontery and was even more irritated that he did not seem to be aware of the snub. "Summon all department heads—"

"Lan Te is on the eastern continent."

"Send out the summons." She made no other comment but raised her long hand in a gesture he could not overlook as meaning dismissal.

For several minutes she sat playing with her personal recorder, slipping it back and forth in her fingers as she thought, trying to fit one bit of information to another in order to form the whole upon which a decision must be based.

Then she spoke to the voice box at her right hand.

"Send in the one who waits—"

The woman who appeared in answer to that abrupt summons wore a shabby spacer uniform, its badges proclaiming her a communication expert, but those were tarnished. In all she gave the appearance of one perhaps bumped from a berth and unable to make a new connection.

Her face was bloated, the cheeks distended and shivers ran over her body. The Veep studied her.

"Very, very good, Ho-Sing. An excellent disguise. And what do you have for me?"

"The Zacathan and his guard were kidnapped and have left planet on a Tssekian Force fighter. It seems that one of the Horde Commanders, Sopt s'Qu, took him from his quarters at the Auroa Inn. They did it by flitter and loaded the prisoners on board at once—they had been stassed—the guard looked near death. The ship lifted them as soon as possible."

When the woman stopped speaking Tetempra clicked her long nails on the tabletop.

"We knew that the Tssekians might try this," she said, "they moved fast."

"They had another passenger also, Veep."

The nails were now motionless.

"Who?"

"A woman of Asborgan—one of those trained to give pleasure—and of the highest rank—those called Jewelbright."

"Ah—" What Zarn had parted with in the way of knowledge, besides the jewels, was now to be added to the picture. That was the one he had spoken of at their second meeting, the one to whom the Guild, in the manner of speaking, owed the increase on their fee.

"What do they say was the purpose of this Jewelbright's visit to Tssek?"

The woman shrugged. "What could her purpose be? She was a gift to the Holder. Doubtless she was to whisper into his ear at the proper moments any word her sponsor would wish passed on."

"Tssek—" Tetempra's nails began to tap again. "Four shipments of arms to the far west there—and a different touchdown, not a true port for any of them. The rebels made an excellent deal and they must be very close to the

fruition of their plans. It may go hard with the Zacathan—
and his guard, if he survives the trip—should Arn's'Dunn
win this squabble. What is the latest news?"

"None as yet, Veep. We have the eyes out, the ears
ready. Wayright is covered."

"When there is news, bring it at once."

With no parting salute the woman turned and was gone.
That one was to be depended upon, Tetempra considered
with satisfaction. She had handpicked her herself and the
reward which had been dangled was very great. Nor would
it be skimped—this one was well worth her hire.

There was nothing to do now but wait. But she could
find plenty otherwise to deal with. There was the matter
of the ship they would need, if and when they could
get the Zacathan away from Tssek and once more on
the move along the path THEY chose—though the fool
thought it was all his doing. It showed that even such
as a Zacathan could be subtly managed into obeying the
desires of another. All had been going so well until these
mire-eaters of Tssek interfered. Though if Guild calculations were right about Arn's'Dunn, the Illustrious Holder
and any henchman of his would speedily have very little
to say about anything.

She would present at the conference the bargain with
Zarn and she had no expectation of anything but success.

It was a ten-ten of days later that Tetempra's chamber
safe alarm brought her awake. This Farcar Inn was Guild
owned, through a proxy, of course, and had a number of
additions for the comfort and convenience of its occupants.
The Veep pressed a button set in the frame of her bed,
pulled around her a length of thick blue-green cloth and
stalked over to the wall farthest from the window.

At her touch the concealed door opened, and, slipping
into the very dim light of the room, was the woman she
had interviewed before.

"What has happened?"

"Opher has reported in—not from the port, Veep. No,
there was the landing of a service courier and on board were

all three of those you wish knowledge of—the Zacathan, his guard, and the play woman."

"A service courier! They were under some form of arrest?"

"The signs were not of that. An antigrav was summoned and they all went to the same inn where the Zacathan was staying when the Tssekians took them. Also—Opher reports that they have a Jat."

"Sigsman gave that to the Holder four seasons ago when we wished certain privileges. But—a Jat does not leave its bond master. That needs some thinking about also.

"Tssek must have come to a boil. But why this woman with them? She is a new complication."

"What we can learn, Veep, we shall."

"You continue to do very well, Ho-Sing. I am well pleased."

"One asks no more than that, Veep. I have already ordered that a strict watch be kept."

It was the third day after their return to Wayright and Zurzal had been summoned twice to service headquarters. He returned each time with a flaring frill and a refusal to talk for a while after pacing the room like a caged orzal. The scanner had been carefully returned to the guardianship of the hive as if the Zacathan feared that it might disappear were he to leave it out of safekeeping.

Jofre had known something of impatience also. He needed weapons. Even the Makwire was lost to him now and he felt almost as if he had been stripped of his clothing as well. On the third morning he ventured to break into Zurzal's preoccupation with a mention of this point.

"Of course!" Zurzal was immediately attentive. "A man must always be supplied with the tools of his trade if he is to be set to work. But this is not a place where I have the proper contacts—"

"There is one Istarn of Vega." The cool voice of Taynad somewhat startled them both. "It is said that he offers weapons from half a hundred worlds to those who take pleasure in collecting such things."

Though Zurzal had urged her to gather a new wardrobe, she had made no effort to return to the rich garments of her supposed trade. She had selected a second spacer suit, lacking any insignia, and seemed, when wearing it, to be able to take on a kind of enwarping drabness. Jofre knew that she was summoning her own form of the Shadows invisibility.

Only her hair remained to mark her as different from any woman crew member on leave, for, though she kept it braided tightly, it still formed a heavy crown for her head. That, Jofre also knew, she would not part with willingly, for it was a weapon she might call upon in need.

"Istarn," Zurzal repeated first a little blankly as if he had not heard the name before, and then added with more force, "Istarn—but of course—it was he who turned up the Balakan mirror dispatcher that Zanquat has in his collection. I have never met the man but I thought he dealt mainly in antiques—not the weapons of this day."

"Learned One," Jofre said, "we of the issha have been trained with weapons those of these strange worlds believe to be primitive, for the use of barbarians only. However, it might be that this Istarn would put a collector's price on what he has to offer and that would be too great to pay."

"Istarn himself does not deal here on Wayright," Taynad continued to impart information the other two began to wonder how she gathered. "His shop is on the Second Way—where those bored while they wait for their ships spend time and money on things which seem strange and new to them, but have little real value. We have the knowledge to pick from among rubbish that which will serve."

Zurzal gave his hissing laugh. "I do not know how you got this information—"

For the first time Jofre saw Taynad's lips curve in a true smile. "Learned One, I listened—after asking a question or two. Yan," she patted the head of the Jat that, as usual, was clutching at the edge of her tunic, "is very much an interest to the maidservants. They have come and asked to see our little one. And they talk freely when doing so. I have learned of the best shops, those which have quality merchandise and do not put up the prices when a passenger ship planets, the eating places and the speciality of each, again where one may expect to get the best service for the credit outlay. So eventually I learned of Istarn."

"To our benefit," Zurzal returned. "Very well, let us off to this establishment and I shall leave it to the two of you to equip yourselves with what you believe will be most useful."

In the arms courts of the Lairs a weapon was judged for efficiency. The truth of a blade was in its forging and edging, of all other implements for battle in their usability and strength. Valley lords of Asborgan might prance about with gem-hilted sidearms. A hilt wrapped with well-seasoned lacing to keep it from slipping in the hand was what the issha-trained judged by—and no one could fault the value of any Lair wrought blade, lance, hand hook or the like, that value rested in the weapon itself and not in any ornamentation.

What confronted Jofre in the shop of this so-called weapon merchant were not the tools of his trade but rather trumped-up bits of glitter misnamed for the blades he knew. He stared at the display of what the shopkeeper spoke of as "swords of value from Vega" and thought privately that one good blow from any one of those would speedily separate blade from hilt, perhaps even shattering the blade. These caught the eye most certainly but not the eye of a warrior. What did he care if a hilt was of tri-gold in the form of a washawk with emerald eyes—or something of the same stupid description when he could see very well that the blade attached was not nine times forged, or even six times worked!

"These are toys," he said in Lair tongue to Taynad. "What does any want with such—unless to pick out the jewels, melt down those hilts and use the blades for hide scraping?"

"Those off-worlders who are the buyers here do not intend to USE them," she replied as softly. "They are for show only. But there is a second display beyond. Perhaps—"

He was impatient enough to move away and lost any other word she might have said.

Yes, there was a second display—or rather it was not an arranged display to show off the offered weapons, rather a pile, in a darkish corner, of dull metal, long uncared for, with nothing in that mass to catch the untaught eye. Only when he stopped there and looked for himself—could he mark possibilities. This clutter might be what was tossed aside in some smith's forge, things to be melted down and reworked—at least that is what it looked to be at first sight.

However—no arms master would have been so quick to devalue—that! His gaze fixed upon the peeling leather sheaths, twins, and the matched blades they sheltered. He plucked one forth. Dulled, needing a honing, yes. But the steel—ah—that he knew for what it was. Heartened, Jofre drew the second knife and found it as sound as its twin.

Taynad was busied separating a choice of her own from the rusty jumble. Luckily the proprietor had been detached from them by the entrance of several off-worlders whose rich robing proclaimed hearty credit ratings and who were fascinated by the gemmed display.

At the end of some careful choosing, even a bit of surreptitious testing of the elasticity of blade, Jofre had at his hand for bargaining the twin knives, a short sword, and a collection of wicked-looking hooks which, when wedded to a length of chain he had loosed from the pile, would make a Makwire far more suitable even than that which had served him on Tssek. Unfortunately other familiar aids to a guardsman were not to be found. Perhaps he was lucky that he had discovered as much as were useful among these apparent discards as he had.

Taynad had a blade which was near the length of a short sword encased in a sheath once covered with a grimy brocade which was now peeling from it in strips. At the top of the scabbard showed also the hilts of two small knives and she had worked one out of the damaged sheath to show, unrusted, an almost needle-thin weapon perhaps as long as her hand. Such were perhaps meant for eating purposes but they were close to those weapons the Sisters were well-known to hide in hair coils or hanging sleeves, and Jofre had no doubt that she would be able to put them to the best service. She also had a Makwire chain, which she was twisting about now inch by inch to test it, for there were stains of rust on her fingers where she handled it. However, beneath that surface flaking it appeared to be strong enough to satisfy her.

"Gentlehomo and—Gentlefem—" The salesman looked at Taynad as if she were indeed an oddity in such a place, or else her air of knowing exactly what she wanted from this dingy heap was a surprise to the seller. "Have you made some discovery—? But this—this is of second rating. You would be better with the swords from Lanker, or the ruby-headed daggers of Grath. Now those are proud weapons."

"They are," Jofre returned, "but not to our purpose—"

"No," Taynad struck in, "we do not seek weapons of fine show, but rather ones we can use to demonstrate various forms of fighting. We think to display combat for show."

"So? Are you then from the Arms Court of Assherbal? It is known that his battle displays are very lifelike—close to the real—blood spilled, even."

"Something like is what we aim to do." Jofre picked up her hint quickly. "No, Gentlehomo, what price is put on these?" He indicated what they had set aside. The salesman eyed their selections with a disdain he did not attempt to conceal. Certainly his attitude had become brusque—that of one dealing with persons below the social rating of those he commonly served.

He quoted a price well within the credits Zurzal had transferred to Jofre's new account and for the first time Jofre made use of that ever-present aid to off-world living.

Their selections were bundled into a sack in a hurry as if the salesman did not want it seen that such dingy wares were going out of his shop, and they returned to the open street.

They were passing by one open-fronted shop where there was a sprouting of tables edging out into the thoroughfare and for each some stools. The aroma of food was strong enough to combat and defeat the scents wafting from a place of perfumes across the way.

Jofre nodded towards one of the tables. "It smells good," he said simply. For it did, better somehow than the exotic dishes which were constantly offered them at the inn. Taynad gave a heavy sniff and then showed him again that very fleeting smile.

"So it does, and no Shadow food either. Yes, let us try it to see if it tastes as good as it smells."

They seated themselves at one of the tables, Jofre allowing the package of weapons to lie on the floor between his feet, and consulted the menu printed in trade and displayed as part of the tabletop between them.

Not too far away a woman in a spacer's uniform chose a table and settled into a seat there. The occupant who was already there greeted her with a nod. He was humanoid to about the fifth degree, but his heavily furred body, erect pointed ears, and wide well-toothed mouth, showed he did not share his companion's Terran breed.

"Those then." He did not look at Jofre and Taynad, and his voice was very soft, nearly a growl.

"Those. I pass them on to you, Lenoil. She wants them well watched. And do not take them lightly, they are of a trained-for-fighting breed—the most feared on their home world."

"One world among many," her companion replied. "We all have our champions. Sometimes such do not survive—"

"No! No interference with them, only watching," the woman said swiftly. "Watch and report—you are staying at the Auroa as are they; therefore, you have better chance to keep an eye on them. Be sure that eye is ever there."

22

THE ZACATHAN WALKED IN UPON A SCENE OF CON-
centrated industry. His three companions were seated
on the floor and each was busy. The Jat was drawing
back and forth through a length of oil-stained cloth a
supple chain. Beside him Taynad honed the narrow blade
of a very small knife and opposite them both Jofre was
fitting another chain, thicker, well able to support such
a burden, with a series of wicked-looking hooks, pausing
now and then to test his work with a swing or two of the
metal line.

"Luck, Learned One?" They had all three looked up at
his coming but it was Jofre who asked that.

"As yet none. Almost one could believe that there was
some pattern we are not able to understand—" He paused
as if not knowing just how to put his thoughts into words.

"A warn off by the Patrol!" Jofre suggested.

"I hardly think so. We seek Free Traders, and they
do not take kindly to official warning unless those are
delivered with force. Two such ships have planeted within
the last ten days. One is already chartered by a party of
engineer-techs to transport them and their equipment to
Helga. The other carries no passengers and is mainly an
asteroid mining ferry."

"It may be a long wait, Learned One." Taynad had not halted work on her knife while she listened. "It seems you deal with the whims of fortune now and that is always sheer chance."

"Yet there is no better place to await any transportation than here," Zurzal returned. "I have spread the word as to what I wish. And this is on route to Lochan—which is why I chose it as a base in the beginning. Have you consulted those?" He indicated the three tapes lying on the tabletop beside the reader.

"It seems a place about which very little is known," Taynad commented, "if that is all which we have to consult, Learned One."

"A barren land," Jofre struck in, not that that was any deterrent as far as he was concerned. The northern stretches of Asborgan were certainly sere and stripped enough. "It seems to be mainly desert—"

"As far as we know. Yes, that is all the information on file," Zurzal assented. "It does not have too promising a reputation—there is no great trade to be found there—small stuff—some strange furs, odd minerals—"

Taynad fitted the newly sharpened knife into a small sheath of her own devising, one actually woven from strands of her hair. "Then why should anyone go there—or is it that this Lochan might have other uses for outworlders—a hidden base, perhaps?"

"Guild dealings?" Zurzal shook his head. "It was well combed for any off-world activity after the failure of Desmond's expedition. There is no defense against Patrol sensors, unless the establishment would be a major one and Lochan certainly could not support such."

"Treasure?" Taynad submitted another surmise.

"Not the kind which would draw the average trader. Though it was the matter of some artifacts turning up in the cargo of such a one which first directed us to Lochan. What we seek there is another kind of treasure than would draw Guild interest—knowledge. There is good reason to think there may be one of the Forerunner respositories there."

"The Guild seeks knowledge, too——" Taynad commented. "Is it not rumored that they discover what they can which may be put to their own uses?"

"The scanner!" Jofre had fastened his last hook and was coiling the chain to accommodate those additions.

"Which will not serve them," Zurzal answered. "We learned long ago to protect our tools from wrongful use. Were any other to attempt to use the scanner, it would destruct. That is built into every tool of the sort which we lift from our own world."

"How long a wait then, Learned One, until such a ship as you wish sets down here?"

"Not too long. There is one which made the run to Lochan five planet months ago. It has made two runs and each time to a near planet. The ship is old, the captain not one, I have been told, who is ready to push into any other territory. We can expect the *Haren Hound* to be in port soon if all goes to the past pattern."

Jofre had moved to the wide window-door which gave upon the balcony servicing this portion of the floor.

"We are being watched," he said flatly. "I do not think we are off the Patrol's hook yet."

"The watcher?" Zurzal demanded quickly.

"Differs. We could slip them if we wish. We would rather learn who they are and why eyes and ears are set on us. To learn that perhaps it is well to let them go about this Shadow business for a space longer."

Tetempra was already seated at the head of the table in the wide room which could be entered only through her personal office. There were five of her staff flanking her and at the other end of the table, awaiting any orders, Ho-Sing.

"They have rearmed themselves, this guard and the woman, with barbarian weapons—such as can only be used in hand-to-hand combat. Doubtless they prepare so for the wastes of Lochan. Our people cannot penetrate into their suites because of the Jat—it is very quick to sense anyone who is not friendly to its bond-mates."

"It can be removed—" came the suggestion from an obese and warty-skinned member to her right.

"And give them warning? Nusa, have your brains begun to addle already? I thought your skin-shed season was yet well off. No, we do not move against them. But there is this other matter—the message—the order to be given to the Asborgan woman. So far we have not been able to separate her from her companions. But a bargain is a bargain and this one must be carried out. Ho-Sing, have you any new thoughts on reaching the woman long enough to pass a message without the others knowing what has happened?"

"This morning the room maid spoke to her of the Fra-grance baths—she showed interest. The maid receives a percentage of what any guest spends at the Tri-lily—she will endeavor to send this woman there. The maid's in debt to Dabblu; she may be reached through that—though the hotel staff are supposed to be incorruptible."

"Excellent. This you will move on, Ho-Sing. When this one goes to the Tri-lily one will meet with her—seemingly by accident—to the beholders—but for our purposes. Let it so be arranged."

"The ship, Veep Tetempra?" Salanten being officious once again, her eyes slitted to mere threads though she did not turn those on him, rather focused her attention on a small com before her.

"The Learned One is waiting for the *Haren Hound*. We have prepared the way very well in that direction. Gosal is due in very shortly—the new drive we installed in his buck-et of rusted bolts has delighted him; he is very willing to be able to pay for it in service. Which is well since any cargo he has lifted in the past could not pay for a wind wheel!"

"Do the Patrol have a watch on them?" One of silent others spoke. "The Tssek business could not have made the authorities happy."

"Ho-Sing?" Tetempra looked to the head of her Shadow service.

"None we have picked up and Everad has scanned for them. But—"

"But what?" Tetempra demanded when the other continued to hesitate.

"I think that they—at least the guard—the woman—guess that they are under observation. We have been using the utmost care and they have done nothing to throw us off—"

"Still you sense it yourself, Ho-Sing?" the Veep concluded for her. "Very well, have one of your force make some error which will suggest he is Patrol or planet force inspired. They may well be expecting that and will go about their business freely. I can leave that well to you."

"Why does that priesthood on Asborgan want the guard so much they offered us such a price?" Again it was Salanten pushing himself forward.

"He has been outlawed by them. All these priesthoods and religious overlords turn vicious if any of their followers begin to think for themselves. I gather they wish to make an example of him. He seems to be on passable terms with the woman at present but once we pass on Zarn's message we may cause complications for them all."

"It is a thing that travelers indulge themselves in," Taynad said as they shared their meal on the terrace. "I think," she continued, "that the maid is probably paid a small fee for suggesting that one goes—if one *DOES* go thereafter."

"We are not just travelers," Jofre said sharply. Their few excursions into the whirl of the city round them had been all for very practical reasons, the obtaining of weapons, clothing, finding out from information sources what they could about possible transportation and the planet Zurzal wanted to explore.

"This might be a chance," the Zacathan said slowly, "to discover more about those shadows you believe are hovering around your trail. Yes, I know it would mean that Taynad would take off on her own, but I believe that there is that in issha training which favors the individual over even a duo. By all means, Jewelbright, try this new sensation, you may have something to import to Asborgan on your return."

He did not like it. Jofre was opposed to her going out alone even at midday and in a city so well policed that no casual crime had existed for years. Nothing must disturb the well-being and peace of the travelers on whom all Wayright's industry was centered. Why did he have this inner warning? Did he fear some improbable attack on Taynad? Certainly all his training would turn him against such a thought—issha did not doubt the skill and ability of issha—she was very well able to take care of herself.

Then—what was it? The fact which had been nibbling at him now for days, that she seemed to accept the Zacathan's offer of employment with no thought that her home Lair might see matters very differently? She had not been oathed to this as was he, and without the oath— Then there was a freedom which could turn to enmity on the demand of a Lair Master. That she could not return to Asborgan without assistance was true. But it would take time for the happenings on Tssek to filter back to that world and meanwhile she had to live. There was the Jat and the linkage; Jofre kept coming back to that for assurance. Surely the creature linked so to them both would display uneasiness, perhaps even more, if Taynad did not mean exactly what she had said to Zurzal. Still—

There was no use in following her to this Tri-lily for it was a luxury establishment for females only. He was also somehow sure that she would know what he was doing if he tried to follow her, at least to the door. For the moment there was nothing Jofre could do and he resented it.

To escape his own thoughts he started a practice session, concentrating on learning just what could be done with his new weapons, the Jat squatting on a cushion to watch him with very round eyes.

*   *   *

The establishment of the Tri-lily was imposing but in an oddly discreet way, as might a Jewelbright slide into a mixed company and subtly let her presence there dawn slowly on those about her. There was a living doorguard, not a robot voice box, to bow Taynad into a room which somehow wrapped one around with a feeling of relaxation and peace. How this effect was accomplished she had no idea, and indeed her issha suspicion tightened. There would be no wearing away of her own core of control, no matter what outward signs of enjoyment she might need to summon.

"Gracious and Illustrious One—" A slender female shape moved from between two misty blue-green wall hangings.

They were prepared to pile it on; Taynad's professional interest sifted it all. Greeting suitable to some highborn, but delivered with apparently complete sincerity. She gave several points to the manager here—perhaps even a Jewel House Mistress might be impressed.

"Bright day," she responded pleasantly, but allowed to creep into her voice a faint tone of uneasiness as if indeed she were a little daunted by such ceremony. "I have heard— there is a maid at the Auroa who spoke highly of the restful value of your services. Such are new to me—but—"

"You were interested enough, Illustrious, to come and see what there is to be offered? We have many services— but since you have not visited us before, perhaps it is well that you begin by making your season choice—"

"Season choice?"

"Yes, it is known that beings differ greatly in their reaction to environmental changes. Perhaps on your world spring is the season which holds the strongest meaning for you—during which you feel at the best. Or you may look forward to the ripeness of summer—the soothing warmth— the cloudless skies under which living things rise to their fruitfulness. There are those also who find autumn stimulating—the first crispness of freshening winds, the savor of the land which has been touched faintly by frost. And there are those, though they are fewer in number, who like the bracing of storms, the clear cold of mornings when ice begems twigs and branches. We have these, Illustrious, ready for your service."

Taynad was intrigued. For a moment she held a flash of memory—of being young—running barefooted across a dew-wet strip of tiny mountain meadow to sniff the first star flowerets of the year.

"I think I choose spring," she found herself saying.

"If you will come this way, Illustrious, you shall meet spring—"

One of the curtain panels on the wall was looped aside and she stepped ahead of the attendant into a narrow corridor not more than three strides long, and so came into a second room. Or was it a room? She could not actually see any walls except a fraction of the one embracing the door behind her. There was a mass of greenery to the sides, and, centering, a pool into which flowed liquid. She might have come out into the open of one of those mountain valleys she knew so well, except this had no skin roughening winds tunneling down it, and the softness of the air was a caress on her flesh. There were fragrances carried by those lightest of breezes, clean, fresh scents of newly awakened growth reaching for new life and renewal.

The attendant beckoned her on to the side of the pool. There were places there for sitting, cleverly hollowed into the seeming stone. Some were so placed they would allow entrance into the pool. The attendant indicated one larger rock.

"You place the fingers so, Illustrious. Within is the spring robe for your use, also there are certain balms and essences. The spring maid will be with you when you are ready— only touch this," she touched another spot on the rock chest, "and she will come at once. What is your pleasure, Illustrious, as to other refreshment? We can offer the spring drinks of near a hundred worlds—"

Certainly not the one of the Lairs, Taynad thought, at

least not that which was left in the spring—the sour dregs which survived a winter's supply.

"Something light—kind to the inner parts—" Taynad was sure she could detect any danger from a drink meant for some other species.

"Lily dew, then. This is collected from flower petals at dawn, Illustrious. It lightens the spirit, calms and soothes—" She produced a flask carved from green stone and poured a portion into a crystal flower shaped glass which she half filled before passing it to Taynad, who cradled the fanciful container between her hands and took a deep sniff of its contents. She could detect nothing save a faint sweetness akin to the perfume of a slowly opening flower.

"Your thanks." Taynad raised the cup toward the attendant in a small salute and sipped. It was good—holding the chill of a mountain stream, with a faintest shadowing of flower honey.

"May you enjoy your spring, Illustrious. The maid will come at your call." The other bowed her head and then disappeared behind those curiously veiling bushes.

Taynad, glass in hand, went to survey the contents of the coffer in the rock. There was a shelf set in its raised lid which supported a number of locked-in bottles and boxes. And in the coffer itself were the folds of a green robe.

She must follow the custom, she supposed, though she shed her clothing a little reluctantly. The robe was as fragile as one of her Jewelbright gowns and as transparent. She made no effort to unbraid her hair. What she carried within that concealment she intended to keep with her.

Having folded her clothing into the coffer, she hesitated about pressing the summons for the promised maid. Instead she sipped slowly at the drink which had been poured for her and took two steps down to one of the curved seats where she could slip her feet into the pool. The water was flesh warm.

Jewelbrights were accustomed to the highest forms of luxury Asborgan knew—many of the noted ones could command more service and pampering than lords' ladies.

Yet this place somehow offered too much—it was a Jewel House carried to the highest degree but she had no duty to hold her here.

She still had not summoned the promised maid, wanting to settle herself into the sensations this place summoned, but there was movement behind her and she looked around swiftly.

From here, the rise of greenery hid even the door through which she had come. Now out of the hiding of that stepped a tall, nearly bone-thin figure, certainly by her strange clothing no employee of the Tri-lily, or at least Taynad did not believe so. That clothing appeared to consist only of long strips of thick furry material of a brilliant scarlet, which stood out in eye-aching intensity against the smooth green, wound about her, to Taynad's reckoning, abnormally thin frame. Her long neck seemed too fragile to keep aloft the huge mass of her head where a large turban covered three-quarters of any skull she might have, its folds hung with a dripping of dazzling gems. Two of which, Taynad noted quickly, were ayzem stones—from Asborgan—and of the first water—the kind which the Shagga kept jealously in their hidden treasure places.

This newcomer moved stiffly, as if her knobby joints did not have the easy play known to most humanoids, and she came directly to stand before Taynad who had risen to meet her.

The long fingers of the one hand lifted lazily from the other's side to sketch a sign. So—Taynad waited, calling on all her training to show no sign of surprise. That signal she had never expected to see off her own world. It was an identification she could not deny.

23

THOSE STRANGE EYES WITH THEIR DOUBLE EYELIDS made her secretly uncomfortable. It was as if this alien stranger possessed some unnamed sense which could sift into her mind. Yet Taynad was not otherwise aware of any such invasion. She had never met any save the Jat and a very few of the highest trained Asshi Masters who could do more than pick up emotions their owners wanted hidden. Thought reading might be common somewhere along the star ways, but she had never heard of any who had encountered it. Which did not mean that it could not exist. Taynad suppressed thought quickly, closing off the way to the Inner Center.

"Gentlefem"—though it might give the other the advantage at their meeting, Taynad chose to break the silence first—"you have come to me. What is your wish?"

"You are direct—that is an attitude I like," the other returned. "What I come for is a matter of business—your business, Jewelbright. I gather that your work on Tssek came to an unfortunately abrupt end—though, of course, through no fault of yours. Sopt s'Qu was not noted for complex mental labor at any time, and he reached well above his abilities in that matter. Since you are now free, I bring you a message." One of those long hands burrowed beneath a looping of the body scarves to seek a hidden pocket and produce two small sticks, shorter than the fingers that offered them.

Taynad accepted them with a reluctance she would not allow to be seen. She slipped first one and then the other between the balls of her thumb and forefinger, the small markings making an impression on her flesh that she could read.

Zarn again! But this time he had called in formidable backing. She was quick to read the mark of the First Sister of her own Lair. This was official, then. They had selected her for a new mission.

"You are to inform me—" she said slowly.

"By Zarn's word you already know what is wished for. This guard who has attached himself to the Zacathan— it seems he has proven traitor to your people, or so Zarn puts it. They wish him returned."

Taynad twiddled the twigs between her fingers.

"And to return him from off-world?"

The alien slitted her inner eyes. "That will be arranged for. However, not at present. Zarn will have his wishes fulfilled but at OUR timing. And that is not yet. I have heard of this oathing of your people, that you cannot break such a bond once it is taken. Have you oathed with the Zacathan as this renegade has done?"

"No, I have merely pledged my help in another matter—"

"Which is suitable. Render him that best of services; he must be made grateful to you. Perhaps then the loss of his guard shall not be too regretted. But you know best your own business, Sister to Shadows."

"And your part in this?" Taynad refused to be cowed by the other's air of complete control of the situation.

"Nothing to interfere with yours, Shadow. We have in part a common goal and your people have seen fit to recognize that. Good hunting—when the time comes."

The stranger turned and vanished behind one of the bush curtains. Taynad was left with the feeling that she had just met a wielder of power—akin to a Lair Master. And who would have such power and yet be interested in them? There was only one answer she could assume—the Guild. So they were taking a hand in some game still not plain to the players?

However, did that one who had just gone have the right to pass along a Shadow order? There were these message sticks she herself held now—Zarn and those behind him would never have entrusted such to this alien unless they considered there had been an oathing—though not directly between Taynad and any employer. And such a situation she found doubtful.

She had to think this out, and carefully. Tucking the two small rune sticks carefully into the hiding places her braid offered, Taynad sat for a very long moment staring into the pool before her. Then she turned and pressed the button for the attendant she had been assured was waiting. As long as she was here she might well make use of the amenities spring had to offer before she went back into the world where decisions waited.

Jofre sat at the small walk side table. The Jat perched on the second chair beside him. Those passing back and forth on errands of their own were an ever-changing show of strangers, enough to hold the interest of any idle spectator. But he was wondering where, in that shifting series of strollers and tourists, lurked the stalker he was very sure was interested only in *HIM*.

"Watch—"

A thread of thought—but Jofre had carefully schooled himself during the past few days to receive such without showing that he knew. Taynad was better at communiction with the Jat than he, but the creature could reach him at times. He fished into the depths of the glass before him, speared one of the tart-sweet wedges of fruit which had been floating on the liquid and brought it out, holding the tidbit to the Jat, whose paw flashed forth to seize it.

"Where?" Jofre tightened and strengthened his thought question to his best ability.

"Red—" It was almost no use. The Jat was obviously communicating more, but all Jofre could pick up was that one exasperating word.

Red—what was red—so much so that the Jat could use mention of the color as a guide—around them?

Red—It was a common enough color—he had caught sight of at least two feminine robes, a short jacket—even a head covering of that shade during the past few minutes. But those had been passing. Since he had settled here, surely his tracker would be more or less anchored nearby.

Red—and he could not look for it obviously. The Jat pawed at his arm—wanting another fruit? Perhaps, but Jofre's senses were alert, perhaps something more. He turned his head a fraction that he might look more closely at his small companion and saw one of those ears twitch as if an insect had dared to alight there. Red—

At that far table. And it was a red, unusual enough to rivet the attention all right, yet he dared not risk a direct glance.

Instead he turned the glass which held the dregs of the drink and went to fishing for another fruit bit. The shiny material of that container was opaque—reflective— he had a smeary sort of mirror which he could watch with impunity.

The man at the other table was humanoid in proportions and stance as far as Jofre could judge. But the general whole of his appearance was alien indeed. Instead of the usual clothing, which here planetside followed a pattern mostly akin to travel suits, this diner (for the stranger was consuming with very apparent gusto small, frantically wriggling creatures it plucked up from a platter before it) had limited wearing apparel to a kiltlike garment reaching to the knee and below that boots which were so tightly modeled to the legs and feet one could see the play of muscles through the substance of their making. The area of displayed skin was a dull black but the head, shoulders and a wedge descending the back in the form of a manelike growth were covered by long thickish bristles of a deep crimson.

That such an easily noted being could have been selected as a "shadow" amazed Jofre now that his attention had been directed to him. The features were decidedly human in character and there were ruffles of the bristle growth over each eye. As far as Jofre could judge the other was paying no attention to either him or the Jat. Yet Jofre trusted Yan that this was someone to be watched.

If he had even Taynad here to back him, he would have departed with the attitude of one about some business and so make sure that the maned one did leave his meal to follow. But Taynad was not here and he wondered how long it would be before she did arrive. The Fragrance place was six shops farther along the avenue and it seemed to him that she had been there a very long time.

The maned man finished his plate of wrigglers, patted his middle and gave a belch. No matter what race or species he might be his public manners left much to be desired.

Jofre fished the last fruit out of his glass and presented it to Yan, leaving that drinking vessel placed so he still had a distorted glimpse of the other diner. But Yan suddenly gave a cry of pleasure, both of his ears swung forward and he wriggled off the chair to run to meet Taynad.

Fragrance indeed! Jofre picked up a mingling of scents as she came along, moving with that languorous glide that he had not seen her use since they had left the great hall on Tssek. She had slipped well back into her Jewelbright armor again.

"It was a pleasure?" he asked, rising to greet her as she arrived, the Jat holding to one of her hands.

"It was spring—" she said, and sighed. "Truly there is much to be learned when one travels. So you missed me, little one?" She smiled down at Yan. "Did not this tall warrior treat you well?"

"We should be getting back." Jofre had taken a step or two closer to her, presenting his back to the maned one and making a quick signal to alert her.

"Time flees when one is at ease," she answered. "Yes, perhaps it is well to return. Zurzal may at last have news for us."

She had made no sign that she had understood his signal but Jofre was sure she had. Now, for quicker passage through the crowd that was thickening on the street as the afternoon advanced, he swung the Jat up to his shoulders and felt the paw hands take a good grip on his turban. Though he had not gone back to the full head covering of the Lairs he had once more assumed a style which made him feel more comfortable.

Taynad let him get a stride or so ahead, stopped as if to adjust a boot buckle, then she light-footedly joined them.

Her forefinger moved. The maned one was following. But for now they had no reason to try and evade him since they were only returning to their temporary quarters.

"This place is stifling," she broke out suddenly. "I find myself thinking with a strong desire of the slopes of Three Claws, or even the Grey Wastes. How can one live ever in such a turmoil?"

Jofre was surprised. He himself had been suffering from the feeling of one entrapped in some lord's vor stockyard with the herd turned in to share it with him. There was always something new to be seen, that he would agree, but one tires of constant change and variety. Also of this enforced idleness. Though issha discipline taught patience and he had thought that he had learned all the Lair lessons well. But perhaps what she had said gave him a chance to discover answers for a question or two which had been plaguing him.

"If there comes word from Asborgan—you are not oathed—"

"No." Her answer was almost harshly abrupt. "But my mission was meant to be one of some length when I left Su-ven-ugen. They will not think of me as being free now and the message which the Patrol promised to deliver will take some time to reach the First Sister. Perhaps because I am without funds, since those of Tssek saw fit to confiscate what I had, I am in debt to the Learned One and it may well be that in the end the Elders will decide that I must work out what is owed. Anyway, oathed or not, I have promised the Zacathan that I will return service for service as long as he needs me."

"It will be a different kind of service than that you trained for—" Jofre was partly convinced that she meant exactly what she had just said.

"It is well to have more than one kind of experience," she remarked. "Do you think that the Learned One will succeed in what he wishes? I know that his scanner showed the past on Tssek, but what of Lochan? It seems to me to be as much of a gamble as when one tosses kust stones for wager."

The Zacathan was not in the suite when they entered and Jofre made his meticulous search through the rooms and across their section of the balcony terrace as he always did, the Jat trotting behind him as if it too could sniff out any hidden danger. Was the red-maned one lounging in the lobby below? And what did whoever set him on their trail want? Was it a ploy of the Guild? That was a point to be very well considered. From all he had ever heard Jofre rated the Guild very, very high as a potential enemy.

When the Zacathan returned his frill was standing high, not flushed scarlet as from anger or frustration but the green-blue of satisfaction with the world.

"Fortune favors us at last," he began even before the door had closed behind him. "The trader who has made the Lochan run twice has planeted. Not only planeted, but the captain is ready for a return. It seems that he took one of those chances which the Free Traders often do and managed to barter directly with one of the desert tribes. What he picked up are a new type of gem—good enough value to have one of the auction houses take on sale.

"One cannot keep such a find a secret; he well knows that there will be others heading in there now—since the trade rights for Lochan have never been auctioned. The Patrol may take a hand—but they cannot by law deny the captain a return trip to realize on his own discovery. He will want to harvest all he can before the rush begins. Which means he is already loading supplies—"

"But will he take passengers also?" Jofre wanted to know. If the Free Trader had an outstanding discovery to exploit, its crew might well be jealously on guard against everyone.

"I had already had contact with him before his last voyage. He knows well that what I would accomplish there will have nothing to do with his business. I have sent him a message and I expect a quick answer. If he wishes to lift soon, we must be able to move—perhaps at a moment's notice. It would be best we think of packing now."

Zurzal's enthusiasm was such he was sweeping them along with him. Though Jofre took time out to make a very careful inspection of the arms he had acquired, together with the stunner which Zurzal had managed to secure for him with a permit near twisted out of the Patrol, the same for himself, and Taynad.

The Jat squatted on a wide pillow watching the girl do her packing in her own quarters. A fast move—her hand went to the braid wreathing her head to touch the ends of the twigs there. Perhaps this was best—if she could stall a little until this ship swept them away— She shook her head at her own thoughts. Why did she resent and shrink from this order which had been delivered?

Because it was not an oathing such as she had always been taught was right? Because it had been so delivered to her by one she knew was Guild? That the Shagga would turn to the Guild for aid went against her deepest beliefs. She was a trained killer, a weapon in the hands of those whom she was sworn to serve. But the Guild was not the Lairs with their old tradition of a certain rigid honor. Also—Zarn said that this Jofre was an outlaw, a traitor— the story he had told her was one she had come fully to believe, having had time to observe this man over days and through sharp demands made on him and his skills.

There was nothing about him to make her think that he was in any way enemy to the Lairs. Rather, it seemed to her,

it was the spite of some priest which lay behind it. Then—
why had they not killed him out of hand? Taynad stood
very still, a half-folded undergarment in her hands. The
basic oath of them all—Brother—Sister—do not delight
in the blood of their kind. Perhaps that priest had been
afraid to kill Jofre openly lest he be called to account for
that—perhaps he had hoped that the harsh season in the
mountains would do it for him. As for the reason for such
a strong hatred—it lay encoiled in what she had sensed—
that in this issha there were surely the seeds of Assha. Yes,
the Shagga would never allow a leader of off-world blood
among them; they were too fixed in the ancient ways. So
they wanted him—but they wanted him returned so that
he could die now under their hands and only so would they
feel safe.

Now she could understand those orders. She dropped the
garment and freed the twigs from their hiding place in her
hair, running them once more to be touch read. Betray him
to the Guild, see him safely taken.

An order—but not an oath! Her head went up as if
she faced the First Sister in her own Lair. She was not
oathed by the mere words of Zarn's sending—there must
be the ritual and blood must flow—she would be one who
betrayed.

They would say she was not oathed to the Zacathan,
but she was indebted to him. And those of the Shadows
paid debts, blood signed or not. No, she was not going to
make any attempt to contact that woman from the Guild—
perhaps time would favor them all and see them aboard
this trader before she could be met again with any more
demands.

For a moment Taynad stretched the twigs between her
fingers. Almost she applied enough pressure to snap them.
But she did not follow through—there was enough of custom to hold her from doing that. She tucked them back
into hiding and determined to let the future arrange itself
into its own patterns.

24

"**P**ASSAGE, YES, THAT YOU MAY BUY. ONCE ON planet you shall be on your own, and Lochan is not friendly." The voice was a deep-chested growl, sounding oddly from this undersized man who eyed them upward from beneath heavy bushy brows as if he was highly suspicious. In contrast to those unduly thick brows his skull was bare of even a fringe of hair, the space-browned flesh of it sprinkled over with darker patches of skin here and there. Captain Gosal was far from being attractive personally any more than his rusted and worn, space-battered ship.

Jofre, his shoulders planted against the wall of the small cabin, was not only unimpressed but wary. If it were his choice, he would be off the *Haren Hound* and as far from its battered length as he could get. But it would seem that Zurzal had discovered they had no choice. It was either this ship or perhaps no chance at all, and since the debacle on Tssek the Zacathan was apparently ridden more and more by the need to get to the goal he had tried so long to reach.

"You have a flitter—" His frill was fluttering. Jofre could actually feel the effort Zurzal was making to keep his emotions under strict control.

"That will be in use. You have heard my terms." This captain was favoring the Zacathan with none of the honorifics which bare courtesy would have suggested he use. Instead he was deliberately trying, Jofre was certain, to make any contract with him as unpleasant as possible.

"It will be necessary for us to strike inland—near the Shattered Land—" Zurzal's hissing was more apparent but he still spoke on a level note as if he did not really understand the captain's hostility.

"Go where you will after we planet. I am not an arranger for travelers—I do not offer tours— There are plenty here who are eager for such as you to come to them."

"For approved planets only." Zurzal still held tightly to his emotions but the flush of color was rising in his frill. "This is a matter of exploration, or discovery. I understand you yourself have recently made a lucky discovery on this same world. Well, such as you are about to exploit I have no interest in. I seek old places—those of the Forerunners."

"You are confederation backed—why then do you come to me? Where is your First-In ship? I am a trader, not a searcher—"

"Perhaps not a searcher for the same things," Zurzal returned. "But, yes, I have cleared this voyage with the authorities—on the *Haren Hound*—"

The captain's head snapped up. Under that brush of brows his eyes showed a reddish glint.

"You cannot make any Free Trader rise to your will unless it is under charter, and I am not—for all your official clearance!"

"There is the matter of time," Zurzal pointed out. "When is your rumored auction—tonight! You have forced that into a rush, which means you need to get planet free very soon. There will be those ready to sniff along your trail and see what they can pick up for themselves."

The captain did not answer at once. His full-lipped mouth was closed as a trap might spring upon a victim and there was a dusky flush spreading up from the unlatched collar of his tunic to color even that bare dome of skull.

"So—by the thrice-damned rules you force yourselves on board—knowing that I must be accountable for your arrival on Lochan. Very well, you have set up the stars in this game, but perhaps the comets lie in other hands. You will pay—"

"I fully intend to," the Zacathan returned. "Full voyage accounts for four."

"Four?" The captain glanced from Zurzal to Jofre and back again as if trying to separate each of those fronting him into a second.

"A party of four. You will find it listed with the port authorities. It has been so listed for a ten days—"

"You were very sure, lizard lord."

"I have had news of your voyaging for some two planet years, Captain Gosal. Lochan has long been my destination as it has also attracted you."

The captain spread his hands palm flat on the small table already untidy with a drift of tapes and a speaker.

"Very well. But you will take us as you find us, without complaint. We are no wallowing passenger liner. Your quarters will be tight and you will give vouchers for your own supplies to our steward. Also—the license runs only while you are on board. On Lochan you make your own way, for there the law favors me. I need not detach from this ship any personnel nor equipment which I need for my own use. And all of what we have is so needed. So think about that, lizard lord, before you move in."

"What if it is as he says?" Jofre asked as they boarded the port flitter to return to the inner city. "He could dump us in some wilderness and not have any questions asked? Does it work that way?"

"It can. However," Zurzal did not seem in the least upset by such a dubious glimpse into the future, "there are other factors. I have made a study of Lochan as far as is possible. Unfortunately, as you know, the discoveries of the single expedition whose path we would follow were lost in the fate which overtook them. But the First-In Scout's report was on record in our own archives and with it similar data gathered by traders such as Gosal, but not having this luck that he has apparently had with the new find of his.

"He may not be willing to provide us with transportation once on planet, but the landing he heads for is known—and there is a port there. It is not manned by off-worlders but there seems to have grown up something of a trading settlement about it. And where there are traders there are those to visit and supply the trade. We have the Jat—"

"Yan? But what has it to do with—?"

"Communication, Jofre. All we must do must be begun by communication. And there have been some hints that certain of the rulers of the rovers in the lands we would visit have been intrigued by the sparse off-world contact which has been. Oh, I believe it truly"—he turned his head to face Jofre squarely and his frill was up, flaring blue-green—"I was meant to do this—and I shall!" There was an aura about him which Jofre recognized. Just so had it been with an issha-trained when he was oathed for a mission. He could only trust blindly for now that the Zacathan could carry this through and follow his lead—but in reality he had no other choice—he was oathed.

Oddly enough when they had picked up Taynad, Yan, and their baggage and returned to the ship they found a different reception waiting them. Gosal, who was apparently hurried, paused to actually welcome them aboard with a thin veneer of courtesy. They were shown to the two cramped cabins far down in the ship, Taynad and the Jat bunking down in one, Jofre and the Zacathan in the other. The stowing of their baggage took some time and some of it had to be given room in the cargo hold. Jofre expected trouble over that but the crewman who aided him in stowing it away so was ready enough, if not talkative.

Jofre was surprised when the captain, with special invitation, made them free of the other small cabin which served as a gathering place for off-duty members of the crew. He felt it necessary to accompany the Zacathan whenever Zurzal took advantage of that hospitality but he found it almost as claustrophobic as their own quarters.

Gosal seemed to have, now he was in space and as it might be master, changed his opinion of the Zacathan.

He not only willingly answered the other's questions concerning Lochan to the best of his ability, but twice summoned his cargo master and his steward to supply various items which they were the more conversant with, having dealt with the natives for supplies and met with the local traders.

Once free of Wayright the captain was in a good humor, even talking freely about his own good fortune in discovering the new gems which would make his fortune and that of the *Haren Hound*. He had kept back from the port auction a couple which he displayed. Even in the rough, without any cutting or polishing, Jofre, as unused to such wealth as he was, could detect their unusual flash of color.

"Koris stones now," Gosal had said at that display. "They bring a high price—'course that is mainly because they give off scent when one wears them against the skin. The *Solar Queen*—they made such a killing with them as brought one of the Companies after them—a nasty scrape that was. So far we're in luck. We're registered and the auction credit—most of that—goes to the planet bid. We've got us nearly two planet years and we're going to make the most of 'em!"

"Where were these found?" Zurzal asked.

Gosal laughed. "Now that would be tellin', wouldn't it? Not that I think the likes of you, lizard lord, would be any threat to this deal. But a trader keeps his secrets—they're as good as credit units on the register."

He and the steward both had stories of the trading parties who came in from the outlands to the port. Though they both said frankly that they found the aliens difficult to deal with—that there were rigid customs and certain patterns to be followed in any attempt at communication.

While Jofre and the Zacathan listened to traveler's advice in the leisure cabin, Taynad kept closely to her own appointed cubby. She felt some of the same claustrophobia as plagued Jofre. The mountain-born of the Lair were not at home in situations which seemed too much either prisons or traps.

She had been so sure that she would have been approached again by some emissary of the Guild acting for Zarn before she had left. But that had not happened. Did such neglect mean that they had taken as a matter of course she had accepted their mission? But if she were to entice Jofre into some type of trap, should that not happen on Wayright, where there were many ships lifting daily and he could be returned to Asborgan with the least difficulty?

Gosal had made very plain that the only exit from Lochan would be this ship she now traveled by. It was a puzzle, and puzzles were never to her liking.

She spent much time with the Jat, trying to tighten the mind ties between them. Once or twice the creature actually sent her a mind picture which held, if mistily, for a fraction of time. Taynad worked carefully, fighting down her own determination and eagerness to perfect what she could do with Yan.

When the Zacathan was busied with his own calculations for the scanner, which seemed to occupy him by fits and starts, Jofre would come visiting and though she distrusted the wisdom of doing so the Jat himself drew the guard into their experiments. They discovered that reception was far clearer when Jofre and Taynad were linked by touch and both concentrating on Yan at once. So this they tried to perfect and hone as they would their selected weapons.

Jofre wondered at these crewmen, most of whom spent the longer parts of their lives encased in these metal wombs. He felt that a man would go out of his mind facing day after artificial day and night of this imprisonment. He had his mental exercises, his work with Taynad and the Jat, even the necessity of making mental notes for anything picked up in the conversation concerning Lochan which could be put to future use. Also there was the knowledge that sooner or later this was going to come to an end.

It did at last: the orders came to strap down for entrance. And the settling of the ship on its fins was as steady as if it had planeted on a recognized landing port.

Jofre longed to see what lay beyond the shell of the ship, to be able to breathe again more than the stale air which seemed to give one always a dull headache. He went through the ritual of checking his weapons, so much a part of his drill that he no longer was truly conscious of it.

They had their cabin luggage to secure. Jofre hoped that they would spend no more time aboard than was necessary though he had not the least idea where they would shelter on Lochan.

As they came out on the runway which stretched beyond the slice of heated ground where they had ridden the tail flames down, he was astounded by what lay about. The port on Asborgan was two planet generations old. There were a number of off-world buildings which had come into existence there for the convenience of travelers.

Wayright was a whole planet of ports, it existed only because it was a travel center, and all its resources were gathered to support and provide for those using the star ways.

What he looked out on, over the Zacathan's shoulder, was dull rock, fairly smooth in the vicinity of the ship and seared with the burnoffs of other landings. Beyond the edge of that was an undulating stretch of plain which appeared to reach to the horizon without any break except a huddle of what might be very rude shelters a good distance from them. The sun was blazing hot, even though it could not have been more than mid morning. And heat, which was more than that just born from the rocket-scorched earth, reflected back to them. There seemed to be no vegetation which he could identify as such—unless the uniform dull yellow of the ground was some low-growing herbage. The sky overhead was a palish blue with a hint of green. It was a forbidding place, doubly so to one mountain bred.

"There you have it, lizard lord." Gosal swept a thick-fingered hand in the direction of that smudge on the desolate prairie land. "That is the one and only city on Lochan that I have ever heard tell of. I think you will find accommodations limited there. There is a welcoming party coming—"

There was indeed movement away from those blots on the yellow land, heading in the direction of the ship. Jofre had expected the captain to have out the flitter and ready that to reach the distant settlement but he seemed perfectly willing to await the arrival of the native party. Though he did unhook a com from his belt and hold it ready for speaking, thumbing the on button in a moment or two.

What he jabbered into the mike was either code or native tongue, totally incomprehensible to his listeners. Jofre had little liking for that action. He did not know what he feared, but he had that alert within that this unknown was not to be trusted.

They had seen all the tapes on Lochan that Zurzal had had to offer, but the material the Zacathan had been able to locate had not dealt with this scrub of a port but rather with the planet at large. Jofre knew that the greater part of the continent on which they had landed was this stretch of plains land, arid for most of the year. It supported some nomadic tribes who traveled to find herbage for flocks of weird creatures upon whose meat and fleece they built their existence.

It was to the northward that Zurzal's interest was centered. There, somewhere beyond present sighting, were the remains of a very ancient earth turmoil, ragged beds of age-worn lava once vomited forth by a narrow chain of now eroded mountains. It was a land even more sere than that they could see now. And, knowing that, Jofre was even more uneasy. Had the obsession of the Zacathan brought them, badly prepared, into such country wherein no off-worlder could hope to survive? Had they the use of the flitter they might have had a chance, but he could see none if they attempted to strike into the unknown with any other form of transportation.

The cackle of conversation between Gosal and his unknown contact continued at intervals. Zurzal had transversed the rock of the landing field to the edge of the yellow line, Jofre with him. He was right, the guard saw, as they came to the ragged edge. The ground ahead was thickly grown with a carpet of vegetation which was more like long and ragged moss than grass. Also it was busy with life as there were small puffs of insects which arose at their coming, circled and settled again.

Jofre jerked as one of those winged dots which had alighted on his hand delivered what was either a sting or a bite. He hoped that the immune shots they had all gone through on Wayright would help and that nothing more than that single sharp pain was going to plague him in consequence.

The caravan from the "port" reached them at last. They had withdrawn into that small shelter the shadow of the ship offered, for the beat of the sun was strong. Jofre had seen many aliens on Wayright but the motley party which straggled now from the plain across the rock to the ship seemed to him to unite all the possible whims nature might have indulged in during a fantastic dream.

They were not carried on antigrav plates, nor were the mounts they rode akin to anything Jofre had imagined might exist. In the first place these bearers did not run four-footed, but walked erect using two trunk-thick back legs for propulsion. Their skin was bare of any hair or fur he could distinguish and seemed to be merely warty and puffy flesh, dark in color, nearly approaching the shade of the rock over which they now padded. Their heads were out of proportion to the rest of them, too small, and yet in a way disgustingly close to human though there was no sign of intelligence in their tiny eyes. Across their shoulders rested wide and heavy yokes which ended in loops of dangling chain that supported flat plates somewhat like the boards of swings. These they constantly steadied as they went with their great balls of hands. And in those bobbing swings rode the rest of the party.

On the first mount one of the beings transported a passenger who was clearly humanoid, perhaps even of distant Terran descent, dressed in what was almost a parody of a port commander's uniform. His companion who had the other swing of this first bearer startled Jofre. That dull black skin, the bristle of fire red hair—this might have been the twin of that alien—the man himself who had been watching him back on Wayright—except there was no possible way that the other could have reached Lochan before them, nor was there any place in the cramped quarters of the trader where he could have been concealed.

The human stared at Zurzal.

"I am Wok Bi, Commandant of Lochan Port," he announced in a voice which had a metallic quality. "This is a closed port—there can be no visitors."

"I have this." Zurzal held out a small coil of message tape already snapped into a reader hardly larger than a ring.

Wok Bi's glare did not diminish but he took the tape, gingerly, as if he feared that it might be an explosive device of some kind. Zurzal appeared to have no doubts of the efficacy of what he had brought in the way of introduction.

25

THE SELF-ANNOUNCED PORT COMMANDER ACTIVATED the tiny reader, though he seemed uneasy about taking his eyes from the Zacathan and Jofre long enough to absorb the message there, giving a couple of quick glances in their direction and losing nothing of the scowl with which he had welcomed them. Meanwhile Jofre made a study of the commander's force.

There were four of the huge transport creatures. And each had two passengers. Besides the red-maned one, there were three others of the same general appearance, save that their manes, instead of being flaming red, were of the same yellow shade as the land over which they had traveled. Jofre thought that if they lay facedown in that moss stuff, they might even be invisible. Another of the group from the "city" was closer to the conventional humanoid and unlike his companions wore an enveloping robe of grey, like the rock underfoot, over which there sprawled a pattern of meaningless and formless lines. His round skull was as hairless as that of Captain Gosal and the skin was yellow as Haperian honey, with a sleek overcasting as if he had been carefully rubbed down with a doubtful grease. His features were blunter than those of the maned men, his mouth so wide and lipless in appearance that it might have been merely a slit cut in the puffed skin.

His eyeballs protruded until Jofre wondered if he were able to close the wrinkled lids entirely over them. And the eyes seemed to be like surface mirrors, giving nothing away as they met Jofre's and swept on. His alienness was even more apparent than that of his maned companions, but it would seem that he occupied some position of authority among them, for two had hurried to aid him from his traveling sling and fell in a pace or so behind as he waddled towards the commander.

The last two of the party slid off their swings but made no move to advance. Like the greasy one they wore robes of grey but these lacked any touch of pattern. One swung back an arm as if impatient of that covering and Jofre saw muscular yellow flesh—but more, a weapons belt from which hung a curved blade as brightly kept as any of his own steel.

Though they wore robes, they remained aloof from their fellow in the like garb. However, their faces had something of the same general traits—the wide mouths, the protruding eyes. Only these boasted head decorations of a kind, a ragged kind of crest running from between the eyes on the forehead back to the nape of the neck. Jofre could not distinguish whether that was artifical or, as Zurzal's frill, a natural flap of skin.

"You presume much—" The voice of the commander jerked his attention back to the Zacathan and the man who fronted him.

"I do not presume, Commander. I ask no more than what the Central Control has for centuries of your time granted my people. We are the Keepers—"

It was plain that the commander was impressed against his will, either by the unperturbed attitude of the Zacathan or by whatever credentials had been a part of the message on the reader.

"This is a closed planet, Learned One. We have no facilities for expeditions, nor would such be allowed if we did. There is life out there"—he swept a hand towards the horizon—"which considers any stranger rich prey. You are truly a fool if you believe that you can reach even the edge of the Shattered Land."

For the first time the oily one took part in the conversation. He gabbled a stream of squeaks, high and thin, and very strange when proceeding from his massive body. Zurzal made a quick grasp at the array of tools hanging from his belt he had equipped with care just before their landing. His taloned hand swept out of its loop a disc which he swung up before the speaker. The man gave a squeal and backed off a step, while those two who had established themselves as his attendants snarled, showing fangs as sharp as the knives which had appeared, apparently out of nowhere, in their hands.

"A translator—my speech to you, yours to me," Zurzal stated calmly, though Jofre was at his shoulder, ready to move if those two yellow-maned toughs did dare an attack.

There was a squeaking from the disc and the oily one started as if a fassnake had arisen from the ground at his very feet and was weaving its war dance in the air. Then those huge eyes blinked. One of the puffy hands sketched a gesture in the air between them. Jofre thought he needed no translation for that—this native of Lochan was warding off evil.

"Off-world evil!" The squeakings suddenly made sense. "Who are you—serpent skin—to travel our land? What do you seek? It can be nothing good."

"I seek knowledge, and that is better than ignorance, Worshipful One. What I may be able to find will be freely shared with your learned ones. Are you not one such yourself?"

Again those huge eyes blinked. The hand trembled as if again he would form the ward sign, but he did not carry that through. Instead the tip of a green tongue appeared between those narrow lips and ran from side to side as if to prepare the way for some important message.

"To share knowledge—" the squeaking became words. "That is always to be desired. But what knowledge can you give us, off-worlder, which will be of use to us? Your own laws will not allow you to bring things which are of your high knowledge—have we not been told this many times over?" There had come about a change in the priest, if priest the man was, and Jofre thought he could recognize the type by now. He did not need any translator to understand that the other, once past his first repudiation of another and doubtless to him inferior sorcery, was now busy calculating what could be accomplished by a show of, if not friendship, then neutral acceptance.

"There is knowledge and knowledge, Worshipful One. Some it is lawful to share, and that I would open to any who wished to learn."

"To every bargain there are two sides," the disc translated. The squeals had an almost impatient sound as if the priest felt Zurzal was refusing to come to the point. "For what you give, what must you receive?"

"That we can discuss together—at a better time and place," the Zacathan said firmly, before turning to the commander. "We are prepared to follow the regulations, Commander, even as you. You have seen our credentials. Do you question them?"

The man who had given his name as Wok Bi glanced from the Zacathan to the priest. He eyed the latter with some surprise, Jofre believed, as if he had not expected such a response from the native.

"No question," he said brusquely. "We have little in the way of accommodation—but there is part of a warehouse in which you may camp. Follow the Deves, they will see you back to the port."

He turned his shoulder a little, shutting them out as he approached Gosal.

The two robed men were back in the swings, their huge carriers already turning to depart. Jofre shrugged on his shoulder pack and helped the Zacathan adjust his and a sling which held the scanner. Taynad came down the last few feet of the ramp, Yan running beside her, her own pack in place. They would have to depend upon Gosal to see to the arrival of the rest of their supplies.

As they tramped from the rock to the thick moss their heavy space boots crushed well into it and the insects arose. The Jat whistled and slapped at its arms and legs and Jofre swept the small creature up to hold onto his pack, settling his own shoulders under that increased burden and trying not to feel the sharp sting of the bites as he went.

The bearers made better time than those who trailed behind, but since they knew their goal, the four off-worlders did not try to stretch their pace any. The constant attacks of the moss insects was irritating, but Zurzal's scaled skin apparently protected him against the worst of the bites. Only Jofre and Taynad had to call upon their stoicism to tramp that path. The Jat was apparently now free of such attacks, since the disturbed life, so busily defending its territory, did not rise high above the moss.

Closer to hand the "port" did not make any more of an impressive sight than it had from the ship. The buildings were all low, not more than one story, and apparently constructed of slabs of the same turf over which they had traveled, molded together, the now disturbed moss mottled in color to brown, and a dark red.

There was no pretense at any order, no sign of marked-off streets. Apparently the buildings had been thrown up where needed and to the builder's fancy at the time. At the opposite end of the way they followed there was a wider space in which crouched more of the swing carriers sans their yokes. Several were chewing as a ruminant might on a cud and others were very apparently napping. The breeze from that section brought a thick odor which the off-worlders found unpleasant and which hinted that these were not altogether cleanly citizens—if citizens they were and not animals.

Their guide into town brought them to a slightly larger sod building and, without dismounting, one of the swing riders motioned to the dark open doorway of that before the carrier shuffled on.

"Shelter," Zurzal commented and led the way within.

A long room had been divided by partitions which neither reached completely to the low roof nor clear across the width so that there was a passage running along beside the cubicles which perhaps were meant to serve as separate rooms.

Most of these were filled to corridor openings with bales, large earthenware jars, baskets which appeared to be woven from some manner of reed. And the mingling of smells was nearly overpowering. The Jat set up a wailing cry and pulled at Jofre's head as if to try to turn it around and so move his mount away from this place.

Luckily there was a vacant cubicle only a short distance from the outer door and Zurzal pointed to that.

"Certainly not the most luxurious quarters," he commented. "However, I think the best we can count on for now."

Jofre unlatched the Jat from his hold and handed the small struggling body to Taynad before he made his safety survey of this darkish hole. There was light, certainly far from the brilliancy of any room on Wayright or even the lamplit quarters of the Lair. These wan beams filtered out of bunches of what looked like the herbage of the plains but of a much darker shade, stuck haphazardly along the upper edges of the partitions and the wall behind.

The floor appeared to be an uneven surface of rock as if surface soil and growth had been rolled back to clear the space. It was certainly solid enough to ring under the tread of his space boots and he thought it could conceal no unpleasant surprises. While the walls appeared so thin, he was sure that a determined assault could bring any one of the three down, but it would seem they had no choice.

"That priest," Taynad had soothed the panting Jat and shrugged off her pack, "he is one to be watched." She knew she stated the obvious and she was sure in her own mind that the Zacathan was well aware of it.

"That priest," Zurzal countered, "may be our key to what we wish." He divested himself of his own burdens but he placed the scanner carefully between his feet as he stood, one hand on hip, looking about him. "That one wants power—knowledge is power—it is sometimes simple."

"It sounds simple," Jofre returned, "but the working out is perhaps far more difficult."

At least Gosal saw to the delivery of the rest of their equipment, sending it in on an antigrav which belonged to the ship and which he certainly had not offered to them. Jofre, remembering well-bitten legs, added another mark to his score against the Free Trader.

They saw the inhabitants of the port only in passing. No one came to the warehouse to which they had been so summarily dismissed nor was there any sign of either the commander or the priest. It would appear that their arrival was now a matter for total denial. Though Jofre had sighted at least one of the armed robed ones passing along the stretch of ground outside the warehouse door at rather regular intervals, as if he walked a beat.

Zurzal seemed content to wait. Patience was inborn in his long-lived race, but it was a virtue which the two from Asborgan had learned the hard way to cultivate. Since there was no sign of an eating place, they reluctantly broke open some of their own supplies and ate a very frugal portion as the day swept on toward evening.

More and more of those giants who supplied transportation were returning to the place where off-worlders had seen their fellows relaxing earlier. Some of them were burden carriers and others had their smaller swings occupied with the maned aliens or, once in a while, a robed one.

With the coming of evening and the setting of the sun there was a change in the temperature. The heat which had grown almost to a stifling degree began to dissipate and there arose a wind sweeping in from the north which had a decidedly cold edge. Jofre had taken position on guard at the door of the warehouse itself. There had been no intruders during the afternoon to get at any of what was stored there and they seemed to have it for themselves.

"One—come—" He did not really need the warning of the Jat. It would seem his own battle-honed sense was keen enough here to pick up that feeling that there was a stranger headed for their quarters. Certainly there was no lighting of the "streets" in the dusk but there did seem to be a haze of dim radiance bobbing along towards the doorway at a pace a person might walk.

Jofre did not step into direct sight himself and now he was aware that Taynad was moving in at an angle behind him as might any Brother when the alert was given. One of his hands was on the hilt of a throwing knife. They had set out from Wayright with stunners, only to have theirs put under seal by the captain as contraband on Lochan. Only Zurzal, because of his maiming, had not been deprived of his weapon. Here one was back to the bladed weapons Jofre knew best.

The pinch of light brought a glisten from a round face. If not the priest from the landing site, then another of his kind. And there came through the dark not only an odor which suggested a long-unbathed body but, in addition, a thin whistle.

"Let him in." Zurzal moved out, ready to bid their visitor welcome. Jofre obeyed but fell in on the heels of the Lochanian. He knew without being told that Taynad and the Jat shared sentry duty now and that his place as guard was with the Zacathan.

The light of their cubicle was strong enough to show that this was indeed the one Zurzal had spoken to. In one pudgy hand the fellow held a loose ball of stuff from which spun the thread of feeble light. His bulbous eyes glistened in that glow, as subdued as it was.

Zurzal was ready with the translator. "Greeting, Worshipful One, you have been awaited—the hour grows late." There was a kind of snap in the Zacathan's voice; whether such a nuance was translated into the squealing by the disc Jofre could not guess. But he was very sure that Zurzal was prepared to take a firm stand with this visitor.

Those wide lips puffed forth a breath which was foul. And then squeaked in answer:

"The Axe of Rou comes or goes not at the will of off-worlders. There is little patience—what would you do here, stranger?"

"I seek, as I have said, knowledge. Your world is old—it has seen many changes—is that not so?"

"Rou works as it is willed. The earth and all which forms it is for HIM as the mud of the under leaf is to the maker of pots, as the knuckle of iron to him who fashions a blade. But what do you know of these changes you speak of? You are not one with Rou."

"Rou exists in many forms also," Zurzal answered. "Can it not be that it is by His will we stand here this night? Axe of Rou, would it not be to such a close-held follower as you that revelations would be made? Or is it that the Axe merely speaks for another who is closer to the ear of Rou?"

"I have the ear of Rou." The squealing arose to a high pitch. "Say it to me, off-worlder, and I shall judge whether this be business of Rou's Own or not."

"Very well." The Zacathan stooped and laid a hand lightly on the scanner case. "This I carry, Axe of Rou, is born of long study and the use of very ancient records. It has the power to bring to light matters lost in the long seasons forgotten by men whose memories cannot hold so much. There is a place in the Shattered Land which bears a certain mark. That was discovered by some knowledge seekers before me. But they did not possess such an aid as this one and they were driven away before they could obtain much which they were sure could be learned. Therefore I have come to carry on this work and see into the ages behind—"

"Only Rou can look behind more than one lifetime!"

"So can I not, without this. But it is the learning which Rou allows men that has brought this into being and the glory will be HIS when the great find is made."

The priest wiped the palm of his light-free hand across his triple chin. He was like all of his kind, Jofre believed, seeking what could lie in such a matter which would further his own gain.

"What would you need to do Rou's Will in this matter?" The demand was abrupt. Their needs would also present a bargaining point.

"We need a guide to the Shattered Land, and transportation for ourselves and our gear." Zurzal was as quick to deliver his needs.

"The Shattered Land—it is a place of the Long Dead, of the damned Ones who followed Vunt. You will find no true follower of Rou to enter there. But—" The squeaking voice paused for a moment. Jofre tensed, sensing that what was coming now was of the first importance as far as the priest was concerned.

"There once was land where Rou had *His* place. And— yes, there are very old stories that there was powerful knowledge to be found there—left behind when the Will of Rou twisted that part of the world with fire and the shaking of the earth. But why should we allow such knowledge to fall into the hands of off-worlders? By what right do you claim the knowledge which was once that of Rou's children?"

"None," the Zacathan returned promptly. "I freely surrender all claims to what may be found if those of Rou will it so."

"Then," came back the priest with a rush, "what do *you* gain, off-worlder, if you surrender any knowledge treasure which may be found? Why do you, and these with you, willingly go into the Dead Land if you gain no benefit from your labors?"

"I will make with this," again the Zacathan indicated the scanner, "a record, one which you will be free to see. It is my wish to prove that I can set aside the mists of the past. With such proof I can visit other worlds and on each I can add to the store of ancient knowledge. To my people, Axe, such is the primary work of our lives. We find in any discoveries value, whether it is something which can be seen and handled, or whether it abides only in the minds thereafter."

"There must be a considering of this," the Axe replied. "You will be told what the answer will be." So abruptly he turned and waddled away.

"He has a reason," Jofre ventured. The issha might not be able to read minds but they were aware when alerted to certain emanations of emotion. He was certain that the Axe was indeed taking time out to think and that, behind his assent, if assent it would be, there would also be a scheme set in motion.

"There is one on guard," Taynad said in a low tone from the door to which they had followed, more slowly, their late visitor.

"We could not expect less," Zurzal asserted. "But I think we need fear no more attention until our friend is ready to move."

26

IT WAS ONLY PARTLY IMPATIENCE WHICH RODE JOFRE. He held Zurzal's knowledge to be far above even that of the Shagga priests—and put to better use. However, he also knew that the Zacathan was so fiercely determined to prove the efficiency of the scanner that he might be led to overlook any hidden threats. Its use on Tssek had confirmed for Zurzal that he could do this, but to be able to deliver a find from Lochan would reestablish his credit among his own peers. And that was a situation which Jofre could understand very well, even though he himself could have no hope of a triumphant return to Asborgan and an addition of issha status made by the Shagga.

The sheer mechanics of a crossing of the long tundralike plain to the northern country was always to the fore of his mind. That they could tramp it carrying all their supplies was out of the question. From the scanty tape information they had studied so carefully they knew that the Shattered Land would be a far greater obstacle even than the insect-infested tundra.

"We can make no deal with Gosal?" he asked, though he was sure of the answer. "Even if he would give us use of the one gravity sled—"

"Those carriers," Taynad added as if she had been following some line of reasoning of her own, "are they natives or beasts, servants, slaves—? The Jat has tried to reach them by mind touch—there is nothing there."

"They serve both the maned people and those they call Deves," Jofre commented. "But even with such aid could we reach our goal while our supplies still hold out?"

Zurzal's toothed jaws showed in a grin. "We shall have another visitor," he stated. "One who will come by dark."

And Jofre, who had quickly retaken his place as sentry, was startled as there was a warning from the other end of the warehouse, that where there seemed to be only solid wall. He saw movement and knew that Taynad was on alert, slipping from their cubicle to the door of the next, the Jat close beside her.

"It is all right," Zurzal said, his hissing voice carrying easily. "Bright evening to you, Commander!"

That port official who had been so obstructive at their landing passed close enough to one of the moss torches to show his face, pausing in the light a second or two as if to make sure they recognized him, before he slipped into their quarters and settled himself cross-legged facing the Zacathan.

"You are a fool, Learned One," his voice had the rasp of exasperation in it. "There is no way under the Heavens of Lochan that you can succeed in this."

"Men have succeeded on thinner chances than the one I have been offered, Wok Bi. And you have your orders."

"Orders!" The man flung up his hands in a gesture which suggested that this was indeed folly. "You head willfully into country where one expedition came to a very bloody end. There are what—four of you—one a woman—another a Jat—you would need a squad of Patrol to even venture over the border there. It is madness and you are forcing me to be a part of it."

"Your orders are plain," Zurzal returned placidly. "Yes, we are a small party, but that means we have less to transport. It is the transport that we must now consider."

"No Pungal owner will lease out to you and I cannot make them." There was a small note of satisfaction in that. "And on your own feet there is no possible way to reach your goal before Change-season."

"There are the Gar," Zurzal said.

"Gar!" The way Wok Bi said that name made it sound as if the Zacathan had hissed it.

Gar—Jofre remembered. There had been a brief note concerning them on one of the tapes. They were the nomads of the inner lands and the off-worlders would have to transverse those in order to reach their own goal.

"Yes. Captain Gosal has a mixed cargo. There were Gar dealers to meet us at set down. And those have caravan trails inland. With fresh goods some one of them will be moving out."

"The priests will not hear of it!" Wok Bi fell back on a second objection.

"I think that there will be a change of thought there, too. Now—the Gar caravans must have been transport other than these Punga—"

Wok Bi shook his head. "No, not this side of the Var, but they do have carriers which are steady movers. It is said that sometimes they keep the trail for a full day and a night at a time since their drivers have learned to sleep a-swing. On the other side of the Var—there you would have to take your chance with what the Wild Ones use—they have mounts of a sort—I have seen a couple of specimens of them—running four-legged, with a sweep of horn—and nasty tempered I am told. Also that you might be able to make any deals for a guide or beasts of burden beyond the Var—that is very problematical."

"Commander, you have done your duty in stating frankly all the perils we must face. I shall, of course, give you a tape absolving you of blame which might come from some catastrophe. But go on, we shall."

Again the man threw up his hands. "On your head be it. There is also this—within the Shattered Land none of our coms work. If you are caught in some trouble, you cannot call for any aid—not that we would have any to send you."

"That is also understood," agreed the Zacathan.

"Be it on your own heads then." The commander got up. "I do not expect to see you again. If there is any hope of fortune, may it be yours. But I doubt such exists."

They settled then for the night, Jofre taking the first watch once again, well advised that the warehouse door was under surveillance from the outside. He thought of Zurzal's stubbornness. To an oathed the wishes of his patron were law. He might advise if called upon, but the central core of any operation remained the choice of the one to whom he had pledged himself. After all, men of the Lair had served very threatened causes before, and the triumph of some of them over great odds was the material for the Legend singers. No man could see the future and it was best to live but one day, one night at a time. His fingers sought within his girdle for that small pocket he had fashioned and drew out the stone. There was no heart fire in it, but it was warm and that warmth reached within him, far—banishing the ghosts of foreseeing. He held it so until Taynad moved up to take his place as sentry, closing his hand quickly when he heard those faint stirs in the dark which marked her coming. This was his secret only and he would hold it so.

However, Taynad had thoughts of her own. She had taken the measure of this Zacathan and she believed that if anyone could succeed in what sounded like a fever-born dream quest, it was he. There was something else. She found the twigs of her braids and once more fingering read their message. If not capture—kill! But to take the life of a Brother was to break-oath. And not to follow orders was an even greater break-oath. The Shagga wanted Jofre— they would find the means of contacting her even here— since they had joined forces with the Guild. The latter was as legendary as the issha-trained in achieving what its members were set to do.

Why did they want him? And why, if they could not take him bodily, did they demand blood? By his own tale, which instinct told her was the full truth, he had done nothing to provoke all custom and honor. She must watch, wait, and see what time itself would bring in answer. Kill—her fingernail bit into that last ominous notch. Though perhaps—with Shagga wrath so raised against him, he might welcome death rather than to fall into the hands of the priests.

Priests—it would seem that there were always priests to deal with. Her mouth twisted disdainfully as she thought of the Axe of Rou. But he, she believed, from what she had sensed of him was a relatively simple man—wily in a way, of course, but no match even for the Zacathan. He might well be brought to support them up to a point and right now they could use support.

She stretched. By the Flowers of Moon Valley, how she longed for a dip in one of the Three Pools with the comfort of an oil rub thereafter. Before this journeying was done with the Jewelbright might well be the Jeweldimmed and worth no second look from any man.

The Axe of Rou duly returned, at the first dim light of day, somewhat to the surprise of Jofre and Taynad though it would seem that Zurzal had been expecting him.

"You have taken council?" he greeted the priest.

"What do you offer?" countered the Axe.

"Let one of your own, one whom you trust, go with us—let him bring guards also if you will. What we find—the solid portion will be yours—we shall keep only the record of its finding."

"The trader U-Ky leaves today," the priest said. "It is true I shall be with him as it is necessary that I return to the Walls. And my Deves will bear me company. If you can bargain for transport with U-Ky—then let it be done."

It seemed that the Zacathan had very little trouble striking the bargain with the red-maned trader whom Jofre continued to watch narrowly. The fellow was a double for that alien who had been on Wayright though there was no way he could have made the journey back without their knowing it. It must be that there was such a strong resemblance between members of his race that it was difficult for outsiders to differentiate between them. What Zurzal offered him was a packet of silver pieces, such an exchange allowed by Wok Bi, in whose presence the transaction was done—silver being, it appeared, in rare supply on Lochan.

Their bargaining obtained the use of four of the swing carrying monsters. Zurzal, with the scanner across his knees, occupied the left swing of the first, Jofre the right. Behind them came Taynad with the Jat, balanced by a selection of equal weight of their gear, and the final bearers transported the rest of their equipment.

The heat as they set out was intense but at least, perched on swings, they were above the insect swarms. Though the constant movement of those seats made the off-world riders a little giddy and queasy, inclined to hold on tightly wherever a good anchorage offered.

U-Ky's caravan was a fairly impressive command and he rode to its head. There was also the bearer who balanced the great weight of the Axe against a tall pile of bundles. Swinging along behind the priest were the robed Deves. Strung out behind came some of the maned people, only a few of them red-maned and the rest as yellow-backed as the tundra.

Their rate of progress was no faster than a ponderous walk; apparently the huge bearers kept to what was a steady pace for them and never displayed any change in gait. Under the climbing and burning sun this travel was misery for the off-worlders and Jofre had to fight to hold on to his patience.

The yellow tundra seemed to stretch forever and though the caravan headed confidently forward, there was no trace of trail or road to be seen, nor any markers rising to guide the unknowing. It must be that the natives were like animals or birds on some of the other worlds which possessed ingrown direction skills.

They made no halt for nooning but as the sun shifted westward there began to show a line of dark marking the junction of sky and land ahead. It was toward that they continued doggedly even as the sun set and the quick dusk of Lochan closed in.

Still the caravan showed no signs of coming to a halt and the off-worlders were decidedly uncomfortable and tired. Then, out of the northern shadows, there shot a beam of light which flickered, Jofre decided after a moment's watching, in a distinct pattern. He was aware of movement on the right-hand swing of the bearer ahead of him; the rider there, one of the yellow manes, had raised what looked like a thick stick. From the tip of that flashed in turn an answer to that flare ahead.

So announced they swung on into what was an encampment, nearly as large as the caravan itself as to numbers. There were no sod buildings here, rather stretches of woven reed mats set to form very crude tentlike enclosures. While awaiting them were not only members of the maned race, and robed Deves, but a new type of Lochanian native. These were short in size, hardly larger than the Jat, and armored—or shelled—with dull green carapace-like body covering from which a wide, also shielded head and thin knobby jointed limbs projected. They did not mingle with those who crowded forward to greet the caravaners, rather held off in a party to themselves.

Jofre, catching good sight of one standing just beneath one of the massed luminous moss torches of the camp, recognized this as a tribesman concerning which there had been a very short note in their scant study tapes. This was a Skrem, one of the nomads whose tribes drifted along the very edge of the Shattered land.

The off-worlders were glad to be able to slide down from their shaking conveyances and immediately sought the outer regions of the camp for relief. Even the issha training, Jofre decided, had not prepared him for such a journey as this had been. He drew a deep breath as he relatched his belt; even another fraction of a time mark might have been a disaster.

The small outlander party was left alone. Their luggage had been carelessly dumped as their bearers trudged mechanically away to the assembly of their own kind. There was no offer of any tent covering, but the three united in piling their equipment so that it gave a measure of shelter and they did not try to approach the low-burning fires which marked the fore of those misshapen tents. They had their trail rations and they selected small shares of those, knowing from the start they must take good care of the highly nourishing, if near-tasteless stuff, since living off the land might be impossible.

The caravaners apparently had a more robust meal to suit them. Joints of some unidentifiable meat were spitted over the fires and then portions sawed off with belt knives to please the diner. Bulging skins appeared also and were passed from hand to hand. The Lochanians, Jofre noted, were quite practiced in the tricky maneuver of throwing back the head and allowing a thick curl of liquid to flow from the lower bag end directly into their mouths.

This informal feasting was still in progress when a party of three approached the impromptu campsite of the off-worlders. Against the glow of one of the fires could be made out the unwieldy bulk of one who could only be the Axe of Rou, attended by one of the Deves, and scuttling along at his side one of the Skrem.

The three from off-world arose, the Jat pushing in behind Taynad, peering around her with timid curiosity.

"Well journeyed," Zurzal had the translator at ready. "What does the Axe desire of this company?"

For a moment or so after he came to a halt the priest merely puffed as if he had made the trip across camp at some labor.

"Strangers, Rou frowns upon your travels."

"How so?"

"The season is late, we move too slowly, there is no entering the Shattered Land after the Wild Winds rise."

"Our pace is one set by you and your people, Axe of Rou. Can it be that Rou now requires that we prove ourselves by finding a faster way to satisfy *His* bidding in this matter?"

"There is one." The priest paused as if he were undecided about this, as if he were being forced against his will to come to a decision he distrusted. "The Skrem know another path. This is I'On." He indicated the strange native. There was little to be seen in the way of features on that one's face. The helmet (or the outgrowth of natural skull) reached forward in a visor shape which fully shadowed the eyes. Below those half-hidden pits the face narrowed to a sharp point of chin, the nose joined to that in a beaklike extension.

I'On made no move nor sound to acknowledge the introduction. Instead he stepped ahead of the priest to stand directly before the Zacathan, his head moving slowly up and then down, as if he measured the much taller lizard man from head to foot and back again.

Zurzal could not speak any greeting since the other's speech had not been picked up to be read by the translator.

From the Zacathan, the Skrem turned to Jofre, favored him with the same scrutiny, passed on to Taynad, and last of all shot his head a little forward as if to get a better look at the Jat, which had squeaked and withdrawn nearly behind the girl.

Having submitted them all to some form of his own measurement, the Skrem returned to the Zacathan.

What issued from the beak mouth was a chittering sound not unlike that Jofre had heard the hive man give back on Wayright.

"Why hunt you ghosts?" sputtered the translator.

"To learn," Zurzal returned briefly.

"To learn what?"

"The ways of the past."

"Those of the silences are eaters of men. Would you fill their pots joyfully?"

"I would learn of them—"

"There are always fools in the world." The contempt of that pushed even through the translator. "Well, what have you to offer, fool, to be taken to meet the results of your folly?"

"What do you ask, I'On?"

The Skrem did not answer at once. Rather he turned his head slowly as if to inspect all the pile of their belongings. Then of a sudden, so suddenly, that it brought Jofre to a crouch and ready to defend himself, he turned to the guard.

"This one goes also?"

"He goes," Zurzal assured him.

"He will have a service to offer—when the time is ready. Let him be also ready."

"What service?"

"It shall reveal itself. So be it. The Shattered Land shall be a gate opened to you, fools. We shall claim our price when it is right. Be ready to move out at first light."

He turned and left them, brushing past the Deves and leaving the priest to stare after him before the Axe looked, his big eyes a little narrowed, at the Zacathan, and on to Jofre.

"What does he mean? What service can such as you offer the drifting ones?"

"You heard, Axe, what we heard. It would seem that we have now an open-ended bargain. But it will have to suffice."

For a moment it seemed as if the priest was going to protest further and then he turned away, but not before he shot another look at Jofre which was both speculative and unpleasant.

"Why me?" Jofre actually voiced that question when they were alone again.

He heard Taynad laugh. "Did he not speak of ghosts who want man flesh for their pots? Perhaps he would herd a particularly toothsome dish in their direction. But I think—Learned One," she said slowly, "that Skrem— he has a strong inner sense—he sought. Us he could not touch—but the little one," she stooped and gathered up the trembling Jat, holding its body close, "it knew and feared. I think that we had best be doubly on guard."

"As if we can be anything else," Zurzal returned. "This is indeed perhaps folly, yet I cannot—I cannot stray from what I would do here!"

27

W HAT I'ON HAD TO OFFER ON HIS PART THEY LEARNED the next morning. Though the caravan moved on its way, the off-worlders remained with the Skrem. Two of the Deves also relinquished their traveling swings, though the Axe had gone with the others. It was apparent that the priest fully intended to have his own sources of information—or control—accompanying the Zacathan's party.

The stamping march of the bearers was well away from the overnight campsite when the Skrem went to work. He scrabbled in the mosscarpet some distance away from the trampled ground and came up with three rods which he fitted together—much like the tripod on which the scanner rested. But what was then affixed on top was a round of what appeared to be crystal, backed with an interweaving of the same material as the rods.

As the off-worlders remained by the pile of their gear, the Skrem affixed the platter to the tripod and wriggled it back and forth. Jofre recognized something from the Lair days—their mountain sentries had used burnished mirrors for the flashing of messages overland. This must be a similar form of communication.

Swiftly the Skrem tilted his signal back and forth. Then from the northeast there came a flicker of light in return.

Methodically the Skrem set about dismantling the apparatus and then reburied it, pulling the moss back over it.

How long must they wait? Taynad leaned back against a box of supplies. It seemed to her now that her wits certainly must have been astray when she had joined up with this muddle-headed Zacathan. Jofre was oathed to him, she was not—save by word alone. The mission to Tssek had been her first big one and it had fallen apart through no fault of her own. She had been given those orders—why did she continue to question them this way? She could only return in thought to those moments when she, Jofre, and Yan had been one—as if at that time there had been forged something as strong as a blood oath. It was almost as if her own will had been weakened, that she had been drawn along as one sometimes was in ill dreams when one struggled against an invisible threatening power.

"Power—strong—big—" She had a mind vision of a fire raging up into the sky, heat which was not from any sun, even one as hot as this one. Yan crouched against her. The Jat's paw hand rested over her hand and its large eyes were turned up to view her face. "Power—" Yes, that had sprung from Yan's thinking, not her own. She shot a glance in Jofre's direction.

He was watching the actions of the Skrem with complete absorption as if he expected some trouble to burst from a gesture or action on the part of the alien. No, Jofre must not have been touched by that half-message.

Taynad closed her hand gently about the Jat's. "Power?" She struggled to give all the strength she could to make that word a question.

What she received in return did not altogether surprise her. A wavering, oddly slanted face flashed into her mind—Jofre—as Yan must see him.

"Power?" she asked again in thought.

Flames—shooting flames bursting outward as if a dozen lasers were firing at a single target. She instinctively cringed. Yan was very sure.

The flames were, of course, merely a picturing of punishing force, of that she was certain. The guard could have not smuggled in any weapon that would reveal itself so. In fact she was very sure that she knew exactly the number and style of every piece of armament he had hidden about his person.

There were tales that the Shagga could produce strange effects—bemuse minds—make one see what was not there—even as the issha could protect themselves for short periods of time. But Jofre was not Shagga—to them he was the enemy who must be erased—one way or another.

Why did they want him prisoner, that was a small puzzle—better dead—off-world dead where he would be no problem. Why prisoner—and only dead at the last resort as the instructions passed to her? Or—her thought took another small leap—were those twigs and their messages counterfeit? The Guild was supposed to possess infinite knowledge. She knew that Zarn had been charged with certain delicate negotiations with the Guild. Suppose it was the Guild who wanted Jofre—alive—or dead by her hand?

Her eyes lowered to that hand curved to comfort the Jat. Shadow did not slay Shadow. She must have better reason— Which came back to—

The Jat squirmed closer to her. Another mind picture—blurred—so distorted she could make nothing of it. Except that she was certain that it was an object—something which Jofre owned, or controlled, or—

"They are coming!" Zurzal was on his feet, looking out over the tundra in the direction which that flash had marked. There was certainly movement there and at a speed far transcending the plod of the bearers. As they plowed on through the moss the new party revealed themselves, however, as grotesquely alien to the off-worlders as U-Ky and his caravaners had been.

There were four mounted figures, each leading a line of four-footed creatures but apparently by no lines or reins, the mounts being followed without urging by six of their own kind, in a line behind each of the riders.

They were of the same musty yellow as the tundra, their legs long and thin, their bodies apparently hairless and also nearly skeleton-slender. They held their heads on a straight line with their bodies as they came, and the muzzles ended in sharp points. Those heads were small in proportion to a spread of horns, bending sharply backward, which were flat and shovellike in appearance.

As the runners came pounding up to the deserted campsite Jofre saw that their feet were long and narrow, the fore ones sprouting claws which apparently were not retractable. The Skrem who brought them rode well forward on those slim backs, their hands gripping the edges of the shovel horns.

In height they were close to the size of a small horse such as Jofre had seen used for pleasure riding on Wayright, and on the backs of those without riders there were weavings of odd-looking harness. But there were no saddles; apparently one was to perch like the Skrem, hold on to the horns, and hope for the best.

The Skrem made no move to aid in the loading of the extra mounts, gathering in a knot around I'On and chittering loudly. Fortunately the animals they had brought did not seem to resent the actions of the three in dividing up their gear and stowing it into the baggage nets. Jofre wondered if what they had to haul would not be too heavy a load but the creatures, except for a grunt or two, made no complaint.

At length it was time for they themselves to scramble up, finding that their seats on those ridge-boned backs were not comfortable—but, as with the swings, had to be endured. The riders were back in place, and I'On mounted behind one of those. At some signal the off-worlders did not catch the party wheeled in parade order and headed out, northeast, in the same style as they had arrived, lining up behind the four leaders.

It was a rough jolting, and the hold on the creatures' horns did little to steady one. But at least they went at a good speed and the animals, ridden or laden, apparently were ready to keep to that pace. Within a short time there loomed before them a rise in the land like a wall. The grey stones of it pierced the moss. The Deves, who had done nothing to help with the luggage, and both bestrode one of the animals, uttered a call which blended both of their voices. This was the Var, a natural walling as far as the Lochanians knew, separating the plains from the highlands. It was also a cut across which a bridge had been strung— an exceedingly fragile-looking bridge—by the approaches to which there were both maned men and Deves stationed. However, at the sight of the two Deves with the Skrem party these fell back and the first of the riders was out on the bridge.

At least here their mounts slowed to a walk and ventured out on the swinging support at well separated intervals, so there was a wait on the far side for their party to again assemble. Also here their path led through gullies and there were rising hills. The vegetation changed to a sharp degree. The yellow moss of the tundra was gone. Here were skeleton-thin, branched shrubs, around the roots of which clustered patches of indigo blue, an eye-aching green, and a bloody red growth which put forth bristles, not unlike thorns, and attracted a great many flying things.

Back and forth they wove through these gullies, sometimes seeming even to turn completely around. Ahead, against the sky, there was a rise of taller hills, mountains. As on the tundra Jofre could distinguish no path or road, or even markings, yet their leader did not falter and those who followed showed no lack of confidence in him.

Once in such a land, Jofre thought, how did one win free again? And from what little they had been able to gather the Shattered Land was even more chaotic.

They came to a halt at last, the off-worlders bone-shaken. Zurzal, because of his greater height, must have found it even a tougher ordeal, though he made no complaint. Here was a spring where water rippled through a crevice in the rocks and threaded down into a pool, which in turn fed a stream. There were gauzy winged things dancing over the water, prismatic colors glinting off their wings as if those were formed of fine lace set with tiny jewels.

That rider who had shared his perch with l'On did not dismount as all the rest swung down. Once the other mounts were free they clustered around that leader which ambled at a much slower pace down the stream, leaving the rest of the party behind. The Skrem paid no attention to the off-worlders, rather gathered in a group about l'On, producing bags in which they rummaged to bring forth what looked like handfuls of dried grass. Two of their number went on hands and knees to the stream side and busied themselves flipping over the water-moistened rocks, now and then scooping up what looked like a pallid wriggling grub which they tossed over their shoulders, their finds eagerly pounced upon by their fellows. It would seem that this was a time to eat.

Jofre had had enough training in living off the countryside on Asborgan to have tasted—without any pleasure but most stoically—insects and rough gathered herbs. But he was glad that for now they had their own trail rations.

The mounts were being watered downstream and then turned to foraging on the most purplish of the bristle growth, chewing it vigorously until dark, slimy juice dribbled from their jaws. With a compressed meat biscuit in one hand Zurzal produced with the foreshortened other a square of nearly transparent stuff which had been folded into very tight compress but shook out into a wide strip which Jofre identified as that mapping of the ways on which the Zacathan had worked many hours from time to time ever since he had obtained from the dying spacer the coordinates the other had brought back from his ordeal on Lochan. But that Zurzal could make any sense of what was marked there was a wonder to the guard. This up-and-down land might present landmarks by the thousands to the educated eye, but those would exist for a native, and he doubted whether the spacer had been in a position to sight many.

The Zacathan's head came up and he was staring now
at the north line of heights, which were like broken teeth
gnawing at the sky. They seemed to be paralleling that
line rather than heading directly towards it. But was it the
boundary of the Shattered Land? Jofre was sure that even
Zurzal could not tell.

He got to his feet and walked up and down, to stretch
muscles, battling the various aches and pains their riding had produced. His inner thighs felt raw, chafed by
the constant pressure he had had to keep to hold his
place. But if it were so for him, what had it been for
Taynad?

The girl sat with her back to a lichen-crusted stone. Her
eyes were closed and there was that masklike quietude in
her face which he could understand. One hand, holding
a barely nibbled journey square, lay laxly across her knee
and the other rested on Yan's head.

"Eat!" Jofre moved to stand so that his shadow fell
across her and hid her from the rest of their company.
"Without food, strength goes." Even in his own ears his
voice sounded rough and he must rouse her into seeking
inner strength, for there could be no falling behind. He
did not believe that the Skrem would in any way suit
their form of travel to those in their company. While
any Sister to Shadows had to be issha-tough, her own
training had differed in places from his—and he did not
know, could not judge how much. Why had she agreed
to Zurzal's offer? So far her communication skills had not
been put to any testing. He stood in hesitation—there
was a wish to somehow lend her strength now as he had
when she had brought the Jat out of its catatonic sei-
zure, yet he was at a loss how to do that. He knew very
little of women—that was a subject on which none of the
Masters ever dwelt, and before a boy gained puberty he
was drilled and disciplined into control over the body's
desires.

An issha who had well served on the missions, proved
himself worthy to have his bloodline carried on, could be

assigned to a mating by selection. Then he passed into another category of fighter, became a trainer, or an advisor. But otherwise women played no part in his life.

It had been growing on him that there was indeed a difference between them, issha-trained though they were. She would have been as disciplined to meet him as a battle comrade only had they been on a double oathing. As a Jewelbright she was a warrior of an entirely different breed. He felt rough-handed, as unskilled as a boy at his first mustering in the arms court.

However, he slipped down beside her now. The Jat stirred and looked at him. Reaching across the girl, who had not moved, Yan caught at Jofre's hand, keeping its own grip also on Taynad.

Heat, first a warmth and then a flame against his ribs. The stone from Qaw-en-itter—he knew it too well now to doubt that it was so making known its presence. Power? Jofre's free hand slipped inside his girdle, his fingers closed on that source of warmth.

Power—strength—his thought fastened on that. Flow of strength—he fought to draw upon it even as he had in the battle to win the Jat. And it was coming—up his arm—across his body—into that other hand—the paw which held him in such a grip. And beyond—though he could not trace it any further than Yan, he was sure that the Jat was channeling it into Taynad.

Her eyes opened and focused on him. There was the faintest trace of a frown troubling the mask of her face.

"Draw—" He spoke that single word as an order.

The flow was continuing, not as heavy as it had been before, but steady. Then her hand jerked away from the Jat, breaking the chain.

"Who—what are you?" She demanded that sharply, straightening her shoulders, pulling herself away from the rock support.

"Issha feeds issha when there is need," he returned, drawing his hand away from his girdle. Why would he not share the secret of his find with her? He could not tell except there seemed to be a guard on his tongue, a shutter in his mind when he thought of it.

"It is well." Once more she showed him the mask. "It seems I am too far, too long from the Lair." He thought he could detect a measure of resentment in her speech and she was using the language of the Lair which had many inflections and subtle shadings. Yes, she could well resent the fact that she had displayed signs of fatigue.

"It is always well to give." He used the formal speech of an instructor. "Is it not written so in the Laws of Kak?"

What answer she might have made to that he was not to know, for Zurzal roused from the studying of his flimsy map and there was the clatter of feet on gravel as their mounts headed back upstream in their direction.

Remounted, their leader swung them on along the stream for a space and then there was a scramble up a slope and for the first time the dim marks of a true trail—which turned and twisted up into the heights beyond. This was far harder riding than even the gully wandering had been and the holds they must keep on the horns of their mounts in order not to slip from their seats crooked their fingers with aching cramps. Jofre concentrated on looking only at those horns and making sure that his hold was the best he could grip. To look out into the empty air, down, or even at the length of the slope ahead was disheartening.

They hit at last what seemed to be a pass and on either side the rock walls towered. There was a searching wind, as chill as the tundra plain had been hot. Yet there was life of a sort clinging here, for both walls were festooned with weblike binding and Jofre, daring for the moment to look beyond his hands, saw a shaking of those lines. Climbing down was a ball-like body, hardly to be distinguished from the rocks in color, legs as thin and apparently as supple as the webbing sprouting from under the round of its body.

Jofre caught the sudden action of the Skrem bestriding the lead mount. Both he and I'On, seated behind, made throwing gestures. The ball thing gave a convulsive leap which left it dangling from the webbing by only two of its legs, the rest jerking frenziedly in the air. Protruding from the round back Jofre sighted two small shafts. Then the ball lost its last hold, fell squashily and was sent farther on by a kick from his own mount which nearly unseated him.

There appeared to be no further danger as they won through the pass to the northern end. There their line of mounts halted, only those bearing riders gathering closer to the downward grade as if they consciously wished those they carried to see what lay ahead.

What did was such a frozen convulsion of nature that Jofre, though he had somewhat been prepared for such a sight by the tapes, thought could hardly exist on any world.

They called this the Shattered Land and they were very right in that description. It was all sharp ridges of rock, looking knife-sharp from above, with dark drops between. As if one of the Storm Gods of the old days had taken a sword half as wide as the sky and deliberately cut and recut the earth, turning soil where that weapon touched into the traps of blade-edged lava.

How could any man find a way through such a country? The expedition which had come to grief here had been borne by flitter—though Jofre wondered about the downdrafts and wind changes over such a territory. But on foot? This was one of those impossible tasks given to the Older Heroes in order for them to achieve immortality. One could perhaps achieve a measure of that, to be sure, in another way, by simply dying here, Jofre thought.

The mount bearing I'On as one rider had edged up beside the Zacathan.

"Here is the country you seek, stranger. Now what do you seek in it?"

Zurzal was busy with one of the belongings taken from his belt, a small oval into which he now most carefully inserted a pellet. He held it out towards that riven world.

A moment later, to be heard even above the strange echoing cries of the wind through those broken vales below, came a small sharp sound. The Zacathan turned his hand slowly, with infinite care, and the signal strengthened.

"What we seek lies there." He pointed to the north.

Though they could not see the Skrem's eyes, Jofre thought that the alien might be staring at Zurzal's instrument with surprise. He chittered and was answered by his fellow rider. Then he turned to Zurzal with another question.

"How far?"

"That we must learn for ourselves," the Zacathan replied, "but the signal is strong. We cannot be too far."

One of the Deves joined them now, having dismounted. The wind whipped his cloak about, fluttering his head comb.

"No one enters this." He spoke the trade tongue but so heavily accented that it was difficult to understand.

The Skrem shifted around on his mount. It seemed that the heavy head covering kept him from turning his head easily.

He chittered and Zurzal's com picked up his speech even though that was not directed to the off-worlders.

"The Skrem ride where they will. We would see what this one seeks. If it is of value—so shall it be valued."

And without another word the rider seated before I'On pressed down on the horns of his beast and the creature took the first step down the line of broken ledges leading into the Shattered Land.

28

WHAT MIGHT BE THE NATURE OF ZURZAL'S GUIDE Jofre could not guess but certainly the attitude of the Zacathan would lead anyone to believe that he trusted in it implicitly. The guard thought back to that meeting with the dying man on Asborgan. Had what he had passed to Zurzal then come to lead them now?

However, this was no country into which to venture as that night was drawing in. The broken, knife-edged lava remains formed a constant threat. From what Jofre could see bubbles must have formed in the molten rock, to burst, leaving jagged teeth to threaten any unwary step.

Apparently the Skrem were well aware of this danger. Once they had reached the end of the downslope, they clustered on a semilevel space, making no move to enter the broken maze even though the signal Zurzal carried sent forth its constant assertion that what was to be sought did lie ahead.

It was a cramped and uncomfortable camp they set up. The rugged lava flow provided some small shelter and once again the party separated naturally into three. While the off-worlders worked at getting their gear free from the baggage beasts they were left alone, each animal as it was unloaded moving away to join its fellows. The Skrem hunkered down without looking to their mounts, gathering in a knot about a spot of fire the Zacathan could have covered with his two hands.

Between the Skrem and the off-worlders the two Deves found a resting place. They made no move toward any fire, only bundled their robes more tightly about them, and Jofre noted that they drew hoods from the folds of those robes over their heads as they settled back-to-back, one facing the Skrem gathering, one Zurzal's party, as if they fully intended to keep full watch on all those they companied with.

Zurzal himself moved around restlessly for a space, the instrument in his hand not only clicking in a broken rhythm as he turned this way and that, but giving forth a glow which grew the brighter as the daylight failed.

At last he dropped down between Jofre and Taynad. "We must be closer than I reckoned." He was hissing as he did when excited and the stir of his neck frill was constant, as if being ruffled by some wind.

"This is bad land to cross." Jofre had made his own close inspection of the edge of the way in which that guide would send them. To transverse those glasslike splinters would take time and very careful study of any path ahead.

"But—there are flowers!" Taynad pointed.

Indeed there was life here. That bristly growth which had covered the ground on the other side of the pass had changed to another kind of vegetation, closer in some ways to the tundra moss, yet with a characteristic very much its own. This did sprout thread-thin stems, hardly as long as a finger, so lifting high small white stars of flowers which seemed to lose no color in the closing dusk but rather to glow.

Beyond a clump of these there appeared to emerge from rock itself tiny lacy fringed leaves of a faintly reddish hue. While above this display there winged minute flutterers that moved from one star flower to another, as might the night spirits of the oldest legends.

Yan was entranced, moving away from Taynad and squatting down, now and then tentatively advancing a paw hand but never quite touching the display. Jofre picked up the faint touch of wonder which the Jat emitted. Then to the guard's surprise Yan reached up and caught at his own dangling hand, while the tall-eared head moved up and right as if that pushed-in, wrinkled nose was picking up some scent. Yan scrambled up, not losing touch with Jofre, and pattered on along the rock. They came to a place where the lava wall was taller and there Yan halted and pointed with the free paw.

Whatever attracted its attention must be above. Jofre moved closer to the surface of the wall, intent on a search for any such disastrous surprises as a webbing inhabited by the round ball bodies. But there was none to be seen.

He loosed his hand from Yan's grip and pulled himself up, to discover that he was now on the edge of a cup ringed about with the star flowers in thick profusion, so thick that he was aware of a delicate scent. And they were clustered about a bowl-sized pool of what appeared to be water though there was no sign of a spring, nor could there be in this land, he thought.

They had filled their water canteens at the spring over the mountain, and he would not disturb this small pocket— nor could they be sure it might not be tainted by some mineral. But to look down upon it was like looking into a miniature garden, to his eyes nearly as beautiful as that exotic lounging place the Holder had kept.

"Come," he called softly but he need not have done so, for Yan's summons must have reached her before his and Taynad was already at the base of the wall finding a way to join him.

A moment later her shoulder brushed against his. "It—is like the Moon Garden!" she exclaimed. "Perfect—as only the things made by the true spirit can be perfect. A thing to be fixed in memory forever!"

Jofre had reached down and pulled up Yan, settling the small furred body against his as the Jat leaned forward in his hold and made a soft crooning sound which blended with what they looked upon and became a perfect part of it.

"Food, explorers—" Zurzal's hiss from below brought them back into the world of here and now and they returned to the rough base camp.

They were careful with their supplies, rationing themselves strictly, being doubly saving of the water. The Skrem had not stirred far from their own chosen places and the two Deves still sat back-to-back. If they had eaten, it was in the shadow of their cloaks, a secret business.

The off-worlders followed their now set pattern of dividing the night into thirds, one to keep watch during each. Zurzal took the first watch since he said he wished to check on both the scanner (which he would have to do by touch in this lack of light) and keep an eye on the guide.

Jofre rolled in his covering, watching the shadowy movements of the Zacathan until sleep hit and he was caught in an ever-thickening darkness.

However, there was no mindless rest awaiting him. There was a stirring—first of memories which became oddly distorted dreams and then suddenly cleared into a real pattern. Once more he lay among mountain rocks and there crept upon him an unseen enemy. He fought to still his body, to seem the soundly sleeping one until that skulker came within hand's reach— There came a fumbling at his girdle— knife—

Jofre was awake with the speed of a threatened issha in enemy territory. His left hand had shot out to tighten on the one who had come like a thief, tightened with a crushing force, and in instant reply there was a scream of pain which sounded not only in his ears but in his head.

Sharp teeth scored his flesh. He had just time to deflect the knife blow delivered by his own hand so that that blade was not buried in the small body now squirming half across his middle. Yan! But why—?

"What are you doing?" Taynad was at him now, and her long nails cut skin below his eye.

"What is this one doing?" Jofre spat in return. He was

reaching his knees now and had warded off a second attack from Taynad with force enough to send her back against the astounded Zacathan.

Jofre loosed his hold on Yan with a lightning-fast move, transferring it from the Jat's wrist to the nape of its neck so that he was able to hold it away from him. But what caught his attention first was the paw he had just released, for the whole of it was now aglow—so lit that one could see bones within the skin and flesh. And that paw was fast gripped about—

The stone! The Jat had somehow attempted to steal his secret! Why? There was one answer—Jofre glanced for only a second toward Taynad. There was more light now—he had slept past the twin moon rise and even the lava appeared to reflect some of that downward glow.

Jofre's lips flattened across his set teeth. The Jat—so in tune with this issha-trained—she must have set Yan on him.

"Give." His hand closed over that of Yan.

The Jat whimpered, shivered as if whipped around by a bitter wind, but it obeyed, releasing the stone into Jofre's grip. Some of the radiance died during that exchange, but enough was left to make it certain that what the guard now held was nothing ordinary.

"So you would have the creature thieve?" Jofre said slowly, trying to make his contempt edge each word. "What else have the Shagga ordered to be done? Am I now fair game for any Shadow?"

She brushed her hand across her mouth. Above that her eyes seemed very large and empty as if she had raised a strong barrier. He might well know that he would have no truth out of her—unless such was pertinent to the game she had been set to play. He had thought from the first that what he had found at the ancient Lair was indeed powerful, but he had not suspected that he would be hunted off-world for it.

"What is it?" The hissing of the Zacathan's voice was pronounced. He had put out an arm and steadied the girl against his body. Now he added, in a lower tone, "There are other eyes and ears here."

Jofre swallowed, called on control for the stifling of rage and, yes, the odd sense of betrayal. In all his life he had trusted very few, and the last to have his full allegiance was the dead Master. Yan whimpered again and tried to pull away and Jofre freed him but did not yet hide the stone. Why should he? They had seen it. Taynad must know very well what he carried and had been given her orders. But why had she waited so long? On Wayright she must have had countless chances for the Jat to despoil him and then she could have disappeared out of their lives, or else passed her loot on so that she would not be suspected.

"Power—warm—" The thought kindled a picture of flames in his mind; it must have done the same to Taynad. But it was to the Jat that he aimed and steadied his answering thought.

"Why—take—" He wanted to scream that demand; he had to school himself to shape it in mind, to throttle himself into set control so that the Jat's fear would lessen enough to allow him contact. He certainly had no desire to send the small one back into the locking nonlife which had gripped it on Tssek.

"Power—" It seemed that the creature found it impossible to advance beyond that thought. Zurzal took a hand now.

"What do you have?"

Jofre tensed but the Zacathan had every right to ask that. With the issha oath-bound to him there could be no concealment. But what did he have? He could not honestly say. Now he tried to sort out his thoughts in some form. There might well be the chance that Taynad knew more about this than he did—what would happen if it fell into her hands and she did know how to put it to use? It heightened issha powers—it had kept him alive during his early captivity on the Tssekian ship. He felt warm, good, confident when he held it. But what was it?

"I do not know," he responded with the exact truth. "It

is a finding, brought to me by chance, as I once told you. I only know that it sharpens issha powers—it is perhaps a protection of sorts."

"Where did it come from?"

"Out of Qaw-en-itter—a dead Lair—just as I said." Again Jofre gave him the truth. "I nighted there through a mountain storm—and found it by chance—"

He had heard the sharp inhale of breath from Taynad. The names of all the dead Lairs were commonly known and he had doubly damned himself by admitting he had sheltered within such disaster-darkened walls.

Now the Zacathan looked toward the girl. "What is it?"

Jofre awaited her answer eagerly. He believed he could separate false from true if she tried to evade a flat answer.

"It—it seems a Lair stone—or a part of one," she answered in a strange voice, as if she inwardly did doubt the truth of her own words. "It—is Assha—"

Jofre's hand jerked, almost the glowing stone slipped between his fingers. If she spoke the truth, and surely she did as she saw it, then—then what was he? All knew that Assha power was a fortune-gift and that it came after long searching. When a Lair Master died and the stone of that still lived it was the stone itself that selected the next Master—the one it warmed to would be its voice. But that was also a dangerous trial—would-be Assha had been known to be blasted, fire-seared, when they assayed that chance.

This could only be a fraction of the Lair stone that had been. Perhaps its power was lessened by the lack of size, the fact it was not properly set in place. Yet he could not truthfully deny to himself now that what he felt when he held it was a welcoming, not condemnation of some reckless and overambitious action.

"May I?" Zurzal held out his one hand.

For a moment Jofre hesitated. It was as if the thing clung to him. But he allowed it to slip from his hold into the Zacathan's. The glow which it had shown faded as might fire sinking into ash. Zurzal held it closer to his eyes. His frill lifted and his dark tongue flickered out almost as if he wished to taste what he held.

"Radiation, yes." He turned it around slowly. "Of what kind—who can tell? Part of a Lair stone—"

"Part of a Lair stone," Jofre repeated firmly and glanced again at Taynad. "Did they lay oath on you—against me— to bring that back? The Shagga are jealous of the stones— they cannot use them—only the Masters can—and no Shagga can be assha—they walk another road. I do not claim to be a Master—nor Assha. But, see you!" He plucked the stone away from Zurzal and it glowed again. "Would you?"

Now he deliberately held it out to Taynad. She shook her head. "It is a thing of ill fortune out of a place accursed. I do not know why it should answer to any true issha—"

"Ah, but if you have listened to the Shagga, to the story I myself told you, Shadow Sister, you would know that I am not deemed true issha—my rights have been stripped from me—"

He had spread his palm, the stone resting flat upon it. It was as if the heart of its dull red there held a sturdy core of fire—not blazing as it had when the Jat laid paw on it, but alive as it had not been in the Zacathan's hold.

"What task have they laid on you?" Jofre swept swiftly back to his original demand. "My death—the taking of this? And this little one—Yan is your tool?"

"No!" She shook her head and that tightly braided hair loosened somewhat. "I did not set Yan on you this night! It tried to tell me that you have some power; I think it wished to prove it to me. Yes, the Shagga would hunt you down. They have out their nets." She raised one hand and pulled at the fore of her braid loop, freeing the twigs. "They have given orders—"

Jofre stepped back a pace. He crooked his finger and Yan obeyed. Into the Jat's forepaws he dropped the stone.

"I take no advantage," he said. "What would you? Knives by choice?"

It had come so suddenly—though, yes, he had had his

suspicions of her. But somehow he had never guessed that it would end in blade against blade. They were probably evenly matched enough—since they must keep to the single weapon agreed upon—and she was issha-trained. Also the knife was the first weapon for the Sisters, even as the sword or spear might be for the Brothers.

"Stop!" Zurzal was between them. "You are oathed to me," he added sharply to Jofre. "While that oath holds you are not allowed to seek a private quarrel. Is that not part of the oathing?"

"For issha—yes," Jofre returned slowly. "But now it is said I am not issha—otherwise the Sister would not take mission against me."

"I refuse to accept such a quibble," Zurzal hissed. His frill, flushing darkly, was a fan behind his head. "You are my oathed. And you," he looked now to Taynad, "I did not oath you but you accepted a bargain—were you already then playing another game? Had you taken oath to bring down this man?"

Slowly the girl shook her head. "No, Learned One, when I said I would come with you they had not sent any message to me. It was only afterward—"

"I have heard much of issha honor on Asborgan," Zurzal continued. "No, I did not formally oath you to my service, Taynad. But you accepted my offer freely. Does one need a ritual to keep full faith?"

Jofre saw her tongue tip show between her set lips. The heavy lids nearly veiled her eyes and for a moment she was silent as one who weighs one matter against another.

"Learned One, what I accepted I shall keep to for as long as this venture lasts—"

Jofre's hand moved away from the hilt of his knife. So until another day this would go unsettled. But he also knew well that issha word was unbending; she would hold only to a truce and that for the time the Zacathan would set.

"We had better settle down," Zurzal said, "before some of our companions grow interested and come to see what we are doing. I think none of us would want them to know about that." And he pointed to what blazed brightly in the Jat's hold. Swiftly Jofre recovered his treasure and tucked it away into hiding.

"I take the watch," he said, knowing that he could not sleep now, not until he had thought, weighed, and decided all he could about the days ahead.

29

Howerver, MORNING LIGHT FOUND HIM WITH NO TRUE decision. What he could foresee was only what concerned his own actions; he could not know what Taynad might think or do. Realizing this, Jofre forced the whole matter to the back of his mind. What lay before them now was another kind of action. He had mistrusted this ragged land from the start and to work their way across it might well be beyond what any living thing—without wings—could do.

The Skrem broke their own camp and herded their beasts down to be packed by the off-worlders, the Deves still holding themselves apart, though keeping a close eye, Jofre noted, on both parties. There was a suggestion in this that they were not altogether ready to play trail comrades with the Skrem.

Though Zurzal's guide pointed out into those knife-edged ridges, he did not lead in that direction, rather paced a little south, pausing often to check on the com he held. Perhaps with other knowledge he had not shared with them he had some idea there was a way into this stark country which could be taken on foot. Though Jofre remembered that the party whose directions they now depended upon had come by flitter and so had not had to face that impossible terrain.

The ranges of massed lava about them took on color as the sun arose. Those patches of small growth on them were in vivid contrast, but the small flowers which had greeted the night seemed now to be tightly closed. It was indeed a weird country, for the rock in places seemed to have been worked into faces which grinned, or grimaced, or gaped widely at passersby.

Out of their whole company the Jat seemed the most at ease for some reason. Its usual timidity had vanished and from where it rode perched before Taynad it made eager gestures and murmurs which sometimes sounded like small muted cries. Jofre began to wonder about the world from which Yan had been stolen—had it borne some resemblance to this riven countryside so that the Jat felt it had come home?

Suddenly the Zacathan brought his mount to a halt with a jerk on its horns, swung it around to face into the lava stretch. The com was giving forth a sharp series of notes, so close together they almost formed a kind of scream.

"Here—we strike cross-country here."

He said that as if he were suggesting no more than they cross one of the thoroughfares of Wayright. But there was certainly no road ahead—only a round wall which rose well above their heads. Zurzal swung off the beast, which snorted as if registering a strong protest to what it now faced.

"A foot march—over there? We cannot push the beasts into it!" Jofre moved up beside him.

"No other way. Let's take a look." He slipped the cord attached to one end of the com over his head and started to climb. Jofre was prompt to follow. Taynad had moved in at their backs, and, for now, he believed he could depend upon her to see that none of the natives would interfere without warning.

The porous material over which they scrambled had hand and footholds enough, but they had to be very wary of the cutting edges of broken-off pieces. Luckily it was not a long ordeal and when Jofre pulled up beside the already standing Zacathan he stared out on something he had not expected.

Through some ancient level of the land here the flow of the lava had narrowed into a river. Beyond that was another kind of rock, darker in color, not showing the threat of the broken edges. The distance between them and that island was not too wide to be spanned, though they would have to take great care in their going, perhaps somehow fashioning extra covers for hands and feet, or provide an advance guard to chop out the worst of the edges. It could be done, and for the first time Jofre saw that Zurzal was not totally brain-twisted by his desire to reach that goal.

On returning to the edge of the flow below they reported to Skrem and Deves what they had discovered.

"This you search for—it lies there?" I'On demanded.

In answer Zurzal had simply held forward the com, so that they could all catch its chatter, which was now steady.

"The ochs cannot go." The Skrem indicated their mounts.

"That is so. We must go on foot, carrying with us what is needful. But what we would find is not in the fields of broken rock, it is on firm and older land." The Zacathan spoke with the authority of one who might well have seen exactly what he was describing.

"We think—" I'On made a gesture and withdrew, the rest of the Skrem close with him. They squatted in a circle some distance away, and Jofre could hear no sound from them. However, he did not doubt they were in debate over Zurzal's plan for the venture on foot.

It was one of the robed Deves who came up to the Zacathan now.

"Only the mad walk the Shattered Land." His shrill voice formed words via the translator. "Why do you urge death on us—take it upon yourself?"

Zurzal waved his hand toward the wall of the flow. "Climb and see. There are islands in the flow—it is not all as you see it before you here."

For a moment it looked as if the Deve would do just that—climb to see for himself. But then he wheeled quickly and swung up on the mount his fellow, already on his own beast, had herded toward him.

Without any other answer the two started away. The knot of Skrem broke apart and scrambled toward their own beasts, as if fearing the creatures might follow the two which the Deves bestrode. Their chittering reached the height of screams as they swung up to follow the runaways.

"That," commented Zurzal after a moment, "seems to be that. At least we still have the supplies."

Jofre wondered what good the small amount they had brought with them would do if they were left without transportation. On the other hand it might well be that I'On and his fellows would catch the Deves and return. There was no way they, the three of them, could aid or hinder that chase at present. And he fell to checking over the woven containers which held all the equipment they had been able to assemble.

They made up three packs of the main essentials. Zurzal had used a knife and cut from his suit the half-empty sleeve covering his regrowing left arm. It was in length now a little past the elbow of his right one and the fingers of the hand on that side, when he flexed them, seemed to be as ready for work as those of his right. It was that miniature left hand which steadied the scanner in its web carrier.

Jofre had taken as much of the foodstuff and concentrates as he could crowd in his pack and knew he could shoulder. And Taynad worked with him putting together a burden of her own. His last addition was a roll of sleep coverings which he knotted into a rope, the other end of which he could tie to his weapons belt and carry up with him.

The Jat jumped to the side of the Zacathan as they began their climb—there had been no sign nor sound of the return of their fellow travelers. And it was Yan who had a ready paw to steady the scanner and aid the heavily laden Zurzal to make the top.

Once there Jofre jerked up the bundle of coverings and they all three set to work slitting them into strips and binding them thickly, not only around their own feet but around those of the Jat also, for with their other burdens they could not hope to carry Yan across that strip of lava flow ready and waiting to saw to pieces any flesh unaware enough to trust foot to it.

It was taking them a long time; the sun was well along towards setting. Jofre wanted to make that rock point which offered all the safety they could hope for before darkness closed in. Moonlight—under the two moons of Lochan, which whirled in orbit around each other as they passed— would not be enough to lighten all the pitfalls.

They selected what they believed was the narrowest of that anciently frozen flow and started their wavering path, for they could not keep to a straight line across it. As it was, the extra covering shredded from their feet, and they had to keep their pace to a crawl.

But there comes an end to every trial, Jofre thought thankfully, when at last he could put out a hand and touch the rock of the spur the flow had not engulfed. Again they must climb, first squatting to loose the tattered coverings from their feet and making sure that their packs were roped well together to be lifted once they had reached the top.

The Jat took the lead, again flapping its large ears and uttering cries as if it recognized the place, something of its exuberance urging them on. Then they were safely aloft and looking out into a stretch of country where the Shattered Land was not what it had been called.

They had reached a height and that widened out into a vast plateau where the fury of the mountain fire had not left any such scars as it had below. To the north, a little aslant of what might be the center of this open stretch of rock, gravelly sand, and a few stubborn patches of the yellow tundra grass, was a hill, the crown of which had been flattened off except for some humps here and there. It had a different look to it than the other heights around—as if it had not come directly from the shaping of nature by wind and time.

The sound of the Zacathan's trail guide was now a steady drone and he headed out towards that hillock with the certain stride of someone knowing exactly where he was going. Nor had they been led astray, for, as they neared the truncated cone, they saw that the tundra grass had withered patches, that there were small heaps of the turf which had been peeled back so that the ground below could be trenched and trenched it had been, in narrow ditches. These no longer stood out clearly, for it was plain that they had been exposed to the weather for some time, but Jofre recognized the site as it had appeared on one dim tape. This was the doomed camp of the expedition which had made the first discovery.

It was only seconds later that they were fully shown what had happened. There were a series of rocks placed in a half circle about the edges of those ditches and mounted on each rough base formed by one of those was a skull. And they seemed to grin with a ghastly promise as the off-worlders drew near.

There were no other signs of any visitors—no remains of any camp structure if there had been such. Nor, as Jofre discovered as he circled the eerie site, any other signs of other bones. But not far beyond the ditches with their ghostly guardians there was a sinking of the plain which occurred abruptly and could not be sighted until one was almost on it.

Where the rest of the plateau stretching so far about them suggested a desert country, this slash in the rock allowed them to gaze down into a narrow file as different from the land above as one planet might differ from another.

There was a thick growth of fleshy-leaved plants, large near their first rooting at the foot of the rise, dwindling in size as they climbed. The leaves each grew in a rosette which was centered by a thick red stem—the leaves being a sickly yellow-green. And on the stem was a trumpet-shaped growth which might be a bloom yet certainly gave no pleasure to the eye.

What was more important was that these plant beds bordered a stream of dark water—at least it seemed to flow like water, if a little sluggishly. Though, Jofre decided, they would hold off testing it as long as possible. There was something about this dank seam in the earth which repelled.

Dusk would soon be upon them and they must establish some type of camp. The threat of the skulls was ominous enough to make them sure they should select a site which they could defend—against what—or whom—they could not be sure.

They found the best cover the countryside had to offer farther on towards the cone hill where there were small bumps in the ground and Jofre, with a scout's trained eye, picked out three such which could form a rough triangle, their pack gear and stones dragged up to give some seeming of walls, low as those had to be.

Even Yan helped with the dragging of stones, and pawed up sods of the tundra grass to plaster between the loose rocks. They worked as fast as they could, though they tried to make certain they did not scant any loophole. A small fire, set in a hollow scooped in their rude fortress, could not be sighted across the plain top—though it would be visible from the hillock but to that he had no answer.

However, the night winds were chill enough that they must have a measure of heat. To keep that cup of flame alive during the night would be one of the duties of the sentry. And they carried to pile against one of their shelter rocks dried vines which crisscrossed the tundra growth and were thick enough to be broken into respectable sticks.

Once more they ate their limited rations slowly. Zurzal sat with the scanner between his outstretched legs, his good hand more occupied with examining that than by conveying the ration strips to his mouth. Jofre chewed as he squatted by another of their chosen boulders, staring out across that ill-omened stretch of trenches and the guardian skulls, back across the country they had come.

If the Skrem and the Deves, he thought with a resigned logic, really wanted to be rid of them, all they need do was to leave them marooned here. There was no way he could see that they would ever be able to make a return journey. Twice he was nearly moved to say that aloud but then decided that his own dire predictions must indeed be shared by all of them since they possessed the intelligence of sentinent beings—even the Jat must feel that they must have indeed come to the end of the trail.

Still you had the perkiness of one at home with the surroundings. Earlier it had surveyed the skulls round-eyed and Jofre had been able to pick up a glimmer of disgust from the creature's mind. But there was no shadow of fear.

"Tomorrow"—Zurzal gave the scanner a final pat as if it were a pet animal ready to offer good service—"we need wait no longer. Tomorrow!" There was exultation in his voice and his frill waved and stiffened, dark color flooding up through its ribbing.

Neither Jofre nor Taynad made answer. They were concerned with more than just tomorrow—the time which stretched beyond that. It might serve Zurzal completely that he prove for all time his contention was right—the ancient and unknown past might be made clear, recorded for the reading of others but they were still engaged in living and preparing to continue that state.

Jofre took first watch. The Zacathan did not seem prepared to either settle down to rest or put himself to camp routine. He had edged out into the night as Jofre crouched tensely trying to follow his movements, as well as pick up any threat which might lie hid. Back and forth along those trenches Zurzal had strode, the com in his hand, until at last he seemed to find some point he had been hunting and stood there for some time.

There was something about that hillock which was now a backdrop for their own camp which kept nudging at Jofre. He had absorbed enough of the time scanted instructions the Zacathan had given on Wayright and during their flight to Lochan to believe that that rise might indeed hide ruins, part of a city or a single fortress. Yet those who had come here had not delved there but rather dug their trenches at its foot.

It was a place which could be defended—against anything but an air attack. Between quick glances at the Zacathan to make sure that he was safe, the guard began to set himself the problem of how that rise might be made to serve them best should those who collected skulls come to see what stirred here now.

Zurzal had returned when Jofre reached over to touch Taynad's shoulder, signal her for second guard duty. The double moons gave strange light to this barren country— it was wholly alien and more to be mistrusted for that.

"There is a watcher," she whispered. "Yan knows. See."

Her gritty fingers touched the back of the hand Jofre had reached to awaken her. And he did understand. The sending was very dim, but it was there. They were indeed under observation.

"Yan will know," she said. "Rest while you can."

Mistrust rippled in his mind and he repelled it. With her promise to the Zacathan she meant no ill, nor would she deliver any attack until she formally ended that courtesy tie. He could rely that she and the Jat would do just as he had been doing—stand guard.

So they won through to day again. Taynad reported that the watcher had withdrawn sometime in the early predawn and that the Jat had shown no fear concerning it.

They had to insist that Zurzal eat—he was as a child before a feast day—so eager to be at what he would do that nothing else mattered. With Jofre's help the scanner was once more mounted and then there was a tedious space of waiting as the Zacathan applied measurements and adjustments, making sure that the instrument aimed directly down, not across the central one of those ditches.

30

THEY WERE NOT PREPARED FOR WHAT CAME WITH less warning than a mountain storm. The sound tore through the brazen sky, something totally foreign to this place which had so been forgotten by time.

A shadow swept over the plateaus like a giant Kag preparing to dive on prey—though that airborne craft did not indeed skim as close to them as the sound suggested.

Jofre had thrown himself flat, taking Zurzal down with him, half covering the Zacathan's body with his own. He was prepared in one instant of recognition to feel the sear of laser fire catching them both.

But the flitter's occupants had not taken their advantage and the aircraft swept on, over the hump of the cone—northward. They had been such easy prey that Jofre could not believe for an instant or two that they seemed to have been ignored.

It was a screaming cry from the Jat which brought him up to his knees, half-slewed around. Yan was pulling at Taynad, striving to drag her from where she had prudently gone prone at the passing of the flitter, toward them. Why became understandable almost immediately.

The edge of that cut which bisected the plateau suddenly had developed a series of humps along its edge, moving things which flowed up and over as if they were part of some giant flood imprisoned below and determined now to be free.

Sword-knife in one hand, the barbed length of chain in the other, Jofre tried to settle his weight evenly, be prepared to meet that dash. The Zacathan had drawn his stunner but against this wave that would be little good. Taynad moved in, the Jat leaping up and down at her side and screaming. It stooped to scrabble up an armload of stones, nursing those against its small body as potential weapons.

The creatures from the chasm resembled Skrem—but of a different kind than those who had companied with them earlier. These were larger; they did not ride but scuttled at a speed which hardly seemed possible toward the beleaguered off-worlders.

The Zacathan's weapon hissed and the first line of the charge twisted and went down, frozen in the cords of stass. However, that was only a portion of those arranged against them.

Jofre's eyes narrowed, he measured distances, the footing before him, and then with the ear-splitting, heart-stopping cry of the issha, he went into action, meeting the first three of those who had tramped over their kind with the whirling hooked chain. One of those hooks caught under the edge of the helmetlike head covering of the foremost, and the force of the swing whirled the native off his feet, smashing him into his closest fellow.

Jofre was back in a crouch. The tip of his knife had caught the third at the point where a human would have had a chin and sent it down as cleanly as the chain had taken the others.

A rock flew past Jofre to strike another Skrem flat on the head so it staggered and fell. Then another and another such projectile flew with skillful aim. It was not only Yan who was the marksman. Taynad had joined him, proving herself an expert with even such crude weapons. Still they came.

Zurzal had had time to thumb another charge into his hand weapon and this he now discharged, adding to the line of motionless bodies.

The Skrem had made no sound when they attacked; only Jofre's cry had broken the silence. Now they could hear again the beat of the flitter engine. Jofre's shoulders stiffened. They had them at their mercy, those in the flitter, for he was very sure that the crew of that was not coming to their rescue.

Yet, it would seem that he had been wrong. The Skrem milled around on the edge of the cut, now forming another attack line. Yan was screaming again, jumping up, trying to catch at the Zacathan's maimed arm, draw his attention. Zurzal attempted to fend off the Jat and still keep his weapon poised.

Once more the flitter banked, withdrew towards the hillock, and the wild Skrem gathered. How many charges they could hold off Jofre dared not try to guess. He believed he did know what those in the flitter had in mind—the wearing down, even the death of him and his companions, whereupon they could move in and take what they wanted. Yet surely those aloft must have superior arms on board—why this cat-and-mouse play with them and the wild Skrem? Except perhaps that they needed Zurzal to operate the machine and so were willing to keep their attackers at bay for now lest they destroy the scanner.

The Jat turned away from Zurzal and threw itself at the scanner while Zacathan, with a hissing cry, his neck frill an engorged crimson, clutched vainly after him. But the maneuver of the Jat brought the Zacathan's hand down on the controls.

There was a sound which drowned out the flitter. Jofre saw that machine tremble in the air, dip sidewise, as if its equilibrium was disturbed. Color, sound burst from behind. Jofre, by the very weight of that blow on his ears, was pushed against one of the rocks which had been part of their shelter for the night. It took some seconds for his eyes to adjust to the flow of images, so merged one with the other that it was difficult to see any one clearly. There appeared to be beings mounted and riding. Someone dressed not unlike the Axe was haranguing a mob of people into which the mounted warriors flowed and comingled—then the whole scene began to flicker at the edges—

Jofre was half knocked from his place by the thud of a small body against him. He threw out an arm to fend the Jat off, still so bemused by that swirl of pictures before him that he did not defend himself fully against that scrabbling paw.

Yan was gone, swallowed up by the play of pictures in the air fanning out farther and farther from the center point of the cone hill which was no longer that, but a great, towered keep more imposing than the largest of the Lairs.

The—the stone—the stone was gone! Jofre stumbled away from the rock support. Yan had taken his stone. Then—

There was no more change, weaving, misting about what he was watching. Instead it steadied into a clear stretch of a different world. The mounted warriors charged the crowd gathered around the priest. People who resembled the maned natives of the present produced weapons from beneath their robes, cut at the mounts, dragged riders like the Skrem from their beasts.

It was so real! Jofre edged closer to the rock and felt a body beside him. Taynad's breath came fast against his cheek. Forgotten was the attack from the chasm beasts. There was certainly no flitter in the air over this battle which they watched rage back and forth across a city so long lost that there was not even a dim memory of it left.

From the towered citadel issued more troops—these on foot. They were real, three-dimensional. Jofre could see them as well as if he had been there on the day when all this had happened.

Footmen fought footmen; those who were the priest's followers showed such ferocity one could only believe that they had good reason to hate the fortress guard. There were leaders standing out among them now. The priest was swept from his command position by a red-maned warrior who was a woman! Jofre could hear ancient screams, echoing from so far down the corridors of time that they were but whispers.

On and on it went. Then there was the seeming of a curtain which dropped between them and that wild scene. Figures moved within that mist but not so violently, and it seemed to Jofre that they did not war—that the struggle was perhaps now ended or else time had jumped and it had not yet begun.

There were clearings of that curtain now and then but only for very short periods of time, just enough to give hints of a city fallen into decay. Afterwards strangers unlike any Jofre had seen on Lochan moved through those crumbling ruins. Until at last there was a final flicker and once more they were in the ruins under the heavy sun.

Zurzal knelt by the scanner, his hand out to the machine, not quite touching it. His frill seemed made of iridescent color, as if one emotion mingled with another to set it so agleam. His eyes were on the stretch of country before him as if they still saw all which had swirled there.

"Sssssssseee, sssseee—" his voice was a jubilant hiss.

However, Jofre had pulled Taynad around so that they both faced, not the country across which that picture had brought life, but the edge of the chasm. Those Skrem who had been brought down, either by Zurzal's weapon or their own efforts, still lay there. One or two not locked into stass were crawling towards the tip of the cut. For the rest—they were gone even as if they had also been swept away by the winds of the past.

"It—it was the Lair stone—" Taynad's voice was uneven, she breathed as one who had been running. "Did you not see—Yan, the Lair stone—the Jat took it—put it in the scanner for power. How did it know what to do? Why the Lair stone?"

She looked to Jofre as might a child who needed some answer to an important question.

Yan squatted still by the scanner. As the Zacathan, the Jat was staring out to the dregs of the past. Jofre had no answer for her. Yan had been fascinated by the stone, he had sensed it in Jofre's possession before he had ever tried to take it in the night. But why had the creature known that it must be fitted into the scanner? How much had Yan ever understood about their quest and what they wanted to do here?

"Yan knows more than we can tell. He has his own reasons—perhaps sometime he will share those with us—"

She had gotten only so far when they heard again the sound of the flitter beat—coming out of the north. To bring on them again the horde from the chasm?

Certainly those in the flitter had done nothing to help them ward off the attack from the chasm; therefore, they were not to be depended upon now.

"Down—take cover—" Jofre had just time to shout that warning when the Jat streaked at a speed they had never seen it produce before, straight for the guard. Yan leaped, aiming for his head and shoulders. This was an attack for which the man had in no way been prepared. At the same time he staggered backward, trying to claw with one hand to free himself from the furry body pressed close enough to blind him, the forepaws which enwrapped his neck, there came another blow.

Jofre whirled around, fighting to keep his feet, but his bones might have softened in an instant. He crumpled to the ground, half bouncing off a rock. But even that encounter failed to scrape the Jat away and its body was now a lump-load on his chest. The guard found it sheer agony to get a breath, and he realized that, for the second time, he had taken a bolt from a stass stunner, leaving him easy prey for any attack.

He did not lose consciousness; though, for a period of time he could not measure, he strove somehow to shift the body of Yan, hoping that would let him breathe easier. The fact that he did have some small movement in his neck was a faint promise that he could do this. Had the

Jat taken to itself part of the charge of that weapon, thus giving Jofre the slimmest of chances? But again, how did the creature—?

"Be still—not move—" the thought struck into his mind. Yan's head was squeezed a little down so that the Jat's forehead pressed against Jofre's. The contact—could it be what aided their transfer of thought?

He had managed to edge his head around a fraction, something he certainly could not have done had he taken the full force of the ray. Now he could breathe—and hear—

But he could not see, save for a hair-fringed, tiny slit of what was beyond. The Zacathan's boots were within that very limited range of vision and that was all. Now—he must fight in his own way, as he had aboard the Tssekian ship, call upon his inner strength. And this time he lacked the Lair stone to amplify what powers he could summon.

The drone of the flitter was very loud; the craft must be setting down somewhere near. They had not stassed Zurzal for some reason. Taynad—? Apparently the Jat was not unconscious. It might well be as locked as he into helplessness of body but its mind was alert. Could he somehow reach Taynad through that furry head resting against his own?

"Learned One," it was a strange voice, speaking trade tongue, "you are to be congratulated on a most impressive display from your invention—or discovery—or whatever you claim it to be. We were duly made aware of just what this discovery has to offer—for our purposes, of course."

Zurzal's boots had not moved in that narrow slit of sight allowed Jofre.

"One success does not make for a continued series of them—" the hissing note in the Zacathan's answer had the fury of a reptilian arousal. "You play games, let us come to the point. I take it you are Guild."

"But of course," the smooth voice returned. "We tried to discuss matters with you some time back but it appears that you are a very stubborn lizard, Learned One. It was then decided that, until we had real proof of what you were able to do, we would just wait and see. We even helped you along the way—Gosal's ship was ready when you needed transportation, and if you had not won out of Tssek through your own efforts, we had plans to assist you there also. Yes, we have a number of work hours tied up in you and your affairs, Learned One. Now it is time to collect payment."

"Take the scanner if you wish," Zurzal returned. Jofre could see a slight movement as if he shifted weight from one foot to the other. "It will do you no good. That summoning of the past you saw burned out the charge."

"Oh, but surely that can be easily corrected. You yourself, Learned One, will be only too glad to lend your full assistance."

"I hardly think so," Zurzal returned.

"You are a master of knowledge—or so you Zacathans claim. But do not underrate others. We have our sources also. I think you will be most eager to give us any aid within your power. Opgor, let us have a demonstration of your marksmanship."

Jofre could not mistake the crackle of a blaster. He saw those two firmly planted feet tremble, totter out of his line of sight. And there was a smell—the smell of cooked meat.

A hissing like that of a snake about to strike.

"Excellent beam control, Opgor. Now, Learned One, you may not have the use of that right hand of yours, and your other is not much good. But you can direct others in providing the agile fingers needed. Also—understand this, we know very well that if you cannot be provided with the proper regeneration treatment in time you are *NOT* going to regrow *that* one. So your cooperation is necessary. It really is very simple, isn't it? We shall see that you have proper accommodations and tending just as long as you give us in exchange some of the vaunted knowledge of yours.

"And it will not be limited to just the use of your scanner. Oh, no, a chance such as this comes perhaps once in

a being's lifetime. You will provide our information experts
with the sites of suitable delvings for the future. You see,
in the end, the game is ours."

"Is it?" Taynad—what was she doing using that voice,
addressing this Guild leader as she would a lesser servant?

"We have not indeed forgotten you, my dear. Guild
bargains hold. You have been dispatched to ensnare one
of your own kind—though a traitor. He is freely yours
and in such condition that you will not have to worry
about any guards. You will be lifted from here, returned
to the port with your catch. Gosal shall again obey orders
and see that you and this lump of meat will be returned
to Wayright. What happens beyond that, I leave to your
own people. We have done as we were paid to do."

"It would seem, Veep," the Taynad Jofre could not see
answered, "that you have taken into consideration every
point except one. Your knowledge may run deep but I do
not think that it encompasses the oaths of the issha breed.
I gave the Learned One my promise to be one with him
until this adventure was finished—"

"It is finished." There was a note of impatience in that.
"The lizard has done what he desired—proved the useful-
ness of this time reader of his. Therefore, you are now freed.
We will proceed as planned—"

"The lizard—Lord Rang—he is dying!"

Those words were like a jolt—as sharp a jolt of fear and
energy as any the Assha stone had ever delivered. Jofre
reached for strength from the Center, and that responded.
He knew he could move again, but how greatly would the
stass hinder that movement? He could only test it by the
swiftest action he could summon.

His arm swept under the Jat's flaccid body.

"No watch now—" Those three words fed Jofre's energy
another, if shorter, jolt. They believed him entirely out of
the picture. Well, they would discover what an issha could
do to revenge his oath!

There was a babble of voices to which he closed his
ears. That rock he had slid down against at the first attack

gave him a solid base against which he shifted now. Then he flung aside the Jat and was up, his back to the stone. And he had been right! Their attackers were gathered some distance away about a body on the ground and one of them knelt beside it, an open medical kit to hand.

Taynad? She was in the midst of them, Zurzal's frilled head on her knee. But her eyes sought farther afield—found Jofre. He tensed—she would cry out—

He had already picked his man. By the clothing and the way orders sprouted from him, this was the leader. His back was to Jofre, whom they had totally dismissed from their minds.

The guard inched forward. Had he been able to throw off all the effects of the stass, he might well have gone into action. However, his arms and legs did not respond to the orders his raging mind gave. Rage—anger—it was fuel, it could burn away doubts, increase energy if it were so used. Jofre allowed, in a sudden snap of control, his rage to flare.

He was behind that Guild leader, the clawed chain out, about the man's throat, its hooks biting into the other's thick flesh.

"Now," Jofre said in a set, quiet voice, "there is a new payment, life for life. You die, brother of all evil."

31

"**B**LOOD PRICE—"

They had frozen as if a stass had taken them all, though they did not collapse. Jofre tightened hold with his left hand on the chain, though he was not yet ready to supply the final twist. His right flashed around and gripped the blaster in his captive's holster, flicking it out into the open.

One of that group of four about the prone Zacathan rolled and was on his feet, running towards the flitter. Jofre fired. A scream which tore the air was his answer. That would-be escape ended with a sobbing, screeching body rolling on the earth, beating at smoldering clothing.

The man Jofre held jerked, and then uttered a cry of his own as one of the hooks tore into his flesh. He who had tried for the flitter now lay quiet.

"Blood price—" Jofre repeated and his voice seemed battle shrill in the heavy silence.

Taynad moved, setting Zurzal's head gently aside. As she pulled up to her feet her hand skimmed along the side of the man beside her, neatly disarming him. Jofre waited. He could kill now with one twist of his wrist and burn down those others in a wide-armed sweep, but such would take in Taynad.

She held her own weapon steady but did not try to aim at Jofre. Perhaps she did not dare, for, even as she crisped him, she would be destroying also the leader he held.

"Drop your weapons!" It was she who said that and the blaster was on the other three.

Perhaps the precarious position of their leader might not have brought such instant obedience, but the fact that they, too, were now within range of a blast which could not miss made them indeed draw their weapons and drop them to the ground.

"Kick them—" Jofre took a quick hand in the game, though he was not yet sure by which rules Taynad was playing—"out!"

That man who had continued to kneel by the Zacathan with the medical kit picked his sidearm up by the barrel and hurled it in Jofre's direction. The other kicked as ordered, sending his weapons in the same direction.

Taynad turned again to the man she had already disarmed. Still holding the blaster at ready, her other hand grabbed at his dangling arm, ran down the sleeve there and now held a knife by the blade. This she tossed after the blasters.

"There is no blood price yet." For the first time she addressed Jofre directly. "The Learned One still lives—if that one can keep life in his body." She nodded toward the one with the medic's bag.

"Do so," Jofre snapped. At the same time he brought the barrel of the blaster around behind the ear of the man he held in the chain noose. That one crumpled so suddenly that he nearly took Jofre down with him before the guard could loosen his grasp.

He stood over that unconscious prisoner for a moment, eyeing Taynad. But she was no longer looking in his direction; her attention was all for the two men she covered with her blaster.

Jofre dared believe that, at least for now, they were on the same side. He used the chain for another purpose, in spite of the cruelty of the embedded hooks, and fastened the wrists of his captive securely behind him before dragging them down so that the hooks on the other end could be caught firmly in the boots, leaving the other's body arched as a bow.

With that one as secure as he could make him, the guard rounded one of the rocks to the side of the man from whose sleeve Taynad had dislodged the hidden knife. A blow delivered with the edge of his hand sent that one sprawling and his own belt was used to truss him up.

That left the medic, but Taynad was standing over him now as he worked on the Zacathan. Jofre saw that charred stump and his breath hissed between his teeth as if he shared some of Zurzal's reptilian blood.

"I guard," he told the girl. "There is Yan—"

"Yes," she agreed but she did not put away the blaster. With that still swinging in one hand she hurried to that small brown form curled at the foot of the rock.

"You!" Jofre demanded attention from the medic who had been keeping his head down, working quickly and, Jofre thought, with practiced skill at the Zacathan's burn. Perhaps, seeing who he companioned with, he had plenty of skill in such matters.

"Tell me," the guard demanded, "what can you do to bring the Jat out of stass?"

"For humanoids there is an injection," the man answered, though he did not look up. "Whether that will work for a Jat—who knows?" He shrugged.

"You for one had better," Jofre said. He watched the last of the elastic casing applied to Zurzal's wound and then he gestured to the Jat. "Be about your business there now."

Zurzal slowly opened his large eyes. They did not seem to focus on Jofre, but before him, straight up into the sky. "The legions rode—" he said and his frill fluttered, save for where the weight of his head pinned it to the ground. "The legions of the lost rode—we saw them."

Jofre went down on one knee. "We did, Learned One. No man can now say that you are a fool—for we have seen the past alive because of you." He did not know why he chose those words, only they seemed to come without summoning as what must be said now.

"What—I am—" His right arm trembled, raised, and he turned his head that he might look down the length of his body to survey that wound of horror.

"You are alive, Learned One. And they are prisoners."

"But—you were in stass—"

"The Jat—it put itself between—now—" Jofre looked beyond Zurzal to where Taynad held Yan within the crook of one arm while the medic readied an infusion punch against the furred upper limb now dropping so limply over Taynad's knee. "Now, that medic of theirs tries revival."

"Little one—" Not words of voice, words of mind— Taynad's mind.

Jofre moved again to the girl's side. He no longer had the Assha stone; did that mean that he could give no more aid? He could only try. But he laid the blaster well within reach as he took Taynad into his hold much as she had the Jat.

"Little one—" She was mind calling, and he added to that call as best he could. There was a passage of power between them, he could feel the flow of it. "Little one, come back to us—"

Jofre's lips shaped the same words as blazed now in his mind. His rage had been expended in the attack, so he did not have that fuel for the inner fire. But there were other emotions besides rage. Yan had offered himself for a life shield—that was the act not of any animal Jofre knew, but the action of a man. Therefore all the emotion which could pass between battle comrades could—must come—NOW!

"Yan—dark—Yan—lost—" A trail of thought so tenuous he might almost believe it a wisp of his own imagination. But he felt Taynad seize instantly upon it as one might seize upon a rope to pull to safety some climber who had lost footing on a treacherous slope.

"Yan! Come—come—!"

At first no answer and then—yes, that line was holding. Jofre poured what power he could into their linkage, and Taynad, Taynad was a very anchor of strength!

There was a little moaning cry and Yan's head turned against the girl's shoulder.

Jofre gently withdrew his support. He felt as if he had spent long hours in the arms court, tired to weakness, near dizzy when he tried to turn his full sight on anyone. Yet— there was much to be done.

Somehow he got on his feet and went back to Zurzal. The Zacathan had managed to use his growing left arm and hand to lever himself to a sitting position and now he stretched that small fist of immature fingers toward the scanner.

Jofre looked beyond. The man he had burned down lay in a patch of charred tundra grass—the flitter near him. They had three captives on their hands—perhaps it might be well to put the medic in bonds too—and they had the flitter.

But suppose they were to load their prisoners and themselves on that? He was no flitter pilot, he doubted very much that Taynad had such training—and certainly Zurzal, even if he knew how to manage the controls, could not do so now. Also, supposing that fortune was to favor them very wildly, and they managed to make the flight back to the port—that might well mean they would simply be walking into a trap. On Lochan he could not help but believe that they were without any friends.

Something dangerous and foolhardy might be done using at least the leader of this expedition as a bargaining point but at present Jofre could not see his way into such a maze. He would have to know the value of his captive and whom he was going to have to bargain with. Certainly none of the prisoners would voluntarily supply him with that information.

It was now the time to reckon up just what their resources were. He looked to Taynad still cradling the Jat, though he noted that she kept one hand near her blaster and one eye on the medic, who appeared very busy fitting various things into the bag on the ground between them.

So sweeping was Jofre's gaze that he caught sight again of that wave of Skrem out of the chasm. Their bodies were still inert. But how they could handle the stass he could not tell. Perhaps, being of another species, they were dead when exposed to even the low wave Zurzal's weapon used.

Also he saw but four in the Guild squad. Certainly no one else had issued from the flitter to counter his attack, nor had a weapon set within the craft been used to burn him down. But that did not mean that there could not be some nasty surprise waiting there.

Jofre spoke to the girl. "Those Skrem—if they rise again—"

She nodded briskly. "I shall watch, Shadow. There is also the flitter—"

"Which I shall see to now." Jofre glanced to the Zacathan, who now sat with his back against one of the rocky mounds. It was plain Zurzal had reached that position with an effort which left him panting, but his eyes were open and aware.

The two in bonds still lay quiet. Now Jofre moved in on the medic. Best make sure.

"Hands behind," he ordered.

"You haven't a chance—" The other set his bag aside and did place his hands behind his back. "They are going to come looking for us. Praspar"—he jerked a nod towards the chained man—"is to broadcast in a measured time. If they don't hear from him—" He shrugged.

Jofre did not answer. He had sacrificed most of his girdle to be torn into strips and he made use of those well. No one was going to slip out of those.

His first assay must be to the flitter. Taynad could watch the chasm and the fringe of bodies at the edge of that. Were there any stirring she would sound the alarm.

He approached the landed craft with all the expertise of a scout exploring enemy territory, fully expecting at any moment to have some surprise confront him. The door of the cabin had been left slid well open when the squad had disembarked. He could hear no sound from within. Nor, when he reached out with that other carefully honed sense, could he pick up any suggestion that there was someone in concealment there.

Blaster in hand he made a final short dash from an angle which exposed as little of his body as he could hope and then was within, his back against the cabin wall, quick to survey all which lay about.

The accommodations were of more generous size than one would gauge from the exterior of the craft. There were six seats and behind those a space left free—perhaps meant to transport gear, though there was nothing there now.

Aimed through a small port on the right side of the first pair of seats was a piece of armament which might be either a larger form of blaster or a stunner—he half guessed the latter—and it was this which must have brought him down when the flitter came in for a landing. He had seen enough of such weapons of a smaller size that he knew the procedure for disarming the thing, and with two swift movements he did just that, rolling between his fingers the cylinder which made it workable.

There was a chatter of noise which sent him again into a fighting half-crouch, blaster ready. The sound came from a box mounted before the same seat that the gunner must have occupied. The com—if he could only give the answer! But that was beyond him and he knew that he could not trust the medic. This was like Tssek, like much of Wayright—the machines were highly evolved— this one might even be able to report back on its own that there were difficulties. He would take no risks, no matter how slight.

Jofre brought the butt of the blaster down on the box which returned a screeching cry, as if it had indeed a life of its own, and then puffed out choking smoke which drove him to the door of the flitter.

His problem was no closer to solution. He stood now in a form of transportation which could save them all—but he could not put it to use. And to retrace by foot the way they had come, Zurzal suffering from that maiming, three prisoners—the Jat—

The issha were taught to act as individuals; their whole
way of life made them first and foremost dependent upon
themselves and wary of losing any of that independence.
He shook his head as if to scatter out thoughts he could
not arrange in the proper pattern.

At least he could see one thing—set against the wall of
the flitter was a rack holding water flasks. Sighting those
his thirst awoke. He worked free the nearest and forced
himself to take only three sips, not enough to wash the
gravelly dryness from his tongue and mouth. But with that
and two others swinging on their slings from his shoulder
he returned to the party by the rocks.

"The Skrem are dead," Taynad greeted him. "Yan says
so—" The Jat was still snuggled against her but now it
squeaked with some vigor.

"Well enough." But at the moment that was far down
the list of Jofre's immediate concerns. He handed one of
the water flasks to the girl and took another to where the
Zacathan half sat, half lay.

Somehow Zurzal had managed to wriggle around to get
a hold on the time scanner with his small hand. He was
fumbling now at that part of the mechanism which held
the power coil and, as Jofre came up, that yielded to his
struggle. A wisp of smoke answered.

"Gone—burnt out—"

The Assha stone, Jofre thought. Power—it had given the
power to hold that vivid return of life. But it was shattered
into—he ran his finger into the small chamber of the coil—
heat and dust—only dust—

"It needed only greater power!" The Zacathan was leaning away from his rock support. "Now we know!"

"And, Learned One, what good will that do us?" Jofre
was going to make no pretense of covering the gloom of
his own speculations concerning their future. "I am no
pilot, you cannot handle the flitter. If I loose any one of
these," he nodded towards the captives, "we cannot trust
them to deliver us anywhere save the place they wish.
And overland—" He gazed out over the plateau toward

the breakage of the lava river, "we have no chance."

"You have no chance anyway, Slip-shadow," the leader of the squad rasped. "They will come when we do not report in. If you think to make a deal with me—with that lame-brain," he glanced toward the man Taynad had disarmed, "or Yager here—forget it. The Guild doesn't deal—they'll simply fly over and stass us all and then pick up what they want and leave the—"

"Jofre!" Taynad was on her feet, looking north, "they come—in the air—"

He caught it, too, the hum of another flitter. He could try—it was so small a chance but the only one he had—Jofre called upon his full energy and made for the cone hill. Fear as well as rage fed him now. He pulled and threw himself from hold to hold. Somehow he reached the crest and crouched, panting heavily behind one of those smaller mounds. But he was not too exhausted to steady the barrel of the blaster on the top of that mound, ready himself for the single small chance he might have for a beam at the flitter as it bore in to stass them as the squad leader had promised. He was not even sure that if the beam hit it would cause enough damage to bring the craft down; he could only hope.

The craft did not swoop in, but made a circle well above where he waited. Then it slipped sidewise and his fingers tightened until he willed them fiercely to relax. He had a single second to see that emblazoned sign on the side of the flitter, to depress the barrel of his weapon. The flare of fire shot across the cone crest, it did not touch that machine.

There was no return—either of stass beam or weapon fire. The flitter dipped where the others were, and then lifted for a space to set down near the other flitter. Jofre drew a ragged breath as he watched the uniformed passengers emerge, take evasive action.

The first of those silvered helms reached the Guild flitter. Then they were all past it. One halted briefly beside the body, but only for a moment. Jofre turned and started down the hill, his body still shaking from the stress of that charge to reach the heights. He found it far more difficult going. No one appeared to notice him until he made the final drop to the level where the Patrol troopers had the three from the Guild in tangle cords and their officer was fronting Zurzal.

"—a good catch," the officer was saying.

The Zacathan's frill darkened, his eyes were coldly reptilian. "Bait, Captain? Then we were bait all the time? Well, that explains some incidents I wondered at."

"Bait?" returned the officer coolly. "You greatly desired this expedition, Learned One. You wished to prove something, I believe. We merely allowed you to fulfill what you desired. You did get the results you wanted, did you not? We have some video-casts which are certainly amazing. And I do not think that you need fear any more attentions from the Guild. They have lost a great deal—including an in-port that they were very eager to establish in secret. On the whole, a most successful operation, do you not agree?"

Zurzal lifted his maimed arm. "One well paid for," he returned.

The Patrol officer lost a little of his confident calm. "We have regenerative facilities, Learned One. Our command ship carries a medic with the techniques. You shall be given every attention. We are most indebted to you—"

Jofre felt drained. There was no longer any need for an oathed man. He had completed his service and in a very checkered fashion. It seemed to him now, and painfully, that he certainly had not shown well as an isshi—in many ways.

Issha—Taynad. At that moment he remembered what the Guild leader had said. Taynad had been sent to take him captive and deliver him to the Shagga. Well, enough of the issha was left in him that he would not be so easily disposed of.

"Friend—friend—"

Something tugged at his sleeve and he looked down to see that Yan had him fast. But the Jat was still in Taynad's arms, she had moved that close to him. He tensed.

"Friend—" It was imperative—it was a demand for understanding.

Jofre looked to the girl. "But you are oathed—"

She stooped and allowed Yan to slide out of her hold. Her hands went to her braids and she pulled out the notched twigs, showing them clearly to him.

"They sent me these on Wayright. I was ordered—but I gave no oath before the High Altar."

"They will hold you to it anyway. I know the Shagga."

She looked at him proudly. "The Shagga may order; they do not oath."

"They will oath against you then, unless—" He started away from the rock against which he had been leaning, a new energy building in him. "Your sleeve knife, Sister— give it!" He held out his hand.

She stared at him, not understanding. Yan pulled at her other hand and looked up into her face, uttering one of those small coaxing mews.

Slowly Taynad drew that most precious, most intimate weapon and held it a little away from her. Jofre put out his hand and closed it about the bared blade.

"Pull!" he ordered and almost instinctively she answered. He felt that smart as its keen edge met his flesh and cut. Then she was holding a bloodstained knife, looking from it to him in wonder, as he brought his own hand up to lick the blood welling in that cut.

"You have done as ordered," he said, "my blood dims your blade. So can you swear and no one, Lair Master or Shagga, can hold you wrong!"

The mask which she ever wore cracked. For the first time he saw more of the one who wore it than he ever thought he might.

"It is so—Shadow Brother," she said in a half whisper.

"It is so!" he told her firmly. "Shadow Sister."

"Jofre, Taynad!"

They awoke to the present and and answered Zurzal's call.

"My coworkers. Captain," the Zacathan said. "It is thanks to them that the Guild did not put an end to these games you all have been playing before your somewhat late arrival. Now, I think, we should be shown some of this gratitude which you mentioned is owed to us."

They were off Lochan, aboard the Patrol cruiser and in the sickbed where the Zacathan lay with his maimed arm under a roofing bubble which kept in the fine spray bathing the charred wrist, before they were together again in private.

"You were oathed to me for this venture now ended," Zurzal spoke first to Jofre. "I declare you have fulfilled your oath. Unless—"

"Unless?" Jofre asked.

"Unless you wish to make it a life burden?"

"Never a burden!" Since he had knelt to say farewell to the Lair Master in Ho-Le-Far he had not felt exactly like this. There was no question in him but what the Zacathan offered him now was all he could wish.

"Taynad Jewelbright," Zurzal seemed to need no more words from Jofre but looked past him to her.

"Not Jewelbright." She shook her head. "I think there are other roads."

"There is one we may take together," Zurzal said. "What we did on Lochan is only the beginning—there are treasures out of time beyond all reckoning—it is up to us to find our share of them!"

Jofre's bandaged hand arose—his fingers shaped "Greeting to Shadow Comrade," which seldom, if ever, in his lifetime, an oathed issha could pattern.

Taynad's hand reached into his full sight—"So let it be." Her fingers gave assent.

"We deal then no more with the shadows of others," he spoke aloud, "only those which shall be our own."

And into his wounded hand slipped a paw—a paw for Taynad also. The last link closed tight.

AVONOVA PRESENTS
AWARD-WINNING NOVELS
FROM MASTERS OF SCIENCE FICTION

WULFSYARN
by Phillip Mann   71717-4/ $4.99 US

MIRROR TO THE SKY
by Mark S. Geston   71703-4/ $4.99 US/ $5.99 Can

THE DESTINY MAKERS
by George Turner   71887-1/ $4.99 US/ $5.99 Can

A DEEPER SEA
by Alexander Jablokov   71709-3/ $4.99 US/ $5.99 Can

BEGGARS IN SPAIN
by Nancy Kress   71877-4/ $4.99 US/ $5.99 Can

FLYING TO VALHALLA
by Charles Pellegrino   71881-2/ $4.99 US/ $5.99 Can

THE MAGICAL *XANTH* SERIES!

PIERS ANTHONY

QUESTION QUEST
75948-9/ $4.99 US/ $5.99 Can

ISLE OF VIEW
75947-0/ $4.99 US/ $5.99 Can

VALE OF THE VOLE
75287-5/ $4.95 US/ $5.95 Can

HEAVEN CENT
75288-3/ $4.99 US/ $5.99 Can

MAN FROM MUNDANIA
75289-1/ $4.95 US/ $5.95 Can

THE COLOR OF HER PANTIES
75949-7/ $4.99 US/ $5.99 Can